BISON FRONTIERS OF IMAGINATION

THE GIRL IN THE
GOLDEN ATOM

BY

RAY CUMMINGS

Introduction to the Bison Books Edition by Jack Williamson

University of Nebraska Press
Lincoln and London

Introduction © 2005 by the Board of Regents of the University of
Nebraska
Manufactured in the United States of America

First Nebraska paperback printing: 2005

Library of Congress Cataloging-in-Publication Data
Cummings, Ray.
The girl in the golden atom / Ray Cummings; introduction by Jack
Williamson.
p.   cm.—(Bison frontiers of imagination)
ISBN-13: 978-0-8032-6457-1 (pbk.: alk. paper)
ISBN-10: 0-8032-6457-7 (pbk.: alk. paper)
1. Chemists—Fiction.   2. Atoms—Fiction.   I. Title.   II. Series.
PS3505.U339G57   2005
813'.52—dc22   2005008981

INTRODUCTION

JACK WILLIAMSON

Tales of fantasy and imagination have fascinated us forever. The term "science fiction" was coined in 1929 by Hugo Gernsback to name the contents of *Science Wonder Stories*, the magazine he founded to replace *Amazing Stories*, where he had called the genre "scientifiction"—but the genre was by no means new.

The popular pulp magazines published by Frank A. Munsey, beginning in 1882 with the *The Golden Argosy*, identified science fiction as "different stories" or "unusual stories." The great early novels of H. G. Wells had been "scientific romances." Jules Verne wrote of "extraordinary voyages." Mary Shelley and Jonathan Swift had used no specific label at all.

Before radio and TV, people read for entertainment. The most popular magazines, such as the *Saturday Evening Post*, were known as "slicks" because they were printed on slick white paper. Subsidized by advertising dollars and edited for everybody, the *Post* sold for a nickel a copy and paid popular writers up to a dollar a word. The "pulps," with little advertising and edited for smaller, specialized audiences, were printed on cheap, gray wood pulp, wrapped in slick covers, and cost four or five times as much. *Argosy* was paying A. Merritt five or six cents a word in the 1920s, though in a changing world I got only $1\frac{1}{4}$ cent a word for stories I sold them in the 1930s.

Not yet for everybody, fantasy found a home in the pulps. Ray Cummings (1887–1957) was a pioneer among the foremost founders of science fiction. "The Girl in the Golden Atom" first appeared in 1919 in Munsey's *All Story Weekly*, and its sequel, "The People of the Golden Atom," in 1920.

This edition is a reprint of the original, which combines the two stories, published by Harper and Brothers in 1923. Hyperion Press reprinted it in 1948 with the new introduction by Thyrill H. Ladd, who met Cummings and described him as a modest and genial gentlemen. I must have seen Cummings myself, since we were both among the two hundred or so at the first World Science Fiction Convention in New York in 1939, but I don't recall him.

My family lived on isolated farms and ranches, and I grew up a daydreamer, hungry for the imagined adventure of good fantasy. But we were far from bookstores or libraries, and fantasy literature was hard for me to find. I'd been fascinated by a stray copy of Edgar Allen Poe's *Tales* and the time travel in Mark Twain's *A Connecticut Yankee in King Arthur's Court*, but I failed to discover science fiction until after Gernsback's *Amazing Stories* began reprinting the classics in 1926.

I first learned of *The Girl in the Golden Atom* from the letters set in tiny type in the back pages of the magazines, letters begging for the reprint of remembered classics. The story had made Ray Cummings a star in the legendary group producing "different stories" for the Munsey pulps. The best-loved were Edgar Rice Burroughs, creator of Tarzan and "A Princess of Mars" and A. Merritt, with the enchantments of "The Moon Pool" and "The Face in the Abyss." Austin Hall and Homer Eon Flint won mythic status for the mystery and wonder of "The Blind Spot," but it was a disappointment to me when I finally found it, the mysteries never resolved.

That legendary group also included George Allan England, Charles B. Stilson, Francis Stevens, and J. J. Giesy. The youngest must have been Murray Leinster (William Fitzgerald Jenkins, 1896–1975), who sold his first story to *Argosy* in 1919, while still in his teens.

Cummings had worked for several years as a laboratory assistant to the genius inventor Thomas Alva Edison and had married his daughter. Edison held patents on more than a thousand inventions, including the phonograph, the electric light, and motion picture equipment. Cummings was not so innovative. His writing career grew out of his success with a single idea, the theme of big and little, that he began exploiting with *The Girl in the Golden Atom*.

Hardly new, the idea had shaped such satires as Jonathan Swift's *Gulliver's Travels* and Voltaire's *Micromegas*. Cummings was no satirist; his novel follows the pattern of popular romance. Adventure in size became a theme that he repeated in story after story, but *The Girl in the Golden Atom* remains his most famous and most innovative work. His early popularity declined as the years went by, but he continued to write and published some 750 stories in several genres under various pen names.

The notion of the atom as a micro–solar system was given a certain plausibility at the time by the Rutherford-Bohr model that placed the atom as a central nucleus surrounded by electrons in orbit. Cummings, however, makes an effort to deal with such technical matters as the conservation of energy and mass or the manifest problems of reaching any electron planet. Instead, in the manner of Robert Louis Stevenson's Dr. Jekyll, he simply uses two drugs, one for growth and the other for shrinking.

Cummings dedicated the book to "My friend and mentor, Robert H. Davis, with grateful acknowledgment of his encouragement and practical assistance to which I owe my initial success." I used to hear Bob Davis praised as a veteran editor of the Munsey pulps and one of the ablest and most respected in the field. The dedication makes me wonder if he didn't suggest the story idea to Cummings.

With no effort at disguise, Cummings takes H. G. Wells's *The Time Machine* as a model for his characters, style, and story structure. The Wells novel begins with a group of friends at the dinner table listening to the never-named time traveler discussing time as a fourth dimension and his plan to travel along it. Cummings begins with a very similar group with the Chemist discussing the dimension of size and revealing his plan for his own expedition.

The Wells group includes the Medical Man, the Psychologist, the Provincial Mayor, and the Very Young Man. Besides his venturesome Chemist, Cummings's group includes the Doctor, the Big Business Man, and the same Very Young Man. Wells's traveler exhibits his machine, which he rides in the way that Wells himself rode his bicycle around the familiar dimensions of his London suburb.

The Chemist's story begins in 1910 when he becomes fascinated with "another world—the world of the infinitely small" (2). He invents a microscope with a thousand times the power of the one he has been using, and through it he sees a beautiful girl. This scene may have been influenced by "The Diamond Lens," a classic story published in 1858 by Fitz-James O'Brien. O'Brien's scientist invents a super-microscope, discovers a beautiful girl in a drop of water, and sees her doomed as it evaporates. Cummings's Chemist loses sight of the girl when his largest lens inexplicably explodes. The parallels seem obvious to me, though I think critics are often too certain about perceived sources. In fact, given the same problem, two different minds can arrive independently at the same solution.

The novel is more fantastic than scientific, but Cummings followed Wells's method of fantasy. A storyline known to writers dating back to Daniel Defoe, it asks the reader to accept one single assumption or premise and make the whole story a chain of its logical consequences, keeping everything else as familiar and believable as possible. Here the entire novel follows naturally from the Chemist's glimpse of that unreachable girl. Nuclear physics has taken giant strides since 1919, but Cummings never troubles readers with lectures on science. He spins his illusion of reality with convincing details of place, sense, emotion, and action, with no obvious gaps in story logic. The idea had more of a novelty appeal in 1919 than it has today. He keeps the story running smoothly, with no obvious gaps in the story logic. Creating such a tale is a game that he must have enjoyed, and the story earned its popularity.

In spite of the similar openings, the Cummings novel is vastly different from *The Time Machine*. Wells had been a Fabian socialist and had learned evolution from T. H. Huxley. He was writing to fictionalize his serious speculations about the future evolution of mankind and the earth itself. His Eloi, the childlike people living above ground, are descendants of the leisure class. They have forgotten how to care for themselves. The gray Morlocks are the future workers. They live underground, run the machines, and cannibalize the Eloi.

Cummings wrote with a very different purpose. Under the guidance of Bob Davis, he was composing a fantastic romance designed to entertain the readers of *All Story*. He did that with memorable success. After the introductory scenes and after they have promised to return, the Chemist and the time traveler vanish on their respective expeditions into size and future time. Any further similarities between the two novels are hard to spot.

Modes of popular fiction have changed since 1919, but Cummings's writing has survived the test of time. His story is sharply imagined, and he makes skillful use of convincing specifics. The Chemist's account of his laboratory work on the size-changing drug may reflect the author's own experience in Edison's lab. To prove the effects to his friends, he feeds the growth drug to a fly, which he crushes before it becomes dangerous, and then feeds the other drug to another fly that shrinks under the lens until it disappears. Throughout the novel Cummings takes care to support his marvels with plausible details. He weaves an engaging and suspenseful narrative.

When the Chemist is ready and equipped with bottles of the two pills, he reserves a room for himself and his friends at the club to make sure of absolute privacy for forty-eight hours. He lays the gold ring on a silk handkerchief under the light and has marked the spot at the edge of a scratch on the ring where the microscope was focused when he saw the girl. He takes a shrinkage pill and leaves his friends watching as he dwindles, walks across the black handkerchief, climbs astride the ring, and disappears into the scratch.

His friends keep a vigil in the room until he climbs out of the scratch and grows to his normal size. Wells's time traveler had asked for champagne and food when he got back. Cummings's Chemist wants brandy and time to eat before he tells his story.

Cummings's ring has no atomic structure; it is solid gold all the way through. The crack becomes a canyon that widens and deepens as the Chemist climbs down toward a rugged and perilous path at the bottom. He passes though tunnels until he comes to a cave where he falls into an exhausted sleep until the girl awakens him.

They are on the concave inner surface of a hollow world that curves upward into distance. He estimates that it is about the size of earth. There is no sun, but its entire mass is softly luminous. The girl's people are the Oroids. Like Wells's Eloi they seem to live in state of childlike innocence, though they are able to govern their socialistic utopia and care for themselves.

The girl, melodiously named Lylda, may be taken as a counterpart to Wells's little Weena, though Lylda is the king's daughter and a person of authority. She yields to the Chemist's ardent kisses as immediately as she masters his language. With her in his arms, the Chemist finds himself happily located in her paradise.

An eden has no drama, however, without a serpent. The Chemist finds the Oroids under attack by the Malites. Not quite Wells's cannibalistic Morlocks, they are still selfish and vicious enemies. He makes himself a modern Gulliver among the Lilliputians and tramples the Malite army. Time flows faster for the Oroids than in the larger world. Though only two days have passed for his friends, the Chemist experienced five Oroid days. Once he tells his tale to his friends, he returns to Lylda for good.

That's the first story. Five years pass for his waiting friends, who have placed the ring in a museum to keep it safe and have rigged it with an alarm device to alert them if he should return. The sequel begins when the Doctor gathers his friends to read a sealed letter the Chemist had entrusted to him.

With it is the formula for the drugs and a supply of the chemical required to make them. The letter is dated September 14, 1918, when World War I was still in progress, and is not to be opened until September 4, 1923. The Chemist forbids them to make any other use of the drugs except to follow him into the ring. He urges them to do so and sets a date when he will meet them.

The Doctor burns the letter as requested and undertakes the adventure. The Big Business Man and the Very Young Man go with him, while the elderly Banker, recalling that time moves faster in the atom, elects to stay behind. The drugs compounded, they destroy the equipment and test the shrinkage drug on a sparrow and a lizard. A cockroach gets an accidental dose of the growth drug and become a hideous monster before they kill it.

When all is ready, with the ring lying on a handkerchief, the three take shrinkage pills. They dwindle almost too fast to reach the ring, and the Banker picks up the rings and lays it closer to them. He watches them dwindle into it until they vanish on their way to reach the Chemist and "the people of the golden atom."

Cummings's other works are too numerous for any complete list. *The Girl in the Golden Atom* is the matter segment of a trilogy, Matter, Space, and Time. The space segment includes "The Princess of the Atom" and "The Fire People," and the time segment includes "The Man Who Mastered Time," "The Shadow Girl," and "The Exile of Time." Most of the stories were first published in *Argosy*. Cummings was a highly competent pulp craftsman, but he failed to adapt as the genre evolved. None of his later works gained the popularity of *The Girl in the Golden Atom.*

CONTENTS

Contents

THE GIRL IN THE GOLDEN ATOM

CHAPTER 1

A UNIVERSE IN AN ATOM

"THEN you mean to say there is no such thing as the *smallest* particle of matter?" asked the Doctor.

"You can put it that way if you like," the Chemist replied. "In other words, what I believe is that things can be infinitely small just as well as they can be infinitely large. Astronomers tell us of the immensity of space. I have tried to imagine space as finite. It is impossible. How can you conceive the edge of space? Something must be beyond—something or nothing, and even that would be more space, wouldn't it?"

"Gosh," said the Very Young Man, and lighted another cigarette.

The Chemist resumed, smiling a little. "Now, if it seems probable that there is no limit to the immensity of space, why should we make its smallness finite? How can you say that the atom cannot be divided? As a matter of fact, it already has been. The most powerful microscope will show you realms of smallness to which you can penetrate no other way. Multiply that power a thousand times, or ten thousand times, and who shall say what you will see?"

The Chemist paused, and looked at the intent little group around him.

He was a youngish man, with large features and horn-rimmed glasses, his rough English-cut clothes hanging loosely over his broad, spare frame.   The Banker drained his glass and rang for the waiter.

"Very interesting," he remarked.

"Don't be an ass, George," said the Big Business Man. "Just because you don't understand, doesn't mean there is no sense to it."

"What I don't get clearly"—began the Doctor.

"None of it's clear to me," said the Very Young Man.

The Doctor crossed under the light and took an easier chair.   "You intimated you had discovered something unusual in these realms of the infinitely small," he suggested, sinking back luxuriously.   "Will you tell us about it?"

"Yes, if you like," said the Chemist, turning from one to the other.   A nod of assent followed his glance, as each settled himself more comfortably.

"Well, gentlemen, when you say I have discovered something unusual in another world—in the world of the infinitely small—you are right in a way.   I have seen something and lost it.   You won't believe me probably," he glanced at the Banker an instant, "but that is not important.   I am going to tell you the facts, just as they happened."

The Big Business Man filled up the glasses all around, and the Chemist resumed:

"It was in 1910, this problem first came to interest me. I had never gone in for microscopic work very much, but now I let it absorb all my attention.   I secured larger, more powerful instruments—I spent most of my money," he smiled ruefully, "but never could I come to the end of the space into which I was looking.   Something was always hidden beyond—something I could almost, but not quite, distinguish.

"Then I realized that I was on the wrong track. My instrument was not merely of insufficient power, it was not one-thousandth the power I needed.

"So I began to study the laws of optics and lenses. In 1913 I went abroad, and with one of the most famous lens-makers of Europe I produced a lens of an entirely different quality, a lens that I hoped would give me what I wanted. So I returned here and fitted up my microscope that I knew would prove vastly more powerful than any yet constructed.

"It was finally completed and set up in my laboratory, and one night I went in alone to look through it for the first time. It was in the fall of 1914, I remember, just after the first declaration of war.

"I can recall now my feelings at that moment. I was about to see into another world, to behold what no man had ever looked on before. What would I see? What new realms was I, first of all our human race, to enter? With furiously beating heart, I sat down before the huge instrument and adjusted the eyepiece.

"Then I glanced around for some object to examine. On my finger I had a ring, my mother's wedding ring, and I decided to use that. I have it here." He took a plain gold band from his little finger and laid it on the table.

"You will see a slight mark on the outside. That is the place into which I looked."

His friends crowded around the table and examined a scratch on one side of the band.

"What did you see?" asked the Very Young Man eagerly.

"Gentlemen," resumed the Chemist, "what I saw staggered even my own imagination. With trembling hands I put the ring in place, looking directly down into that scratch. For a moment I saw nothing. I was like a person coming suddenly out of the sunlight into a darkened room. I knew there was something visible in my view, but my eyes did not seem able to receive the impressions. I realize now they were not yet adjusted to the new form of light. Gradually, as I looked, objects of definite shape began to emerge from the blackness.

"Gentlemen, I want to make clear to you now—as clear as I can—the peculiar aspect of everything that I saw under this microscope. I seemed to be inside an immense cave. One side, near at hand, I could now make out quite clearly. The walls were extraordinarily rough and indented, with a peculiar phosphorescent light on the projections and blackness in the hollows. I say phosphorescent light, for that is the nearest word I can find to describe it—a curious radiation, quite different from the reflected light to which we are accustomed.

"I said that the hollows inside of the cave were blackness. But not blackness—the absence of light—as we know it. It was a blackness that seemed also to radiate light, if you can imagine such a condition; a blackness that seemed not empty, but merely withholding its contents just beyond my vision.

"Except for a dim suggestion of roof over the cave, and its floor, I could distinguish nothing. After a moment this floor became clearer. It seemed to be—well, perhaps I might call it black marble—smooth, glossy, yet somewhat translucent. In the foreground the floor was apparently liquid. In no way did it differ in appearance from the solid part, except that its surface seemed to be in motion.

"Another curious thing was the outlines of all the shapes in view. I noticed that no outline held steady when I looked at it directly; it seemed to quiver. You see something like it when looking at an object through water—only, of course, there was no distortion. It was also like looking at something with the radiation of heat between.

"Of the back and other side of the cave, I could see nothing, except in one place, where a narrow effulgence of light drifted out into the immensity of the distance behind.

"I do not know how long I sat looking at this scene; it may have been several hours. Although I was obviously in a cave, I never felt shut in—never got the impression of being in a narrow, confined space.

"On the contrary, after a time I seemed to feel the vast immensity of the blackness before me. I think perhaps it may have been that path of light stretching out into the distance. As I looked it seemed like the reversed tail of a comet, or the dim glow of the Milky Way, and penetrating to equally remote realms of space.

"Perhaps I fell asleep, or at least there was an interval of time during which I was so absorbed in my own thoughts I was hardly conscious of the scene before me.

"Then I became aware of a dim shape in the foreground—a shape merged with the outlines surrounding it. And as I looked, it gradually assumed form, and I saw it was the figure of a young girl, sitting beside the liquid pool. Except for the same waviness of outline and phosphorescent glow, she had quite the normal aspect of a human being of our own world. She was beautiful, according to our own standards of beauty; her long braided hair a glowing black, her face, delicate of feature and winsome in expression. Her lips were a deep red, although I felt rather than saw the colour.

"She was dressed only in a short tunic of a substance I might describe as gray opaque glass, and the pearly whiteness of her skin gleamed with iridescence.

"She seemed to be singing, although I heard no sound.

Once she bent over the pool and plunged her hand into it, laughing gaily.

"Gentlemen, I cannot make you appreciate my emotions, when all at once I remembered I was looking through a microscope. I had forgotten entirely my situation, absorbed in the scene before me. And then, abruptly, a great realization came upon me—the realization that everything I saw was inside that ring. I was unnerved for the moment at the importance of my discovery.

"When I looked again, after the few moments my eye took to become accustomed to the new form of light, the scene showed itself as before, except that the girl had gone.

"For over a week, each night at the same time I watched that cave. The girl came always, and sat by the pool as I had first seen her. Once she danced with the wild grace of a wood nymph, whirling in and out the shadows, and falling at last in a little heap beside the pool.

"It was on the tenth night after I had first seen her that the accident happened. I had been watching, I remember, an unusually long time before she appeared, gliding out of the shadows. She seemed in a different mood, pensive and sad, as she bent down over the pool, staring into it intently. Suddenly there was a tremendous cracking sound, sharp as an explosion, and I was thrown backward upon the floor.

"When I recovered consciousness—I must have struck my head on something—I found the microscope in ruins. Upon examination I saw that its larger lens had exploded —flown into fragments scattered around the room. Why I was not killed I do not understand. The ring I picked up from the floor; it was unharmed and unchanged.

"Can I make you understand how I felt at this loss? Because of the war in Europe I knew I could never replace my lens—for many years, at any rate. And then, gentlemen, came the most terrible feeling of all; I knew at last that the scientific achievement I had made and lost counted for little with me. It was the girl. I realized then that the only being I ever could care for was living out her life with her world, and, indeed, her whole universe, in an atom of that ring."

The Chemist stopped talking and looked from one to the other of the tense faces of his companions.

"It's almost too big an idea to grasp," murmured the Doctor.

"What caused the explosion?" asked the Very Young Man.

"I do not know." The Chemist addressed his reply to the Doctor, as the most understanding of the group. "I can appreciate, though, that through that lens I was magnifying tremendously those peculiar light-radiations that I have described. I believe the molecules of the lens were shattered by them—I had exposed it longer to them that evening than any of the others."

The Doctor nodded his comprehension of this theory.

Impressed in spite of himself, the Banker took another drink and leaned forward in his chair. "Then you really think that there is a girl now inside the gold of that ring?" he asked.

"He didn't say that necessarily," interrupted the Big Business Man.

"Yes, he did."

"As a matter of fact, I do believe that to be the case," said the Chemist earnestly. "I believe that every particle of matter in our universe contains within it an equally complex and complete a universe, which to its inhabitants seems as large as ours. I think, also that the whole realm of our interplanetary space, our solar system and all the remote stars of the heavens are contained within the atom of some other universe as gigantic to us as we are to the universe in that ring."

"Gosh!" said the Very Young Man.

"It doesn't make one feel very important in the scheme of things, does it?" remarked the Big Business Man dryly.

The Chemist smiled. "The existence of no individual, no nation, no world, nor any one universe is of the least importance."

"Then it would be possible," said the Doctor, "for this gigantic universe that contains us in one of its atoms, to be itself contained within the atom of another universe, still more gigantic, and so on."

"That is my theory," said the Chemist.

"And in each of the atoms of the rocks of that cave there may be other worlds proportionately minute?"

"I can see no reason to doubt it."

"Well, there is no proof, anyway," said the Banker. "We might as well believe it."

"I intend to get proof," said the Chemist.

"Do you believe all these innumerable universes, both larger and smaller than ours, are inhabited?" asked the Doctor.

"I should think probably most of them are. The existence of life, I believe, is as fundamental as the existence of matter without life."

"How do you suppose that girl got in there?" asked the Very Young Man, coming out of a brown study.

"What puzzled me," resumed the Chemist, ignoring the question, "is why the girl should so resemble our own race. I have thought about it a good deal, and I have reached the conclusion that the inhabitants of any universe in the next smaller or larger plane to ours probably resemble us fairly closely. That ring, you see, is in the same—shall we say—environment as ourselves. The same forces control it that control us. Now, if the ring had been created on Mars, for instance, I believe that the universes within its atoms would be inhabited by beings like the Martians—if Mars has any inhabitants. Of course, in planes beyond those next to ours, either smaller or larger, changes would probably occur, becoming greater as you go in or out from our own universe."

"Good Lord! It makes one dizzy to think of it," said the Big Business Man.

"I wish I knew how that girl got in there," sighed the Very Young Man, looking at the ring.

"She probably didn't," retorted the Doctor. "Very likely she was created there, the same as you were here."

"I think that is probably so," said the Chemist. "And yet, sometimes I am not at all sure. She was very human." The Very Young Man looked at him sympathetically.

"How are you going to prove your theories?" asked the Banker, in his most irritatingly practical way.

The Chemist picked up the ring and put it on his finger. "Gentlemen," he said. "I have tried to tell you facts, not theories. What I saw through that ultramicroscope was not an unproven theory, but a fact. My theories you have brought out by your questions."

"You are quite right," said the Doctor; "but you did mention yourself that you hoped to provide proof."

The Chemist hesitated a moment, then made his decision. "I will tell you the rest," he said.

"After the destruction of the miscroscope, I was quite at a loss how to proceed. I thought about the problem for many weeks. Finally I decided to work along another altogether different line—a theory about which I am surprised you have not already questioned me."

He paused, but no one spoke.

"I am hardly ready with proof to-night," he resumed after a moment. "Will you all take dinner with me here at the club one week from to-night?" He read affirmation in the glance of each.

"Good. That's settled," he said, rising. "At seven, then."

"But what was the theory you expected us to question you about?" asked the Very Young Man.

The Chemist leaned on the back of his chair.

"The only solution I could see to the problem," he said slowly, "was to find some way of making myself sufficiently small to be able to enter that other universe. I have found such a way and one week from to-night, gentlemen, with your assistance, I am going to enter the surface of that ring at the point where it is scratched!"

CHAPTER II

THE cigars were lighted and dinner over before the Doctor broached the subject uppermost in the minds of every member of the party.

"A toast, gentlemen," he said, raising his glass. "To the greatest research chemist in the world. May he be successful in his adventure to-night."

The Chemist bowed his acknowledgment.

"You have not heard me yet," he said smiling.

"But we want to," said the Very Young Man impulsively.

"And you shall." He settled himself more comfortably in his chair. "Gentlemen, I am going to tell you, first, as simply as possible, just what I have done in the past two years. You must draw your own conclusions from the evidence I give you.

"You will remember that I told you last week of my dilemna after the destruction of the microscope. Its loss and the impossibility of replacing it, led me into still bolder plans than merely the visual examination of this minute world. I reasoned, as I have told you, that because of its physical proximity, its similar environment, so to speak, this outer world should be capable of supporting life identical with our own.

"By no process of reasoning can I find adequate refutation of this theory. Then, again, I had the evidence of my own eyes to prove that a being I could not tell from one of my own kind was living there. That this girl, other than in size, differs radically from those of our race, I cannot believe.

"I saw then but one obstacle standing between me and this other world—the discrepancy of size. The distance separating our world from this other is infinitely great or infinitely small, according to the viewpoint. In my present size it is only a few feet from here to the ring on that plate. But to an inhabitant of that other world, we are as remote as the faintest stars of the heavens, diminished a thousand times."

He paused a moment, signing the waiter to leave the room.

"This reduction of bodily size, great as it is, involves no deeper principle than does a light contraction of tissue, except that it must be carried further. The problem, then, was to find a chemical, sufficiently unharmful to life, that would so act upon the body cells as to cause a reduction in bulk, without changing their shape. I had to secure a uniform and also a proportionate rate of contraction of each cell, in order not to have the body shape altered.

"After a comparatively small amount of research work, I encountered an apparently insurmountable obstacle. As you know, gentlemen, our living human bodies are held together by the power of the central intelligence we call the mind. Every instant during your lifetime your subconscious mind is commanding and directing the individual life of each cell that makes up your body. At death this power is withdrawn; each cell is thrown under its own individual command, and dissolution of the body takes place.

"I found, therefore, that I could not act upon the cells separately, so long as they were under control of the mind. On the other hand, I could not withdraw this power of the subconscious mind without causing death.

"I progressed no further than this for several months. Then came the solution. I reasoned that after death the body does not immediately disintegrate; far more time elapses than I expected to need for the cell-contraction. I devoted my time, then to finding a chemical that would temporarily withhold, during the period of cell-contraction, the power of the subconscious mind, just as the power of the conscious mind is withheld by hypnotism.

"I am not going to weary you by trying to lead you through the maze of chemical experiments into which I plunged. Only one of you," he indicated the Doctor, "has the technical basis of knowledge to follow me. No one had been before me along the path I traversed. I pursued the method of pure theoretical deduction, drawing my conclusions from the practical results obtained.

"I worked on rabbits almost exclusively. After a few weeks I succeeded in completely suspending animation in one of them for several hours. There was no life apparently existing during that period. It was not a trance or coma, but the complete simulation of death. No harmful results followed the revivifying of the animal. The contraction of the cells was far more difficult to accomplish; I finished my last experiment less than six months ago."

"Then you really have been able to make an animal infinitely small?" asked the Big Business Man.

The Chemist smiled. "I sent four rabbits into the unknown last week," he said.

"What did they look like going?" asked the Very Young Man. The Chemist signed him to be patient.

"The quantity of diminution to be obtained bothered me considerably. Exactly how small that other universe is, I had no means of knowing, except by the computations I made of the magnifying power of my lens. These figures, I know, must necessarily be very inaccurate.   Then, again, I have no means of judging by the visual rate of diminution of these rabbits, whether this contraction is at a uniform rate or accelerated.   Nor can I tell how long it is prolonged, for the quantity of drug administered, as only a fraction of the diminution has taken place when the animal passes beyond the range of any microscope I now possess.

"These questions were overshadowed, however, by a far more serious problem that encompassed them all.

"As I was planning to project myself into this unknown universe and to reach the exact size proportionate to it, I soon realized such a result could not be obtained were I in an unconscious state.   Only by successive doses of the drug, or its retardent about which I will tell you later, could I hope to reach the proper size.   Another necessity is that I place myself on the exact spot on that ring where I wish to enter and to climb down among its atoms when I have become sufficiently small to do so. Obviously, this would be impossible to one not possessing all his faculties and physical strength."

"And did you solve that problem, too?" asked the Banker.

"I'd like to see it done," he added, reading his answer in the other's confident smile.

The Chemist produced two small paper packages from his wallet.   "These drugs are the result of my research," he said.   "One of them causes contraction, and the other expansion, by an exact reversal of the process.   Taken together, they produce no effect, and a lesser amount of one retards the action of the other."   He opened the papers, showing two small vials.   "I have made them as you see, in the form of tiny pills, each containing a minute quantity of the drug.   It is by taking them successively in unequal amounts that I expect to reach the desired size."

"There's one point that you do not mention," said the Doctor. "Those vials and their contents will have to change size as you do. How are you going to manage that?"

"By experimentation I have found," answered the Chemist, "that any object held in close physical contact with the living body being contracted is contracted itself at an equal rate. I believe that my clothes will be affected also. These vials I will carry strapped under my armpits."

"Suppose you should die, or be killed, would the contraction cease?" asked the Doctor.

"Yes, almost immediately," replied the Chemist. "Apparently, though I am acting through the subconscious mind while its power is held in abeyance, when this power is permanently withdrawn by death, the drug no longer affects the individual cells. The contraction or expansion ceases almost at once."

The Chemist cleared a space before him on the table. "In a well-managed club like this," he said, "there should be no flies, but I see several around. Do you suppose we can catch one of them?"

"I can," said the Very Young Man, and forthwith he did.

The Chemist moistened a lump of sugar and laid it on the table before him. Then, selecting one of the smallest of the pills, he ground it to powder with the back of a spoon and sprinkled this powder on the sugar.

"Will you give me the fly, please?"

The Very Young Man gingerly did so. The Chemist held the insect by its wings over the sugar. "Will someone lend me one of his shoes?"

The Very Young Man hastily slipped off a dancing pump.

"Thank you," said the Chemist, placing it on the table with a quizzical smile.

The rest of the company rose from their chairs and gathered around, watching with interested faces what was about to happen.

"I hope he is hungry," remarked the Chemist, and placed the fly gently down on the sugar, still holding it by the wings. The insect, after a moment, ate a little.

Silence fell upon the group as each watched intently. For a few moments nothing happened. Then, almost imperceptibly at first, the fly became larger. In another minute it was the size of a large horse-fly, struggling to release its wings from the Chemist's grasp. A minute more and it was the size of a beetle. No one spoke. The Banker moistened his lips, drained his glass hurriedly and moved slightly farther away. Still the insect grew; now it was the size of a small chicken, the multiple lens of its eyes presenting a most terrifying aspect, while its ferocious droning reverberated through the room. Then suddenly the Chemist threw it upon the table, covered it with a napkin, and beat it violently with the slipper. When all movement had ceased he tossed its quivering body into a corner of the room.

"Good God!" ejaculated the Banker, as the white-faced men stared at each other. The quiet voice of the Chemist brought them back to themselves. "That, gentlemen, you must understand, was only a fraction of the very first stage of growth. As you may have noticed, it was constantly accelerated. This acceleration attains a speed of possibly fifty thousand times that you observed. Beyond that, it is my theory, the change is at a uniform rate." He looked at the body of the fly, lying inert on the floor. "You can appreciate now, gentlemen, the importance of having this growth cease after death."

"Good Lord, I should say so!" murmured the Big Business Man, mopping his forehead. The Chemist took the lump of sugar and threw it into the open fire.

"Gosh!" said the Very Young Man, "suppose when we were not looking, another fly had——"

"Shut up!" growled the Banker.

"Not so skeptical now, eh, George?" said the Big Business Man.

"Can you catch me another fly?" asked the Chemist. The Very Young Man hastened to do so. "The second demonstration, gentlemen," said the Chemist, "is less spectacular, but far more pertinent than the one you have just witnessed." He took the fly by the wings, and prepared another lump of sugar, sprinkling a crushed pill from the other vial upon it.

"When he is small enough I am going to try to put him on the ring, if he will stay still," said the Chemist.

The Doctor pulled the plate containing the ring forward until it was directly under the light, and every one crowded closer to watch; already the fly was almost too small to be held. The Chemist tried to set it on the ring, but could not; so with his other hand he brushed it lightly into the plate, where it lay, a tiny black speck against the gleaming whiteness of the china.

"Watch it carefully, gentlemen," he said, as they bent closer.

"It's gone," said the Big Business Man.

"No, I can still see it," said the Doctor. Then he raised the plate closer to his face. "Now it's gone," he said.

The Chemist sat down in his chair. "It's probably still there, only too small for you to see. In a few minutes, if it took a sufficient amount of the drug, it will be small enough to fall between the molecules of the plate."

"Do you suppose it will find another inhabited universe down there?" asked the Very Young Man.

"Who knows," smiled the Chemist. "Very possibly it will. But the one we are interested in is here," he added, touching the ring.

"Is it your intention to take this stuff yourself tonight?" asked the Big Business Man.

"If you will give me your help, I think so, yes. I have made all arrangements. The club has given us this room in absolute privacy for forty-eight hours. Your meals will be served here when you want them, and I am going to ask you, gentlemen, to take turns watching and guarding the ring during that time. Will you do it?"

"I should say we would," cried the Doctor, and the others nodded assent.

"It is because I wanted you to be convinced of my entire sincerity that I have taken you so thoroughly into my confidence. Are those doors locked?" The Very Young Man locked them.

"Thank you," said the Chemist, starting to disrobe. In a moment he stood before them attired in a woolen bathing-suit of pure white. Over his shoulders was strapped tightly a narrow leather harness, supporting two silken pockets, one under each armpit. Into each of these he placed one of the vials, first laying four pills from one of them upon the table.

At this point the Banker rose from his chair and selected another in the further corner of the room. He sank into it a crumpled heap and wiped the beads of perspiration from his face with a shaking hand.

"I have every expectation," said the Chemist, "that this suit and harness will contract in size uniformly with me. If the harness should not, then I shall have to hold the vials in my hand."

On the table, directly under the light, he spread a large

silk handkerchief, upon which he placed the ring. He then produced a teaspoon, which he handed to the Doctor.

"Please listen carefully," he said, "for perhaps the whole success of my adventure, and my life itself, may depend upon your actions during the next few minutes. You will realize, of course, that when I am still large enough to be visible to you I shall be so small that my voice may be inaudible. Therefore, I want you to know, now, just what to expect.

"When I am something under a foot high, I shall step upon that handkerchief, where you will see my white suit plainly against its black surface. When I become less than an inch high, I shall run over to the ring and stand beside it. When I have diminished to about a quarter of an inch, I shall climb upon it, and, as I get smaller, will follow its surface until I come to the scratch.

"I want you to watch me very closely. I may miscalculate the time and wait until I am too small to climb upon the ring. Or I may fall off. In either case, you will place that spoon beside me and I will climb into it. You will then do your best to help me get on the ring. Is all this quite clear?"

The Doctor nodded assent.

"Very well, watch me as long as I remain visible. If I have an accident, I shall take the other drug and endeavor to return to you at once. This you must expect at any moment during the next forty-eight hours. Under all circumstances, if I am alive, I shall return at the expiration of that time.

"And, gentlemen, let me caution you most solemnly, do not allow that ring to be touched until that length of time has expired. Can I depend on you?"

"Yes," they answered breathlessly.

"After I have taken the pills," the Chemist continued, "I shall not speak unless it is absolutely necessary. I do not know what my sensations will be, and I want to follow them as closely as possible." He then turned out all the lights in the room with the exception of the center electrolier, that shone down directly on the handkerchief and ring.

The Chemist looked about him. "Good-by, gentlemen," he said, shaking hands all round. "Wish me luck," and without hesitation he placed the four pills in his mouth and washed them down with a swallow of water.

Silence fell on the group as the Chemist seated himself and covered his face with his hands. For perhaps two minutes the tenseness of the silence was unbroken, save by the heavy breathing of the Banker as he lay huddled in his chair.

"Oh, my God! He *is* growing smaller!" whispered the Big Business Man in a horrified tone to the Doctor. The Chemist raised his head and smiled at them. Then he stood up, steadying himself against a chair. He was less than four feet high. Steadily he grew smaller before their horrified eyes. Once he made as if to speak, and the Doctor knelt down beside him. "It's all right, good-by," he said in a tiny voice.

Then he stepped upon the handkerchief. The Doctor knelt on the floor beside it, the wooden spoon ready in his hand, while the others, except the Banker, stood behind him. The figure of the Chemist, standing motionless near the edge of the handkerchief, seemed now like a little white wooden toy, hardly more than an inch in height.

Waving his hand and smiling, he suddenly started to walk and then ran swiftly over to the ring. By the time he reached it, somewhat out of breath, he was little more than twice as high as the width of its band. Without pausing, he leaped up, and sat astraddle, leaning over and holding to it tightly with his hands. In another moment he was on his feet, on the upper edge of the ring, walking carefully along its circumference towards the scratch.

The Big Business Man touched the Doctor on the shoulder and tried to smile. "He's making it," he whispered. As if in answer the little figure turned and waved its arms. They could just distinguish its white outline against the gold surface underneath.

"I don't see him," said the Very Young Man in a scared voice.

"He's right near the scratch," answered the Doctor, bending closer. Then, after a moment, "He's gone." He rose to his feet. "Good Lord! Why haven't we a microscope!"

"I never thought of that," said the Big Business Man, "we could have watched him for a long time yet."

"Well, he's gone now," returned the Doctor, "and there is nothing for us to do but wait."

"I hope he finds that girl," sighed the Very Young Man, as he sat chin in hand beside the handkerchief.

CHAPTER III

THE Banker snored stertorously from his mattress in a corner of the room. In an easy-chair near by, with his feet on the table, lay the Very Young Man, sleeping also.

The Doctor and the Big Business Man sat by the handkerchief conversing in low tones.

"How long has it been now?" asked the latter.

"Just forty hours," answered the Doctor; "and he said that forty-eight hours was the limit. He should come back at about ten to-night."

"I wonder if he *will* come back," questioned the Big Business Man nervously. "Lord, I wish *he* wouldn't snore so loud," he added irritably, nodding in the direction of the Banker.

They were silent for a moment, and then he went on: "You'd better try to sleep a little while, Frank. You're worn out. I'll watch here."

"I suppose I should," answered the Doctor wearily. "Wake up that kid, he's sleeping most of the time."

"No, I'll watch," repeated the Big Business Man. "You lie down over there."

The Doctor did so while the other settled himself more comfortably on a cushion beside the handkerchief, and prepared for his lonely watching.

The Doctor apparently dropped off to sleep at once, for he did not speak again. The Big Business Man sat staring steadily at the ring, bending nearer to it occasionally. Every ten or fifteen minutes he looked at his watch.

Perhaps an hour passed in this way, when the Very Young Man suddenly sat up and yawned. "Haven't they come back yet?" he asked in a sleepy voice.

The Big Business Man answered in a much lower tone. "What do you mean—they?"

"I dreamed that he brought the girl back with him," said the Very Young Man.

"Well, if he did, they have not arrived. You'd better go back to sleep. We've got six or seven hours yet— maybe more."

The Very Young Man rose and crossed the room. "No, I'll watch a while," he said, seating himself on the floor. "What time is it?"

"Quarter to three."

"He said he'd be back by ten to-night. I'm crazy to see that girl."

The Big Business Man rose and went over to a dinner-tray, standing near the door. "Lord, I'm hungry. I must have forgotten to eat to-day." He lifted up one of the silver covers. What he saw evidently encouraged him, for he drew up a chair and began his lunch.

The Very Young Man lighted a cigarette. "It will be the tragedy of my life," he said, "if he never comes back."

The Big Business Man smiled. "How about *his* life?" he answered, but the Very Young Man had fallen into a reverie and did not reply.

The Big Business Man finished his lunch in silence and was just about to light a cigar when a sharp exclamation brought him hastily to his feet.

"Come here, quick, I see something." The Very Young Man had his face close to the ring and was trembling violently.

The other pushed him back. "Let me see. Where?"

"There, by the scratch; he's lying there; I can see him."

The Big Business Man looked and then hurriedly woke the Doctor.

"He's come back," he said briefly; "you can see him there." The Doctor bent down over the ring while the others woke up the Banker.

"He doesn't seem to be getting any bigger," said the Very Young Man; "he's just lying there. Maybe he's dead."

"What shall we do?" asked the Big Business Man, and made as if to pick up the ring. The Doctor shoved him away. "Don't do that!" he said sharply. "Do you want to kill him?"

"He's sitting up," cried the Very Young Man. "He's all right."

"He must have fainted," said the Doctor. "Probably he's taking more of the drug now."

"He's much larger," said the Very Young Man; "look at him!"

The tiny figure was sitting sideways on the ring, with its feet hanging over the outer edge. It was growing perceptibly larger each instant, and in a moment it slipped down off the ring and sank in a heap on the handkerchief.

"Good Heavens! Look at him!" cried the Big Business Man. "He's all covered with blood."

The little figure presented a ghastly sight. As it steadily grew larger they could see and recognize the Chemist's haggard face, his cheek and neck stained with blood, and his white suit covered with dirt.

"Look at his feet," whispered the Big Business Man. They were horribly cut and bruised and greatly swollen.

The Doctor bent over and whispered gently, "What can I do to help you?" The Chemist shook his head.

His body, lying prone upon the handkerchief, had torn it apart in growing. When he was about twelve inches in length he raised his head. The Doctor bent closer. "Some brandy, please," said a wraith of the Chemist's voice. It was barely audible.

"He wants some brandy," called the Doctor. The Very Young Man looked hastily around, then opened the door and dashed madly out of the room. When he returned, the Chemist had grown to nearly four feet. He was sitting on the floor with his back against the Doctor's knees. The Big Business Man was wiping the blood off his face with a damp napkin.

"Here!" cried the Very Young Man, thrusting forth the brandy. The Chemist drank a little of it. Then he sat up, evidently somewhat revived.

"I seem to have stopped growing," he said. "Let's finish it up now. God! how I want to be the right size again," he added fervently.

The Doctor helped him extract the vials from under his arm, and the Chemist touched one of the pills to his tongue. Then he sank back, closing his eyes. "I think that should be about enough," he murmured.

No one spoke for nearly ten minutes. Gradually the Chemist's body grew, the Doctor shifting his position several times as it became larger. It seemed finally to have stopped growing, and was apparently nearly its former size.

"Is he asleep?" whispered the Very Young Man.

The Chemist opened his eyes.

"No," he answered. "I'm all right now, I think." He rose to his feet, the Doctor and the Big Business Man supporting him on either side.

"Sit down and tell us about it," said the Very Young Man. "Did you find the girl?"

The Chemist smiled wearily.

"Gentlemen, I cannot talk now. Let me have a bath and some dinner. Then I will tell you all about it."

The Doctor rang for an attendant, and led the Chemist to the door, throwing a blanket around him as he did so. In the doorway the Chemist paused and looked back with a wan smile over the wreck of the room.

"Give me an hour," he said. "And eat something yourselves while I am gone." Then he left, closing the door after him.

When he returned, fully dressed in clothes that were ludicrously large for him, the room had been straightened up, and his four friends were finishing their meal. He took his place among them quietly and lighted a cigar.

"Well, gentlemen, I suppose that you are interested to hear what happened to me," he began. The Very Young Man asked his usual question.

"Let him alone," said the Doctor. "You will hear it all soon enough."

"Was it all as you expected?" asked the Banker. It was his first remark since the Chemist returned.

"To a great extent, yes," answered the Chemist. "But I had better tell you just what happened." The Very Young Man nodded his eager agreement.

"When I took those first four pills," began the Chemist in a quiet, even tone, "my immediate sensation was a sudden reeling of the senses, combined with an extreme nausea. This latter feeling passed after a moment.

"You will remember that I seated myself upon the floor and closed my eyes. When I opened them my head had steadied itself somewhat, but I was oppressed by a curious feeling of drowsiness, impossible to shake off.

"My first mental impression was one of wonderment when I saw you all begin to increase in size. I remember standing up beside that chair, which was then half again its normal size, and you"—indicating the Doctor—

"towered beside me as a giant of nine or ten feet high.

"Steadily upward, with a curious crawling motion, grew the room and all its contents. Except for the feeling of sleep that oppressed me, I felt quite my usual self. No change appeared happening to me, but everything else seemed growing to gigantic and terrifying proportions.

"Can you imagine a human being a hundred feet high? That is how you looked to me as I stepped upon that huge expanse of black silk and shouted my last good-bye to you!

"Over to my left lay the ring, apparently fifteen or twenty feet away. I started to walk towards it, but although it grew rapidly larger, the distance separating me from it seemed to increase rather than lessen. Then I ran, and by the time I arrived it stood higher than my waist—a beautiful, shaggy, golden pit.

"I jumped upon its rim and clung to it tightly. I could feel it growing beneath me, as I sat. After a moment I climbed upon its top surface and started to walk towards the point where I knew the scratch to be.

"I found myself now, as I looked about, walking upon a narrow, though ever broadening, curved path. The ground beneath my feet appeared to be a rough, yellowish quartz. This path grew rougher as I advanced. Below the bulging edges of the path, on both sides, lay a shining black plain, ridged and indented, and with a sunlike sheen on the higher portions of the ridges. On the one hand this black plain stretched in an unbroken expanse to the horizon. On the other, it appeared as a circular valley, enclosed by a shining yellow wall.

"The way had now become extraordinarily rough. I bore to the left as I advanced, keeping close to the outer edge. The other edge of the path I could not see. I clambered along hastily, and after a few moments was confronted by a row of rocks and bowlders lying directly across my line of progress. I followed their course for a short distance, and finally found a space through which I could pass.

"This transverse ridge was perhaps a hundred feet deep. Behind it and extending in a parallel direction lay a tremendous valley. I knew then I had reached my first objective.

"I sat down upon the brink of the precipice and watched the cavern growing ever wider and deeper. Then I realized that I must begin my descent if ever I was to reach the bottom. For perhaps six hours I climbed steadily downwards. It was a fairly easy descent after the first little while, for the ground seemed to open up before me as I advanced, changing its contour so constantly that I was never at a loss for an easy downward path.

"My feet suffered cruelly from the shaggy, metallic ground, and I soon had to stop and rig a sort of protection for the soles of them from a portion of the harness over my shoulder. According to the stature I was when I reached the bottom, I had descended perhaps twelve thousand feet during this time.

"The latter part of the journey found me nearing the bottom of the cañon. Objects around me no longer seemed to increase in size, as had been constantly the case before, and I reasoned that probably my stature was remaining constant.

"I noticed, too, as I advanced, a curious alteration in the form of light around me. The glare from above (the sky showed only as a narrow dull ribbon of blue) barely penetrated to the depths of the cañon's floor. But all about me there was a soft radiance, seeming to emanate from the rocks themselves.

"The sides of the cañon were shaggy and rough, beyond anything I had ever seen. Huge bowlders, hundreds of feet in diameter, were embedded in them. The bottom also was strewn with similar gigantic rocks.

"I surveyed this lonely waste for some time in dismay, not knowing in what direction lay my goal. I knew that I was at the bottom of the scratch, and by the comparison of its size I realized I was well started on my journey.

"I have not told you, gentlemen, that at the time I marked the ring I made a deeper indentation in one portion of the scratch and focused the microscope upon that. This indentation I now searched for. Luckily I found it, less than half a mile away—an almost circular pit, perhaps five miles in diameter, with shining walls extending downwards into blackness. There seemed no possible way of descending into it, so I sat down near its edge to think out my plan of action.

"I realized now that I was faint and hungry, and whatever I did must be done quickly. I could turn back to you, or I could go on. I decided to risk the latter course, and took twelve more of the pills—three times my original dose."

The Chemist paused for a moment, but his auditors were much too intent to question him. Then he resumed in his former matter-of-fact tone.

"After my vertigo had passed somewhat—it was much more severe this time—I looked up and found my surroundings growing at a far more rapid rate than before. I staggered to the edge of the pit. It was opening up and widening out at an astounding rate. Already its sides were becoming rough and broken, and I saw many places where a descent would be possible.

"The feeling of sleep that had formerly merely oppressed me, combined now with my physical fatigue and the larger dose of the drug I had taken, became almost intolerable. I yielded to it for a moment, lying down on a crag near the edge of the pit. I must have become almost immediately unconscious, and remained so for a considerable time. I can remember a horrible sensation of sliding headlong for what seemed like hours. I felt that I was sliding or falling downward. I tried to rouse but could not. Then came absolute oblivion.

"When I recovered my senses I was lying partly covered by a mass of smooth, shining pebbles. I was bruised and battered from head to foot—in a far worse condition than you first saw me when I returned.

"I sat up and looked around. Beside me, sloped upward at an apparently increasing angle a tremendous glossy plane. This extended, as far as I could see, both to the right and left and upward into the blackness of the sky overhead. It was this plane that had evidently broken my fall, and I had been sliding down it, bringing with me a considerable mass of rocks and bowlders.

"As my senses became clearer I saw I was lying on a fairly level floor. I could see perhaps two miles in each direction. Beyond that there was only darkness. The sky overhead was unbroken by stars or light of any kind. I should have been in total darkness except, as I have told you before, that everything, even the blackness itself, seemed to be self-luminous.

"The incline down which I had fallen was composed of some smooth substance suggesting black marble. The floor underfoot was quite different—more of a metallic quality with a curious corrugation. Before me, in the dim distance, I could just make out a tiny range of hills.

"I rose, after a time, and started weakly to walk towards these hills. Though I was faint and dizzy from my fall and the lack of food, I walked for perhaps half an hour, following closely the edge of the incline. No change in my visual surroundings occurred, except that I seemed gradually to be approaching the line of hills.

My situation at this time, as I turned it over in my mind, appeared hopelessly desperate, and I admit I neither expected to reach my destination nor to be able to return to my own world.

"A sudden change in the feeling of the ground underfoot brought me to myself; I bent down and found I was treading on vegetation—a tiny forest extending for quite a distance in front and to the side of me. A few steps ahead a little silver ribbon threaded its way through the trees. This I judged to be water.

"New hope possessed me at this discovery. I sat down at once and took a portion of another of the pills.

"I must again have fallen asleep. When I awoke, somewhat refreshed, I found myself lying beside the huge trunk of a fallen tree. I was in what had evidently once been a deep forest, but which now was almost utterly desolated. Only here and there were the trees left standing. For the most part they were lying in a crushed and tangled mass, many of them partially embedded in the ground.

"I cannot express adequately to you, gentlemen, what an evidence of tremendous superhuman power this scene presented. No storm, no lightning, nor any attack of the elements could have produced more than a fraction of the destruction I saw all around me.

"I climbed cautiously upon the fallen tree-trunk, and from this elevation had a much better view of my surroundings. I appeared to be near one end of the desolated area, which extended in a path about half a mile wide and several miles deep. In front, a thousand feet away, perhaps, lay the unbroken forest.

"Descending from the tree-trunk I walked in this direction, reaching the edge of the woods after possibly an hour of the most arduous traveling of my whole journey.

"During this time almost my only thought was the necessity of obtaining food. I looked about me as I advanced, and on one of the fallen tree-trunks I found a sort of vine growing. This vine bore a profusion of small gray berries, much like our huckleberries. They proved similar in taste, and I sat down and ate a quantity.

"When I reached the edge of the forest I felt somewhat stronger. I had seen up to this time no sign of animal life whatever. Now, as I stood silent, I could hear around me all the multitudinous tiny voices of the woods. Insect life stirred underfoot, and in the trees above an occasional bird flitted to and fro.

"Perhaps I am giving you a picture of our own world. I do not mean to do so. You must remember that above me there was no sky, just blackness. And yet so much light illuminated the scene that I could not believe it was other than what we would call daytime. Objects in the forest were as well lighted—better probably than they would be under similar circumstances in our own world.

"The trees were of huge size compared to my present stature; straight, upstanding trunks, with no branches until very near the top. They were bluish-gray in color, and many of them well covered with the berry-vine I have mentioned. The leaves overhead seemed to be blue —in fact the predominating color of all the vegetation was blue, just as in our world it is green. The ground was covered with dead leaves, mould, and a sort of gray moss. Fungus of a similar color appeared, but of this I did not eat.

"I had penetrated perhaps two miles into the forest when I came unexpectedly to the bank of a broad, smooth-flowing river, its silver surface seeming to radiate waves of the characteristic phosphorescent light. I found it cold, pure-tasting water, and I drank long and deeply. Then I remember lying down upon the mossy bank, and in a moment, utterly worn out, I again fell asleep."

CHAPTER IV

LYLDA

"I WAS awakened by the feel of soft hands upon my head and face. With a start I sat up abruptly; I rubbed my eyes confusedly for a moment, not knowing where I was. When I collected my wits I found myself staring into the face of a girl, who was kneeling on the ground before me. I recognized her at once—she was the girl of the microscope.

"To say I was startled would be to put it mildly, but I read no fear in her expression, only wonderment at my springing so suddenly into life. She was dressed very much as I had seen her before. Her fragile beauty was the same, and at this closer view infinitely more appealing, but I was puzzled to account for her older, more mature look. She seemed to have aged several years since the last evening I had seen her through the microscope. Yet, undeniably, it was the same girl.

"For some moments we sat looking at each other in wonderment. Then she smiled and held out her hand, palm up, speaking a few words as she did so. Her voice was soft and musical, and the words of a peculiar quality that we generally describe as liquid, for want of a better term. What she said was wholly unintelligible, but whether the words were strange or the intonation different 'from anything I had ever heard I could not determine.

"Afterwards, during my stay in this other world, I found that the language of its people resembled English quite closely, so far as the words themselves went. But

33

the intonation with which they were given, and the gestures accompanying them, differed so widely from our own that they conveyed no meaning.

"The gap separating us, however, was very much less than you would imagine. Strangely enough, though, it was not I who learned to speak her tongue, but she who mastered mine."

The Very Young Man sighed contentedly.

"We became quite friendly after this greeting," resumed the Chemist, "and it was apparent from her manner that she had already conceived her own idea of who and what I was.

"For some time we sat and tried to communicate with each other. My words seemed almost as unintelligible to her as hers to me, except that occasionally she would divine my meaning, clapping her hands in childish delight. I made out that she lived at a considerable distance, and that her name was Lylda. Finally she pulled me by the hand and led me away with a proprietary air that amused and, I must admit, pleased me tremendously.

"We had progressed through the woods in this way, hardly more than a few hundred yards, when suddenly I found that she was taking me into the mouth of a cave or passageway, sloping downward at an angle of perhaps twenty degrees. I noticed now, more graphically than ever before, a truth that had been gradually forcing itself upon me. Darkness was impossible in this new world. We were now shut in between narrow walls of crystalline rock, with a roof hardly more than fifty feet above.

"No artificial light of any kind was in evidence, yet the scene was lighted quite brightly. This, I have explained, was caused by the phosphorescent radiation that apparently emanated from every particle of mineral matter in this universe.

"As we advanced, many other tunnels crossed the one

we were traveling. And now, occasionally, we passed other people, the men dressed similarly to Lylda, but wearing their hair chopped off just above the shoulder line.

"Later, I found that the men were generally about five and a half feet in stature: lean, muscular, and with a grayer, harder look to their skin than the iridescent quality that characterized the women.

"They were fine-looking chaps these we encountered. All of them stared curiously at me, and several times we were held up by chattering groups. The intense whiteness of my skin, for it looked in this light the color of chalk, seemed to both awe and amuse them. But they treated me with great deference and respect, which I afterwards learned was because of Lylda herself, and also what she told them about me.

"At several of the intersections of the tunnels there were wide open spaces. One of these we now approached. It was a vast amphitheater, so broad its opposite wall was invisible, and it seemed crowded with people. At the side, on a rocky niche in the wall, a speaker harangued the crowd.

"We skirted the edge of this crowd and plunged into another passageway, sloping downward still more steeply. I was so much interested in the strange scenes opening before me that I remarked little of the distance we traveled. Nor did I question Lylda but seldom. I was absorbed in the complete similarity between this and my own world in its general characteristics, and yet its complete strangeness in details.

"I felt not the slightest fear. Indeed the sincerity and kindliness of these people seemed absolutely genuine, and the friendly, naïve, manner of my little guide put me wholly at my ease. Towards me Lylda's manner was one of childish delight at a new-found possession. Towards those of her own people with whom we talked, I found she preserved a dignity they profoundly respected.

"We had hardly more than entered this last tunnel when I heard the sound of drums and a weird sort of piping music, followed by shouts and cheers. Figures from behind us scurried past, hastening towards the sound. Lylda's clasp on my hand tightened, and she pulled me forward eagerly. As we advanced the crowd became denser, pushing and shoving us about and paying little attention to me.

"In close contact with these people I soon found I was stronger than they, and for a time I had no difficulty in shoving them aside and opening a path for us. They took my rough handling in all good part, in fact, never have I met a more even-tempered, good-natured people than these.

"After a time the crowd became so dense we could advance no further. At this Lylda signed me :c bear to the side. As we approached the wall of the cavern she suddenly clasped her hands high over her head and shouted something in a clear, commanding voice. Instantly the crowd fell back, and in a moment I found myself being pulled up a narrow flight of stone steps in the wall and out upon a level space some twenty feet above the heads of the people.

"Several dignitaries occupied this platform. Lylda greeted them quietly, and they made place for us beside the parapet. I could see now that we were at the intersection of a transverse passageway, much broader than the one we had been traversing. And now I received the greatest surprise I had had in this new world, for down this latter tunnel was passing a broad line of men who obviously were soldiers.

"The uniformly straight lines they held; the glint of

light on the spears they carried upright before them; the weird, but rhythmic, music that passed at intervals, with which they kept step; and, above all, the cheering enthusiasm of the crowd, all seemed like an echo of my own great world above.

"This martial ardor and what it implied came as a distinct shock. All I had seen before showed the gentle kindliness of a people whose life seemed far removed from the struggle for existence to which our race is subjected. I had come gradually to feel that this new world, at least, had attained the golden age of security, and that fear, hate, and wrongdoing had long since passed away, or had never been born.

"Yet, here before my very eyes, made wholesome by the fires of patriotism, stalked the grim God of War. Knowing nothing yet of the motive that inspired these people, I could feel no enthusiasm, but only disillusionment at this discovery of the omnipotence of strife.

"For some time I must have stood in silence. Lylda, too, seemed to divine my thoughts, for she did not applaud, but pensively watched the cheering throng below. All at once, with an impulsively appealing movement, she pulled me down towards her, and pressed her pretty cheek to mine. It seemed almost as if she was asking me to help.

"The line of marching men seemed now to have passed, and the crowd surged over into the open space and began to disperse. As the men upon the platform with us prepared to leave, Lylda led me over to one of them. He was nearly as tall as I, and dressed in the characteristic tunic that seemed universally worn by both sexes. The upper part of his body was hung with beads, and across his chest was a thin, slightly convex stone plate.

"After a few words of explanation from Lylda, he laid

his hands on my shoulders near the base of the neck, smiling with his words of greeting. Then he held one hand before me, palm up, as Lylda had done, and I laid mine in it, which seemed the correct thing to do.

"I repeated this performance with two others who joined us, and then Lylda pulled me away. We descended the steps and turned into the broader tunnel, finding near at hand a sort of sleigh, which Lylda signed me to enter. It was constructed evidently of wood, with a pile of leaves, or similar dead vegetation, for cushions. It was balanced upon a single runner of polished stone, about two feet broad, with a narrow, slightly shorter outrider on each side.

"Harnessed to the shaft were two animals, more resembling our reindeers than anything else, except that they were gray in color and had no horns. An attendant greeted Lylda respectfully as we approached, and mounted a seat in front of us when we were comfortably settled.

"We drove in this curious vehicle for over an hour. The floor of the tunnel was quite smooth, and we glided down its incline with little effort and at a good rate. Our driver preserved the balance of the sleigh by shifting his body from side to side so that only at rare intervals did the siderunners touch the ground.

"Finally, we emerged into the open, and I found myself viewing a scene of almost normal, earthly aspect. We were near the shore of a smooth, shining lake. At the side a broad stretch of rolling country, dotted here and there with trees, was visible. Near at hand, on the lake shore, I saw a collection of houses, most of them low and flat, with one much larger on a promontory near the lake.

"Overhead arched a gray-blue, cloudless sky, faintly

star-studded, and reflected in the lake before me I saw that familiar gleaming trail of star-dust, hanging like a huge straightened rainbow overhead, and ending at my feet."

CHAPTER V

THE Chemist paused and relighted his cigar. "Perhaps you have some questions," he suggested.

The Doctor shifted in his chair.

"Did you have any theory at this time"—he wanted to know—"about the physical conformation of this world? What I mean is, when you came out of this tunnel were you on the inside or the outside of the world?"

"Was it the same sky you saw overhead when you were in the forest?" asked the Big Business Man.

"No, it was what he saw in the microscope, wasn't it?" said the Very Young Man.

"One at a time, gentlemen," laughed the Chemist. "No, I had no particular theory at this time—I had too many other things to think of. But I do remember noticing one thing which gave me the clew to a fairly complete understanding of this universe. From it I formed a definite explanation, which I found was the belief held by the people themselves."

"What was that?" asked the Very Young Man.

"I noticed, as I stood looking over this broad expanse of country before me, one vital thing that made it different from any similar scene I had ever beheld. If you will stop and think a moment, gentlemen, you will realize that in our world here the horizon is caused by a curvature of the earth below the straight line of vision. We are on a convex surface. But as I gazed over this landscape, and even with no appreciable light from the sky

I could see a distance of several miles, I saw at once that quite the reverse was true. I seemed to be standing in the center of a vast shallow bowl. The ground curved upward into the distance. There was no distant horizon line, only the gradual fading into shadow of the visual landscape. I was standing obviously on a concave surface, on the inside, not the outside of the world.

"The situation, as I now understand it, was this: According to the smallest stature I reached, and calling my height at that time roughly six feet, I had descended into the ring at the time I met Lylda several thousand miles, at least. By the way, where is the ring?"

"Here is it," said the Very Young Man, handing it to him. The Chemist replaced it on his finger. "It's pretty important to me now," he said, smiling.

"You bet!" agreed the Very Young Man.

"You can readily understand how I descended such a distance, if you consider the comparative immensity of my stature during the first few hours I was in the ring. It is my understanding that this country through which I passed is a barren waste—merely the atoms of the mineral we call gold.

"Beyond that I entered the hitherto unexplored regions within the atom. The country at that point where I found the forest, I was told later, is habitable for several hundred miles. Around it on all sides lies a desert, across which no one has ever penetrated.

"This surface is the outside of the Oroid world, for so they call their earth. At this point the shell between the outer and inner surface is only a few miles in thickness. The two surfaces do not parallel each other here, so that in descending these tunnels we turned hardly more than an eighth of a complete circle.

"At the city of Arite, where Lylda first took me, and where I had my first view of the inner surface, the curvature is slightly greater than that of our own earth, although, as I have said, in the opposite direction."

"And the space within this curvature—the heavens you have mentioned—how great do you estimate it to be?" asked the Doctor.

"Based on the curvature at Arite it would be about six thousand miles in diameter."

"Has this entire inner surface been explored?" asked the Big Business Man.

"No, only a small portion. The Oroids are not an adventurous people. There are only two nations, less than twelve million people all together, on a surface nearly as extensive as our own."

"How about those stars?" suggested the Very Young Man.

"I believe they comprise a complete universe similar to our own solar system. There is a central sun-star, around which many of the others revolve. You must understand, though, that these other worlds are infinitely tiny compared to the Oroids, and, if inhabited, support beings nearly as much smaller than the Oroids, as they are smaller than you."

"Great Cæsar!" ejaculated the Banker. "Don't let's go into that any deeper!"

"Tell us more about Lylda," prompted the Very Young Man.

"You are insatiable on that point," laughed the Chemist. "Well, when we left the sleigh, Lylda took me directly into the city of Arite. I found it an orderly collection of low houses, seemingly built of uniformly cut, highly polished gray blocks. As we passed through the streets, some of which were paved with similar blocks, I was reminded of nothing so much as the old jingles of Spotless Town. Everything was immaculately, inordinately clean. Indeed, the whole city seemed built of some curious form of opaque glass, newly scrubbed and polished.

"Children crowded from the doorways as we advanced, but Lylda dispersed them with a gentle though firm, command. As we approached the sort of castle I have mentioned, the reason for Lylda's authoritative manner dawned upon me. She was, I soon learned, daughter of one of the most learned men of the nation and was—handmaiden, do you call it?—to the queen."

"So it was a monarchy?" interrupted the Big Business Man. "I should never have thought that."

"Lylda called their leader a king. In reality he was the president, chosen by the people, for a period of about what we would term twenty years; I learned something about this republic during my stay, but not as much as I would have liked. Politics was not Lylda's strong point, and I had to get it all from her, you know.

"For several days I was housed royally in the castle. Food was served me by an attendant who evidently was assigned solely to look after my needs. At first I was terribly confused by the constant, uniform light, but when I found certain hours set aside for sleep, just as we have them, when I began to eat regularly, I soon fell into the routine of this new life.

"The food was not greatly different from our own, although I found not a single article I could identify. It consisted principally of vegetables and fruits, the latter of an apparently inexhaustible variety.

"Lylda visited me at intervals, and I learned I was awaiting an audience with the king. During these days she made rapid progress with my language—so rapid that I shortly gave up the idea of mastering hers.

"And now, with the growing intimacy between us and our ability to communicate more readily, I learned the simple, tragic story of her race—new details, of course, but the old, old tale of might against right, and the tragedy of a trusting, kindly people, blindly thinking others as just as themselves.

"For thousands of years, since the master life-giver had come from one of the stars to populate the world, the Oroid nation had dwelt in peace and security. These people cared nothing for adventure. No restless thirst for knowledge led them to explore deeply the limitless land surrounding them. Even from the earliest times no struggle for existence, no doctrine of the survival of the fittest, hung over them as with us. No wild animals harassed them; no savages menaced them. A fertile boundless land, a perfect climate, nurtured them tenderly.

"Under such conditions they developed only the softer, gentler qualities of nature. Many laws among them were unnecessary, for life was so simple, so pleasant to live, and the attainment of all the commonly accepted standards of wealth so easy, that the incentive to wrongdoing was almost non-existent.

"Strangely enough, and fortunately, too, no individuals rose among them with the desire for power. Those in command were respected and loved as true workers for the people, and they accepted their authority in the same spirit with which it was given. Indolence, in its highest sense the wonderful art of doing nothing gracefully, played the greatest part in their life.

"Then, after centuries of ease and peaceful security, came the awakening. Almost without warning another nation had come out of the unknown to attack them.

"With the hurt feeling that comes to a child unjustly treated, they all but succumbed to this first onslaught. The abduction of numbers of their women, for such seemed the principal purpose of the invaders, aroused them sufficiently to repel this first crude attack. Their manhood challenged, their anger as a nation awakened for the first time, they sprang as one man into the horror we call war.

"With the defeat of the Malites came another period of ease and security. They had learned no lesson, but went their indolent way, playing through life like the kindly children they were. During this last period some intercourse between them and the Malites took place. The latter people, whose origin was probably nearly opposite them on the inner surface, had by degrees pushed their frontiers closer and closer to the Oroids. Trade between the two was carried on to some extent, but the character of the Malites, their instinctive desire for power, for its own sake, their consideration for themselves as superior beings, caused them to be distrusted and feared by their more simple-minded companion nation.

"You can almost guess the rest, gentlemen. Lylda told me little about the Malites, but the loathing disgust of her manner, her hesitancy, even to bring herself to mention them, spoke more eloquently than words.

"Four years ago, as they measure time, came the second attack, and now, in a huge arc, only a few hundred miles from Arite, hung the opposing armies."

The Chemist paused. "That's the condition I found, gentlemen," he said. "Not a strikingly original or unfamiliar situation, was it?"

"By Jove!" remarked the Doctor thoughtfully, "what a curious thing that the environment of our earth should so affect that world inside the ring. It does make you stop and think, doesn't it, to realize how those infinitesimal creatures are actuated now by the identical motives that inspire us?"

"Yet it does seem very reasonable, I should say," the Big Business Man put in.

"Let's have another round of drinks," suggested the Banker—"this is dry work!"

"As a scientist you'd make a magnificent plumber, George!" retorted the Big Business Man. "You're about as helpful in this little gathering as an oyster!"

The Very Young Man rang for a waiter.

"I've been thinking——" began the Banker, and stopped at the smile of his companion. "Shut up!"—he finished—"that's cheap wit, you know!"

"Go on, George," encouraged the other, "you've been thinking——"

"I've been tremendously interested in this extraordinary story"—he addressed himself to the Chemist—"but there's one point I don't get at all. How many days were you in that ring do you make out?"

"I believe about seven, all told," returned the Chemist.

"But you were only away from us some forty hours. I ought to know, I've been right here." He looked at his crumpled clothes somewhat ruefully.

"The change of time-progress was one of the surprises of my adventure," said the Chemist. "It is easily explained in a general way, although I cannot even attempt a scientific theory of its cause. But I must confess that before I started the possibility of such a thing never even occurred to me."

"To get a conception of this change you must analyze definitely what time is. We measure and mark it by years, months, and so forth, down to minutes and seconds, all based upon the movements of our earth around its sun. But that is the measurement of time, not time itself. How would you describe time?"

The Big Business Man smiled. "Time," he said, "is what keeps everything from happening at once."

"Very clever," laughed the Chemist.

The Doctor leaned forward earnestly. "I should say," he began, "that time is the rate at which we live—the speed at which we successively pass through our existence from birth to death. It's very hard to put intelligibly, but I think I know what I mean," he finished somewhat lamely.

"Exactly so. Time is a rate of life-progress, different for every individual, and only made standard because we take the time-duration of the earth's revolution around the sun, which is constant, and arbitrarily say: 'That is thirty-one million five hundred thousand odd seconds.'"

"Is time different for every individual?" asked the Banker argumentatively.

"Think a moment," returned the Chemist. "Suppose your brain were to work twice as fast as mine. Suppose your heart beat twice as fast, and all the functions of your body were accelerated in a like manner. What we call a second would certainly seem to you twice as long. Further than that, it actually would be twice as long, so far as you were concerned. Your digestion, instead of taking perhaps four hours, would take two. You would eat twice as often. The desire for sleep would overtake you every twelve hours instead of twenty-four, and you would be satisfied with four hours of unconsciousness instead of eight. In short, you would soon be living a cycle of two days every twenty-four hours. Time then, as we measure it, for you at least would have doubled—you would be progressing through life at twice the rate that I am through mine."

"That may be theoretically true," the Big Business Man put in. "Practically, though, it has never happened to any one."

"Of course not, to such a great degree as the instance I put. No one, except in disease, has ever doubled our average rate of life-progress, and lived it out as a balanced, otherwise normal existence. But there is no question that to some much smaller degree we all of us differ one from the other. The difference, however, is so comparatively slight, that we can each one reconcile it to the standard measurement of time. And so, outwardly, time is the same for all of us. But inwardly, why, we none of us conceive a minute or an hour to be the same! How do you know how long a minute is to me? More than that, time is not constant even in the same individual. How many hours are shorter to you than others? How many days have been almost interminable? No, instead of being constant, there is nothing more inconstant than time."

"Haven't you confused two different issues?" suggested the Big Business Man. "Granted what you say about the slightly different rate at which different individuals live, isn't it quite another thing, how long time seems to you. A day when you have nothing to do seems long, or, on the other hand, if you are very busy it seems short. But mind, it only *seems* short or long, according to the preoccupation of your mind. That has nothing to do with the speed of your progress through life."

"Ah, but I think it has," cried the Chemist. "You forget that we none of us have all of the one thing to the exclusion of the other. Time seems short; it seems long, and in the end it all averages up, and makes our rate of progress what it is. Now if any of us were to go through life in a calm, deliberate way, making time seem as long as possible, he would live more years, as we measure them, than if he rushed headlong through the days, accomplishing always as much as possible. I mean in neither case to go to the extremes, but only so far as would be consistent with the maintenance of a normal standard of health. How about it?" He turned to the Doctor. "You ought to have an opinion on that."

"I rather think you are right," said the latter thoughtfully, "although I doubt very much if the man who took it easy would do as much during his longer life as the other with his energy would accomplish in the lesser time allotted to him."

"Probably he wouldn't," smiled the Chemist; "but that does not alter the point we are discussing."

"How does this apply to the world in the ring?" ventured the Very Young Man.

"I believe there is a very close relationship between the dimensions of length, breadth, and thickness, and time. Just what connection with them it has, I have no idea. Yet, when size changes, time-rate changes; you have only to look at our own universe to discover that."

"How do you mean?" asked the Very Young Man.

"Why, all life on our earth, in a general way, illustrates the fundamental fact that the larger a thing is, the slower its time-progress is. An elephant, for example, lives more years than we humans. Yet how quickly a fly is born, matured, and aged! There are exceptions, of course; but in a majority of cases it is true.

"So I believe that as I diminished in stature, my time-progress became faster and faster. I am seven days older than when I left you day before yesterday. I have lived those seven days, gentlemen, there is no getting around that fact."

"This is all tremendously interesting," sighed the Big Business Man; "but not very comprehensible."

CHAPTER VI

"IT was the morning of my third day in the castle," began the Chemist again, "that I was taken by Lylda before the king. We found him seated alone in a little anteroom, overlooking a large courtyard, which we could see was crowded with an expectant, waiting throng. I must explain to you now, that I was considered by Lylda somewhat in the light of a Messiah, come to save her nation from the destruction that threatened it.

"She believed me a supernatural being, which, indeed, if you come to think of it, gentlemen, is exactly what I was. I tried to tell her something of myself and the world I had come from, but the difficulties of language and her smiling insistence and faith in her own conception of me, soon caused me to desist. Thereafter I let her have her own way, and did not attempt any explanation again for some time.

"For several weeks before Lylda found me sleeping by the river's edge, she had made almost a daily pilgrimage to that vicinity. A maidenly premonition, a feeling that had first come to her several years before, told her of my coming, and her father's knowledge and scientific beliefs had led her to the outer surface of the world as the direction in which to look. A curious circumstance, gentlemen, lies in the fact that Lylda clearly remembered the occasion when this first premonition came to her. And in the telling, she described graphically the scene in the cave, where I saw her through the microscope." The Chemist paused an instant and then resumed.

"When we entered the presence of the king, he greeted me quietly, and made me sit by his side, while Lylda knelt on the floor at our feet. The king impressed me as a man about fifty years of age. He was smooth-shaven, with black, wavy hair, reaching his shoulders. He was dressed in the usual tunic, the upper part of his body covered by a quite similar garment, ornamented with a variety of metal objects. His feet were protected with a sort of buskin; at his side hung a crude-looking metal spear.

"The conversation that followed my entrance, lasted perhaps fifteen minutes. Lylda interpreted for us as well as she could, though I must confess we were all three at times completely at a loss. But Lylda's bright, intelligent little face, and the resourcefulness of her gestures, always managed somehow to convey her meaning. The charm and grace of her manner, all during the talk, her winsomeness, and the almost spiritual kindness and tenderness that characterized her, made me feel that she embodied all those qualities with which we of this earth idealize our own womanhood.

"I found myself falling steadily under the spell of her beauty, until—well, gentlemen, it's childish for me to enlarge upon this side of my adventure, you know; but—Lylda means everything to me now, and I'm going back for her just as soon as I possibly can."

"Bully for you!" cried the Very Young Man. "Why didn't you bring her with you this time?"

"Let him tell it his own way," remonstrated the Doctor. The Very Young Man subsided with a sigh.

"During our talk," resumed the Chemist, "I learned from the king that Lylda had promised him my assistance in overcoming the enemies that threatened his country. He smilingly told me that our charming little interpreter had assured him I would be able to do this. Lylda's blushing face, as she conveyed this meaning to me, was so thoroughly captivating, that before I knew it, and quite without meaning to, I pulled her up towards me and kissed her.

"The king was more surprised by far than Lylda, at this extraordinary behavior. Obviously neither of them had understood what a kiss meant, although Lylda, by her manner evidently comprehended pretty thoroughly.

"I told them then, as simply as possible to enable Lylda to get my meaning, that I could, and would gladly aid in their war. I explained then, that I had the power to change my stature, and could make myself grow very large or very small in a short space of time.

"This, as Lylda evidently told it to him, seemed quite beyond the king's understanding. He comprehended finally, or at least he agreed to believe my statement.

"This led to the consideration of practical questions of how I was to proceed in their war. I had not considered any details before, but now they appeared of the utmost simplicity. All I had to do was to make myself a hundred or two hundred feet high, walk out to the battle-lines, and scatter the opposing army like a set of small boys' playthings."

"What a quaint idea!" said the Banker. "A modern 'Gulliver.'"

The Chemist did not heed this interruption.

"Then like three children we plunged into a discussion of exactly how I was to perform these wonders, the king laughing heartily as we pictured the attack on my tiny enemies.

"He then asked me how I expected to accomplish this change of size, and I very briefly told him of our larger world, and the manner in which I had come from it into his. Then I showed the drugs that I still carried carefully strapped to me. This seemed definitely to convince the king of my sincerity. He rose abruptly to his feet, and strode through a doorway on to a small balcony overlooking the courtyard below.

"As he stepped out into the view of the people, a great cheer arose. He waited quietly for them to stop, and then raised his hand and began speaking. Lylda and I stood hand in hand in the shadow of the doorway, out of sight of the crowd, but with it and the entire courtyard plainly in our view.

"It was a quadrangular enclosure, formed by the four sides of the palace, perhaps three hundred feet across, packed solidly now with people of both sexes, the gleaming whiteness of the upper parts of their bodies, and their upturned faces, making a striking picture.

"For perhaps ten minutes the king spoke steadily, save when he was interrupted by applause. Then he stopped abruptly and, turning, pulled Lylda and me out upon the balcony. The enthusiasm of the crowd doubled at our appearance. I was pushed forward to the balcony rail, where I bowed to the cheering throng.

"Just after I left the king's balcony, I met Lylda's father. He was a kindly-faced old gentleman, and took a great interest in me and my story. He it was who told me about the physical conformation of his world, and he seemed to comprehend my explanation of mine.

"That night it rained—a heavy, torrential downpour, such as we have in the tropics. Lylda and I had been talking for some time, and, I must confess, I had been making love to her ardently. I broached now the principal object of my entrance into her world, and, with an eloquence I did not believe I possessed, I pictured the wonders of our own great earth above, begging her to come back with me and live out her life with mine.

"Much of what I said, she probably did not understand, but the main facts were intelligible without question. She listened quietly. When I had finished, and waited for her decision, she reached slowly out and clutched my shoulders, awkwardly making as if to kiss me. In an instant she was in my arms, with a low, happy little cry.

CHAPTER VII

A MODERN GULLIVER

"THE clattering fall of rain brought us to ourselves. Rising to her feet, Lylda pulled me over to the window-opening, and together we stood and looked out into the night. The scene before us was beautiful, with a weirdness almost impossible to describe. It was as bright as I had ever seen this world, for even though heavy clouds hung overhead, the light from the stars was never more than a negligible quantity.

"We were facing the lake—a shining expanse of silver radiation, its surface shifting and crawling, as though a great undulating blanket of silver mist lay upon it. And coming down to meet it from the sky were innumerable lines of silver—a vast curtain of silver cords that broke apart into great strings of pearls when I followed their downward course.

"And then, as I turned to Lylda, I was struck with the extraordinary weirdness of her beauty as never before. The reflected light from the rain had something the quality of our moonlight. Shining on Lylda's body, it tremendously enhanced the iridescence of her skin. And her face, upturned to mine, bore an expression of radiant happiness and peace such as I had never seen before on a woman's countenance."

The Chemist paused, his voice dying away into silence as he sat lost in thought. Then he pulled himself together with a start. "It was a sight, gentlemen, the memory of which I shall cherish all my life.

"The next day was that set for my entrance into the war. Lylda and I had talked nearly all night, and had decided that she was to return with me to my world. By morning the rain had stopped, and we sat together in the window-opening, silenced with the thrill of the wonderful new joy that had come into our hearts.

"The country before us, under the cloudless, starry sky, stretched gray-blue and beautiful into the quivering obscurity of the distance. At our feet lay the city, just awakening into life. Beyond, over the rolling meadows and fields, wound the road that led out to the battle-front, and coming back over it now, we could see an endless line of vehicles. These, as they passed through the street beneath our window, I found were loaded with soldiers, wounded and dying. I shuddered at the sight of one cart in particular, and Lylda pressed close to me, pleading with her eyes for my help for her stricken people.

"My exit from the castle was made quite a ceremony. A band of music and a guard of several hundred soldiers ushered me forth, walking beside the king, with Lylda a few paces behind. As we passed through the streets of the city, heading for the open country beyond, we were cheered continually by the people who thronged the streets and crowded upon the housetops to watch us pass.

"Outside Arite I was taken perhaps a mile, where a wide stretch of country gave me the necessary space for my growth. We were standing upon a slight hill, below which, in a vast semicircle, fully a hundred thousand people were watching.

"And now, for the first time, fear overcame me. I realized my situation—saw myself in a detached sort of way—a stranger in this extraordinary world, and only the power of my drug to raise me out of it. This drug you must remember, I had not as yet taken. Suppose it were not to act? Or were to act wrongly?

"I glanced around. The king stood before me, quietly waiting my pleasure. Then I turned to Lylda. One glance at her proud, happy little face, and my fear left me as suddenly as it had come. I took her in my arms and kissed her, there before that multitude. Then I set her down, and signified to the king I was ready.

"I took a minute quantity of one of the drugs, and as I had done before, sat down with my eyes covered. My sensations were fairly similar to those I have already described. When I looked up after a moment, I found the landscape dwindling to tiny proportions in quite as astonishing a way as it had grown before. The king and Lylda stood now hardly above my ankle.

"A great cry arose from the people—a cry wherein horror, fear, and applause seemed equally mixed. I looked down and saw thousands of them running away in terror.

"Still smaller grew everything within my vision, and then, after a moment, the landscape seemed at rest. I kneeled now upon the ground, carefully, to avoid treading on any of the people around me. I located Lylda and the king after a moment; tiny little creatures less than an inch in height. I was then, I estimated, from their viewpoint, about four hundred feet tall.

"I put my hand flat upon the ground near Lylda, and after a moment she climbed into it, two soldiers lifting her up the side of my thumb as it lay upon the ground. In the hollow of my palm, she lay quite securely, and very carefully I raised her up towards my face. Then, seeing that she was frightened, I set her down again.

"At my feet, hardly more than a few steps away, lay the tiny city of Arite and the lake. I could see all around the latter now, and could make out clearly a line of hills on the other side. Off to the left the road wound up out of sight in the distance. As far as I could see, a line of soldiers was passing out along this road—marching four abreast, with carts at intervals, loaded evidently with supplies; only occasionally, now, vehicles passed in the other direction. Can I make it plain to you, gentlemen, my sensations in changing stature? I felt at first as though I were tremendously high in the air, looking down as from a balloon upon the familiar territory beneath me. That feeling passed after a few moments, and I found that my point of view had changed. I no longer felt that I was looking down from a balloon, but felt as a normal person feels. And again I conceived myself but six feet tall, standing above a dainty little toy world. It is all in the viewpoint, of course, and never, during all my changes, was I for more than a moment able to feel of a different stature than I am at this present instant. It was always everything else that changed.

"According to the directions I had received from the king, I started now to follow the course of the road. I found it difficult walking, for the country was dotted with houses, trees, and cultivated fields, and each footstep was a separate problem.

"I progressed in this manner perhaps two miles, covering what the day before I would have called about a hundred and thirty or forty miles. The country became wilder as I advanced, and now was in places crowded with separate collections of troops.

"I have not mentioned the commotion I made in this walk over the country. My coming must have been told widely by couriers the night before, to soldiers and peasantry alike, or the sight of me would have caused utter demoralization. As it was, I must have been terrifying to a tremendous degree. I think the careful way in which I picked my course, stepping in the open as much as possible, helped to reassure the people. Behind me, whenever I turned, they seemed rather more curious than fearful, and once or twice when I stopped for a few moments they approached my feet closely. One athletic young soldier caught the loose end of the string of one of my buskins, as it hung over my instep close to the ground and pulled himself up hand over hand, amid the enthusiastic cheers of his comrades.

"I had walked nearly another mile, when almost in front of me, and perhaps a hundred yards away, I saw a remarkable sight that I did not at first understand. The country here was crossed by a winding river running in a general way at right angles to my line of progress. At the right, near at hand, and on the nearer bank of the river, lay a little city, perhaps half the size of Arite, with its back up against a hill.

"What first attracted my attention was that from a dark patch across the river which seemed to be woods, pebbles appeared to pop up at intervals, traversing a little arc perhaps as high as my knees, and falling into the city. I watched for a moment and then I understood. There was a siege in progress, and the catapults of the Malites were bombarding the city with rocks.

"I went up a few steps closer, and the pebbles stopped coming. I stood now beside the city, and as I bent over it, I could see by the battered houses the havoc the bombardment had caused. Inert little figures lay in the streets, and I bent lower and inserted my thumb and forefinger between a row of houses and picked one up. It was the body of a woman, partly mashed. I set it down again hastily.

"Then as I stood up, I felt a sting on my leg. A pebble had hit me on the shin and dropped at my feet. I picked it up. It was the size of a small walnut—a huge bowlder six feet or more in diameter it would have been in Lylda's eyes. At the thought of her I was struck with a sudden fit of anger. I flung the pebble violently down into the wooded patch and leaped over the river in one bound, landing squarely on both feet in the woods. It was like jumping into a patch of ferns.

"I stamped about me for a moment until a large part of the woods was crushed down. Then I bent over and poked around with my finger. Underneath the tangled wreckage of tiny-tree trunks, lay numbers of the Malites. I must have trodden upon a thousand or more, as one would stamp upon insects.

"The sight sickened me at first, for after all, I could not look upon them as other than men, even though they were only the length of my thumb-nail. I walked a few steps forward, and in all directions I could see swarms of the little creatures running. Then the memory of my coming departure from this world with Lylda, and my promise to the king to rid his land once for all from these people, made me feel again that they, like vermin, were to be destroyed.

"Without looking directly down, I spent the next two hours stamping over this entire vicinity. Then I ran two or three miles directly toward the country of the Malites, and returning I stamped along the course of the river for a mile or so in both directions. Then I walked back to Arite, again picking my way carefully among crowds of Oroids, who now feared me so little that I had difficulty in moving without stepping upon them.

"When I had regained my former size, which needed two successive doses of the drug, I found myself surrounded by a crowd of the Oroids, pushing and shoving each other in an effort to get closer to me. The news of my success over their enemy have been divined by them, evidently. Lord knows it must have been obvious enough what I was going to do, when they saw me stride away, a being four hundred feet tall.

"Their enthusiasm and thankfulness now were so

mixed with awe and reverent worship of me as a divine being, that when I advanced towards Arite they opened a path immediately. The king, accompanied by Lylda, met me at the edge of the city. The latter threw herself into my arms at once, crying with relief to find me the proper size once more.

"I need not go into details of the ceremonies of rejoicing that took place this afternoon. These people seemed little given to pomp and public demonstration. The king made a speech from his balcony, telling them all I had done, and the city was given over to festivities and preparations to receive the returning soldiers."

The Chemist pushed his chair back from the table, and moistened his dry lips with a swallow of water. "I tell you, gentlemen," he continued, "I felt pretty happy that day. It's a wonderful feeling to find yourself the savior of a nation."

At that the Doctor jumped to his feet, overturning his chair, and striking the table a blow with his fist that made the glasses dance.

"By God!" he fairly shouted, "that's just what you can be here to us."

The Banker looked startled, while the Very Young Man pulled the Chemist by the coat in his eagerness to be heard. "A few of those pills," he said in a voice that quivered with excitement, "when you are standing in France, and you can walk over to Berlin and kick the houses apart with the toe of your boot."

"Why not?" said the Big Business Man, and silence fell on the group as they stared at each other, awed by the possibilities that opened up before them.

CHAPTER VIII

"I MUST GO BACK"

THE tremendous plan for the salvation of their own suffering world through the Chemist's discovery occupied the five friends for some time. Then laying aside this subject, that now had become of the most vital importance to them all, the Chemist resumed his narrative.

"My last evening in the world of the ring, I spent with Lylda, discussing our future, and making plans for the journey. I must tell you now, gentlemen, that never for a moment during my stay in Arite was I once free from an awful dread of this return trip. I tried to conceive what it would be like, and the more I thought about it, the more hazardous it seemed.

"You must realize, when I was growing smaller, coming in, I was able to climb down, or fall or slide down, into the spaces as they opened up. Going back, I could only imagine the world as closing in upon me, crushing me to death unless I could find a larger space immediately above into which I could climb.

"And as I talked with Lylda about this and tried to make her understand what I hardly understood myself, I gradually was brought to realize the full gravity of the danger confronting us. If only I had made the trip out once before, I could have ventured it with her. But as I looked at her fragile little body, to expose it to the terrible possibilities of such a journey was unthinkable.

"There was another question, too, that troubled me. I had been gone from you nearly a week, and you were only to wait for me two days. I believed firmly that I was living at a faster rate, and that probably my time with you had not expired. But I did not know. And suppose, when I had come out on to the surface of the ring, one of you had had it on his finger walking along the street? No, I did not want Lylda with me in that event.

"And so I told her—made her understand—that she must stay behind, and that I would come back for her. She did not protest. She said nothing—just looked up into my face with wide, staring eyes and a little quiver of her lips. Then she clutched my hand and fell into a low, sobbing cry.

"I held her in my arms for a few moments, so little, so delicate, so human in her sorrow, and yet almost superhuman in her radiant beauty. Soon she stopped crying and smiled up at me bravely.

"Next morning I left. Lylda took me through the tunnels and back into the forest by the river's edge where I had first met her. There we parted. I can see, now, her pathetic, drooping little figure as she trudged back to the tunnel.

"When she had disappeared, I sat down to plan out my journey. I resolved now to reverse as nearly as possible the steps I had taken coming in. Acting on this decision, I started back to that portion of the forest where I had trampled it down.

"I found the place without difficulty, stopping once on the way to eat a few berries, and some of the food I carried with me. Then I took a small amount of one of the drugs, and in a few moments the forest trees had dwindled into tiny twigs beneath my feet.

"I started now to find the huge incline down which I had fallen, and when I reached it, after some hours of wandering, I followed its bottom edge to where a pile of rocks and dirt marked my former landing-place. The rocks were much larger than I remembered them, and so I knew I was not so large, now, as when I was here before.

"Remembering the amount of the drug I had taken coming down, I took now twelve of the pills. Then, in a sudden panic, I hastily took two of the others. The result made my head swim most horribly. I sat or lay down, I forget which. When I looked up I saw the hills beyond the river and forest coming towards me, yet dwindling away beneath my feet as they approached. The incline seemed folding up upon itself, like a telescope. As I watched, its upper edge came into view, a curved, luminous line against the blackness above. Every instant it crawled down closer, more sharply curved, and its inclined surface grew steeper.

"All this time, as I stood still, the ground beneath my feet seemed to be moving. It was crawling towards me, and folding up underneath where I was standing. Frequently I had to move to avoid rocks that came at me and passed under my feet into nothingness.

"Then, all at once, I realized that I had been stepping constantly backward, to avoid the inclined wall as it shoved itself towards me. I turned to see what was behind, and horror made my flesh creep at what I saw. A black, forbidding wall, much like the incline in front, entirely encircled me. It was hardly more than half a mile away, and towered four or five thousand feet overhead.

"And as I stared in terror, I could see it closing in, the line of its upper edge coming steadily closer and lower. I looked wildly around with an overpowering impulse to run. In every direction towered this rocky wall, inexorably swaying in to crush me.

"I think I fainted. When I came to myself the scene had not greatly changed. I was lying at the bottom and against one wall of a circular pit, now about a thousand feet in diameter and nearly twice as deep. The wall all around I could see was almost perpendicular, and it seemed impossible to ascend its smooth, shining sides. The action of the drug had evidently worn off, for everything was quite still.

"My fear had now left me, for I remembered this circular pit quite well. I walked over to its center, and looking around and up to its top I estimated distances carefully. Then I took two more of the pills.

"Immediately the familiar, sickening, crawling sensation began again. As the walls closed in upon me, I kept carefully in the center of the pit. Steadily they crept in. Now only a few hundred feet away! Now only a few paces—and then I reached out and touched both sides at once with my hands.

"I tell you, gentlemen, it was a terrifying sensation to stand in that well (as it now seemed), and feel its walls closing up with irresistible force. But now the upper edge was within reach of my fingers. I leaped upward and hung for a moment, then pulled myself up and scrabbled out, tumbling in a heap on the ground above. As I recovered myself, I looked again at the hole out of which I had escaped; it was hardly big enough to contain my fist.

"I knew, now, I was at the bottom of the scratch. But how different it looked than before. It seemed this time a long, narrow cañon, hardly more than sixty feet across. I glanced up and saw the blue sky overhead, flooded with light, that I knew was the space of this room above the ring.

"The problem now was quite a different one than getting out of the pit, for I saw that the scratch was so deep in proportion to its width that if I let myself get too big,

I would be crushed by its walls before I could jump out. It would be necessary, therefore, to stay comparatively small and climb up its side.

"I selected what appeared to be an especially rough section, and took a portion of another of the pills. Then I started to climb. After an hour the buskins on my feet were torn to fragments, and I was bruised and battered as you saw me. I see, now, how I could have made both the descent into the ring, and my journey back with comparatively little effort, but I did the best I knew at the time.

"When the cañon was about ten feet in width, and I had been climbing arduously for several hours, I found myself hardly more than fifteen or twenty feet above its bottom. And I was still almost that far from the top. With the stature I had then attained, I could have climbed the remaining distance easily, but for the fact that the wall above had grown too smooth to afford a foothold. The effects of the drug had again worn off, and I sat down and prepared to take another dose. I did so—the smallest amount I could—and held ready in my hand a pill of the other kind in case of emergency. Steadily the walls closed in.

"A terrible feeling of dizziness now came over me. I clutched the rock beside which I was sitting, and it seemed to melt like ice beneath my grasp. Then I remembered seeing the edge of the cañon within reach above my head, and with my last remaining strength, I pulled myself up, and fell upon the surface of the ring. You know the rest. I took another dose of the powder, and in a few minutes was back among you."

The Chemist stopped speaking, and looked at his friends. "Well," he said, "you've heard it all. What do you think of it?"

"It is a terrible thing to me," sighed the Very

Young Man, "that you did not bring Llyda with you."

"It would have been a terrible thing if I had brought her. But I am going back for her."

"When do you plan to go back?" asked the Doctor after a moment.

"As soon as I can—in a day or two," answered the Chemist.

"Before you do your work here? You must not," remonstrated the Big Business Man. "Our war here needs you, our nation, the whole cause of liberty and freedom needs you. You cannot go."

"Lylda needs me, too," returned the Chemist. "I have an obligation towards her now, you know, quite apart from my own feelings. Understand me, gentlemen," he continued earnestly, "I do not place myself and mine before the great fight for democracy and justice being waged in this world. That would be absurd. But it is not quite that way, actually; I can go back for Lylda and return here in a week. That week will make little difference to the war. On the other hand, if I go to France first, it may take me a good many months to complete my task, and during that time Lylda will be using up her life several times faster than I. No, gentlemen, I am going to her first."

"That week you propose to take," said the Banker slowly, "will cost this world thousands of lives that you could save. Have you thought of that?"

The Chemist flushed. "I can recognize the salvation of a nation or a cause," he returned hotly, "but if I must choose between the lives of a thousand men who are not dependent on me, and the life or welfare of one woman who is, I shall choose the woman."

"He's right, you know," said the Doctor, and the Very Young Man agreed with him fervently.

Two days later the company met again in the privacy

of the club-room. When they had finished dinner, the Chemist began in his usual quiet way:

"I am going to ask you this time, gentlemen, to give me a full week. There are four of you—six hours a day of watching for each. It need not be too great a hardship. You see," he continued, as they nodded in agreement, "I want to spend a longer period in the ring world this time. I may never go back, and I want to learn, in the interest of science, as much about it as I can. I was there such a short time before, and it was all so strange and remarkable, I confess I learned practically nothing.

"I told you all I could of its history. But of its arts, its science, and all its sociological and economic questions, I got hardly more than a glimpse. It is a world and a people far less advanced than ours, yet with something we have not, and probably never will have—the universally distributed milk of human kindness. Yes, gentlemen, it is a world well worth studying."

The Banker came out of a brown study. "How about your formulas for these drugs?" he asked abruptly; "where are they?" The Chemist tapped his forehead smilingly. "Well, hadn't you better leave them with us?" the Banker pursued. "The hazards of your trip— you can't tell——"

"Don't misunderstand me, gentlemen," broke in the Chemist. "I wouldn't give you those formulas if my life and even Lylda's depended on it. There again you do not differentiate between the individual and the race. I know you four very well. You are my friends, with all the bond that friendship implies. I believe in your integrity—each of you I trust implicitly. With these formulas you could crush Germany, or you could, any one of you, rule the world, with all its treasures for your own. These drugs are the most powerful thing for good in the world to-day. But they are equally as powerful for evil. I would stake my life on what you would do, but I will not stake the life of a nation."

"I know what I'd do if I had the formulas," began the Very Young Man.

"Yes, but I don't know what you'd do," laughed the Chemist. "Don't you see I'm right?" They admitted they did, though the Banker acquiesced very grudgingly.

"The time of my departure is at hand. Is there anything else, gentlemen, before I leave you?" asked the Chemist, beginning to disrobe.

"Please tell Lylda I want very much to meet her," said the Very Young Man earnestly, and they all laughed.

When the room was cleared, and the handkerchief and ring in place once more, the Chemist turned to them again. "Good-by, my friends," he said, holding out his hands. "One week from to-night, at most." Then he took the pills.

No unusual incident marked his departure. The last they saw of him he was calmly sitting on the ring near the scratch.

Then passed the slow days of watching, each taking his turn for the allotted six hours.

By the fifth day, they began to hourly expect the Chemist, but it passed through its weary length, and he did not come. The sixth day dragged by, and then came the last —the day he had promised would end their watching. Still he did not come, and in the evening they gathered, and all four watched together, each unwilling to miss the return of the adventurer and his woman from another world.

But the minutes lengthened into hours, and midnight found the white-faced little group, hopeful yet hopeless, with fear tugging at their hearts. A second week passed, and still they watched, explaining with an optimism they could none of them feel, the non-appearance of their friend. At the end of the second week they met again to talk the situation over, a dull feeling of fear and horror possessing them. The Doctor was the first to voice what now each of them was forced to believe. "I guess it's all useless," he said. "He's not coming back."

"I don't hardly dare give him up," said the Big Business Man.

"Me, too," agreed the Very Young Man sadly.

The Doctor sat for some time in silence, thoughtfully regarding the ring. "My friends," he began finally, "this is too big a thing to deal with in any but the most careful way. I can't imagine what is going on inside that ring, but I do know what is happening in our world, and what our friend's return means to civilization here. Under the circumstances, therefore, I cannot, I will not give him up.

"I am going to put that ring in a museum and pay for having it watched indefinitely. Will you join me?" He turned to the Big Business Man as he spoke.

"Make it a threesome," said the Banker gruffly. "What do you take me for?" and the Very Young Man sighed with the tragedy of youth.

CHAPTER IX

FOUR men sat in the club-room, at their ease in the luxurious leather chairs, smoking and talking earnestly. Near the center of the room stood a huge mahogany table. On its top, directly in the glare of light from an electrolier overhead, was spread a large black silk handkerchief. In the center of this handkerchief lay a heavy gold band—a woman's wedding-ring.

An old-fashioned valise stood near a corner of the table. Its sides were perforated with small brass-rimmed holes; near the top on one side was a small square aperture covered with a wire mesh through which one might look into the interior. Altogether, from the outside, the bag looked much like those used for carrying small animals.

As it lay on the table now its top was partly open. The inside was brightly lighted by a small storage battery and electric globe, fastened to the side. Near the bottom of the bag was a tiny wire rack, held suspended about an inch from the bottom by transverse wires to the sides. The inside of the bag was lined with black plush.

On an arm of the Doctor's chair lay two white tin boxes three or four inches square. In his hand he held an opened envelope and several letter pages.

"A little more than five years ago to-night, my friends," he began slowly, "we sat in this room with that"—he indicated the ring—"under very different circumstances." After a moment, he went on:

71

"I think I am right when I say that for five years the thought uppermost in our minds has always been that ring and what is going on within one of its atoms."

"You bet," said the Very Young Man.

"For five years now we have had the ring watched," continued the Doctor, "but Rogers has never returned."

"You asked us here to-night because you had something special to tell us," began the Very Young Man, with a questioning look at the valise and the ring.

The Doctor smiled. "I'm sorry," he said, "I don't mean to be aggravating."

"Go ahead in your own way, Frank," the Big Business Man put in. "We'll wait if we have to."

The Doctor glanced at the papers in his hand; he had just taken them from the envelope. "You are consumed with curiosity, naturally, to know what I have to say—why I have brought the ring here to-night. Gentlemen, you have had to restrain that curiosity less than five minutes; I have had a far greater curiosity to endure—and restrain—for over five years.

"When Rogers left us on his last journey into the ring, he gave into my keeping, unknown to you, this envelope." The Doctor held it up.

"He made me swear I would keep its existence secret from every living being, until the date marked upon it, at which time, in the event of his not having returned, it was to be opened. Look at it." The Doctor laid the envelope on the table.

"It is inscribed, as you see, 'To be opened by Dr. Frank Adams at 8 P. M. on September 4th, 1923.' For five years, gentlemen, I kept that envelope, knowing nothing of its contents and waiting for the moment when I might, with honor, open it. The struggle has been a hard one. Many times I have almost been able to persuade myself, in justice to our friend's safety—his very life, probably—

that it would be best to disregard his instructions. But I did not; I waited until the date set and then, a little more than a month ago, alone in my office, I opened the envelope."

The Doctor leaned forward in his chair and shuffled the papers he held in his hand. His three friends sat tense, waiting.

"The envelope contained these papers. Among them is a letter in which I am directed to explain everything to you as soon as I succeed in doing certain other things. Those things I have now accomplished. So I have sent for you. I'll read you the letter first."

No one spoke when the Doctor paused. The Banker drew a long breath. Then he bit the end off a fresh cigar and lit it with a shaking hand. The Doctor shifted his chair closer to the table under the light.

"The letter is dated September 14th, 1918. It begins: 'This will be read at 8 P. M. on September 4th, 1923, by Dr. Frank Adams with no one else present. If the envelope has been opened by him previous to that date I request him to read no further. If it has fallen into other hands than his I can only hope that the reader will immediately destroy it unread.'" The Doctor paused an instant, then went on.

"Gentlemen, we are approaching the most important events of our lives. An extraordinary duty—a tremendous responsibility, rests with us, of all the millions of people on this earth. I ask that you listen most carefully."

His admonition was quite unnecessary, for no one could have been more intent than the three men silently facing him.

The Doctor continued reading: " 'From Dr. Frank Adams, I exact the following oath, before he reads further. You, Dr. Adams, will divulge to no one, for a period of thirty days, the formulas set down in **these** papers; you will follow implicitly the directions given you; you will do nothing that is not expressly stated here. Should you be unable to carry out these directions, you will destroy this letter and the formulas, and tell no one of their ever having been in existence. I must have your oath, Dr. Adams, before you proceed further.' "

The Doctor's voice died away, and he laid the papers on the table.

"Gentlemen," he went on, "later on in the letter I am directed to consult with you three, setting before you this whole matter. But before I do so I must exact a similar oath from each of you. I must have your word of honor, gentlemen, that you will not attempt to transgress the instructions given us, and that you will never, by word or action, allow a suggestion of what passes between us here in this room to-night, to reach any other person. Have I your promise?"

Each of his three hearers found voice to agree. The Banker's face was very red, and he mopped his forehead nervously with his handkerchief.

The Doctor picked up the papers. "The letter goes on: 'I am about to venture back into the unknown world of the ring. What will befall me there I cannot foretell. If by September 4th, 1923, I have not returned, or no other mortal has come out of the ring, it is my desire that you and the three gentlemen with you at the time of my departure, use this discovery of mine for the benefit of humanity in your world, or the world in the ring, exactly as I myself would have used it were I there.

" 'Should the European war be in progress at that time, I direct that you four throw your power on the side of the United States for the defeat of the Central Powers. That you will be able to accomplish that defeat I cannot doubt.

" 'If, on September 4th, 1923, the United States is formally at peace with the powers of the world, you are forbidden to use these chemicals for any purpose other than joining me in the world of the ring. If any among you wish to make the venture, which I hope may be the case, I request that you do so.

" 'Among these pages you will find a list of fourteen chemicals to be used by Dr. Frank Adams during the month following September 4, 1923, for the compounding of my powders. Seven of these chemicals (marked A), are employed in the drug used to diminish bodily size. Those seven marked B are for the drug of opposite action.

" 'You will find here a separate description of each chemical. Nine are well known and fairly common. Dr. Adams will be able to purchase each of them separately without difficulty. Three others will have to be especially compounded and I have so stated in the directions for each of them. Dr. Adams can have them prepared by any large chemical manufacturer; I suggest that he have not more than one of them compounded by the same company.

" 'The two remaining chemicals must be prepared by Dr. Adams personally. Their preparation, while intricate, demands no complicated or extensive apparatus. I have tried to explain thoroughly the making of these two chemicals, and I believe no insurmountable obstacle will be met in completing them.

" 'When Dr. Adams has the specified quantities of each of these fourteen chemicals in his possession, he will proceed according to my further directions to compound the two drugs. If he is successful in making these drugs, I direct that he make known to the three other men referred to, the contents of this letter, after first exacting an oath from each that its provisions will be carried out.

" 'I think it probable that Dr. Adams will succeed in

compounding these two drugs. It also seems probable that at that time the United States no longer will be at war. I make the additional assumption that one or more of you gentlemen will desire to join me in the ring. Therefore, you will find herewith memoranda of my first journey into the ring which I have already described to you; I give also the quantities of each drug to be taken at various stages of the trip. These notes will refresh your memory and will assist you in your journey.

"'I intend to suggest to Dr. Adams to-day when I hand him this letter, that in the event of my failure to return within a week, he make some adequate provision for guarding the ring in safety. And I must caution you now, before starting to join me, if you conclude to do so, that you continue this provision, so as to make possible your safe return to your own world.

"'If our country is at war at the time you read this, your duty is plain. I have no fears regarding your course of action. But if not, I do not care to influence unduly your decision about venturing into this unknown other world. The danger into which I personally may have fallen must count for little with you, in a decision to hazard your own lives. I may point out, however, that such a journey successfully accomplished cannot fail but be the greatest contribution to science that has ever been made. Nor can I doubt but that your coming may prove of tremendous benefit to the humanity of this other equally important, though, in our eyes, infinitesimal world.

"'I therefore suggest, gentlemen, that you start your journey into the ring at 8 P. M. on the evening of November 4, 1923. You will do your best to find your way direct to the city of Arite, where, if I am alive, I will be awaiting you.'"

CHAPTER X

TESTING THE DRUGS

THE Doctor laid his papers on the table and looked up into the white faces of the three men facing him. "That's all, gentlemen," he said.

For a moment no one spoke, and on the face of each was plainly written the evidence of an emotion too deep for words. The Doctor sorted out the papers in silence, glanced over them for a moment, and then reached for a large metal ash tray that stood near him on the table. Taking a match from his pocket he calmly lighted a corner of the papers and dropped them burning into the metal bowl. His friends watched him in awed silence; only the Very Young Man found words to protest.

"Say now, wait," he began, "why——"

The Doctor looked at him. "The letter requests me to do that," he said.

"But I say, the formulas——" persisted the Very Young Man, looking wildly at the burning papers.

The Doctor held up one of the white tin boxes lying on the arm of his chair.

"In these tins," he said, "I have vials containing the specified quantity of each drug. It is ample for our purpose. I have done my best to memorize the formulas. But in any event, I was directed to burn them at the time of reading you the letter. I have done so."

The Big Business Man came out of a brown study.

"Just three weeks from to-night," he murmured, "three weeks from to-night. It's too big to realize."

The Doctor put the two boxes on the table, turned his chair back toward the others, and lighted a cigar.

"Gentlemen, let us go over this matter thoroughly," he began. "We have a momentous decision to make. Either we destroy those boxes and their contents, or three weeks from to-night some or all of us start our journey into the ring. I have had a month to think this matter over; I have made my decision.

"I know there is much for you to consider, before you can each of you choose your course of action. It is not my desire or intention to influence you one way or the other. But we can, if you wish, discuss the matter here to-night; or we can wait, if you prefer, until each of you has had time to think it out for himself."

"I'm going," the Very Young Man burst out.

His hands were gripping the arms of his chair tightly; his face was very pale, but his eyes sparkled.

The Doctor turned to him gravely.

"Your life is at stake, my boy," he said, "this is not a matter for impulse."

"I'm going whether any one else does or not," persisted the Very Young Man. "You can't stop me, either," he added doggedly. "That letter said——"

The Doctor smiled at the youth's earnestness. Then abruptly he held out his hand.

"There is no use my holding back my own decision. I am going to attempt the trip. And since, as you say, I cannot stop you from going," he added with a twinkle, "that makes two of us."

They shook hands. The Very Young Man lighted a cigarette, and began pacing up and down the room, staring hard at the floor.

"I can remember trying to imagine how I would feel," began the Big Business Man slowly, "if Rogers had asked me to go with him when he first went into the ring. It is

not a new idea to me, for I have thought about it many
times in the abstract, during the past five years. But now
that I am face to face with it in reality, it sort of———"
He broke off, and smiled helplessly around at his companions.

The Very Young Man stopped in his walk. "Aw,
come on in," he began, "the———"

"Shut up," growled the Banker, speaking for the first
time in many minutes.

"I'm sure we would all like to go," said the Doctor.
"The point is, which of us are best fitted for the trip."

"None of us are married," put in the Very Young Man.

"I've been thinking———" began the Banker. "Suppose we get into the ring—how long would we be gone,
do you suppose?"

"Who can say?" answered the Doctor smiling. "Perhaps a month—a year—many years possibly. That is
one of the hazards of the venture."

The Banker went on thoughtfully. "Do you remember that argument we had with Rogers about time? Time
goes twice as fast, didn't he say, in that other world?"

"Two and a half times faster, if I remember rightly,
he estimated," replied the Doctor.

The Banker looked at his skinny hands a moment. "I
owned up to sixty-four once," he said quizzically. "Two
years and a half in one year. No, I guess I'll let you
young fellows tackle that; I'll stay here in this world
where things don't move so fast."

"Somebody's got to stay," said the Very Young Man.
"By golly, you know if we're all going into that ring it
would be pretty sad to have anything happen to it while
we were gone."

"That's so," said the Banker, looking relieved. "I
never thought of that."

"One of us should stay at least," said the Doctor. "We

cannot take any outsider into our confidence. One of us must watch the others go, and then take the ring back to its place in the Museum. We will be gone too long a time for one person to watch it here."

The Very Young Man suddenly went to one of the doors and locked it.

"We don't want any one coming in," he explained as he crossed the room and locked the others.

"And another thing," he went on, coming back to the table. "When I saw the ring at the Biological Society the other day, I happened to think, suppose Rogers was to come out on the underneath side? It was lying flat, you know, just as it is now." He pointed to where the ring lay on the handkerchief before them. "I meant to speak to you about it," he added.

"I thought of that," said the Doctor. "When I had that case built to bring the ring here, you notice I raised it above the bottom a little, holding it suspended in that wire frame."

"We'd better fix up something like that at the Museum, too," said the Very Young Man, and went back to his walk.

The Big Business Man had been busily jotting down figures on the back of an envelope. "I can be in shape to go in three weeks," he said suddenly.

"Bully for you," said the Very Young Man. "Then it's all settled." The Big Business Man went back to his notes.

"I knew what your answer would be," said the Doctor. "My patients can go to the devil. This is too big a thing."

The Very Young Man picked up one of the tin boxes. "Tell us how you made the powders," he suggested.

The Doctor took the two boxes and opened them. Inside each were a number of tiny glass vials. Those in one box were of blue glass; those in the other were red.

"These vials," said the Doctor, "contain tiny pellets of the completed drug. That for diminishing size I have put in the red vials; those of blue are the other drug.

"I had rather a difficult time making them—that is, compared to what I anticipated. Most of the chemicals I bought without difficulty. But when I came to compound those two myself"—the Doctor smiled—"I used to think I was a fair chemist in my student days. But now —well, at least I got the results, but only because I have been working almost night and day for the past month. And I found myself with a remarkably complete experimental laboratory when I finished," he added. "That was yesterday; I spent nearly all last night destroying the apparatus, as soon as I found that the drugs had been properly made."

"They do work?" said the Very Young Man anxiously.

"They work," answered the Doctor. "I tried them both very carefully."

"On yourself?" said the Big Business Man.

"No, I didn't think that necessary. I used several insects."

"Let's try them now," suggested the Very Young Man eagerly.

"Not the big one," said the Banker. "Once was enough for that."

"All right," the Doctor laughed. "We'll try the other if you like."

The Big Business Man looked around the room. "There's a few flies around here if we can catch one," he suggested.

"I'll bet there's a cockroach in the kitchen," said the Very Young Man, jumping up.

The Doctor took a brass cneck from his pocket. "I thought probably you'd want to try them out. Will you get that box from the check-room?" He handed the check to the Very Young Man, who hurried out of the room. He returned in a moment, gingerly carrying a cardboard box with holes perforated in the top. The Doctor took the box and lifted the lid carefully. Inside, the box was partitioned into two compartments. In one compartment were three little lizards about four inches long; in the other were two brown sparrows. The Doctor took out one of the sparrows and replaced the cover.

"Fine," said the Very Young Man with enthusiasm.

The Doctor reached for the boxes of chemicals.

"Not the big one," said the Banker again, apprehensively.

"Hold him, will you," the Doctor said.

The Very Young Man took the sparrow in his hands.

"Now," continued the Doctor, "what we need is a plate and a little water."

"There's a tray," said the Very Young Man, pointing with his hands holding the sparrow.

The Doctor took a spoon from the tray and put a little water in it. Then he took one of the tiny pellets from a red vial and crushing it in his fingers, sprinkled a few grains into that water.

"Hold that a moment, please." The Big Business Man took the proffered spoon.

Then the Doctor produced from his pocket a magnifying glass and a tiny pair of silver callipers such as are used by jewelers for handling small objects.

"What's the idea?" the Very Young Man wanted to know.

"I thought I'd try and put him on the ring," explained the Doctor. "Now, then hold open his beak."

The Very Young Man did so, and the Doctor poured

the water down the bird's throat. Most of it spilled; the sparrow twisted its head violently, but evidently some of the liquid had gone down the bird's throat.

Silence followed, broken after a moment by the scared voice of the Very Young Man. "He's getting smaller, I can feel him. He's getting smaller."

"Hold on to him," cautioned the Doctor. "Bring him over here." They went over to the table by the ring, the Banker and the Big Business Man standing close beside them.

"Suppose he tries to fly when we let go of him," suggested the Very Young Man almost in a whisper.

"He'll probably be too confused," answered the Doctor. "Have you got him?" The sparrow was hardly bigger than a large horse-fly now, and the Very Young Man was holding it between his thumb and forefinger.

"Better give him to me," said the Doctor. "Set him down."

"He might fly away," remonstrated the Very Young Man.

"No, he won't."

The Very Young Man put the sparrow on the handkerchief beside the ring and the Doctor immediately picked it up with the callipers.

"Don't squeeze him," cautioned the Very Young Man.

The sparrow grew steadily smaller, and in a moment the Doctor set it carefully on the rim of the ring.

"Get him up by the scratch," whispered the Very Young Man.

The men bent closer over the table, as the Doctor looking through his magnifying glass shoved the sparrow slowly along the top of the ring.

"I can't see him," said the Banker.

"I can," said the Very Young Man, "right by the scratch." Then after a moment, "he's gone."

"I've got him right over the scratch," said the Doctor, leaning farther down. Then he raised his head and laid the magnifying glass and the callipers on the table. "He's gone now."

"Gosh," said the Very Young Man, drawing a long breath.

The Banker flung himself into a chair as though exhausted from a great physical effort.

"Well, it certainly does work," said the Big Business Man, "there's no question about that."

The Very Young Man was shaking the cardboard box in his hands and lifting its cover cautiously to see inside. "Let's try a lizard," he suggested.

"Oh, what's the use," the Banker protested wearily, "we know it works."

"Well, it can't hurt anything to try it, can it?" the Very Young Man urged. "Besides, the more we try it, the more sure we are it will work with us when the time comes. You don't want to try it on yourself, now, do you?" he added with a grin.

"No, thank you," retorted the Banker with emphasis.

"I think we might as well try it again," said the Big Business Man.

The Very Young Man took one of the tiny lizards from the box, and in a moment they had dropped some water containing the drug down its throat. "Try to put him on the scratch, too," said the Very Young Man.

When the lizard was small enough the Doctor held it with the callipers and then laid it on the ring.

"Look at him walk; look at him walk," whispered the Very Young Man excitedly. The lizard, hardly more than an eighth of an inch long now, but still plainly visible, was wriggling along the top of the ring. "Shove him up by the scratch," he added.

In a moment more the reptile was too small for any but the Doctor with his glass to see. "I guess he got there," he said finally with a smile, as he straightened up. "He was going fast."

"Well, *that's* all right," said the Very Young Man with a sigh of relief.

The four men again seated themselves; the Big Business Man went back to his figures.

"When do you start?" asked the Banker after a moment.

"November 4th—8 P. M.," answered the Doctor. "Three weeks from to-night."

"We've a lot to do," said the Banker.

"What will this cost, do you figure?" asked the Big Business Man, looking up from his notes.

The Doctor considered a moment.

"We can't take much with us, you know," he said slowly. Then he took a sheet of memoranda from his pockets. "I have already spent for apparatus and chemicals to prepare the drugs"—he consulted his figures—"seventeen hundred and forty dollars, total. What we have still to spend will be very little, I should think. I propose we divide it three ways as we have been doing with the Museum?"

"Four ways," said the Very Young Man. "I'm no kid any more. I got a good job—that is," he added with a rueful air, "I had a good job. To-morrow I quit."

"Four ways," the Doctor corrected himself gravely. "I guess we can manage that."

"What can we take with us, do you think?" asked the Big Business Man.

"I think we should try strapping a belt around our waists, with pouches in it," said the Doctor. "I doubt if it would contract with our bodies, but still it might. If it didn't there would be no harm done; we could leave it behind."

"You want food and water," said the Banker. "Remember that barren country you are going through."

"And something on our feet," the Big Business Man put in.

"I'd like to take a revolver, too," said the Very Young Man. "It might come in awful handy."

"As I remember Rogers's description," said the Doctor thoughtfully, "the trip out is more difficult than going down. We mustn't overlook preparations for that; it is most imperative we should be careful."

"Say, talking about getting back," burst out the Very Young Man. "I'd like to see that other drug work first. It would be pretty rotten to get in there and have it go back on us, wouldn't it? Oh, golly!" The Very Young Man sank back in his chair overcome by the picture he had conjured up.

"I tried it," said the Doctor. "It works."

"I'd like to see it again with something different," said the Big Business Man. "It can't do any harm." The Banker looked his protest, but said nothing.

"What shall we try, a lizard?" suggested the Very Young Man. The Doctor shrugged his shoulders.

"What'll we kill it with? Oh, I know." The Very Young Man picked up a heavy metal paper-weight from the desk. "This'll do the trick, fine," he added.

Then, laying the paper-weight carefully aside, he dipped up a spoonful of water and offered it to the Doctor.

"Not that water this time," said the Doctor, shaking his head with a smile.

The Very Young Man looked blank.

"Organisms in it," the Doctor explained briefly. "All

right for them to get small from the other chemical, but
we don't want them to get large and come out at us, do
we?"

"Holy Smoke, I should say not," said the Very Young
Man, gasping; and the Banker growled:

"Something's going to happen to us, playing with fire
like this."

The Doctor produced a little bottle. "I boiled this
water," he said. "We can use this."

It took but a moment to give the other drug to one of
the remaining lizards, although they spilled more of the
water than went down its throat.

"Don't forget to hit him, and don't you wait very
long," said the Banker warningly, moving nearer the
door.

"Oh, I'll hit him all right, don't worry," said the Very
Young Man, brandishing the paper-weight.

The Doctor knelt down, and held the reptile pinned to
the floor; the Very Young Man knelt beside him. Slowly
the lizard began to increase in size.

"He's growing," said the Banker. "Hit him, boy,
what's the use of waiting; he's growing."

The lizard was nearly a foot long now, and struggling
violently between the Doctor's fingers.

"You'd better kill him," said the Doctor, "he might get
away from me." The Very Young Man obediently
brought his weapon down with a thump upon the reptile's
head.

"Keep on," said the Banker. "Be sure he's dead."

The Very Young Man pounded the quivering body for
a moment. The Big Business Man handed him a napkin from the tray and the Very Young Man wrapped up
the lizard and threw it into the waste-basket.

Then he rose to his feet and tossed the paper-weight on
to the desk with a crash.

"Well, gentlemen," he said, turning back to them with flushed face, "those drugs sure do work. We're going into the ring all right, three weeks from to-night, and nothing on earth can stop us."

CHAPTER XI

THE ESCAPE OF THE DRUG

FOR the next hour the four friends busily planned their preparations for the journey. When they began to discuss the details of the trip, and found themselves face to face with so hazardous an adventure, each discovered a hundred things in his private life that needed attention.

The Doctor's phrase, "My patients can go to the devil," seemed to relieve his mind of all further responsibility towards his personal affairs.

"That's all very well for you," said the Big Business Man, "I've too many irons in the fire just to drop everything—there are too many other people concerned. And I've got to plan as though I were never coming back, you know."

"Your troubles are easy," said the Very Young Man. "I've got a girl. I wonder what she'll say. Oh, gosh, I can't tell her where I'm going, can I? I never thought of that." He scratched his head with a perplexed air. "That's tough on her. Well, I'm glad I'm an orphan, anyway."

The actual necessities of the trip needed a little discussion, for what they could take with them amounted to practically nothing.

"As I understand it," said the Banker, "all I have to do is watch you start, and then take the ring back to the Museum."

"Take it carefully," continued the Very Young Man. "Remember what it's got in it."

"You will give us about two hours to get well started down," said the Doctor. "After that it will be quite safe to move the ring. You can take it back to the Society in that case I brought it here in."

"Be sure you take it yourself," put in the Very Young Man. "Don't trust it to anybody else. And how about having that wire rack fixed for it at the Museum," he added. "Don't forget that."

"I'll have that done myself this week," said the Doctor.

They had been talking for perhaps an hour when the Banker got up from his chair to get a fresh cigar from a box that lay upon the desk. He happened to glance across the room and on the floor in the corner by the closed door he saw a long, flat object that had not been there before. It was out of the circle of light and being brown against the polished hardwood floor, he could not make it out clearly. But something about it frightened him.

"What's that over there?" he asked, standing still and pointing.

The Big Business Man rose from his seat and took a few steps in the direction of the Banker's outstretched hand. Then with a muttered oath he jumped to the desk in a panic and picking up the heavy paper-weight flung it violently across the room. It struck the panelled wall with a crash and bounded back towards him. At the same instant there came a scuttling sound from the floor, and a brown shape slid down the edge of the room and stopped in the other corner.

All four men were on their feet in an instant, white-faced and trembling.

"Good God," said the Big Business Man huskily, "that thing over there—that——"

"Turn on the side lights—the side lights!" shouted the Doctor, running across the room.

In the glare of the unshaded globes on the wall the room was brightly lighted. On the floor in the corner the horrified men saw a cockroach nearly eighteen inches in length, with its head facing the angle of wall, and scratching with its legs against the base board as though about to climb up. For a moment the men stood silent with surprise and terror. Then, as they stared they saw the cockroach was getting larger. The Big Business Man laid his hand on the Doctor's arm with a grip that made the Doctor wince.

"Good God, man, look at it—it's growing," he said in a voice hardly above a whisper.

"It's growing," echoed the Very Young Man; *"it's growing!"*

And then the truth dawned upon them, and brought with it confusion, almost panic. The cockroach, fully two feet long now, had raised the front end of its body a foot above the floor, and was reaching up the wall with its legs.

The Banker made a dash for the opposite door. "Let's get out of here. Come on!" he shouted.

The Doctor stopped him. Of the four men, he was the only one who had retained his self-possession.

"Listen to me," he said. His voice trembled a little in spite of his efforts to control it. "Listen to me. That—that—thing cannot harm us yet." He looked from one to the other of them and spoke swiftly. "It's gruesome and —and loathsome, but it is not dangerous—yet. But we cannot run from it. We must kill it—here, now, before it gets any larger."

The Banker tore himself loose and started again towards the door.

"You fool!" said the Doctor, with a withering look. "Don't you see, it's life or death later. That—that thing will be as big as this house in half an hour. Don't you know that? As big as this house. We've got to kill it now—now."

The Big Business Man ran towards the paper-weight. "I'll hit it with this," he said.

"You can't," said the Doctor, "you might miss. We haven't time. Look at it," he added.

The cockroach was noticeably larger now—considerably over two feet; it had turned away from the wall to face them.

The Very Young Man had said nothing; only stood and stared with bloodless face and wide-open eyes. Then suddenly he stooped, and picking up a small rug from the floor—a rug some six feet long and half as wide—advanced slowly towards the coackroach.

"That's the idea," encouraged the Doctor. "Get it under that. Here, give me part of it." He grasped a corner of the rug. "You two go up the other sides"—he pointed with his free hand—"and head it off if it runs."

Slowly the four men crept forward. The cockroach, three feet long now, was a hideous, horrible object as it stood backed into the corner of the room, the front part of its body swaying slowly from side to side.

"We'd better make a dash for it," whispered the Very Young Man; and jerking the rug loose from the Doctor's grasp, he leaped forward and flung himself headlong upon the floor, with the rug completely under him.

"I've got the damned thing. I've got it!" he shouted. "Help—you. Help!"

The three men leaped with him upon the rug, holding it pinned to the floor. The Very Young Man, as he lay, could feel the curve of the great body underneath, and could hear the scratch of its many legs upon the floor.

"Hold down the edges of the rug!" he cried. "Don't let it out. Don't let it get out. I'll smash it." He raised himself on his hands and knees, and came down heavily. The rug gave under his thrust as the insect flattened out; then they could hear again the muffled scratching of its legs upon the floor as it raised the rug up under the Very Young Man's weight.

"We can't kill it," panted the Big Business Man. "Oh, we can't kill it. Good God, how big it is!"

The Very Young Man got to his feet and stood unsteadily on the bulge of the rug. Then he jumped into the air and landed solidly on his heels. There was a sharp crack as the shell of the insect broke under the sharpness of his blow.

"That did it; that'll do it!" he shouted. Then he leaped again.

"Let me," said the Big Business Man. "I'm heavier"; and he, too, stamped upon the rug with his heels.

They could hear the huge shell of the insect's back smash under his weight, and when he jumped again, the squash of its body as he mashed it down.

"Wait," said the Doctor. "We've killed it."

They eased upon the rug a little, but there was no movement from beneath.

"Jump on it harder," said the Very Young Man. "Don't let's take a chance. Mash it good."

The Big Business Man continued stamping violently upon the rug; joined now by the Very Young Man. The Doctor sat on the floor beside it, breathing heavily; the Banker lay in a heap at its foot in utter collapse.

As they stamped, the rug continued to flatten down; it sank under their tread with a horrible, sickening, squashing sound.

"Let's look," suggested the Very Young Man. "It must be dead"; and he threw back a corner of the rug. The men turned sick and faint at what they saw.

Underneath the rug, mashed against the floor, lay a

great, noisome, semi-liquid mass of brown and white. It covered nearly the entire under-surface of the rug—a hundred pounds, perhaps, of loathsome pulp and shell, from which a stench arose that stopped their breathing.

With a muttered imprecation the Doctor flung back the rug to cover it, and sprang to his feet, steadying himself against a chair.

"We killed it in time, thank God," he murmured and dropped into the chair, burying his face in his hands.

For a time silence fell upon the room, broken only by the labored breathing of the four men. Then the Big Business Man sat up suddenly. "Oh, my God, what an experience!" he groaned, and got unsteadily to his feet.

The Very Young Man helped the Banker up and led him to a seat by the window, which he opened, letting in the fresh, cool air of the night.

"How did the drug get loose, do you suppose?" asked the Very Young Man, coming back to the center of the room. He had recovered his composure somewhat, though he was still very pale. He lighted a cigarette and sat down beside the Doctor.

The Doctor raised his head wearily. "I suppose we must have spilled some of it on the floor," he said, "and the cockroach——" He stopped abruptly and sprang to his feet.

"Good God!" he cried. "Suppose another one——"

On the bare floor beside the table they came upon a few drops of water.

"That must be it," said the Doctor. He pulled his handkerchief from his pocket; then he stopped in thought. "No, that won't do. What shall we do with it?" he added. "We must destroy it absolutely. Good Lord, if that drug ever gets loose upon the world——"

The Big Business Man joined them.

"We must destroy it absolutely," repeated the Doctor. "We can't just wipe it up."

"Some acid," suggested the Big Business Man.

"Suppose something else has got at it already," the Very Young Man said in a scared voice, and began hastily looking around the floor of the room.

"You're right," agreed the Doctor. "We mustn't take any chance; we must look thoroughly."

Joined by the Banker, the four men began carefully going over the room.

"You'd better watch that nothing gets at it," the Very Young Man thought suddenly to say. The Banker obediently sat down by the little pool of water on the floor.

"And I'll close the window," added the Very Young Man; "something might get out."

They searched the room thoroughly, carefully scanning its walls and ceiling, but could see nothing out of the ordinary.

"We'll never be quite sure," said the Doctor finally, "but I guess we're safe. It's the best we can do now, at any rate."

He joined the Banker by the table. "I'll get some nitric acid," he added. "I don't know what else——"

"We'll have to get that out of here, too," said the Big Business Man, pointing to the rug. "God knows how we'll explain it."

The Doctor picked up one of the tin boxes of drugs and held it in his hand meditatively. Then he looked over towards the rug. From under one side a brownish liquid was oozing; the Doctor shuddered.

"My friends," he said, holding up the box before them, "we can realize now something of the terrible power we have created and imprisoned here. We must guard it carefully, gentlemen, for if it escapes—it will destroy the world."

CHAPTER XII

O N the evening of November 4th, 1923, the four
friends again assembled at the Scientific Club for
the start of their momentous adventure. The Doctor was
the last to arrive, and found the other three anxiously
awaiting him. He brought with him the valise containing the ring and a suit-case with the drugs and equipment necessary for the journey. He greeted his friends
gravely.

"The time has come, gentlemen," he said, putting the
suitcase on the table.

The Big Business Man took out the ring and held it in
his hand thoughtfully.

"The scene of our new life," he said with emotion.
"What does it hold in store for us?"

"What time is it?" asked the Very Young Man.
"We've got to hurry. We want to get started on time—
we mustn't be late."

"Everything's ready, isn't it?" asked the Banker.
"Who has the belts?"

"They're in my suit-case," answered the Very Young
Man. "There it is."

The Doctor laid the ring and handkerchief on the floor
under the light and began unpacking from his bag the
drugs and the few small articles they had decided to try
and take with them. "You have the food and water,"
he said.

The Big Business Man produced three small flasks of

water and six flat, square tins containing compressed food. The Very Young Man opened one of them. "Chocolate soldiers we are," he said, and laughed.

The Banker was visibly nervous and just a little frightened. "Are you sure you haven't forgotten something?" he asked, quaveringly.

"It wouldn't make a great deal of difference if we had," said the Doctor, with a smile. "The belts may not contract with us at all; we may have to leave them behind."

"Rogers didn't take anything," put in the Very Young Man. "Come on; let's get undressed.

The Banker locked the doors and sat down to watch the men make their last preparations. They spoke little while they were disrobing; the solemnity of what they were about to do both awed and frightened them. Only the Very Young Man seemed exhilarated by the excitement of the coming adventure.

In a few moments the three men were dressed in their white woolen bathing suits. The Very Young Man was the first to be fully equipped.

"I'm ready," he announced. "All but the chemicals. Where are they?"

Around his waist he had strapped a broad cloth belt, with a number of pockets fastened to it. On his feet were felt-lined cloth shoes, with hard rubber soles; he wore a wrist watch. Under each armpit was fastened the pouch for carrying the drugs.

"Left arm for red vials," said the Doctor. "Be sure of that—we mustn't get them mixed. Take two of each color." He handed the Very Young Man the tin boxes.

All the men were ready in a moment more.

"Five minutes of eight," said the Very Young Man, looking at his watch. "We're right on time; let's get started."

The Banker stood up among them. "Tell me what

I've got to do," he said helplessly. "You're going all but me; I'll be left behind alone."

The Big Business Man laid his hand on the Banker's shoulder affectionately. "Don't look so sad, George," he said, with an attempt at levity. "We're not leaving you forever—we're coming back."

The Banker pressed his friend's hand. His usual crusty manner was quite gone now; he seemed years older.

The Doctor produced the same spoon he had used when the Chemist made his departure into the ring. "I've kept it all this time," he said, smiling. "Perhaps it will bring us luck." He handed it to the Banker.

"What you have to do is this," he continued seriously. "We shall all take an equal amount of the drug at the same instant. I hope it will act upon each of us at the same rate, so that we may diminish uniformly in size, and thus keep together."

"Gosh!" said the Very Young Man. "I never thought of that. Suppose it doesn't?"

"Then we shall have to adjust the difference by taking other smaller amounts of the drug. But I think probably it will.

"You must be ready," he went on to the Banker, "to help us on to the ring if necessary."

"Or put us back if we fall off," said the Very Young Man. "I'm going to sit still until I'm pretty small. Gracious, it's going to feel funny."

"After we have disappeared," continued the Doctor, "you will wait, say, until eleven o'clock. Watch the ring carefully—some of us may have to come back before that time. At eleven o'clock pack up everything"—he looked around the littered room with a smile—"and take the ring back to the Biological Society."

"Keep your eye on it on the way back," warned the

Very Young Man. "Suppose we decide to come out some time later to-night—you can't tell."

"I'll watch it all night to-night, here and at the Museum," said the Banker, mopping his forehead.

"Good scheme," said the Very Young Man approvingly. "Anything might happen."

"Well, gentlemen," said the Doctor, "I believe we're all ready. Come on, Will."

The Big Business Man was standing by the window, looking out intently. He evidently did not hear the remark addressed to him, for he paid no attention. The Doctor joined him.

Through the window they could see the street below, crowded now with scurrying automobiles. The sidewalks were thronged with people—theater-goers, hurrying forward, seeking eagerly their evening's pleasure. It had been raining, and the wet pavements shone with long, blurred yellow glints from the thousands of lights above. Down the street they could see a huge blazing theater sign, with the name of a popular actress spelt in letters of fire.

The Big Business Man threw up the window sash and took a deep breath of the moist, cool air of the night.

"Good-by, old world," he murmured with emotion. "Shall I see you again, I wonder?" He stood a moment longer, silently staring at the scene before him. Then abruptly he closed the window, pulled down the shade, and turned back to the room.

"Come on," said the Very Young Man impatiently. "It's five minutes after eight. Let's get started."

"Just one thing before we start," said the Doctor, as they gathered in the center of the room. "We must understand, gentlemen, from the moment we first take the drug, until we reach our final smallest size, it is imperative, or at least highly desirable, that we keep together.

We start by taking four of the pellets each, according to the memoranda Rogers left. By Jove!" he interrupted himself, "that's one thing important we did nearly forget."

He went to his coat, and from his wallet took several typewritten sheets of paper.

"I made three copies," he said, handing them to his companions. "Put them away carefully; the front pocket will be most convenient, probably.

"It may not be hard for us to keep together," continued the Doctor. "On the other hand, we may find it extremely difficult, if not quite impossible. In the latter event we will meet at the city of Arite.

"There are two things we must consider. First, we shall be constantly changing size with relation to our surroundings. In proportion to each other, we must remain normal in size if we can. Secondly we shall be traveling—changing position in our surroundings. So far as that aspect of the trip is concerned, it will not be more difficult for us to keep together, probably, than during any adventurous journey here in this world.

"If through accident or any unforeseen circumstance we are separated in size, the one being smallest shall wait for the others. That can be accomplished by taking a very small quantity of the other drug—probably merely by touching one of the pellets to the tongue. Do I make myself clear?" His friends nodded assent.

"If any great separation in relative size occurs," the Doctor went on, "a discrepancy sufficient to make the smallest of us invisible for a time to the others, then another problem presents itself. We must be very careful, in that event, not to change our position in space—not to keep on traveling, in other words—or else, when we become the same size once more, we will be out of sight of one another. Geographically separated, so to speak," the Doctor finished with a smile.

"I am so explicit on this point of keeping together," he continued, "because—well, I personally do not want to undertake even part of this journey alone."

"You're darn right—me neither," agreed the Very Young Man emphatically. "Let's get going."

"I guess that's all," said the Doctor, with a last glance around, and finally facing the Banker. "Good-by, George."

The Banker was quite overcome, and without a word he shook hands with each of his friends.

The three men sat beside each other on the floor, close to the handkerchief and ring; the Banker sat in his chair on the other side, facing them, spoon in hand. In silence they each took four of the pellets. Then the Banker saw them close their eyes; he saw the Big Business Man put his hands suddenly on the floor as though to steady himself.

The Banker gripped the arms of his chair firmly. He knew exactly what to expect, yet now when his friends began slowly to diminish in size he was filled with surprise and horror. For several minutes no one spoke. Then the Very Young Man opened his eyes, looked around dizzily for an instant, and began feeling with his hands the belt at his waist, his shoes, wrist-watch, and the pouches under his armpits.

"It's all right," he said with an enthusiasm that contrasted strangely with the tremor in his voice. "The belt's getting smaller, too. We're going to be able to take everything with us."

Again silence fell on the room, broken only by the sound of the three men on the floor continually shifting their positions as they grew smaller. In another moment the Doctor clambered unsteadily to his feet and, taking a step backward, leaned up against the cylindrical mahogany leg of the center-table, flinging his arms around it. His head did not reach the table-top.

The Very Young Man and the Big Business Man were on their feet now, too, standing at the edge of the handkerchief, and clinging to one another for support. The Banker looked down at them and tried to smile. The Very Young Man waved his hand, and the Banker found voice to say: "Good-by, my boy."

"Good-by, sir," echoed the Very Young Man. "We're making it."

Steadily they grew smaller. By this time the Doctor had become far too small for his arms to encircle the leg of the table. The Banker looked down to the floor, and saw him standing beside the table leg, leaning one hand against it as one would lean against the great stone column of some huge building.

"Good-by, Frank," said the Banker. But the Doctor did not answer; he seemed lost in thought.

Several minutes more passed in silence. The three men had diminished in size now until they were not more than three inches high. Suddenly the Very Young Man let go of the Big Business Man's arm and looked around to where the Doctor was still leaning pensively against the table leg. The Banker saw him speak swiftly to the Big Business Man, but in so small a voice he could not catch the words. Then both little figures turned towards the table, and the Banker saw the Very Young Man put his hands to his mouth and shout. And upward to him came the shrillest, tiniest little voice he had ever heard, yet a voice still embodying the characteristic intonation of the Very Young Man.

"Hey, Doctor!" came the words. "You'll never get here if you don't come now."

The Doctor looked up abruptly; he evidently heard the words and realized his situation. (He was by this time not more than an inch and a half in height.) He hesitated only a moment, and then, as the other two little figures waved their arms wildly, he began running towards them. For more than a minute he ran. The Very Young Man started towards him, but the Doctor waved him back, redoubling his efforts.

When he arrived at the edge of the handkerchief, evidently he was nearly winded, for he stopped beside his friends, and stood breathing heavily. The Banker leaned forwards, and could see the three little figures (they were not as big as the joint of his little finger) talking earnestly; the Very Young Man was gesticulating wildly, pointing towards the ring. One of them made a start, but the others called him back.

Then they began waving their arms, and all at once the Banker realized they were waving at him. He leaned down, and by their motions knew that something was wrong—that they wanted him to do something.

Trembling with fright, the Banker left his chair and knelt upon the floor. The Very Young Man made a funnel of his hands and shouted up: "It's too far away. We can't make it—we're too small!"

The Banker looked his bewilderment. Then he thought suddenly of the spoon that he still held in his hand, and he put it down towards them. The three little figures ducked and scattered as the spoon in the Banker's trembling fingers neared them.

"Not that—the ring. Bring it closer. Hurry— Hurry!" shouted the Very Young Man. The Banker, leaning closer, could just hear the words. Comprehending at last, he picked up the ring and laid it near the edge of the handkerchief. Immediately the little figures ran over to it and began climbing up.

The Very Young Man was the first to reach it; the Banker could see him vault upwards and land astraddle upon its top. The Doctor was up in a moment more, and the two were reaching down their hands to help up the Big Business Man. The Banker slid the spoon carefully along the floor towards the ring, but the Big Business Man waved it away. The Banker laid the spoon aside, and when he looked at the ring again the Big Business Man was up beside his companions, standing upright with them upon the top of the ring.

The Banker stared so long and intently, his vision blurred. He closed his eyes for a moment, and when he opened them again the little figures on the top of the ring had disappeared.

The Banker felt suddenly sick and faint in the closeness of the room. Rising to his feet, he hurried to a window and threw up the sash. A gust of rain and wind beat against his face as he stood leaning on the sill. He felt much better after a few moments; and remembering his friends, he closed the window and turned back towards the ring. At first he thought he could just make them out, but when he got down on the floor close beside the ring, he saw nothing.

Almost unnerved, he sat down heavily upon the floor beside the handkerchief, leaning on one elbow. A corner of the handkerchief was turned back, and one side was ruffled where the wind from the opened window had blown it up. He smoothed out the handkerchief carefully.

For some time the Banker sat quiet, reclining uncomfortably upon the hard floor. The room was very still— its silence oppressed him. He stared stolidly at the ring, his head in a turmoil. The ring looked oddly out of place, lying over near one edge of the handkerchief; he had always seen it in the center before. Abruptly he put out his hand and picked it up. Then remembrance of the Doctor's warning flooded over him. In sudden panic he put the ring down again, almost in the same place at the edge of the handkerchief.

Trembling all over, he looked at his watch; it was a quarter to nine. He rose stiffly to his feet and sank into his chair. After a moment he lighted a cigar. The handkerchief lay at his feet; he could just see the ring over the edge of his knees. For a long time he sat staring.

The striking of a church clock near-by roused him. He shook himself together and blinked at the empty room. In his hand he held an unlighted cigar; mechanically he raised it to his lips. The sound of the church bells died away; the silence of the room and the loneliness of it made him shiver. He looked at his watch again. Ten o'clock! Still another hour to wait and watch, and then he could take the ring back to the Museum. He glanced down at the ring; it was still lying by the edge of the handkerchief.

Again the Banker fell into a stupor as he stared at the glistening gold band lying on the floor at his feet. How lonely he felt! Yet he was not alone, he told himself. His three friends were still there, hardly two feet from the toe of his shoe. He wondered how they were making out. Would they come back any moment? Would they ever come back?

And then the Banker found himself worrying because the ring was not in the center of the handkerchief.

He felt frightened, and he wondered why. Again he looked at his watch. They had been gone more than two hours now. Swiftly he stooped, and lifting the ring, gazed at it searchingly, holding it very close to his eyes.. Then he carefully put it down in the center of the handkerchief, and lay back in his chair with a long sigh of relief.   It was all right now; just a little while to **wait,** and then he could take it back to the Museum.   In a moment his eyes blinked, closed, and soon he was fast asleep, lying sprawled out in the big leather chair and breathing heavily.

CHAPTER XIII

PERILOUS WAYS

THE Very Young Man sat on the floor, between his two friends at the edge of the handkerchief, and put the first pellets of the drug to his tongue. His heart was beating furiously; his forehead was damp with the sweat of excitement and of fear. The pellets tasted sweet, and yet a little acrid. He crushed them in his mouth and swallowed them hastily.

In the silence of the room, the ticking of his watch suddenly sounded very loud. He raised his arm and looked at its face; it was just ten minutes past eight. He continued to stare at its dial, wondering why nothing was happening to him. Then all at once the figures on the watch became very sharp and vivid; he could see them with microscopic clearness. A buzzing sounded in his ears.

He remembered having felt the same way just before he fainted. He drew a deep breath and looked around the room; it swam before his gaze. He closed his eyes and waited, wondering if he would faint. The buzzing in his head grew louder; a feeling of nausea possessed him.

After a moment his head cleared; he felt better. Then all at once he realized that the floor upon which he sat was moving. It seemed to be shifting out from under him in all directions. He sat with his feet flat upon the floor, his knees drawn close against his chin. And the floor seemed to be carrying his feet farther out; he constantly had to be pulling them back against him. He put one hand down beside him, and could feel his fingers dragging very slowly as the polished surface moved past. The noise in his head was almost gone now. He opened his eyes.

Before him, across the handkerchief the Banker sat in his chair. He had grown enormously in size, and as the Very Young Man looked he could see him and the chair growing steadily larger. He met the Banker's anxious glance, and smiled up at him. Then he looked at his two friends, sitting on the floor beside him. They alone, of everything within his range of vision, had grown no larger.

The Very Young Man thought of the belt around his waist. He put his hand to it, and found it tight as before. So, after all, they would not have to leave anything behind, he thought.

The Doctor rose to his feet and turned away, back under the huge table that loomed up behind him. The Very Young Man got up, too, and stood beside the Big Business Man, holding to him for support. His head felt strangely confused; his legs were weak and shaky.

Steadily larger grew the room and everything in it. The Very Young Man turned his eyes up to the light high overhead. Its great electric bulbs dazzled him with their brilliancy; its powerful glare made objects around as bright as though in daylight. After a moment the Big Business Man's grip on his arm tightened.

"God, it's weird!" he said in a tense whisper. "Look!"

Before them spread a great, level, shining expanse of black, with the ring in its center—a huge golden circle. Beyond the farther edge of the black they could see the feet of the banker, and the lower part of his legs stretching into the air far above them.

The Very Young Man looked up still higher, and saw

the Banker staring down at him. "Good-by, my boy," said the Banker. His voice came from far away in a great roar to the Very Young Man's ears.

"Good-by, sir," said the Very Young Man, and waved his hand.

Several minutes passed, and still the Very Young Man stood holding to his companion, and watching the expanse of handkerchief widening out and the gleaming ring growing larger. Then he thought of the Doctor, and turned suddenly to look behind him. Across the wide, glistening surface of the floor stood the Doctor, leaning against the tremendous column that the Very Young Man knew was the leg of the center-table. And as the Very Young Man stood staring, he could see this distance between them growing steadily greater. A sudden fear possessed him, and he shouted to his friend.

"Good Lord, suppose he can't make it!" said the Big Business Man fearfully.

"He's coming," answered the Very Young Man. "He's got to make it."

The Doctor was running towards them now, and in a few moments he was beside them, breathing heavily.

"Close call, Frank," said the Big Business Man, shaking his head. "You were the one said we must keep together." The Doctor was too much out of breath to answer.

"This is worse," said the Very Young Man. "Look where the ring is."

More than two hundred yards away across the black expanse of silk handkerchief lay the ring.

"It's almost as high as our waist now, and look how far it is!" added the Very Young Man excitedly.

"It's getting farther every minute," said the Big Business Man. "Come on," and he started to run towards the ring.

"I can't make it. It's too far!" shouted the Doctor after him.

The Big Business Man stopped short. "What'll we do?" he asked. "We've got to get there."

"That ring will be a mile away in a few minutes, at the rate it's going," said the Very Young Man.

"We'll have to get him to move it over here," decided the Doctor, looking up into the air, and pointing.

"Gee, I never thought of that!" said the Very Young Man. "Oh, great Scott, look at him!"

Out across the broad expanse of handkerchief they could see the huge white face of their friend looming four or five hundred feet in the air above them. It was the most astounding sight their eyes had ever beheld; yet so confused were they by the flood of new impressions to which they were being subjected that this colossal figure added little to their surprise.

"We must make him move the ring over here," repeated the Doctor.

"You'll never make him hear you," said the Big Business Man, as the Very Young Man began shouting at the top of his voice.

"We've got to," said the Very Young Man breathlessly. "Look at that ring. We can't get to it now. We're stranded here. Good Lord! What's the matter with him—can't he see us?" he added, and began shouting again.

"He's getting up," said the Doctor. They could see the figure of the Banker towering in the air a thousand feet above the ring, and then with a swoop of his enormous face come down to them as he knelt upon the floor.

With his hands to his mouth, the Very Young Man shouted up: "It's too far away. We can't make it—

we're too small." They waited. Suddenly, without warning, a great wooden oval bowl fifteen or twenty feet across came at them with tremendous speed. They scattered hastily in terror.

"Not that—the ring!" shouted the Very Young Man, as he realized it was the spoon in the Banker's hand that had frightened them.

A moment more and the ring was before them, lying at the edge of the handkerchief—a circular pit of rough yellow rock breast high. They ran over to it and climbed upon its top.

Another minute and the ring had grown until its top became a narrow curving path upon which they could stand. They got upon their feet and looked around curiously.

"Well, we're here," remarked the Very Young Man. "Everything's O.K. so far. Let's get right around after that scratch."

"Keep together," cautioned the Doctor, and they started off along the path, following its inner edge.

As they progressed, the top of the ring steadily became broader; the surface underfoot became rougher. The Big Business Man, walking nearest the edge, pulled his companion towards him. "Look there!" he said. They stood cautiously at the edge and looked down.

Beneath them the ring bulged out. Over the bulge they could see the black of the handkerchief—a sheer hundred-feet drop. The ring curved sharply to the left; they could follow its wall all the way around; it formed a circular pit some two hundred and fifty feet in diameter.

A gentle breeze fanned their faces as they walked. The Very Young Man looked up into the gray of the distance overhead. A little behind, over his shoulder he saw above him in the sky a great, gleaming light many times bigger than the sun. It cast on the ground before him an opaque shadow, blurred about the edges.

"Pretty good day, at that," remarked the Very Young Man, throwing out his chest.

The Doctor laughed. "It's half-past eight at night," he said. "And if you'll remember half an hour ago, it's a very stormy night, too."

The Big Business Man stopped short in his walk. "Just think," he said pointing up into the gray of the sky, with a note of awe in his voice, "over there, not more than fifteen feet away, is a window, looking down towards the Gaiety Theater and Broadway."

The Very Young Man looked bewildered. "That window's a hundred miles away," he said positively.

"Fifteen feet," said the Big Business Man. "Just beyond the table."

"It's all in the viewpoint" said the Doctor, and laughed again.

They had recovered their spirits by now, the Very Young Man especially seeming imbued with the enthusiasm of adventure.

The path became constantly rougher as they advanced.

The ground underfoot—a shaggy, yellow, metallic ore —was strewn now with pebbles. These pebbles grew larger farther on, becoming huge rocks and bowlders that greatly impeded their progress.

They soon found it difficult to follow the brink of the precipice. The path had broadened now so that its other edge was out of sight, for they could see only a short distance amid the bowlders that everywhere tumbled about, and after a time they found themselves wandering along, lost in the barren waste.

"How far is the scratch, do you suppose?" the Very Young Man wanted to know.

They stopped and consulted a moment; then the Very Young Man clambered up to the top of a rock. "There's a range of hills over there pretty close," he called down to them. "That must be the way."

They had just started again in the direction of the hills when, almost without warning, and with a great whistle and roar, a gale of wind swept down upon them. They stood still and looked at each other with startled faces, bracing with their feet against its pressure.

"Oh, golly, what's this?" cried the Very Young Man, and sat down suddenly upon the ground to keep from being blown forward.

The wind increased rapidly in violence until, in a moment, all three of the men were crouching upon the ground for shelter.

"Great Scott, this is a tornado!" ejaculated the Big Business Man. His words were almost lost amid the howling of the blast as it swept across the barren waste of rocks.

"Rogers never told us anything about this. It's getting worse every minute. I——" A shower of pebbles and a great cloud of metallic dust swept past, leaving them choking and gasping for breath.

The Very Young Man got upon his hands and knees.

"I'm going over there," he panted. "It's better."

CHAPTER XIV

L ED by the Very Young Man, the three crawled a few yards to where a cluster of bowlders promised better shelter. Huddled behind this mass of rock, they found themselves protected in a measure from the violence of the storm. Lying there, they could see yellowish-gray clouds of sand go sweeping by, with occasionally a hail of tiny pebbles, blowing almost horizontal. Overhead, the sky was unchanged. Not a vestige of cloud was visible, only the gray-blue of an immense distance, with the huge gleaming light, like an enormous sun, hang-in its center.

The Very Young Man put his hand on the Doctor's arm. "It's going down," he said. Hardly were the words out of his mouth before, with even less warning than it began, the gale abruptly ceased. There remained only the pleasantly gentle breeze of a summer afternoon blowing against their faces. And this came from almost an opposite direction to the storm.

The three men looked at one another in amazement.

"Well, I'll be——" ejaculated the Very Young Man. "What next?"

They waited for some time, afraid to venture out from the rocks among which they had taken refuge. Then, deciding that the storm, however unexplainable, was over for the time at least, they climbed to their feet and resumed their journey with bruised knees, but otherwise none the worse for the danger through which they had passed.

After walking a short distance, they came up a little incline, and before them, hardly more than a quarter of a mile away, they could see a range of hills.

"The scratch must be behind those hills," said the Very Young Man, pointing.

"It's a long distance," said the Big Business Man thoughtfully. "We're still growing smaller—look."

Their minds had been so occupied that for some time they had forgotten the effect of the drug upon their stature. As they looked about them now they could see the rocks around them still increasing steadily in size, and could feel the ground shifting under their feet when they stood still.

"You're right; we're getting smaller," observed the Very Young Man. "How long before we'll stop, do you suppose?"

The Doctor drew the Chemist's memoranda from the pouch of his belt. "It says about five or six hours for the first four pellets," he read.

The Very Young Man looked at his watch. "Quarter to nine. We've been less than an hour yet. Come on, let's keep going," and he started walking rapidly forward.

They walked for a time in silence. The line of hills before them grew visibly in size, and they seemed slowly to be nearing it.

"I've been thinking," began the Doctor thoughtfully as he glanced up at the hills. "There's one theory of Rogers's that was a fallacy. You remember he was quite positive that this change of stature became steadily more rapid, until it reached its maximum rate and then remained constant. If that were so we should probably be diminishing in size more rapidly now than when we first climbed on to the ring. If we had so much trouble getting to the ring then"—he smiled at the remembrance of their difficulty—"I don't see how we could ever get to those hills now."

"Gee, that's so," said the Very Young Man. "We'd never be able to get anywhere, would we?"

"How do you figure it works?" asked the Big Business Man.

The Doctor folded up the paper and replaced it in his belt. "I don't know," he answered. "I think probably it proceeds in cycles, like the normal rate of growth—times of rapid progress succeeded by periods of comparative inactivity."

"I never knew people grew that way," observed the Very Young Man.

"They do," said the Doctor. "And if these drugs pro-duce the same effect we——" He got no further, for suddenly the earth seemed to rise swiftly under them, and they were thrown violently to the ground.

The Very Young Man, as he lay prone, looked upward, and saw the sunlike light above fall swiftly down across the sky and disappear below the horizon, plunging the world about them into the gloom of a semi-twilight. A wind, fiercer than before, swept over them with a roar.

"The end of the world," murmured the Very Young Man to himself. And he wondered why he was not frightened.

Then came the feeling of an extraordinary lightness of body, as though the ground were dropping away from under him. The wind abruptly ceased blowing. He saw the ball of light rise swiftly from the horizon and mount upward in a great, gleaming arc to the zenith, where again it hung motionless.

The three men lay quiet, their heads reeling. Then the

Very Young Man sat up dizzily and began feeling himself all over. "There's nothing wrong with me," he said lugubriously, meeting the eyes of his friends who apparently were also more surprised than hurt. "But—oh, my gosh, the whole universe went nutty!" he added to himself in awe.

"What did that?" asked the Big Business Man. He climbed unsteadily to his feet and sat upon a rock, holding his head in his hands.

The Doctor was up in a moment beside him. "We're not hurt," he said, looking at his companions. "Don't let's waste any more time—let's get into that valley." The Very Young Man could see by his manner that he knew or guessed what had happened.

"But say; what——" began the Very Young Man.

"Come on," interrupted the Doctor, and started walking ahead swiftly.

There was nothing for his two friends to do but to follow. They walked in silence, in single file, picking their way among the rocks. For a quarter of an hour or more they kept going, until finally they came to the ridge of hills, finding them enormous rocks, several hundred feet high, strewn closely together.

"The valley must be right beyond," said the Doctor. "Come on."

The spaces between these huge rocks were, some of them, fifty feet or more in width. Inside the hills the travelers found the ground even rougher than before, and it was nearly half an hour before they emerged on the other side.

Instead of the shallow valley they expected to find, they came upon a precipice—a sheer drop into a tremendous cañon, half as wide possibly as it was deep. They could see down to its bottom from where they stood—the same rocky, barren waste as that through which they had been traveling. Across the cañon, on the farther side, lay another line of hills.

"It's the scratch all right," said the Very Young Man, as they stopped near the brink of the precipice, "but, holy smoke! Isn't it big?"

"That's two thousand feet down there," said the Big Business Man, stepping cautiously nearer to the edge. "Rogers didn't say it was so deep."

"That's because we've been so much longer getting here," explained the Doctor.

"How are we going to get down?" asked the Very Young Man as he stood beside the Big Business Man within a few feet of the brink. "It's getting deeper every minute, don't forget that."

The Big Business Man knelt down and carefully approached to the very edge of the precipice. Then, as he looked over, he got upon his feet with a laugh of relief. "Come here," he said.

They joined him at the edge and, looking over, could see that the jagged roughness of the wall made the descent, though difficult, not exceptionally hazardous. Below them, not more than twenty feet, a wide ledge jutted out, and beyond that they could see other similar ledges and crevices that would afford a foothold.

"We can get down that," said the Very Young Man. "There's an easy place," and he pointed farther along the brink, to where a break in the edge seemed to offer a means of descent to the ledge just below.

"It's going to be a mighty long climb down," said the Big Business Man. "Especially as we're getting smaller all the time. I wonder," he added thoughtfully, "how would it be if we made ourselves larger before we started. We could get big enough, you know, so that it would only be a few hundred feet down there. Then, after we got down, we could get small again."

"That's a thought," said the Very Young Man.

The Doctor sat down somewhat wearily, and again took the papers from his belt. "The idea is a good one," he said. "But there's one thing you overlook. The larger we get, the smoother the wall is going to be. Look, can't you see it changing every moment?"

It was true. Even in the short time since they had first looked down, new crevices had opened up. The descent, though longer, was momentarily becoming less dangerous.

"You see," continued the Doctor, "if the valley were only a few hundred feet deep, the precipice might then be so sheer we could not trust ourselves to it at all."

"You're right," observed the Big Business Man.

"Well, it's not very hard to get down now," said the Very Young Man. "Let's get going before it gets any deeper. Say," he added, "how about stopping our size where it is? How would that work?"

The Doctor was reading the papers he held in his hand. "I think," he said, "it would be our wisest course to follow as closely as possible what Rogers tells us to do. It may be harder, but I think we will avoid trouble in the end."

"We could get lost in size just as easily as in space, couldn't we?" the Big Business Man put in. "That's a curious idea, isn't it?"

"It's true," agreed the Doctor. "It is something we must guard against very carefully."

"Well, come on then, let's get going," said the Very Young Man, pulling the Doctor to his feet.

The Big Business Man glanced at his watch. "Twenty to ten," he said. Then he looked up into the sky. "One hour and a half ago," he added sentimentally, "we were up there. What will another hour bring—I wonder?"

"Nothing at all," said the Very Young Man, "if we don't ever get started.   Come on."

He walked towards the place he had selected, followed by his companions.   And thus the three adventurers began their descent into the ring.

CHAPTER XV

THE VALLEY OF THE SCRATCH

FOR the first half-hour of their climb down into the valley of the scratch, the three friends were too preoccupied with their own safety to talk more than an occasional sentence. They came upon many places that at first glance appeared impassable, or at least sufficiently hazardous to cause them to hesitate, but in each instance the changing contour of the precipice offered some other means of descent.

After thirty minutes of arduous effort, the Big Business Man sat down suddenly upon a rock and began to unlace his shoes.

"I've got to rest a while," he groaned. "My feet are in terrible shape."

His two companions were glad of the opportunity to sit with him for a moment.

"Gosh, I'm all in, too!" said the Very Young Man with a sigh.

They were sitting upon a ledge about twenty feet wide, with the wall down which they had come at their back.

"I'll swear that's as far down there as it ever was," said the Big Business Man, with a wave of his hand towards the valley below them.

"Further," remarked the Very Young Man. "I've known that right along."

"That's to be expected," said the Doctor. "But we're a third the way down, just the same; that's the main thing." He glanced up the rocky, precipitous wall behind them. "We've come down a thousand feet, at least. The valley must be three thousand feet deep or more now."

"Say, how deep does it get before it stops?" inquired the Very Young Man.

The Doctor smiled at him quietly. "Rogers's note put it about twelve thousand," he answered. "It should reach that depth and stop about"—he hesitated a moment, calculating—"about two o'clock," he finished.

"Some climb," commented the Very Young Man. "We could do this a lot better than we're doing it, I think."

For some time they sat in silence. From where they sat the valley had all the appearance of a rocky, barren cañon of their own world above, as it might have looked on the late afternoon of a cloudless summer day. A gentle breeze was blowing, and in the sky overhead they could still see the huge light that for them was the sun.

"The weather is certainly great down here anyway," observed the Very Young Man, "that's one consolation."

The Big Business Man had replaced his shoes, taken a swallow of water, and risen to his feet, preparing to start downward again, when suddenly they all noticed a curious swaying motion, as though the earth were moving under them.

"Now what?" ejaculated the Very Young Man, standing up abruptly, with his feet spread wide apart.

The ground seemed pressing against his feet as if he were weighted down with a heavy load. And he felt a little also as though in a moving train with a side thrust to guard against. The sun was no longer visible, and the valley was plunged in the semidarkness of twilight. A strong wind sprang up, sweeping down upon them from above.

The Very Young Man and the Big Business Man

looked puzzled; the Doctor alone of the three seemed to understand what was happening.

"He's moving the ring," he explained, with a note of apprehension in his voice.

"Oh," ejaculated the Big Business Man, comprehending at last, "so that's the——"

The Very Young Man standing with his back to the wall and his legs spread wide looked hastily at his watch. "Moving the ring? Why, damn it——" he began impetuously.

The Big Business Man interrupted him. "Look there, look!" he almost whispered, awestruck.

The sky above the valley suddenly had become suffused with red. As they watched it seemed to take form, appearing no longer space, but filled with some enormous body of reddish color. In one place they could see it broken into a line of gray, and underneath the gray, two circular holes of light gleamed down at them.

The Doctor shuddered and closed his eyes; his two friends stared upward, fascinated into immobility.

"What—is—that?" the Very Young Man whispered.

Before he could be answered, the earth swayed under them more violently than before. The red faded back out of the sky, and the sun appeared sweeping up into the zenith, where it hung swaying a moment and then poised motionless. The valley was flooded again with light; the ground steadied under them and became quiet. The wind died rapidly away, and in another moment it was as though nothing unusual had occurred.

For a time the three friends stood silent, too astonished for words at this extraordinary experience. The Doctor was the first to recover himself. "He moved the ring," he said hurriedly. "That's twice. We must hurry."

"It's only quarter past ten. We told him not till eleven," protested the Very Young Man.

"Even that is too soon for safety," said the Doctor back over his shoulder, for already he had started downward.

It was nearly twelve o'clock when they stopped again for rest. At this time the valley appeared about seven or eight thousand feet deep: they estimated themselves to be slightly more than half-way down. From eleven until twelve they had momentarily expected some disturbing phenomena attendant upon the removal of the ring by the Banker from the clubroom to its place in the Museum. But nothing unusual had occurred.

"He probably decided to leave it alone for a while," commented the Big Business Man, as they were discussing the matter. "Glad he showed that much sense."

"It would not bother us much now," the Doctor replied. "We're too far down. See how the light is changing."

The sky showed now only as a narrow ribbon of blue between the edges of the cañon's walls. The sun was behind the wall down which they were climbing, out of sight, and throwing their side of the valley into shadow. And already they could begin to see a dim phosphorescence glowing from the rocks near at hand.

The Very Young Man, sitting beside the Doctor, suddenly gripped his friend by the arm. "A bird," he said, pointing down the valley. "See it there?"

From far off they could see a bird coming up the center of the valley at a height apparently almost level with their own position, and flying towards them. They watched it in silence as it rapidly approached.

"Great Scott, it's big!" muttered the Big Business Man in an undertone.

As the bird came closer they saw it was fully fifty feet across the wings. It was flying straight down the valley at tremendous speed. When it was nearly opposite them they heard a familiar "cheep, cheep," come echoing across the valley.

"The sparrow," whispered the Very Young Man. "Oh, my gosh, look how big it is!"

In another moment it had passed them; they watched in silence until it disappeared in the distance.

"Well," said the Very Young Man, "if that had ever seen us——" He drew a long breath, leaving the rest to the imagination of his hearers.

"What a wonderful thing!" said the Big Business Man, with a note of awe in his voice. "Just think—that sparrow when we last saw it was infinitesimally small."

The Doctor laughed. "It's far smaller now than it was then," he said. "Only since we last saw it we have changed size to a much greater extent than it has."

"Foolish of us to have sent it in here," remarked the Big Business Man casually. "Suppose that——" He stopped abruptly.

The Very Young Man started hastily to his feet.

"Oh, golly!" he exclaimed as the same thought occurred to him. "That lizard——" He looked about him wildly.

"It was foolish perhaps." The Doctor spoke quietly. "But we can't help it now. The sparrow has gone. That lizard may be right here at our feet"—The Very Young Man jumped involuntarily—"and so small we can't see it," the Doctor finished with a smile. "Or it may be a hundred miles away and big as a dinosaur." The Very Young Man shuddered.

"It was senseless of us to let them get in here anyway," said the Big Business Man. "That sparrow evidently has stopped getting smaller. Do you realize how big it will be to us, after we've diminished a few hundred more times?"

"We needn't worry over it," said the Doctor. "Even if we knew the lizard got into the valley the chances of our seeing it here are one in a million. But we don't even know that. If you'll remember it was still some distance away from the scratch when it became invisible; I doubt very much if it even got there. No, I think probably we'll never see it again."

"I hope not," declared the Very Young Man emphatically.

For another hour they climbed steadily downward, making more rapid progress than before, for the descent became constantly less difficult. During this time they spoke little, but it was evident that the Very Young Man, from the frequent glances he threw around, never for a moment forgot the possibility of encountering the lizard. The sparrow did not return, although for that, too, they were constantly on the look-out.

It was nearly half-past one when the Big Business Man threw himself upon the ground exhausted. The valley at this time had reached a depth of over ten thousand feet. It was still growing deeper, but the travelers had made good progress and were not more than fifteen hundred feet above its bottom.

They had been under tremendous physical exertion for over five hours, too absorbed in their strange experiences to think of eating, and now all three agreed it was foolish to attempt to travel farther without food and rest.

"We had better wait here an hour or two," the Doctor decided. "Our size will soon remain constant and it won't take us long to get down after we've rested."

"I'm hungry," suggested the Very Young Man, "how about you?"

They ate and drank sparingly of the little store they

had brought with them. The Doctor would not let them have much, both because he wanted to conserve their supply, and because he knew in their exhausted condition it would be bad for them to eat heartily.

It was about two o'clock when they noticed that objects around them no longer were increasing in size. They had finished their meal and felt greatly refreshed.

"Things have stopped growing," observed the Very Young Man. "We've done four pills' worth of the journey anyway," he added facetiously. He rose to his feet, stretching. He felt sore and bruised all over, but with the meal and a little rest, not particularly tired.

"I move we go on down now," he suggested, walking to the edge of the huge crevice in which they were sitting. "It's only a couple of thousand feet."

"Perhaps we might as well," agreed the Doctor, rising also. "When we get to the floor of the valley, we can find a good spot and turn in for the night."

The incongruity of his last words with the scene around made the Doctor smile. Overhead the sky still showed a narrow ribbon of blue. Across the valley the sunlight sparkled on the yellowish crags of the rocky wall. In the shadow, on the side down which they were climbing, the rocks now shone distinctly phosphorescent, with a peculiar waviness of outline.

"Not much like either night or day, is it?" added the Doctor. "We'll have to get used to that."

They started off again, and in another two hours found themselves going down a gentle rocky slope and out upon the floor of the valley.

"We're here at last," said the Big Business Man wearily.

The Very Young Man looked up the great, jagged precipice down which they had come, to where, far above, its edge against the strip of blue marked the surface of the ring.

"Some trip," he remarked. "I wouldn't want to tackle that every day."

"Four o'clock," said the Doctor, "the light up there looks just the same. I wonder what's happened to George."

Neither of his companions answered him. The Big Business Man lay stretched full length upon the ground near by, and the Very Young Man still stood looking up the precipice, lost in thought.

"What a nice climb going back," he suddenly remarked.

The Doctor laughed. "Don't let's worry about that, Jack. If you remember how Rogers described it, getting back is easier than getting in. But the main point now," he added seriously, "is for us to make sure of getting down to Arite as speedily as possible."

The Very Young Man surveyed the barren waste around them in dismay. The floor of the valley was strewn with even larger rocks and bowlders than those on the surface above, and looked utterly pathless and desolate. "What do we do first?" he asked dubiously.

"First," said the Doctor, smiling at the Big Business Man, who lay upon his back staring up into the sky and paying no attention to them whatever, "I think first we had better settle ourselves for a good long rest here."

"If we stop at all, let's sleep a while," said the Very Young Man. "A little rest only gets you stiff. It's a pretty exposed place out here though, isn't it, to sleep?" he added, thinking of the sparrow and the lizard.

"One of us will stay awake and watch," answered the Doctor.

CHAPTER XVI

THE PIT OF DARKNESS

A T the suggestion of the Very Young Man they located without much difficulty a sort of cave amid the rocks, which offered shelter for their rest. Taking turns watching, they passed eight hours in fair comfort, and by noon next day, after another frugal meal they felt thoroughly refreshed and eager to continue the journey.

"We sure are doing this classy," observed the Very Young Man. "Think of Rogers—all he could do was fall asleep when he couldn't stay awake any more. Gosh, what chances he took!"

"We're playing it safe," agreed the Big Business Man.

"But we mustn't take it too easy," added the Doctor.

The Very Young Man stretched himself luxuriously and buckled his belt on tighter. "Well, I'm ready for anything," he announced. "What's next?"

The Doctor consulted his papers. "We find the circular pit Rogers made in the scratch and we descend into it. We take twelve more pills at the edge of the pit," he said.

The Very Young Man leaped to the top of a rock and looked out over the desolate waste helplessly. "How are we going to find the pit?" he asked dubiously. "It's not in sight, that's sure."

"It's down there—about five miles," said the Doctor. "I saw it yesterday as we came down."

"That's easy," said the Very Young Man, and he started off enthusiastically, followed by the others.

In less than two hours they found themselves at the

edge of the pit. It appeared almost circular in form, apparently about five miles across, and its smooth, shining walls extended almost perpendicularly down into blackness. Somewhat awed by the task confronting them in getting down into this abyss, the three friends sat down near its brink to discuss their plan of action.

"We take twelve pills here," said the Doctor. "That ought to make us small enough to climb down into that."

"Do you think we need so many?" asked the Big Business Man thoughtfully. "You know, Frank, we're making an awful lot of work for ourselves, playing this thing so absolutely safe. Think of what a distance down that will be after we have got as small as twelve pills will make us. It might take us days to get to the bottom."

"How did Rogers get down?" the Very Young Man wanted to know.

"He took the twelve pills here," the Doctor answered.

"But as I understand it, he fell most of the way down while he was still big, and then got small afterwards at the bottom." This from the Big Business Man.

"I don't know how about you," said the Very Young Man drily, "but I'd much rather take three days to walk down than fall down in one day."

The Doctor smiled. "I still think," he said, "that we had better stick to the directions Rogers left us. Then at least there is no danger of our getting lost in size. But I agree with you, Jack. I'd rather not fall down, even if it takes longer to walk."

"I wonder——" began the Big Business Man. "You know I've been thinking—it does seem an awful waste of energy for us to let ourselves get smaller than absolutely necessary in climbing down these places. Maybe you don't realize it."

"I do," said the Very Young Man, looking sorrowfully

at the ragged shoes on his feet and the cuts and bruises on his legs.

"What I mean is——" persisted the Big Business Man. "How far do you suppose we have actually traveled since we started last night?"

"That's pretty hard to estimate," said the doctor. "We have walked perhaps fifteen miles altogether, besides the climb down. I suppose we actually came down five or six thousand feet."

"And at the size we are now it would have been twelve thousand feet down, wouldn't it?"

"Yes," answered the Doctor, "it would."

"And just think," went on the Big Business Man, "right now, based on the size we were when we began, we've only gone some six feet altogether from the place we started."

"And a sixteenth of an inch or less since we left the surface of the ring," said the Doctor smiling.

"Gee, that's a weird thought," the Very Young Man said, as he gazed in awe at the lofty heights about them.

"I've been thinking," continued the Big Business Man. "You say we must be careful not to get lost in size. Well, suppose instead of taking twelve pills here, we only take six. That should be enough to get us started—possibly enough to get us all the way down. Then before we moved at all we could take the other six. That would keep it straight, wouldn't it?"

"Great idea," said the Very Young Man. "I'm in favor of that."

"It sounds feasible—certainly if we can get all the way down with six pills we will save a lot of climbing."

"If six aren't enough, we can easily take more," added the Big Business Man.

And so they decided to take only six pills of the drug

and to get down to the bottom of the pit, if possible, without taking more. The pit, as they stood looking down into it now, seemed quite impossible of descent, for its almost perpendicular wall was smooth and shining as polished brass.

They took the drug, standing close together at the edge of the pit. Immediately began again the same crawling sensation underfoot, much more rapid this time, while all around them the rocks began very rapidly increasing in size.

The pit now seemed widening out at an astounding rate. In a few minutes it had broadened so that its opposite side could not be seen. The wall at the brink of which they stood had before curved in a great sweeping arc to enclose the circular hole; now it stretched in a nearly straight, unbroken line to the right and left as far as they could see. Beneath them lay only blackness; it was as though they were at the edge of the world.

"Good God, what a place to go down into," gasped the Big Business Man, after they had been standing nearly half an hour in silence, appalled at the tremendous changes taking place around them.

For some time past the wall before them had become sufficiently indented and broken to make possible their descent. It was the Doctor who first realized the time—or perhaps it should be said, the size—they were losing by their inactivity; and when with a few crisp words he brought them to themselves, they immediately started downward.

For another six hours they traveled downward steadily, stopping only once to eat. The descent during this time was not unlike that down the side of the valley, although towards the last it began rapidly to grow less precipitous.

They now found themselves confronted frequently with

gentle slopes downward, half a mile or more in extent, and sometimes by almost level places, succeeded by another sharp descent.

During this part of the trip they made more rapid progress than at any time since starting, the Very Young Man in his enthusiasm at times running forward and then sitting down to wait for the others to overtake him.

The light overhead gradually faded into the characteristic luminous blackness the Chemist had described. As it did so, the phosphorescent quality of the rocks greatly increased, or at least became more noticeable, so that the light illuminating the landscape became hardly less in volume, although totally different in quality.

The ground underfoot and the rocks themselves had been steadily changing. They had lost now almost entirely the yellowishness, metal look, and seemed to have more the quality of a gray opaque glass, or marble. They appeared rather smoother, too, than before, although the huge bowlders and loosely strewn rocks and pebbles still remained the characteristic feature of the landscape.

The three men were still diminishing in size; in fact, at this time the last dose of the drug seemed to have attained its maximum power, for objects around them appeared to be growing larger at a dizzying rate. They were getting used to this effect, however, to a great extent, and were no longer confused by the change as they had been before.

It was the Big Business Man who first showed signs of weakening, and at the end of six hours or more of steady—and, towards the end, extremely rapid—traveling he finally threw himself down and declared he could go no farther. At this point they rested again several hours, taking turns at watch, and each of them getting some measure of sleep. Of the three, the Very Young Man appeared in the best condition, although possibly it was his enthusiasm that kept him from admitting even to himself any serious physical distress.

It was perhaps ten or twelve hours after they had taken the six pills that they were again ready to start downward. Before starting the three adventurers discussed earnestly the advisability of taking the other six pills. The action of the drug had ceased some time before. They decided not to, since apparently there was no difficulty facing them at this part of the journey, and decreasing their stature would only immeasurably lengthen the distance they had to go.

They had been traveling downward, through a barren land that now showed little change of aspect, for hardly more than another hour, when suddenly, without warning, they came upon the tremendous glossy incline that they had been expecting to reach for some time. The rocks and bowlders stopped abruptly, and they found at their feet, sloping downward at an angle of nearly forty-five degrees, a great, smooth plane. It extended as far as they could see both to the right and left and downward, at a slightly lessening angle, into the luminous darkness that now bounded their entire range of vision in every direction.

This plane seemed distinctly of a different substance than anything they had hitherto encountered. It was, as the Chemist had described it, apparently like a smooth black marble. Yet it was not so smooth to them now as he had pictured it, for its surface was sufficiently indented and ridged to afford foothold.

They started down this plane gingerly, yet with an assumed boldness they were all of them far from feeling. It was slow work at first, and occasionally one or the other of them would slide headlong a score of feet, until a break in the smoothness brought him to a stop. Their rubber-soled shoes stood them in good stead here, for without the aid given by them this part of the journey would have been impossible.

For several hours they continued this form of descent. The incline grew constantly less steep, until finally they were able to walk down it quite comfortably. They stopped again to eat, and after traveling what seemed to them some fifteen miles from the top of the incline they finally reached its bottom.

They seemed now to be upon a level floor—a ground of somewhat metallic quality such as they had become familiar with above. Only now there were no rocks or bowlders, and the ground was smoother and with a peculiar corrugation. On one side lay the incline down which they had come. There was nothing but darkness to be seen in any other direction. Here they stopped again to rest and recuperate, and then they discussed earnestly their next movements.

The Doctor, seated wearily upon the ground, consulted his memoranda earnestly. The Very Young Man sat close beside him. As usual the Big Business Man lay prone upon his back near-by, waiting for their decision.

"Rogers wasn't far from a forest when he got here," said the Very Young Man, looking sidewise at the papers in the Doctor's hand. "And he speaks of a tiny range of hills; but we can't see anything from here."

"We may not be within many miles of where Rogers landed," answered the Doctor.

"No reason why we should be, at that, is there? Do you think we'll ever find Arite?"

"Don't overlook the fact we've got six more pills to take here," called the Big Business Man.

"That's just what I was considering," said the Doctor thoughtfully. "There's no use our doing anything until we have attained the right size. Those hills and the forest and river we are looking for might be here right at our feet and we couldn't see them while we are as big as this."

"We'd better take the pills and stay right here until their action wears off. I'm going to take a sleep," said the Big Business Man.

"I think we might as well all sleep," said the Doctor. "There could not possibly be anything here to harm us."

They each took the six additional pills without further words. Physically exhausted as they were, and with the artificial drowsiness produced by the drug, they were all three in a few moments fast asleep.

CHAPTER XVII

THE WELCOME OF THE MASTER

IT was nearly twelve hours later, as their watches showed them, that the first of the weary adventurers awoke. The Very Young Man it was who first opened his eyes with a confused sense of feeling that he was in bed at home, and that this was the momentous day he was to start his journey into the ring. He sat up and rubbed his eyes vigorously to see more clearly his surroundings.

Beside him lay his two friends, fast asleep. With returning consciousness came the memory of the events of the day and night before. The Very Young Man sprang to his feet and vigorously awoke his companions.

The action of the drug again had ceased, and at first glance the scene seemed to have changed very little. The incline now was some distance away, although still visible, stretching up in a great arc and fading away into the blackness above. The ground beneath their feet still of its metallic quality, appeared far rougher than before. The Very Young Man bent down and put his hand upon it. There was some form of vegetation there, and, leaning closer, he could see what appeared to be the ruins of a tiny forest, bent and trampled, the tree-trunks no larger than slender twigs that he could have snapped asunder easily between his fingers.

"Look at this," he exclaimed. "The woods—we're here."

The others knelt down with him.

"Be careful," cautioned the Doctor. "Don't move around. We must get smaller." He drew the papers from his pocket.

"Rogers was in doubt about this quantity to take," he added. "We should be now somewhere at the edge or in the forest he mentions. Yet we may be very far from the point at which he reached the bottom of that incline. I think, too, that we are somewhat larger than he was. Probably the strength of our drug differs from his to some extent."

"How much should we take next, I wonder?" said the Big Business Man as he looked at his companions.

The Doctor took a pill and crushed it in his hand. "Let us take so much," he said, indicating a small portion of the powder. The others each crushed one of the pills and endeavored to take as nearly as possible an equal amount.

"I'm hungry," said the Very Young Man. "Can we eat right after the powder?"

"I don't think that should make any difference," the Doctor answered, and so accustomed to the drug were they now that, quite nonchalantly, they sat down and ate.

After a few moments it became evident that in spite of their care the amounts of the drug they had taken were far from equal.

Before they had half finished eating, the Very Young Man was hardly more than a third the size of the Doctor, with the Big Business Man about half-way between. This predicament suddenly struck them as funny, and all three laughed heartily at the effect of the drug.

"Hey, you, hurry up, or you'll never catch me," shouted the Very Young Man gleefully. "Gosh, but you're big!" He reached up and tried to touch the Doctor's shoulder. Then, seeing the huge piece of chocolate in his friend's hand and comparing it with the little one in his own, he added: "Trade you chocolate. That's a regular meal you got there."

"That's a real idea," said the Big Business Man, ceasing his laughter abruptly. "Do you know, if we ever get really low on food, all we have to do is one of us stay big and his food would last the other two a month."

"Fine; but how about the big one?" asked the Very Young Man, grinning. "He'd starve to death on that plan, wouldn't he?"

"Well, then he could get much smaller than the other two, and they could feed him. It's rather involved, I'll admit, but you know what I mean," the Big Business Man finished somewhat lamely.

"I've got a much better scheme than that," said the Very Young Man. "You let the food stay large and you get small. How about that?" he added triumphantly. Then he laid carefully on the ground beside him a bit of chocolate and a few of the hard crackers they were eating. "Stay there, little friends, when you grow up, I'll take you back," he added in a gleeful tone of voice.

"Strange that should never have occurred to us," said the Doctor. "It's a perfect way of replenishing our food supply," and quite seriously both he and the Big Business Man laid aside some of their food.

"Thank me for that brilliant idea," said the Very Young Man. Then, as another thought occurred to him, he scratched his head lugubriously. "Wouldn't work very well if we were getting bigger, would it? Don't let's ever get separated from any food coming out."

The Doctor was gigantic now in proportion to the other two, and both he and the Big Business Man took a very small quantity more of the drug in an effort to equalize their rate of bodily reduction. They evidently hit it about right, for no further change in their relative size occurred.

All this time the vegetation underneath them had been

growing steadily larger.   From tiny broken twigs it grew
to sticks bigger than their fingers, then to the thickness of
their arms.   They moved slightly from time to time, letting it spread out from under them, or brushing it aside
and clearing a space in which they could sit more comfortably.   Still larger it grew until the tree-trunks, thick
now almost as their bodies, were lying broken and twisted,
all about them.   Over to one side they could see, half a
mile away, a place where the trees were still standing—
slender saplings, they seemed, growing densely together.

In half an hour more the Very Young Man announced
he had stopped getting smaller.   The action of the drug
ceased in the others a few minutes later.   They were still
not quite in their relative sizes, but a few grains of the
powder quickly adjusted that.

They now found themselves near the edge of what once
was a great forest.   Huge trees, whose trunks measured
six feet or more in diameter, lay scattered about upon the
ground; not a single one was left standing.   In the distance they could see, some miles away, where the untrod-
den forest began.

They had replaced the food in their belts some time before, and now again they were ready to start.   Suddenly
the Very Young Man spied a huge, round, whitish-brown
object lying beside a tree-trunk near by.   He went over
and stood beside it.   Then he called his friends excitedly.
It was irregularly spherical in shape and stood higher than
his knees—a great jagged ball.   The Very Young Man
bent down, broke off a piece of the ball, and, stuffing it
into his mouth, began chewing with enthusiasm.

"Now, what do you think of that?" he remarked with
a grin.   "A cracker crumb I must have dropped when
we first began lunch!"

They decided now to make for the nearest part of the
unbroken forest.   It was two hours before they reached

it, for among the tangled mass of broken, fallen trees their progress was extremely difficult and slow.   Once inside, among the standing trees, they felt more lost than ever.   They had followed implicitly the Chemist's directions, and in general had encountered the sort of country they expected.   Nevertheless, they all three realized that it was probable the route they had followed coming in was quite different from that taken by the Chemist; and in what direction lay their destination, and how far, they had not even the vaguest idea, but they were determined to go on.

"If ever we find this city of Arite, it'll be a miracle sure," the Very Young Man remarked as they were walking along in silence.

They had gone only a short distance farther when the Big Business Man, who was walking in front, stopped abruptly.

"What's that?" he asked in a startled undertone.

They followed the direction of his hand, and saw, standing rigid against a tree-trunk ahead, the figure of a man little more than half as tall as themselves, his grayish body very nearly the color of the blue-gray tree behind him.

The three adventurers stood motionless, staring in amazement.

As the Big Business Man spoke, the little figure, which had evidently been watching them for some time, turned irresolutely as though about to run.   Then with gathering courage it began walking slowly towards them, holding out its arms with the palm up.

"He's friendly," whispered the Very Young Man; and they waited, silent, as the man approached.

As he came closer, they could see he was hardly more than a boy, perhaps twenty years of age.   His lean, gray body was nearly naked.   Around his waist he wore a drab-colored tunic, of a substance they could not identify. His feet and legs were bare. On his chest were strapped a thin stone plate, slightly convex. His thick, wavy, black hair, cut at the base of his neck, hung close about his ears. His head was uncovered. His features were regular and pleasing; his smile showed an even row of very white teeth.

The three men did not speak or move until, in a moment, more, he stood directly before them, still holding out his hands palm up. Then abruptly he spoke.

"The Master welcomes his friends," he said in a soft musical voice. He gave the words a most curious accent and inflexion, yet they were quite understandable to his listeners.

"The Master welcomes his friends," he repeated, dropping his arms to his sides and smiling in a most friendly manner.

The Very Young Man caught his breath. "He's been sent to meet us; he's from Rogers. What do you think of that? We're all right now!" he exclaimed excitedly.

The Doctor held out his hand, and the Oroid, hesitating a moment in doubt, finally reached up and grasped it.

"Are you from Rogers?" asked the Doctor.

The Oroid looked puzzled. Then he turned and flung out his arm in a sweeping gesture towards the deeper woods before them. "Rogers—Master," he said.

"You were waiting for us?" persisted the Doctor; but the other only shook his head and smiled his lack of comprehension.

"He only knows the first words he said," the Big Business Man suggested.

"He must be from Rogers," the Very Young Man put in. "See, he wants us to go with him."

The Oroid was motioning them forward, holding out his hand as though to lead them.

The Very Young Man started forward, but the Big Business Man held him back.

"Wait a moment," he said. "I don't think we ought to go among these people as large as we are. Rogers is evidently alive and waiting for us. Why wouldn't it be better to be about his size, instead of ten-foot giants as we would look now?"

"How do you know how big Rogers is?" asked the Very Young Man.

"I think that a good idea," agreed the Doctor. "Rogers described these Oroid men as being some six inches shorter than himself, on the average."

"This one might be a pygmy, for all we know," said the Very Young Man.

"We might chance it that he's of normal size," said the Doctor, smiling. "I think we should make ourselves smaller."

The Oroid stood patiently by and watched them with interested eyes as each took a tiny pellet from a vial under his arm and touched it to his tongue. When they began to decrease in size his eyes widened with fright and his legs shook under him. But he stood his ground, evidently assured by their smiles and friendly gestures.

In a few minutes the action of the drug was over, and they found themselves not more than a head taller than the Oroid. In this size he seemed to like them better, or at least he stood in far less awe of them, for now he seized them by the arms and pulled them forward vigorously.

They laughingly yielded, and, led by this strange being of another world, they turned from the open places they had been following and plunged into the depths of the forest.

CHAPTER XVIII

FOR an hour or more the three adventurers followed their strange guide in silence through the dense, trackless woods. He walked very rapidly, looking neither to the right nor to the left, finding his way apparently by an intuitive sense of direction. Occasionally he glanced back over his shoulder and smiled.

Walking through the woods here was not difficult, and the party made rapid progress. The huge, upstanding tree-trunks were devoid of limbs for a hundred feet or more above the ground. On some of them a luxuriant vine was growing—a vine that bore a profusion of little gray berries. In the branches high overhead a few birds flew to and fro, calling out at times with a soft, cooing note. The ground—a gray, finely powdered sandy loam —was carpeted with bluish fallen leaves, sometimes with a species of blue moss, and occasional ferns of a like color.

The forest was dense, deep, and silent; the tree branches overhead locked together in a solid canopy, shutting out the black sky above. Yet even in this seclusion the scene remained as light as it had been outside the woods in the open. Darkness indeed was impossible in this land; under all circumstances the light seemed the same—neither too bright nor too dim—a comfortable, steady glow, restful, almost hypnotic in its sameness.

They had traveled perhaps six miles from the point where they met their Oroid guide when suddenly the Very

Young Man became aware that other Oroids were with them. Looking to one side, he saw two more of these strange gray men, silently stalking along, keeping pace with them. Turning, he made out still another, following a short distance behind. The Very Young Man was startled, and hurriedly pointed them out to his companions.

"Wait," called the Doctor to their youthful guide, and abruptly the party came to a halt.

By these signs they made their guide understand that they wanted these other men to come closer. The Oroid shouted to them in his own quaint tongue, words of a soft, liquid quality with a wistful sound—words wholly unintelligible to the adventurers.

The men came forward diffidently, six of them, for three others appeared out of the shadows of the forest, and stood in a group, talking among themselves a little and smiling at their visitors. They were all dressed similarly to Lao—for such was the young Oroid's name—and all of them older than he, and of nearly the same height.

"Do any of you speak English?" asked the Doctor, addressing them directly.

Evidently they did not, for they answered only by shaking their heads and by more smiles.

Then one of them spoke. "The Master welcomes his friends," he said. And all the others repeated it after him, like children in school repeating proudly a lesson newly learned.

The Doctor and his two friends laughed heartily, and, completely reassured by this exhibition of their friendliness, they signified to Lao that they were ready again to go forward.

As they walked onward through the apparently endless and unchanging forest, surrounded by what the Very Young Man called their "guard of honor," they were joined from time to time by other Oroid men, all of whom seemed to know who they were and where they were going, and who fell silently into line with them. Within an hour their party numbered twenty or more.

Seeing one of the natives stop a moment and snatch some berries from one of the vines with which many of the trees were encumbered, the Very Young Man did the same. He found the berries sweet and palatable, and he ate a quantity. Then discovering he was hungry, he took some crackers from his belt and ate them walking along. The Doctor and the Big Business Man ate also, for although they had not realized it, all three were actually famished.

Shortly after this the party came to a broad, smooth-flowing river, its banks lined with rushes, with here and there a little spot of gray, sandy beach. It was apparent from Lao's signs that they must wait at this point for a boat to take them across. This they were glad enough to do, for all three had gone nearly to the limit of their strength. They drank deep of the pure river water, laved their aching limbs in it gratefully, and lay down, caring not a bit how long they were forced to wait.

In perhaps another hour the boat appeared. It came from down the river, propelled close inshore by two members of their own party who had gone to fetch it. At first the travelers thought it a long, oblong raft. Then as it came closer they could see it was constructed of three canoes, each about thirty feet long, hollowed out of tree-trunks. Over these was laid a platform of small trees hewn roughly into boards. The boat was propelled by long, slender poles in the hands of the two men, who, one on each side, dug them into the bed of the river and walked with them the length of the platform.

On to this boat the entire party crowded and they were soon well out on the shallow river, headed for its opposite bank. The Very Young Man, seated at the front end of the platform with his legs dangling over and his feet only a few inches above the silver phosphorescence of the rippling water underneath, sighed luxuriously.

"This beats anything we've done yet," he murmured. "Gee, it's nice here!"

When they landed on the farther bank another group of natives was waiting for them. The party, thus strengthened to nearly forty, started off immediately into the forest, which on this side of the river appeared equally dense and trackless.

They appeared now to be paralleling the course of the river a few hundred yards back from its bank. After half an hour of this traveling they came abruptly to what at first appeared to be the mouth of a large cave, but which afterwards proved to be a tunnel-like passageway. Into this opening the party unhesitatingly plunged.

Within this tunnel, which sloped downward at a considerable angle, they made even more rapid progress than in the forest above. The tunnel walls here were perhaps twenty feet apart—walls of a glistening, radiant, crystalline rock. The roof of the passageway was fully twice as high as its width; its rocky floor was smooth and even.

After a time this tunnel was crossed by another somewhat broader and higher, but in general of similar aspect. It, too, sloped downward, more abruptly from the intersection. Into this latter passageway the party turned, still taking the downward course.

As they progressed, many other passageways were crossed, the intersections of which were wide at the open spaces. Occasionally the travelers encountered other natives, all of them men, most of whom turned and followed them.

The Big Business Man, after over an hour of this rapid walking downward, was again near the limit of his endurance, when the party, after crossing a broad, open square, came upon a sort of sleigh, with two animals harnessed to it. It was standing at the intersection of a still broader, evidently more traveled passageway, and in it was an attendant, apparently fast asleep.

Into this sleigh climbed the three travelers with their guide Lao; and, driven by the attendant, they started down the broader tunnel at a rapid pace. The sleigh was balanced upon a broad single runner of polished stone, with a narrow, slightly shorter outrider on each side; it slid smoothly and easily on this runner over the equally smooth, metallic rock of the ground.

The reindeer-like animals were harnessed by their heads to a single shaft. They were guided by a short, pointed pole in the hands of the driver, who, as occasion demanded, dug it vigorously into their flanks.

In this manner the travelers rode perhaps half an hour more. The passageway sloped steeply downward, and they made good speed. Finally without warning, except by a sudden freshening of the air, they emerged into the open, and found themselves facing a broad, rolling stretch of country, dotted here and there with trees—the country of the Oroids at last.

For the first time since leaving their own world the adventurers found themselves amid surroundings that at least held some semblance of an aspect of familiarity. The scene they faced now might have been one of their own land viewed on an abnormally bright though moonless evening.

For some miles they could see a rolling, open country, curving slightly upward into the dimness of the distance. At their right, close by, lay a broad lake, its surface wrinkled under a gentle breeze and gleaming bright as a great sheet of polished silver.

Overhead hung a gray-blue, cloudless sky, studded with

a myriad of faint, twinkling, golden-silver stars. On the lake shore lay a collection of houses, close together, at the water's edge and spreading back thinly into the hills behind. This they knew to be Arite—the city of their destination.

At the end of the tunnel they left the sleigh, and, turning down the gentle sloping hillside, leisurely approached the city. They were part way across an open field separating them from the nearest houses, when they saw a group of figures coming across the field towards them. This group stopped when still a few hundred yards away, only two of the figures continuing to come forward. They came onward steadily, the tall figure of a man clothed in white, and by his side a slender, graceful boy.

In a moment more Lao, walking in front of the Doctor and his two companions, stopped suddenly and, turning to face them, said quietly, "The Master."

The three travelers, with their hearts pounding, paused an instant. Then with a shout the Very Young Man dashed forward, followed by his two companions.

"It's Rogers—it's Rogers!" he called; and in a moment more the three men were beside the Chemist, shaking his hand and pouring at him excitedly their words of greeting.

The Chemist welcomed them heartily, but with a quiet, curious air of dignity that they did not remember he possessed before. He seemed to have aged considerably since they had last seen him. The lines in his face had deepened; the hair on his temples was white. He seemed also to be rather taller than they remembered him, and certainly he was stouter.

He was dressed in a long, flowing robe of white cloth, gathered in at the waist by a girdle, from which hung a short sword, apparently of gold or of beaten brass. His legs were bare; on his feet he wore a form of sandal with leather thongs crossing his insteps. His hair grew long over his ears and was cut off at the shoulder line in the fashion of the natives.

When the first words of greeting were over, the Chemist turned to the boy, who was standing apart, watching them with big, interested eyes.

"My friends," he said quietly, yet with a little underlying note of pride in his voice, "this is my son."

The boy approached deferentially. He was apparently about ten or eleven years of age, tall as his father's shoulder nearly, extremely slight of build, yet with a body perfectly proportioned. He was dressed in a white robe similar to his father's, only shorter, ending at his knees. His skin was of a curious, smooth, milky whiteness, lacking the gray, harder look of that of the native men, and with just a touch of the iridescent quality possessed by the women. His features were cast in a delicate mold, pretty enough almost to be called girlish, yet with a firm squareness of chin distinctly masculine.

His eyes were blue; his thick, wavy hair, falling to his shoulders, was a chestnut brown. His demeanor was graceful and dignified, yet with a touch of ingenuousness that marked him for the care-free child he really was. He held out his hands palms up as he approached.

"My name is Loto," he said in a sweet, soft voice, with perfect self-possession. "I'm glad to meet my father's friends." He spoke English with just a trace of the liquid quality that characterized his mother's tongue.

"You are late getting here," remarked the Chemist with a smile, as the three travelers, completely surprised by this sudden introduction, gravely shook hands with the boy.

During this time the young Oroid who had guided them down from the forest above the tunnels, had been standing respectfully behind them, a few feet away. A short distance farther on several small groups of natives were gathered, watching the strangers. With a few swift words Loto now dismissed their guide, who bowed low with his hands to his forehead and left them.

Led by the Chemist, they continued on down into the city, talking earnestly, telling him the details of their trip. The natives followed them as they moved forward, and as they entered the city others looked at them curiously and, the Very Young Man thought, with a little hostility, yet always from a respectful distance. Evidently it was night, or at least the time of sleep at this hour, for the streets they passed through were nearly deserted.

CHAPTER XIX

THE city of Arite, as it looked to them now, was strange beyond anything they had ever seen, but still by no means as extraordinary as they had expected it would be. The streets through which they walked were broad and straight, and were crossed by others at regular intervals of two or three hundred feet. These streets paralleled each other with mathematical regularity. The city thus was laid out most orderly, but with one peculiarity; the streets did not run in two directions crossing each other at right angles, but in three, each inclined to an equal degree with the others. The blocks of houses between them, therefore, were cut into diamond-shaped sections and into triangles, never into squares or oblongs.

Most of the streets seemed paved with large, flat gray blocks of a substance resembling highly polished stone, or a form of opaque glass. There were no sidewalks, but close up before the more pretentious of the houses, were small trees growing.

The houses themselves were generally triangular or diamond-shaped, following the slope of the streets. They were, most of them, but two stories in height, with flat roofs on some of which flowers and trellised vines were growing. They were built principally of the same smooth, gray blocks with which the streets were paved. Their windows were large and numerous, without window-panes, but closed now, nearly all of them by shining, silvery curtains that looked as though they might have been woven from the metal itself. The doors were of heavy metal, suggesting brass or gold. On some of the houses tiny low-railed balconies hung from the upper windows out over the street.

The party proceeded quietly through this now deserted city, crossing a large tree-lined square, or park, that by the confluence of many streets seemed to mark its center, and turned finally into another diagonal street that dropped swiftly down towards the lake front. At the edge of a promontory this street abruptly terminated in a broad flight of steps leading down to a little beach on the lake shore perhaps a hundred feet below.

The Chemist turned sharp to the right at the head of these steps, and, passing through the opened gateway of an arch in a low gray wall, led his friends into a garden in which were growing a profusion of flowers. These flowers, they noticed, were most of them blue or gray, or of a pale silvery whiteness, lending to the scene a peculiarly wan, wistful appearance, yet one of extraordinary, quite unearthly beauty.

Through the garden a little gray-pebbled path wound back to where a house stood, nearly hidden in a grove of trees, upon a bluff directly overlooking the lake.

"My home, gentlemen," said the Chemist, with a wave of his hand.

As they approached the house they heard, coming from within, the mellow voice of a woman singing—an odd little minor theme, with a quaint, lilting rhythm, and words they could not distinguish. Accompanying the voice were the delicate tones of some stringed instrument suggesting a harp.

"We are expected," remarked the Chemist with a smile. "Lylda is still up, waiting for us." The Very Young Man's heart gave a leap at the mention of the name.

From the outside, the Chemist's house resembled many

of the larger ones they had seen as they came through the city.   It was considerably more pretentious than any they had yet noticed, diamond-shaped—that is to say, a flattened oblong—two stories in height and built of large blocks of the gray polished stone.

Unlike the other houses, its sides were not bare, but were partly covered by a luxuriant growth of vines and trellised flowers.   There were no balconies under its windows, except on the lake side.   There, at the height of the second story, a covered balcony broad enough almost to be called a veranda, stretched the full width of the house.

A broad door of brass, fronting the garden, stood partly open, and the Chemist pushed it wide and ushered in his friends.   They found themselves now in a triangular hallway, or lobby, with an open arch in both its other sides giving passage into rooms beyond.   Through one of these archways the Chemist led them, into what evidently was the main living-room of the dwelling.

It was a high-ceilinged room nearly triangular in shape, thirty feet possibly at its greatest width.   In one wall were set several silvery-curtained windows, opening out on to the lake.   On the other side was a broad fireplace and hearth with another archway beside it leading farther into the house.   The walls of the room were lined with small gray tiles; the floor also was tiled with gray and white, set in design.

On the floor were spread several large rugs, apparently made of grass or fibre.   The walls were bare, except between the windows, where two long, narrow, heavily embroidered strips of golden cloth were hanging.

In the center of the room stood a circular stone table, its top a highly polished black slab of stone.   This table was set now for a meal, with golden metal dishes, huge metal goblets of a like color, and beautifully wrought table utensils, also of gold. Around the table were several small chairs, made of wicker. In the seat of each lay a padded fiber cushion, and over the back was hung a small piece of embroidered cloth.

With the exception of these chairs and table, the room was practically devoid of furniture. Against one wall was a smaller table of stone, with a few miscellaneous objects on its top, and under each window stood a small white stone bench.

A fire glowed in the fireplace grate—a fire that burned without flame. On the hearth before it, reclining on large silvery cushions, was a woman holding in her hands a small stringed instrument like a tiny harp or lyre. When the men entered the room she laid her instrument aside and rose to her feet.

As she stood there for an instant, expectant, with the light of welcome in her eyes, the three strangers beheld what to them seemed the most perfect vision of feminine loveliness they had ever seen.

The woman's age was at first glance indeterminate. By her face, her long, slender, yet well-rounded neck, and the slim curves of her girlish figure, she might have been hardly more than twenty. Yet in her bearing there was that indefinable poise and dignity that bespoke the more mature, older woman.

She was about five feet tall, with a slender, almost fragile, yet perfectly rounded body. Her dress consisted of a single flowing garment of light-blue silk, reaching from the shoulders to just above her knees. It was girdled at the waist by a thick golden cord that hung with golden tasseled pendants at her side.

A narrower golden cord crossed her breast and shoulders. Her arms, legs, and shoulders were bare. Her skin was smooth as satin, milky white, and suffused with the delicate tints of many colors. Her hair was thick and very black; it was twisted into two tresses that fell forward over each shoulder nearly to her waist and ended with a little silver ribbon and tassel tied near the bottom.

Her face was a delicate oval. Her lips were full and of a color for which in English there is no name. It would have been red doubtless by sunlight in the world above, but here in this silver light of phosphorescence, the color red, as we see it, was impossible.

Her nose was small, of Grecian type. Her slate-gray eyes were rather large, very slightly upturned at the corners, giving just a touch of the look of our women of the Orient. Her lashes were long and very black. In conversation she lowered them at times with a charming combination of feminine humility and a touch of coquetry. Her gaze from under them had often a peculiar look of melting softness, yet always it was direct and honest.

Such was the woman who quietly stood beside her hearth, waiting to welcome these strange guests from another world.

As the men entered through the archway, the boy Loto pushed quickly past them in his eagerness to get ahead, and, rushing across the room, threw himself into the woman's arms crying happily, *"Mita, mita."*

The woman kissed him affectionately. Then, before she had time to speak, the boy pulled her forward, holding her tightly by one hand.

"This is my mother," he said with a pretty little gesture. "Her name is Lylda."

The woman loosened herself from his grasp with a smile of amusement, and, native fashion, bowed low with her hands to her forehead.

"My husband's friends are welcome," she said simply. Her voice was soft and musical. She spoke English perfectly, with an intonation of which the most cultured woman might be proud, but with a foreign accent much more noticeable than that of her son.

"A very long time we have been waiting for you," she added; and then, as an afterthought, she impulsively offered them her hand in their own manner.

The Chemist kissed his wife quietly. In spite of the presence of strangers, for a moment she dropped her reserve, her arms went up around his neck, and she clung to him an instant. Gently putting her down, the Chemist turned to his friends.

"I think Lylda has supper waiting," he said. Then as he looked at their torn, woolen suits that once were white, and the ragged shoes upon their feet, he added with a smile, "But I think I can make you much more comfortable first."

He led them up a broad, curving flight of stone steps to a room above, where they found a shallow pool of water, sunk below the level of the floor. Here he left them to bathe, getting them meanwhile robes similar to his own, with which to replace their own soiled garments. In a little while, much refreshed, they descended to the room below, where Lylda had supper ready upon the table waiting for them.

"Only a little while ago my father and Aura left," said Lylda, as they sat down to eat.

"Lylda's younger sister," the Chemist explained. "She lives with her father here in Arite."

The Very Young Man parted his lips to speak. Then, with heightened color in his cheeks, he closed them again.

They were deftly served at supper by a little native girl who was dressed in a short tunic reaching from waist to knees, with circular discs of gold covering her breasts. There was cooked meat for the meal, a white starchy form of vegetable somewhat resembling a potato, a number of delicious fruits of unfamiliar variety, and for drink the juice of a fruit that tasted more like cider than anything they could name.

At the table Loto perched himself beside the Very Young Man, for whom he seemed to have taken a sudden fancy.

"I like you," he said suddenly, during a lull in the talk.

"I like you, too," answered the Very Young Man.

"Aura is very beautiful; you'll like her."

"I'm sure I will," the Very Young Man agreed soberly.

"What's your name?" persisted the boy.

"My name's Jack.   And I'm glad you like me.   I think we're friends, don't you?"

And so they became firm friends, and, as far as circumstances would permit, inseparable companions.

Lylda presided over the supper with the charming grace of a competent hostess.   She spoke seldom, yet when the conversation turned to the great world above in which her husband was born, she questioned intelligently and with eager interest.   Evidently she had a considerable knowledge of the subject, but with an almost childish insatiable curiosity she sought from her guests more intimate details of the world they lived in.

When in lighter vein their talk ran into comments upon the social life of their own world, Lylda's ready wit, combined with her ingenuous simplicity, put to them many questions which made the giving of an understandable answer sometimes amusingly difficult.

When the meal was over the three travelers found themselves very sleepy, and all of them were glad when the Chemist suggested that they retire almost immediately. He led them again to the upper story into the bedroom they were to occupy.   There, on the low bedsteads, soft

with many quilted coverings, they passed the remainder
of the time of sleep in dreamless slumber, utterly worn
out by their journey, nor guessing what the morning
would bring forth.

CHAPTER XX

THE WORLD OF THE RING

NEXT morning after breakfast the four men sat upon the balcony overlooking the lake, and prepared to hear the Chemist's narrative of what had happened since he left them five years before. They had already told him of events in their world, the making of the chemicals and their journey down into the ring, and now they were ready to hear his story.

At their ease here upon the balcony, reclining in long wicker chairs of the Chemist's own design, as he proudly admitted, they felt at peace with themselves and the world. Below them lay the shining lake, above spread a clear, star-studded sky. Against their faces blew the cool breath of a gentle summer's breeze.

As they sat silent for a moment, enjoying almost with awe the beauties of the scene, and listening to the soft voice of Lylda singing to herself in the garden, the Very Young Man suddenly thought of the one thing lacking to make his enjoyment perfect.

"I wish I had a cigarette," he remarked wistfully.

The Chemist with a smile produced cigars of a leaf that proved a very good substitute for tobacco. They lighted them with a tiny metal lighter of the flint-and-steel variety, filled with a fluffy inflammable wick—a contrivance of the Chemist's own making—and then he started his narrative.

"There is much to tell you, my friends," he began

thoughtfully. "Much that will interest you, shall we say from a socialistic standpoint? I shall make it brief, for we have no time to sit idly talking.

"I must tell you now, gentlemen, of what I think you have so far not even had a hint. . You have found me living here," he hesitated and smiled, "well at least under pleasant and happy circumstances. Yet as a matter of fact, your coming was of vital importance, not only to me and my family, but probably to the future welfare of the entire Oroid nation.

"We are approaching a crisis here with which I must confess I have felt myself unable to cope. With your help, more especially with the power of the chemicals you have brought with you, it may be possible for us to deal successfully with the conditions facing us."

"What are they?" asked the Very Young Man eagerly.

"Perhaps it would be better for me to tell you chronologically the events as they have occurred. As you remember when I left you twelve years ago——"

"Five years," interrupted the Very Young Man.

"Five or twelve, as you please," said the Chemist smiling. "It was my intention then, as you know, to come back to you after a comparatively short stay here."

"And bring Mrs.—er—Lylda, with you," put in the Very Young Man, hesitating in confusion over the Christian name.

"And bring Lylda with me," finished the Chemist. "I got back here without much difficulty, and in a very much shorter time and with less effort than on my first trip. I tried an entirely different method; I stayed as large as possible while descending, and diminished my size materially only after I had reached the bottom."

"I told you——" said the Big Business Man.

"It was a dangerous method of procedure, but I made it successfully without mishap.

"Lylda and I were married in native fashion shortly after I reached Arite."

"How was that; what fashion?" the Very Young Man wanted to know, but the Chemist went on.

"It was my intention to stay here only a few weeks and then return with Lylda. She was willing to follow me anywhere I might take her, because—well, perhaps you would hardly understand, but—women here are different in many ways than you know them.

"I stayed several months, still planning to leave almost at any time. I found this world an intensely interesting study. Then, when—Loto was expected, I again postponed my departure.

"I had been here over a year before I finally gave up my intention of ever returning to you. I have no close relatives above, you know, no one who cares much for me or for whom I care, and my life seemed thoroughly established here.

"I am afraid gentlemen, I am offering excuses for myself—for my desertion of my own country in its time of need. I have no defense. As events turned out I could not have helped probably, very much, but still—that is no excuse. I can only say that your world up there seemed so very—very—far away. Events up there had become to me only vague memories as of a dream. And Lylda and my little son were so near, so real and vital to me. Well, at any rate I stayed, deciding definitely to make my home and to end my days here."

"What did you do about the drugs?" asked the Doctor.

"I kept them hidden carefully for nearly a year," the Chemist replied. "Then fearing lest they should in some way get loose, I destroyed them. They possess a diabolical power, gentlemen; I am afraid of it."

"They called you the Master," suggested the Very Young Man, after a pause. "Why was that?"

The Chemist smiled. "They do call me the Master. That has been for several years. I suppose I am the most important individual in the nation to-day."

"I should think you would be," said the Very Young Man quickly. "What you did, and with the knowledge you have."

The Chemist went on. "Lylda and I lived with her father and Aura—her mother is dead you know—until after Loto was born. Then we had a house further up in the city. Later, about eight years ago, I built this house we now occupy and Lylda laid out its garden which she is tremendously proud of, and which I think is the finest in Arite.

"Because of what I had done in the Malite war, I became naturally the King's adviser. Every one felt me the savior of the nation, which, in a way, I suppose I was. I never used the drugs again and, as only a very few of the people ever understood them, or in fact ever knew of them or believed in their existence, my extraordinary change in stature was ascribed to some supernatural power. I have always since been credited with being able to exert that power at will, although I never used it but that once."

"You have it again now," said the Doctor smiling.

"Yes, I have, thank God," answered the Chemist fervently, "though I hope I never shall have to use it."

"Aren't you planning to go back with us," asked the Very Young Man, "even for a visit?"

The Chemist shook his head. "My way lies here," he said quietly, yet with deep feeling.

A silence followed; finally the Chemist roused himself from his reverie, and went on. "Although I never again changed my stature, there were a thousand different ways in which I continued to make myself—well, famous throughout the land. I have taught these people many things, gentlemen—like this for instance." He indicated his cigar, and the chair in which he was sitting. "You cannot imagine what a variety of things one knows beyond the knowledge of so primitive a race as this.

"And so gradually, I became known as the Master. I have no official position, but everywhere I am known by that name. As a matter of fact, for the past year at least, it has been rather too descriptive a title——" the Chemist smiled somewhat ruefully—"for I have had in reality, and have now, the destiny of the country on my shoulders."

"You're not threatened with another war?" asked the Very Young Man.

"No, not exactly that. But I had better go on with my story first. This is a very different world now, gentlemen, from that I first entered twelve years ago. I think first I should tell you about it as it was then."

His three friends nodded their agreement and the Chemist continued.

"I must make it clear to you gentlemen, the one great fundamental difference between this world and yours. In the evolution of this race there has been no cause for strife—the survival of the fittest always has been an unknown doctrine—a non-existent problem.

"In extent this Inner Surface upon which we are now living is nearly as great as the surface of your own earth. From the earliest known times it has been endowed with a perfect climate—a climate such as you are now enjoying."

The Very Young Man expanded his chest and looked his appreciation.

"The climate, the rainfall, everything is ideal for crops and for living conditions. In the matter of food, one needs in fact do practically nothing. Fruits of a variety ample to sustain life, grow wild in abundance. Vegetables planted are harvested seemingly without blight or hazard of any kind. No destructive insects have ever impeded agriculture; no wild animals have ever existed to harass humanity. Nature in fact, offers every help and no obstacle towards making a simple, primitive life easy to live.

"Under such conditions the race developed only so far as was necessary to ensure a healthful pleasant existence. Civilization here is what you would call primitive: wants are few and easily supplied—too easily, probably, for without strife these people have become—well shall I say effeminate? They are not exactly that—it is not a good word."

"I should think that such an unchanging, unrigorous climate would make a race deteriorate in physique rapidly," observed the Doctor.

"How about disease down here?" asked the Big Business Man.

"It is a curious thing," replied the Chemist. "Cleanliness seems to be a trait inborn with every individual in this race. It is more than godliness; it is the one great cardinal virtue. You must have noticed it, just in coming through Arite. Personal cleanliness of the people, and cleanliness of houses, streets—of everything. It is truly extraordinary to what extent they go to make everything inordinately, immaculately clean. Possibly for that reason, and because there seems never to have been any serious disease germs existing here, sickness as you know it, does not exist."

"Guess you better not go into business here," said the Very Young Man with a grin at the Doctor.

"There is practically no illness worthy of the name," went on the Chemist. "The people live out their lives and, barring accident, die peacefully of old age."

"How old do they live to be?" asked the Big Business Man.

"About the same as with you," answered the Chemist. "Only of course as we measure time."

"Say how about that?" the Very Young Man asked. "My watch is still going—is it ticking out the old time or the new time down here?"

"I should say probably—certainly—it was giving time of your own world, just as it always did," the Chemist replied.

"Well, there's no way of telling, is there?" said the Big Business Man.

"What is the exact difference in time?" the Doctor asked.

"That is something I have had no means of determining. It was rather a curious thing; when I left that letter for you," the Chemist turned to the Doctor—"it never occurred to me that although I had told you to start down here on a certain day, I would be quite at a loss to calculate when that day had arrived. It was my estimation after my first trip here that time in this world passed at a rate about two and two-fifth times faster than it does in your world. That is as near as I ever came to it. We can calculate it more closely now, since we have only the interval of your journey down as an indeterminate quantity."

"How near right did you hit it? When did you expect us?" asked the Doctor.

"About thirty days ago; I have been waiting since then. I sent nearly a hundred men through the tunnels into the forest to guide you in."

"You taught them pretty good English," said the Very Young Man. "They were tickled to death that they knew it, too," he added with a reminiscent grin.

"You say about thirty days; how do you measure time down here?" asked the Big Business Man.

"I call a day, one complete cycle of sleeping and eating," the Chemist replied. "I suppose that is the best translation of the Oroid word; we have a word that means about the same thing."

"How long is a day?" inquired the Very Young Man.

"It seems in the living about the same as your twenty-four hours; it occupies probably about the interval of time of ten hours in your world.

"You see," the Chemist went on, "we ordinarily eat twice between each time of sleep—once after rising—and once a few hours before bedtime. Workers at severe muscular labor sometimes eat a light meal in between, but the custom is not general. Time is generally spoken of as so many meals, rather than days."

"But what is the arbitrary standard?" asked the Doctor. "Do you have an equivalent for weeks, or months or years?"

"Yes," answered the Chemist, "based on astronomy the same as in your world. But I would rather not explain that now. I want to take you, later to-day, to see Lylda's father. You will like him. He is—well, what we might call a scientist. He talks English fairly well. We can discuss astronomy with him; you will find him very interesting."

"How can you tell time?" the Very Young Man wanted to know. "There is no sun to go by. You have no clocks, have you?"

"There is one downstairs," answered the Chemist, "but you didn't notice it. Lylda's father has a very fine one; he will show it to you."

"It seems to me," began the Doctor thoughtfully after a pause, reverting to their previous topic, "that without sickness, under such ideal living conditions as you say exist here, in a very short time this world would be overpopulated."

"Nature seems to have taken care of that," the Chemist answered, "and as a matter of fact quite the reverse is true. Women mature in life at an age you would call about sixteen. But early marriages are not the rule; seldom is a woman married before she is twenty—frequently she is much older. Her period of child-bearing, too, is comparatively short—frequently less than ten years. The result is few children, whose rate of mortality is exceedingly slow."

"How about the marriages?" the Very Young Man suggested. "You were going to tell us."

"Marriages are by mutual consent," answered the Chemist, "solemnized by a simple, social ceremony. They are for a stated period of time, and are renewed later if both parties desire. When a marriage is dissolved children are cared for by the mother generally, and her maintenance if necessary is provided for by the government. The state becomes the guardian also of all illegitimate children and children of unknown parentage. But of both these latter classes there are very few. They work for the government, as do many other people, until they are of age, when they become free to act as they please."

"You spoke about women being different than we knew them; how are they different?" the Very Young Man asked. "If they're all like Lylda I think they're great," he added enthusiastically, flushing a little at his own temerity.

The Chemist smiled his acknowledgment of the compliment. "The status of women—and their character—is I think one of the most remarkable things about this race. You will remember, when I returned from here the first time, that I was much impressed by the kindliness of these people. Because of their history and their government they seem to have become imbued with the milk of human kindness to a degree approaching the Utopian.

"Crime here is practically non-existent; there is nothing over which contention can arise. What crimes are committed are punished with a severity seemingly out of all proportion to what you would call justice. A persistent offender even of fairly trivial wrongdoing is put to death without compunction. There is no imprisonment, except for those awaiting trial. Punishment is a reprimand with the threat of death if the offense is committed again, or death itself immediately. Probably this very severity and the swiftness with which punishment is meted out, to a large extent discourages wrongdoing. But, fundamentally, the capacity for doing wrong is lacking in these people.

"I have said practically nothing exists over which contention can arise. That is not strictly true. No race of people can develop without some individual contention over the possession of their women. The passions of love, hate and jealousy, centering around sex and its problems, are as necessarily present in human beings as life itself.

"Love here is deep, strong and generally lasting; it lacks fire, intensity—perhaps. I should say it is rather of a placid quality. Hatred seldom exists; jealousy is rare, because both sexes, in their actions towards the other, are guided by a spirit of honesty and fairness that is really extraordinary. This is true particularly of the women; they are absolutely honest—square, through and through.

"Crimes against women are few, yet in general they are the most prevalent type we have. They are punishable by death—even those that you would characterize as comparatively slight offenses. It is significant too, that, in judging these crimes, but little evidence is required. A slight chain of proven circumstances and the word of the woman is all that is required.

"This you will say, places a tremendous power in the

hands of women.   It does; yet they realize it thoroughly, and justify it.   Although they know that almost at their word a man will be put to death, practically never, I am convinced, is this power abused.   With extreme infrequency, a female is proven guilty of lying.   The penalty is death, for there is no place here for such a woman!

"The result is that women are accorded a freedom of movement far beyond anything possible in your world. They are safe from harm.   Their morals are, according to the standard here, practically one hundred per cent perfect.   With short-term marriages, dissolvable at will, there is no reason why they should be otherwise.   Curiously enough too, marriages are renewed frequently— more than that, I should say, generally—for 'life-long periods.   Polygamy with the consent of all parties is permitted, but seldom practiced.   Polyandry is unlawful, and but few cases of it ever appear.

"You may think all this a curious system, gentlemen, but it works."

"That's the answer," muttered the Very Young Man. It was obvious he was still thinking of Lylda and her sister and with a heightened admiration and respect.

CHAPTER XXI

A LIFE WORTH LIVING

THE appearance of Lylda at one of the long windows of the balcony, interrupted the men for a moment. She was dressed in a tunic of silver, of curious texture, like flexible woven metal, reaching to her knees. On her feet were little fiber sandals. Her hair was twisted in coils, piled upon her head, with a knot low at the back of the neck. From her head in graceful folds hung a thin scarf of gold.

She stood waiting in the window a moment for them to notice her; then she said quietly, "I am going for a time to the court." She hesitated an instant over the words. The Chemist inclined his head in agreement, and with a smile at her guests, and a little bow, she withdrew.

The visitors looked inquiringly at their host.

"I must tell you about our government," said the Chemist. "Lylda plays quite an important part in it." He smiled at their obvious surprise.

"The head of the government is the king. In reality he is more like the president of a republic; he is chosen by the people to serve for a period of about twenty years. The present king is now in—well let us say about the fifteenth year of his service. This translation of time periods into English is confusing," he interjected somewhat apologetically. "We shall see the king to-morrow; you will find him a most intelligent, likeable man.

"As a sort of congress, the king has one hundred and fifty advisers, half of them women, who meet about once a month. Lylda is one of these women. He also has an inner circle of closer, more intimate counselors consisting of four men and four women. One of these women is the queen; another is Lylda. I am one of the men.

"The capital of the nation is Arite. Each of the other cities governs itself in so far as its own local problems are concerned according to a somewhat similar system, but all are under the central control of the Arite government."

"How about the country in between, the—the rural population?" asked the Big Business Man.

"It is all apportioned off to the nearest city," answered the Chemist. "Each city controls a certain amount of the land around it.

"This congress of one hundred and fifty is the law-making body. The judiciary is composed of one court in each city. There is a leader of the court, or judge, and a jury of forty—twenty men and twenty women. The juries are chosen for continuous service for a period of five years. Lylda is at present serving in the Arite court. They meet very infrequently and irregularly, called as occasion demands. A two-thirds vote is necessary for a decision; there is no appeal."

"Are there any lawyers?" asked the Big Business Man.

"There is no one who makes that his profession, no. Generally the accused talks for himself or has some relative, or possibly some friend to plead his case."

"You have police?" the Doctor asked.

"A very efficient police force, both for the cities and in the country. Really they are more like detectives than police; they are the men I sent up into the forest to meet you. We also have an army, which at present consists almost entirely of this same police force. After the Malite war it was of course very much larger, but of late years it has been disbanded almost completely.

"How about money?" the Very Young Man· wanted to know.

"There is none!" answered the Chemist with a smile.

"Great Scott, how can you manage that?" ejaculated the Big Business Man.

"Our industrial system undoubtedly is peculiar," the Chemist replied, "but I can only say again, it works. We have no money, and, so far, none apparently is needed. Everything is bought and sold as an exchange. For instance, suppose I wish to make a living as a farmer. I have my land——"

"How did you get it?" interrupted the Very Young Man quickly.

"All the land is divided up *pro rata* and given by each city to its citizens. At the death of its owner it reverts to the government, and each citizen coming of age receives his share from the surplus always remaining."

"What about women? Can they own land too?" asked the Very Young Man.

"They have identical rights with men in everything," the Chemist answered.

"But women surely cannot cultivate their own land?" the Doctor said. Evidently he was thinking of Lylda's fragile little body, and certainly if most of the Oroid women were like her, labour in the fields would be for them quite impossible.

"A few women, by choice, do some of the lighter forms of manual labor—but they are very few. Nearly every woman marries within a few years after she receives her land; if it is to be cultivated, her husband then takes charge of it."

"Is the cultivation of land compulsory?" asked the Big Business Man.

"Only when in a city's district a shortage of food is threatened. Then the government decides the amount and kind of food needed, and the citizens, drawn by lot, are ordered to produce it. The government watches very carefully its food supply. In the case of overproduction, certain citizens, those less skillful, are ordered to work at something else.

"This supervision over supply and demand is exercised by the government not only in the question of food but in manufactures, in fact, in all industrial activities. A very nice balance is obtained, so that practically no unnecessary work is done throughout the nation.

"And gentlemen, do you know, as a matter of fact, I think that is the secret of a race of people being able to live without having to work most of its waking hours? If your civilization could eliminate all its unnecessary work, there would be far less work to do.

"I wonder—isn't this balance of supply and demand very difficult to maintain?" asked the Big Business Man thoughtfully.

"Not nearly so difficult as you would think," the Chemist answered. "In the case of land cultivation, the government has a large reserve, the cultivation of which it adjusts to maintain this balance. Thus, in some districts, the citizens do as they please and are never interfered with.

"The same is true of manufactures. There is no organized business in the nation—not even so much as the smallest factory—except that conducted by the government. Each city has its own factories, whose production is carefully planned exactly to equal the demand."

"Suppose a woman marries and her land is far away from her husband's? That would be sort of awkward, wouldn't it?" suggested the Very Young Man.

"Each year at a stated time," the Chemist answered, "transfers of land are made. There are generally enough people who want to move to make satisfactory changes of location practical. And then of course, the government always stands ready to take up any two widely separate pieces of land, and give others in exchange out of its reserve."

"Suppose you don't like the new land as well?" objected the Very Young Man.

"Almost all land is of equal value," answered the Chemist. "And of course, its state of cultivation is always considered."

"You were speaking about not having money," prompted the Very Young Man.

"The idea is simply this: Suppose I wish to cultivate nothing except, let us say, certain vegetables. I register with the government my intention and the extent to which I propose to go. I receive the government's consent. I then take my crops as I harvest them and exchange them for every other article I need."

"With whom do you exchange them?" asked the Doctor.

"Any one I please—or with the government. Ninety per cent of everything produced is turned in to the government and other articles are taken from its stores."

"How is the rate of exchange established?" asked the Big Business Man.

"It is computed by the government. Private exchanges are supposed to be made at the same rate. It is against the law to cut under the government rate. But it is done, although apparently not with sufficient frequency to cause any trouble."

"I should think it would be tremendously complicated and annoying to make all these exchanges," observed the Big Business Man.

"Not at all," answered the Chemist, "because of the governmental system of credits. The financial standing of every individual is carefully kept on record."

"Without any money?   I don't get you," said the Very Young Man with a frown of bewilderment.

The Chemist smiled.   "Well, I don't blame you for that.   But I think I can make myself clear.   Let us take the case of Loto, for instance, as an individual.   When he comes of age he will be allotted his section of land.   We will assume him to be without family at that time, entirely dependent on his own resources."

"Would he never have worked before coming of age?" the Very Young Man asked.

"Children with parents generally devote their entire minority to getting an education, and to building their bodies properly.   Without parents, they are supported by the government and live in public homes.   Such children, during their adolescence, work for the government a small portion of their time.

"Now when Loto comes of age and gets his land, located approximately where he desires it, he will make his choice as to his vocation.   Suppose he wishes not to cultivate his land but to work for the government.   He is given some congenial, suitable employment at which he works approximately five hours a day.   No matter what he elects to do at the time he comes of age the government opens an account with him.   He is credited with a certain standard unit for his work, which he takes from the government in supplies at his own convenience."

"What is the unit?" asked the Big Business Man.

"It is the average work produced by the average worker in one day—purely an arbitrary figure."

"Like our word horse-power?" put in the Doctor.

"Exactly.   And all merchandise, food and labor is valued in terms of it.

"Thus you see, every individual has his financial standing—all in relation to the government.   He can let his balance pile up if he is able, or he can keep it low."

"Suppose he goes into debt?" suggested the Very Young Man.

"In the case of obvious, verified necessity, the government will allow him a limited credit. Persistent—shall I say willful—debt is a crime."

"I thought at first," said the Big Business Man, "that everybody in this nation was on the same financial footing—that there was no premium put upon skill or industriousness. Now I see that one can accumulate, if not money, at least an inordinate amount of the world's goods."

"Not such an inordinate amount," said the Chemist smiling. "Because there is no inheritance. A man and woman, combining their worldly wealth, may by industry acquire more than others, but they are welcome to enjoy it. And they cannot, in one lifetime, get such a preponderance of wealth as to cause much envy from those lacking it."

"What happens to this house when you and Lylda die, if Loto cannot have it?" the Big Business Man asked.

"It is kept in repair by the government and held until some one with a sufficiently large balance wants to buy it."

"Are all workers paid at the same rate?" asked the Doctor.

"No, but their wages are much nearer equal than in your world."

"You have to hire people to work for you, how do you pay them?" the Doctor inquired.

"The rate is determined by governmental standard. I pay them by having the amount deducted from my balance and added to theirs."

"When you built this house, how did you go about doing it?" asked the Big Business Man.

"I simply went to the government, and they built it

for me according to my own ideas and wishes, deducting its cost from my balance."

"What about the public work to be done?" asked the Big Business Man. "Caring for the city streets, the making of roads and all that. Do you have taxes?"

"No," answered the Chemist smiling, "we do not have taxes. Quite the reverse, we sometimes have dividends.

"The government, you must understand, not only conducts a business account with each of its citizens, but one with itself also. The value of articles produced is computed with a profit allowance, so that by a successful business administration, the government is enabled not only to meet its public obligations, but to acquire a surplus to its own credit in the form of accumulated merchandise. This surplus is divided among the people every five years—a sort of dividend."

"I should think some cities might have much more than others," said the Big Business Man. "That would cause discontent, wouldn't it?"

"It would probably cause a rush of people to the more successful cities. But it doesn't happen, because each city reports to the National government and the whole thing is averaged up. You see it is all quite simple," the Chemist finished. "And it makes life here very easy to live, and very worth the living."

Unnoticed by the four interested men, a small compact-looking gray cloud had come sweeping down from the horizon above the lake and was scudding across the sky toward Arite. A sudden sharp crack of thunder interrupted their conversation.

"Hello, a storm!" exclaimed the Chemist, looking out over the lake. "You've never seen one, have you? Come upstairs."

They followed him into the house and upstairs to its flat roof. From this point of vantage they saw that the

house was built with an interior courtyard or *patio*.
Looking down into this courtyard from the roof they
could see a little, splashing fountain in its center, with
flower beds, a narrow gray path, and several small white
benches.

The roof, which was guarded with a breast-high parapet around both its inner and outer edges, was beautifully
laid out with a variety of flowers and with trellised
flower-bearing vines. In one corner were growing a
number of small trees with great fan-shaped leaves of
blue and bearing a large bell-shaped silver blossom.

One end of the roof on the lake side was partially enclosed. Towards this roofed enclosure the Chemist led
his friends. Within it a large fiber hammock hung between two stone posts. At one side a depression in the
floor perhaps eight feet square was filled with what might
have been blue pine needles, and a fluffy bluish moss.
This rustic couch was covered at one end by a canopy of
vines bearing a little white flower.

As they entered the enclosure, it began to rain, and the
Chemist slid forward several panels, closing them in completely. There were shuttered windows in these walls,
through which they could look at the scene outside—a
scene that with the coming storm was weird and beautiful beyond anything they had ever beheld.

The cloud had spread sufficiently now to blot out the
stars from nearly half of the sky. It was a thick cloud,
absolutely opaque, and yet it caused no appreciable darkness, for the starlight it cut off was negligible and the silver radiation from the lake had more than doubled in
intensity.

Under the strong wind that had sprung up the lake assumed now an extraordinary aspect. Its surface was
raised into long, sweeping waves that curved sharply and
broke upon themselves. In their tops the silver phospho-

rescence glowed and whirled until the whole surface of the lake seemed filled with a dancing white fire, twisting, turning and seeming to leap out of the water high into the air.

Several small sailboats, square, flat little catamarans, they looked, showed black against the water as they scudded for shore, trailing lines of silver out behind them.

The wind increased in force. Below, on the beach, a huge rock lay in the water, against which the surf was breaking. Columns of water at times shot into the air before the face of the rock, and were blown away by the wind in great clouds of glistening silver. Occasionally it thundered with a very sharp intense crack accompanied by a jagged bolt of bluish lightning that zigzagged down from the low-hanging cloud.

Then came the rain in earnest, a solid, heavy torrent, that bent down the wind and smoothed the surface of the lake. The rain fell almost vertically, as though it were a tremendous curtain of silver strings. And each of these strings broke apart into great shining pearls as the eye followed downward the course of the raindrops.

For perhaps ten minutes the silver torrent poured down. Then suddenly it ceased. The wind had died away; in the air there was the fresh warm smell of wet and steaming earth. From the lake rolled up a shimmering translucent cloud of mist, like an enormous silver fire mounting into the sky. And then, as the gray cloud swept back behind them, beyond the city, and the stars gleamed overhead, they saw again that great trail of star-dust which the Chemist first had seen through his microscope, hanging in an ever broadening arc across the sky, and ending vaguely at their feet.

CHAPTER XXII

THE TRIAL

IN a few moments more the storm had passed completely; only the wet city streets, the mist over the lake, and the moist warmth of the air remained. For some time the three visitors to this extraordinary world stood silent at the latticed windows, awed by what they had seen. The noise of the panels as the Chemist slid them back brought them to themselves.

"A curious land, gentlemen," he remarked quietly.

"It's—it's weird," the Very Young Man ejaculated.

The Chemist led them out across the roof to its other side facing the city. The street upon which the house stood sloped upwards over the hill behind. It was wet with the rain and gleamed like a sheet of burnished silver. And down its sides now ran two little streams of liquid silver fire.

The street, deserted during the storm, was beginning to fill again with people returning to their tasks. At the intersection with the next road above, they could see a line of sleighs passing. Beneath them, before the wall of the garden a little group of men stood talking; on a rooftop near-by a woman appeared with a tiny naked infant which she sat down to nurse in a corner of her garden.

"A city at work," said the Chemist with a wave of his hand. "Shall we go down and see it?"

His three friends assented readily, the Very Young Man suggesting promptly that they first visit Lylda's father and Aura.

"He is teaching Loto this morning," said the Chemist smiling.

"Why not go to the court?" suggested the Big Business Man.

"Is the public admitted?" asked the Doctor.

"Nothing is secret here," the Chemist answered. "By all means, we will go to the court first, if you wish; Lylda should be through very shortly."

The court of Arite stood about a mile away near the lake shore. As they left the house and passed through the city streets the respect accorded the Chemist became increasingly apparent. The three strangers with him attracted considerable attention, for, although they wore the conventional robes in which the more prominent citizens were generally attired, their short hair and the pallid whiteness of their skins made them objects of curiosity. No crowd gathered; those they passed stared a little, raised their hands to their foreheads and went their way, yet underneath these signs of respect there was with some an air of sullenness, of hostility, that the visitors could not fail to notice.

The Oroid men, in street garb, were dressed generally in a short metallic-looking tunic of drab, with a brighter-colored girdle. The women, most of them, wore only a sort of skirt, reaching from waist to knees; a few had circular discs covering their breasts. There were hardly any children to be seen, except occasionally a little face staring at them from a window, or peering down from a roof-top. Once or twice they passed a woman with an infant slung across her back in a sort of hammock.

The most common vehicle was the curious form of sleigh in which they had ridden down through the tunnels. They saw also a few little two-wheeled carts, with wheels that appeared to be a solid segment of tree-trunk. All the vehicles were drawn by meek-looking little gray animals like a small deer without horns.

The court-house of Arite, though a larger building, from the outside was hardly different than most others in the city. It was distinct, however, in having on either side of the broad doorway that served as its main entrance, a large square stone column.

As they entered, passing a guard who saluted them respectfully, the visitors turned from a hallway and ascended a flight of steps. At the top they found themselves on a balcony overlooking the one large room that occupied almost the entire building. The balcony ran around all three sides (the room was triangular in shape) and was railed with a low stone parapet. On it were perhaps fifty people, sitting quietly on stone benches that lay close up behind the parapet. An attendant stood at each of the corners of the balcony; the one nearest bowed low as the Chemist and his companions entered silently and took their seats.

From the balcony the entire room below was in plain view. At the apex of its triangle sat the judge, on a raised dais of white stone with a golden canopy over it. He was a man about fifty—this leader of the court— garbed in a long loose robe of white. His hair, that fell on his shoulders, was snowy white, and around his forehead was a narrow white band. He held in his hand a sort of scepter of gold with a heavy golden triangle at its end.

In six raised tiers of unequal length, like a triangular flight of stairs across the angle of the room, and directly in front of the judge, was the jury—twenty men and twenty women, seated in alternate rows. The men wore loose robes of gray; the women robes of blue. On a seat raised slightly above the others sat a man who evidently was speaker for the men of the jury. On a similar elevated seat was the woman speaker; this latter was Lylda.

Near the center of the room, facing the judge and jury were two triangular spaces about twenty feet across, enclosed with a breast-high wall of stone. Within each of these enclosures were perhaps ten or twelve people seated on small stone benches. Directly facing the members of the jury and between them and the two enclosures, was a small platform raised about four feet above the floor, with several steps leading up to it from behind.

A number of attendants dressed in the characteristic short tunics, with breastplates and a short sword hanging from the waist, stood near the enclosures, and along the sides of the room.

The Chemist leaned over and whispered to his friends: "Those two enclosed places in the center are for the witnesses. Over there are those testifying for the accused; the others are witnesses for the government. The platform is where the accused stands when——"

He broke off suddenly. An expectant hush seemed to run over the room. A door at the side opened, and preceded and followed by two attendants a man entered, who walked slowly across the floor and stood alone upon the raised platform facing the jury.

He was a man of extraordinarily striking look and demeanor. He stood considerably over six feet in height, with a remarkably powerful yet lean body. He was naked except for a cloth breech clout girdled about his loins. His appearance was not that of an Oroid, for beside his greater height, and more muscular physique, his skin was distinctly of a more brownish hue. His hair was cut at the base of the neck in Oroid fashion; it was black, with streaks of silver running through it. His features were large and cast in a rugged mold. His mouth was cruel, and wore now a sardonic smile. He stood erect with head thrown back and arms folded across his breast, calmly facing the men and women who were to judge him.

The Very Young Man gripped the Chemist by the arm. "Who is that?" he whispered.

The Chemist's lips were pressed together; he seemed deeply affected. "I did not know they caught him," he answered softly. "It must have been just this morning."

The Very Young Man looked at Lylda. Her face was placid, but her breast was rising and falling more rapidly than normal, and her hands in her lap were tightly clenched.

The judge began speaking quietly, amid a deathlike silence. For over five minutes he spoke; once he was interrupted by a cheer, instantly stifled, and once by a murmur of dissent from several spectators on the balcony that called forth instant rebuke from the attendant stationed there.

The judge finished his speech, and raised his golden scepter slowly before him. As his voice died away, Lylda rose to her feet and facing the judge bowed low, with hands to her forehead. Then she spoke a few words, evidently addressing the women before her. Each of them raised her hands and answered in a monosyllable, as though affirming an oath. This performance was repeated by the men.

The accused still stood silent, smiling sardonically. Suddenly his voice rasped out with a short, ugly intonation and he threw his arms straight out before him. A murmur rose from the spectators, and several attendants leaned forward towards the platform. But the man only looked around at them contemptuously and again folded his arms.

From one of the enclosures a woman came, and mounted the platform beside the man. The Chemist whispered, "His wife; she is going to speak for him." But with a muttered exclamation and wave of his arm, the man swept her back, and without a word she descended the steps and re-entered the railed enclosure.

Then the man turned and raising his arms spoke angrily to those seated in the enclosure. Then he appealed to the judge.

The Chemist whispered in explanation: "He refuses any witnesses."

At a sign from the judge the enclosure was opened and its occupants left the floor, most of them taking seats upon the balcony.

"Who is he?" the Very Young Man wanted to know, but the Chemist ignored his question.

For perhaps ten minutes the man spoke, obviously in his own defence. His voice was deep and powerful, yet he spoke now seemingly without anger; and without an air of pleading. In fact his whole attitude seemed one of irony and defiance. Abruptly he stopped speaking and silence again fell over the room. A man and a woman left the other enclosure and mounted the platform beside the accused. They seemed very small and fragile, as he towered over them, looking down at them sneeringly.

The man and woman conferred a moment in whispers. Then the woman spoke. She talked only a few minutes, interrupted twice by the judge, once by a question from Lylda, and once by the accused himself.

Then for perhaps ten minutes more her companion addressed the court. He was a man considerably over middle age, and evidently, from his dress and bearing, a man of prominence in the nation. At one point in his speech it became obvious that his meaning was not clearly understood by the jury. Several of the women whispered together, and one rose and spoke to Lylda. She interrupted the witness with a quiet question. Later the accused himself questioned the speaker until silenced by the judge.

Following this witness came two others. Then the judge rose, and looking up to the balcony where the Chemist and his companions were sitting, motioned to the Chemist to descend to the floor below.

The Very Young Man tried once again with his whispered question "What is it?" but the Chemist only smiled, and rising quietly left them.

There was a stir in the court-room as the Chemist crossed the main floor. He did not ascend the platform with the prisoner, but stood beside it. He spoke to the jury quietly, yet with a suppressed power in his voice that must have been convincing. He spoke only a moment, more with the impartial attitude of one who gives advice than as a witness. When he finished, he bowed to the court and left the floor, returning at once to his friends upon the balcony.

Following the Chemist, after a moment of silence, the judge briefly addressed the prisoner, who stolidly maintained his attitude of ironic defiance.

"He is going to ask the jury to give its verdict now," said the Chemist in a low voice.

Lylda and her companion leader rose and faced their subordinates, and with a verbal monosyllable from each member of the jury the verdict was unhesitatingly given. As the last juryman's voice died away, there came a cry from the back of the room, a woman tore herself loose from the attendants holding her, and running swiftly across the room leaped upon the platform. She was a slight little woman, almost a child in appearance beside the man's gigantic stature. She stood looking at him a moment with heaving breast and great sorrowful eyes from which the tears were welling out and flowing down her cheeks unheeded.

The man's face softened. He put his hands gently upon the sides of her neck. Then, as she began sobbing, he folded her in his great arms. For an instant she clung to him. Then he pushed her away. Still crying softly, she descended from the platform, and walked slowly back across the room.

Hardly had she disappeared when there arose from the street outside a faint, confused murmur, as of an angry crowd gathering. The judge had left his seat now and the jury was filing out of the room.

The Chemist turned to his friends. "Shall we go?" he asked.

"This trial——" began the Big Business Man. "You haven't told us its significance. This man—good God what a figure of power and hate and evil. Who is he?"

"It must have been evident to you, gentlemen," the Chemist said quietly, "that you have been witnessing an event of the utmost importance to us all. I have to tell you of the crisis facing us; this trial is its latest development. That man——"

The insistent murmur from the street grew louder. Shouts arose and then a loud pounding from the side of the building.

The Chemist broke off abruptly and rose to his feet. "Come outside," he said.

They followed him through a doorway on to a balcony, overlooking the street. Gathered before the court-house was a crowd of several hundred men and women. They surged up against its entrance angrily, and were held in check there by the armed attendants on guard. A smaller crowd was pounding violently upon a side door of the building. Several people ran shouting down the street, spreading the excitement through the city.

The Chemist and his companions stood in the doorway of the balcony an instant, silently regarding this ominous scene. The Chemist was just about to step forward, when, upon another balcony, nearer the corner of the building a woman appeared. She stepped close to the edge of the parapet and raised her arms commandingly.

It was Lylda. She had laid aside her court robe and stood now in her glistening silver tunic. Her hair was uncoiled, and fell in dark masses over her white shoulders, blowing out behind her in the wind.

The crowd hesitated at the sight of her, and quieted a little. She stood rigid as a statue for a moment, holding her arms outstretched. Then, dropping them with a gesture of appeal she began to speak.

At the sound of her voice, clear and vibrant, yet soft, gentle and womanly, there came silence from below, and after a moment every face was upturned to hers. Gradually her voice rose in pitch. Its gentle tone was gone now—it became forceful, commanding. Then again she flung out her arms with a dramatic gesture and stood rigid, every line of her body denoting power—almost imperious command. Abruptly she ceased speaking, and, as she stood motionless, slowly at first, the crowd silently dispersed.

The street below was soon clear. Even those onlookers at a distance turned the corner and disappeared. Another moment passed, and then Lylda swayed and sank upon the floor of the balcony, with her head on her arms against its low stone railing—just a tired, gentle, frightened little woman.

"She did it—how wonderfully she did it," the Very Young Man murmured in admiration.

"We can handle them now" answered the Chemist. "But each time—it is harder. Let us get Lylda and go home, gentlemen. I want to tell you all about it." He turned to leave the balcony.

"Who was the man? What was he tried for?" the Very Young Man demanded.

"That trial was the first of its kind ever held," the Chemist answered. "The man was condemned to death. It was a new crime—the gravest we have ever had to face —the crime of treason."

CHAPTER XXIII

BACK home, comfortably seated upon the broad
balcony overlooking the lake, the three men sat waiting to hear their host's explanation of the strange events
they had witnessed. Lylda busied herself preparing a
light noonday meal, which she served charmingly on the
balcony while they talked.

"My friends," the Chemist began. "I tried to give you
this morning, a picture of this world and the life I have
been leading here. I think you understand, although I
did not specifically say so, that all I said related to the
time when I first came here. That you would call this
life Utopia, because of the way I outlined it, I do not
doubt; or at least you would call it a state of affairs as
near Utopian as any human beings can approach.

"All that is true; it was Utopia. But gentlemen, it is
so no longer. Things have been changing of recent
years, until now—well you saw what happened this morning.

"I cannot account for the first cause of this trouble.
Perhaps the Malite war, with its disillusionment to our
people—I do not know. Faith in human kindness was
broken: the Oroids could no longer trust implicitly in each
other. A gradual distrust arose—a growing unrest—a
dissatisfaction, which made no demands at first, nor
seemed indeed to have any definite grievances of any sort.
From it there sprang leaders, who by their greater intelligence created desires that fed and nourished their dis-

satisfaction—gave it a seemingly tangible goal that made it far more dangerous than it ever had been before.

"About a year ago there first came into prominence the man whom you saw this morning condemned to death. His name is Targo—he is a Malite—full-blooded I believe, although he says not. For twenty years or more he has lived in Orlog, a city some fifty miles from Arite. His wife is an Oroid.

"Targo, by his eloquence, and the power and force of his personality, won a large following in Orlog, and to a lesser degree in many other cities. Twice, some months ago, he was arrested and reprimanded; the last time with a warning that a third offence would mean his death."

"What is he after?" asked the Very Young Man.

"The Targos, as they are called, demand principally a different division of the land. Under the present system, approximately one-third of all the land is in the hands of the government. Of that, generally more than half lies idle most of the time. The Targos wish to have this land divided among the citizens. They claim also that most of the city organizations do not produce as large a dividend as the Targos could show under their own management. They have many other grievances that there is no reason for me to detail."

"Why not let them try out their theories in some city?" suggested the Big Business Man.

"They are trying them," the Chemist answered. "There was a revolution in Orlog about six months ago. Several of its officials were assassinated—almost the first murders we have ever had. The Targos took possession of the government—a brother of this man you saw this morning became leader of the city. Orlog withdrew from the Oroid government and is now handling its affairs as a separate nation."

"I wonder——" began the Big Business Man thoughtfully. "Well, why not let them run it that way, if they want to?"

"No reason, if they were sincere. But they are not sincere nor honest fundamentally. Their leaders are for the most part Malites, or Oroids with Malite blood. And they are fooling the people. Their followers are all the more unintelligent, more gullible individuals, or those in whom there lies a latent criminal streak.

"The thing doesn't work. Sexual license is growing in Orlog. Crimes against women are becoming more and more frequent. Offences committed by those prominent, or in authority, go unpunished. Women's testimony is discredited, often by concerted lying on the part of men witnesses.

"Many families are leaving Orlog—leaving their land and their homes deserted. In other cities where the Targos threaten to gain control the same thing is happening. Most of these refugees come to Arite. We cannot take care of them; there is not enough land here."

"Why not take your army and clean them up?" suggested the Very Young Man.

They were seated around a little table, at which Lylda was serving lunch. At the question she stopped in the act of pouring a steaming liquid from a little metal kettle into their dainty golden drinking cups and looked at the Very Young Man gravely.

"Very easy it would be to do that perhaps," she said quietly. "But these Targos, except a few—they are our own people. And they too are armed. We cannot fight them; we cannot kill them—our own people."

"We may have to," said the Chemist. "But you see, I did not realize, I could not believe the extent to which this Targo could sway the people. Nor did I at first realize what evils would result if his ideas were carried out.

He has many followers right here in Arite. You saw that this morning."

"How did you catch him?" interrupted the Very Young Man.

"Yesterday he came to Arite," said Lylda. "He came to speak. With him came fifty others. With them too came his wife to speak here, to our women. He thought we would do nothing; he defied us. There was a fight—this morning—and many were killed. And we brought him to the court—you saw."

"It is a serious situation," said the Doctor. "I had no idea——"

"We can handle it—we must handle it," said the Chemist. "But as Lylda says, we cannot kill our own people—only as a last desperate measure."

"Suppose you wait too long," suggested the Big Business Man. "You say these Targos are gaining strength every day. You might have a very bad civil war."

"That was the problem," answered the Chemist.

"But now you come," said Lylda. "You change it all when you come down to us out of the great beyond. Our people, they call you genii of the Master, they——"

"Oh gee, I never thought of that," murmured the Very Young Man. "What *do* you think of us?"

"They think you are supernatural beings of course," the Chemist said smiling. "Yet they accept you without fear and they look to you and to me for help."

"This morning, there at the court," said Lylda, "I heard them say that Targo spoke against you. Devils, he said, from the Great Blue Star, come here with evil for us all. And they believe him, some of them. It was for that perhaps they acted as they did before the court. In Arite now, many believe in Targo. And it is bad, very bad."

"The truth is," added the Chemist, "your coming, while

it gives us unlimited possibilities for commanding the course of events, at the same time has precipitated the crisis. Naturally no one can understand who or what you are. And as Lylda says, the Targos undoubtedly are telling the people you come to ally yourself with me for evil. There will be thousands who will listen to them and fear and hate you—especially in some of the other cities."

"What does the king say?" asked the Doctor.

"We will see him to-morrow. He has been anxiously waiting for you. But you must not forget," the Chemist added with a smile, "the king has had little experience facing strife or evil-doing of any kind. It was almost unknown until recently. It is I, and you, gentlemen, who are facing the problem of saving this nation."

The Very Young Man's face was flushed, and his eyes sparkled with excitement. "We can do anything we like," he said. "We have the power."

"Ay, that is it," said Lylda. "The power we have. But my friend, we cannot use it. Not for strife, for death; we cannot."

"The execution of Targo will cause more trouble," said the Chemist thoughtfully. "It is bound to make——"

"When will you put him to death?" asked the Big Business Man.

"To-morrow he dies," Lylda answered. "To-morrow, before the time of sleep."

"There will be trouble," said the Chemist again. "We are in no personal danger of course, but, for the people who now believe in Targo, I am afraid——"

"A plan I have made," said Lylda. She sat forward tensely in her chair, brushing her hair back from her face with a swift gesture. "A plan I have made. It is the only way—I now think—that may be there comes no harm to our people. It is that we want to do, if we can."

She spoke eagerly, and without waiting for them to answer, went swiftly on.

"This drug that you have brought, I shall take it. And I shall get big. Oh, not so very big, but big enough to be the height of a man it may be ten times. Then shall I talk to the people—I, Lylda—woman of the Master, and then shall I tell them that this power, this magic, is for good, not for evil, if only they will give up Targo and all who are with him."

"I will take it with you," said the Chemist. "Together we——"

"No, no, my husband. Alone I must do this. Ah, do you not know they say these stranger devils with their magic come for evil? And you too, must you not forget, once were a stranger just as they. That the people know —that they remember.

"But I—I—Lylda—a woman of the Oroids I am— full-blooded Oroid, no stranger. And they will believe me—a woman—for they know I cannot lie.

"I shall tell them I am for good, for kindness, for all we had, that time before the Malite war, when every one was happy. And if they will not believe, if as I say they will not do, then shall my power be indeed for evil, and all who will obey me not shall die. But they will believe —no need will there be to threaten.

"To many cities I will go. And in them, all of those who want to live by Targo's law will I send to Orlog. And all in Orlog who believe him not, will I tell to leave, and to the other cities go to make their homes. Then Orlog shall be Targo's city. And to-morrow he will not die, but go there into Orlog and become their king. For I shall say it may be there are some who like his rule of evil. Or it may be he is good in different fashion, and in time can make us see that his law too, is just and kind.

"Then shall live in Orlog all who wish to stay, and we

shall watch their rule, but never shall we let them pass beyond their borders. For if they do, then shall we kill them.

"All this I can do, my husband, if you but will let me try. For me they will believe, a woman, Oroid all of blood—for they know women do not lie." She stopped and the fire in her eyes changed to a look of gentle pleading. "If you will but let me try," she finished. "My husband—please."

The Chemist glanced at his friends who sat astonished by this flow of eager, impassioned words. Then he turned again to Lylda's intent, pleading face, regarding her tenderly. "You are very fine, little mother of my son," he said gently, lapsing for a moment into her own style of speech. "It could do no harm," he added thoughtfully "and perhaps——"

"Let her try it," said the Doctor. "No harm could come to her."

"No harm to me could come," said Lylda quickly. "And I shall make them believe. I can, because I am a woman, and they will know I tell the truth. Ah, you will let me try, my husband—please?"

The Chemist appealed to the others. "They will believe her, many of them," he said. "They will leave Orlog as she directs. But those in other cities will still hold to Targo, they will simply remain silent for a time. What their feelings will be or are we cannot tell. Some will leave and go to Orlog of course, for Lylda will offer freedom of their leader and to secure that they will seem to agree to anything.

"But after all, they are nothing but children at heart, most of them. To-day, they might believe in Lylda; to-morrow Targo could win them again."

"He won't get a chance," put in the Very Young Man quickly. "If she says we kill anybody who talks for

Targo outside of Orlog, that goes. It's the only way, isn't it?"

"And she might really convince them—or most of them," added the Doctor.

"You will let me try?" asked Lylda softly. The Chemist nodded.

Lylda sprang to her feet. Her frail little body was trembling with emotion; on her face was a look almost of exaltation.

"You *will* let me try," she cried. "Then I shall make them believe. Here, now, this very hour, I shall make them know the truth. And they, my own people, shall I save from sorrow, misery and death."

She turned to the Chemist and spoke rapidly.

"My husband, will you send Oteo now, up into the city. Him will you tell to have others spread the news. All who desire an end to Targo's rule, shall come here at once. And all too, who in him believe, and who for him want freedom, they shall come too. Let Oteo tell them magic shall be performed and Lylda will speak with them.

"Make haste, my husband, for now I go to change my dress. Not as the Master's woman will I speak, but as Lylda—Oroid woman—woman of the people." And with a flashing glance, she turned and swiftly left the balcony.

CHAPTER XXIV

LYLDA ACTS

"SHE'LL do it," the Very Young Man murmured, staring at the doorway through which Lylda had disappeared. "She can do anything."

The Chemist rose to his feet. "I'll send Oteo. Will you wait here gentlemen? And will you have some of the drugs ready for Lylda? You have them with you?" The men nodded.

"How about Lylda carrying the drugs?" asked the Very Young Man. "And what about her clothes?"

"I have already made a belt for Lylda and for myself—some time ago," the Chemist answered. "During the first year I was here I made several experiments with the drugs. I found that almost anything within the immediate—shall I say influence of the body, will contract with it. Almost any garment, even a loose robe will change size. You found that to be so to some extent. Those belts you wore down——"

"That's true," agreed the Doctor, "there seems to be considerable latitude——"

"I decided," the Chemist went on, "that immediately after your arrival we should all wear the drugs constantly. You can use the armpit pouches if you wish; Lylda and I will wear these belts I have made."

Oteo, the Chemist's personal servant, a slim youth with a bright, intelligent face, listened carefully to his master's directions and then left the house hurriedly, running up the street towards the center of the city. Once or twice he stopped and spoke to passers-by for a moment, gathering a crowd around him each time.

The Chemist rejoined his friends on the balcony. "There will be a thousand people here in half an hour," he said quietly. "I have sent a message to the men in charge of the government workshops; they will have their people cease work to come here."

Lylda appeared in a few moments more. She was dressed as the Chemist had seen her first through the microscope—in a short, grey skirt reaching from waist to knees. Only now she wore also two circular metal discs strapped over her breasts. Her hair was unbound and fell in masses forward over her shoulders. Around her waist was a broad girdle of golden cloth with small pouches for holding the chemicals. She took her place among the men quietly.

"See, I am ready," she said with a smile. "Oteo, you have sent him?" The Chemist nodded.

Lylda turned to the Doctor. "You will tell me, what is to do with the drugs?"

They explained in a few words. By now a considerable crowd had gathered before the house, and up the street many others were hurrying down. Directly across from the entrance to Lylda's garden, back of the bluff at the lake front, was a large open space with a fringe of trees at its back. In this open space the crowd was collecting.

The Chemist rose after a moment and from the rooftop spoke a few words to the people in the street below. They answered him with shouts of applause mingled with a hum of murmured anger underneath. The Chemist went back to his friends, his face set and serious.

As he dropped in his chair Lylda knelt on the floor before him, laying her arms on his knees. "I go to do for our people the best I can," she said softly, looking up into his face. "Now I go, but to you I will come back soon." The Chemist tenderly put his hand upon the glossy smoothness of her hair.

"I go—now," she repeated, and reached for one of the vials under her arm. Holding it in her hand, she stared at it a moment, silently, in awe. Then she shuddered like a frightened child and buried her face in the Chemist's lap, huddling her little body up close against his legs as if for protection.

The Chemist did not move nor speak, but sat quiet with his hand gently stroking her hair. In a moment she again raised her face to his. Her long lashes were wet with tears, but her lips were smiling.

"I am ready—now," she said gently. She brushed her tears from her eyes and rose to her feet. Drawing herself to her full height, she tossed back her head and flung out her arms before her.

"No one can know I am afraid—but you," she said. "And I—shall forget." She dropped her arms and stood passive.

"I go now to take the drug—there in the little garden behind, where no one can notice. You will come down?"

The Big Business Man cleared his throat. When he spoke his voice was tremulous with emotion.

"How long will you be gone—Lylda?" he asked.

The woman turned to him with a smile. "Soon will I return, so I believe," she answered. "I go to Orlog, to Raito, and to Tele. But never shall I wait, nor speak long, and fast will I walk. . . . Before the time of sleep has descended upon us, I shall be here."

In the little garden behind the house, out of sight of the crowd on the other side, Lylda prepared to take the drug. She was standing there, with the four men, when Loto burst upon them, throwing himself into his mother's arms.

"Oh, *mamita, mamita,*" he cried, clinging to her. "There in the street outside, they say such terrible things—— Of you *mamita.* 'The master's woman' I heard one say, 'She has the evil magic.' And another spoke of Targo. And they say he must not die, or there will be death for those who kill him."

Lylda held the boy close as he poured out his breathless frightened words.

"No matter, little son," she said tenderly. "To *mamita* no harm can come—you shall see. Did my father teach you well to-day?"

"But *mamita,* one man who saw me standing, called me an evil name and spoke of you, my mother Lylda. And a woman looked with a look I never saw before. I am afraid, *mamita.*"

With quivering lips that smiled, Lylda kissed the little boy tenderly and gently loosening his hold pushed him towards his father.

"The Master's son, Loto, never can he be afraid," she said with gentle reproof. "That must you remember—always."

The little group in the garden close up against the house stood silent as Lylda took a few grains of the drug. The noise and shouts of the crowd in front were now plainly audible. One voice was raised above the others, as though someone were making a speech.

Loto stood beside his father, and the Chemist laid his arm across the boy's shoulder. As Lylda began visibly to increase in size, the boy uttered a startled cry. Meeting his mother's steady gaze he shut his lips tight, and stood rigid, watching her with wide, horrified eyes.

Lylda had grown nearly twice her normal size before she spoke. Then, smiling down at the men, she said evenly, "From the roof, perhaps, you will watch."

"You know what to do if you grow too large," the Doctor said huskily.

"I know, my friend. I thank you all. And good-bye." She met the Chemist's glance an instant. Then abruptly she faced about and walking close to the house, stood at its further corner facing the lake.

After a moment's hesitation the Chemist led his friends to the roof. As they appeared at the edge of the para-pet a great shout rolled up from the crowd below. Nearly a thousand people had gathered. The street was crowded and in the open space beyond they stood in little groups. On a slight eminence near the lake bluff, a man stood haranguing those around him. He was a short, very thickset little man, with very long arms—a squat, ape-like figure. He talked loudly and indignantly; around him perhaps a hundred people stood listening, applauding at intervals.

When the Chemist appeared this man stopped with a final phrase of vituperation and a wave of his fist towards the house.

The Chemist stood silent, looking out over the throng. "How large is she now?" he asked the Very Young Man softly. The Very Young Man ran across the roof to its farther corner and was back in an instant.

"They'll see her soon—look there." His friends turned at his words. At the corner of the house they could just see the top of Lylda's head above the edge of the parapet. As they watched she grew still taller and in another moment her forehead appeared. She turned her head, and her great eyes smiled softly at them across the roof-top. In a few moments more (she had evidently stopped growing) with a farewell glance at her husband, she stepped around the corner of the house into full view of the crowd—a woman over sixty feet tall, standing quietly in the garden with one hand resting upon the roof of the house behind her.

A cry of terror rose from the people as she appeared. Most of those in the street ran in fright back into the field behind. Then, seeing her standing motionless with a gentle smile on her face, they stopped, irresolute. A few held their ground, frankly curious and unafraid. Others stood sullen and defiant.

When the people had quieted a little Lylda raised her arms in greeting and spoke, softly, yet with a voice that carried far away over the field. As she talked the people seemed to recover their composure rapidly. Her tremendous size no longer seemed to horrify them. Those who obviously at first were friendly appeared now quite at ease; the others, with their lessening terror, were visibly more hostile.

Once Lylda mentioned the name of Targo. A scattered shout came up from the crowd; the apelike man shouted out something to those near him, and then, leaving his knoll disappeared.

As Lylda continued, the hostile element in the crowd grew more insistent. They did not listen to her now but shouted back, in derision and defiance. Then suddenly a stone was thrown; it struck Lylda on the breast, hitting her metal breastplate with a thud and dropping at her feet.

As though at a signal a hail of stones flew up from the crowd, most of them striking Lylda like tiny pebbles, a few of the larger ones bounding against the house, or landing on its roof.

At this attack Lylda abruptly stopped speaking and took a step forward menacingly. The hail of stones continued. Then she turned towards the roof-top, where the men and the little boy stood behind the parapet, sheltering themselves from the flying stones.

"Only one way there is," said Lylda sadly, in a soft

whisper that they plainly heard above the noise of the crowd. "I am sorry, my husband—but I must."

A stone struck her shoulder. She faced the crowd again; a gentle look of sorrow was in her eyes, but her mouth was stern. In the street below at the edge of the field the squat little màn had reappeared. It was from here that most of the stones seemed to come.

"That man there—by the road——" The Chemist pointed. "One of Targo's——"

In three swift steps Lylda was across the garden, with one foot over the wall into the street. Reaching down she caught the man between her huge fingers, and held him high over her head an instant so that all might see.

The big crowd was silent with terror; the man high in the air over their heads screamed horribly. Lylda hesitated only a moment more; then she threw back her arm and, with a great great sweep, flung her screaming victim far out into the lake.

CHAPTER XXV

THE ESCAPE OF TARGO

"I AM very much afraid it was a wrong move," said the Chemist gravely.

They were sitting in a corner of the roof, talking over the situation. Lylda had left the city; the last they had seen of her, she was striding rapidly away, over the country towards Orlog. The street and field before the house now was nearly deserted.

"She had to do it, of course," the Chemist continued, "but to kill Targo's brother——"

"I wonder," began the Big Business Man thoughtfully. "It seems to me this disturbance is becoming far more serious than we think. It isn't so much a political issue now between your government and the followers of Targo, as it is a struggle against those of us who have this magic, as they call it."

"That's just the point," put in the Doctor quickly. "They are making the people believe that our power of changing size is a menace that——"

"If I had only realized," said the Chemist. "I thought your coming would help. Apparently it was the very worst thing that could have happened."

"Not for you personally," interjected the Very Young Man. "We're perfectly safe—and Lylda, and Loto." He put his arm affectionately around the boy who sat close beside him. "You are not afraid, are you, Loto?"

"Now I am not," answered the boy seriously. "But this morning, when I left my grandfather, coming home——"

"You were afraid for your mother. That was it, wasn't it?" finished the Very Young Man. "Does your grandfather teach you?"

"Yes—he, and father, and mother."

"I want you to see Lylda's father," said the Chemist. "There is nothing we can do now until Lylda returns. Shall we walk up there?" They all agreed readily.

"I may go, too?" Loto asked, looking at his father.

"You have your lessons," said the Chemist.

"But, my father, it is so very lonely without mother," protested the boy.

The Chemist smiled gently. "Afraid, little son, to stay with Oteo?"

"He's not afraid," said the Very Young Man stoutly.

The little boy looked from one to the other of them a moment silently. Then, calling Oteo's name, he ran across the roof and down into the house.

"Five years ago," said the Chemist, as the child disappeared, "there was hardly such an emotion in this world as fear or hate or anger. Now the pendulum is swinging to the other extreme. I suppose that's natural, but——" He ended with a sigh, and, breaking his train of thought, rose to his feet. "Shall we start?"

Lylda's father greeted them gravely, with a dignity, and yet obvious cordiality that was quite in accord with his appearance. He was a man over sixty. His still luxuriant white hair fell to his shoulders. His face was hairless, for in this land all men's faces were as devoid of hair as those of the women. He was dressed in a long, flowing robe similar to those his visitors were wearing.

"Because—you come—I am glad," he said with a smile, as he shook hands in their own manner. He spoke slowly, with frequent pauses, as though carefully picking his words. "But—an old man—I know not the language of you."

He led them into a room that evidently was his study, for in it they saw many strange instruments, and on a table a number of loosely bound sheets of parchment that were his books. They took the seats he offered and looked around them curiously.

"There is the clock we spoke of," said the Chemist, indicating one of the larger instruments that stood on a pedestal in a corner of the room. "Reoh will explain it to you."

Their host addressed the Chemist. "From Oteo I hear —the news to-day is bad?" he asked with evident concern.

"I am afraid it is," the Chemist answered seriously.

"And Lylda?"

The Chemist recounted briefly the events of the day. "We can only wait until Lylda returns," he finished. "To-morrow we will talk with the king."

"Bad it is," said the old man slowly; "very bad. But— we shall see——"

The Very Young Man had risen to his feet and was standing beside the clock.

"How does it work?" he asked. "What time is it now?"

Reoh appealed to his son-in-law. "To tell of it—the words I know not."

The Chemist smiled. "You are too modest, my father. But I will help you out, if you insist." He turned to the others, who were gathered around him, looking at the clock.

"Our measurement of our time here," he began, "like yours, is based on——"

"Excuse me," interrupted the Very Young Man. "I just want to know first what time it is now?"

"It is in the fourth eclipse," said the Chemist with a twinkle.

The Very Young Man was too surprised by this unex-

pected answer to question further, and the Chemist went
on.

"We measure time by the astronomical movements, just
as you do in your world. One of the larger stars has a
satellite which revolves around it with extreme rapidity.
Here at Arite, this satellite passes nearly always directly
behind its controlling star. In other words, it is eclipsed.
Ten of these eclipses measure the passage of our day.
We rise generally at the first eclipse or about that time.
It is now the fourth eclipse; you would call it late afternoon. Do you see?"

"How is the time gauged here?" asked the Big Business
Man, indicating the clock.

The instrument stood upon a low stone pedestal. It
consisted of a transparent cylinder about twelve inches in
diameter and some four feet high, surmounted by a large
circular bowl. The cylinder was separated from the bowl
by a broad disc of porous stone; a similar stone section
divided the cylinder horizontally into halves. From the
bowl a fluid was dropping in a tiny stream through the
top stone segment into the upper compartment, which was
now about half full. This in turn filtered through the
second stone into the lower compartment. This lower
section was marked in front with a large number of fine
horizontal lines, an equal distance apart, but of unequal
length. In it the fluid stood now just above one of the
longer lines—the fourth from the bottom. On the top
of this fluid floated a circular disc almost the size of the
inside diameter of the cylinder.

The Chemist explained. "It really is very much like
the old hour-glass we used to have in your world. This
filters liquid instead of sand. You will notice the water
filters twice." He indicated the two compartments.
"That is because it is necessary to have a liquid that is
absolutely pure in order that the rate at which it filters

through this other stone may remain constant. The clock is carefully tested, so that for each eclipse the water will rise in this lower part of the cylinder, just the distance from here to here."

The Chemist put his fingers on two of the longer marks.

"Very ingenious," remarked the Doctor. "Is it accurate?"

"Not so accurate as your watches, of course," the Chemist answered. "But still, it serves the purpose. These ten longer lines, you see, mark the ten eclipses that constitute one of our days. The shorter lines between indicate halves and quarter intervals."

"Then it is only good for one day?" asked the Very Young Man. "How do you set it?"

"It resets automatically each day, at the beginning of the first eclipse. This disc," the Chemist pointed to the disc floating on the water in the lower compartment. "This disc rises with the water on which it is floating. When it reaches the top of it, it comes in contact with a simple mechanism—you'll see it up there—which opens a gate below and drains out the water in a moment. So that every morning it is emptied and starts filling up again. All that is needed is to keep this bowl full of water."

"It certainly seems very practical," observed the Big Business Man. "Are there many in use?"

"Quite a number, yes. This clock was invented by Reoh, some thirty years ago. He is the greatest scientist and scholar we have." The old man smiled deprecatingly at this compliment.

"Are these books?" asked the Very Young Man; he had wandered over to the table and was fingering one of the bound sheets of parchment.

"They are Reoh's chronicles," the Chemist answered. "The only ones of their kind in Arite."

"What's this?" The Very Young Man pointed to another instrument.

"That is an astronomical instrument, something like a sextant—also an invention of Reoh's. Here is a small telescope and——" The Chemist paused and went over to another table standing at the side of the room.

"That reminds me, gentlemen," he continued; "I have something here in which you will be greatly interested."

"What you—will see," said Reoh softly, as they gathered around the Chemist, "you only, of all people, can understand. Each day I look, and I wonder; but never can I quite believe."

"I made this myself, nearly ten years ago," said the Chemist, lifting up the instrument; "a microscope. It is not very large, you see; nor is it very powerful. But I want you to look through it." With his cigar-lighter he ignited a short length of wire that burned slowly with a brilliant blue spot of light. In his hand he held a small piece of stone.

"I made this microscope hoping that I might prove with it still more conclusively my original theory of the infinite smallness of human life. For many months I searched into various objects, but without success. Finally I came upon this bit of rock." The Chemist adjusted it carefully under the microscope with the light shining brilliantly upon it.

"You see I have marked one place; I am going to let you look into it there."

The Doctor stepped forward. As he looked they heard his quick intake of breath. After a moment he raised his head. On his face was an expression of awe too deep for words. He made place for the others, and stood silent.

When the Very Young Man's turn came he looked into

the eyepiece awkwardly. His heart was beating fast; for some reason he felt frightened.

At first he saw nothing. "Keep the other eye open," said the Chemist.

The Very Young Man did as he was directed. After a moment there appeared before him a vast stretch of open country. As from a great height he stared down at the scene spread out below him. Gradually it became clearer. He saw water, with the sunlight—his own kind of sunlight it seemed—shining upon it. He stared for a moment more, dazzled by the light. Then, nearer to him, he saw a grassy slope, that seemed to be on a mountainside above the water. On this slope he saw animals grazing, and beside them a man, formed like himself.

The Chemist's voice came to him from far away. "We are all of us here in a world that only occupies a portion of one little atom of the gold of a wedding-ring. Yet what you see there in that stone——"

The Very Young Man raised his head. Before him stood the microscope, with its fragment of stone gleaming in the blue light of the burning wire. He wanted to say something to show them how he felt, but no words came. He looked up into the Chemist's smiling face, and smiled back a little foolishly.

"Every day I look," said Reoh, breaking the silence. "And I see—wonderful things. But never really—can I believe."

At this moment there came a violent rapping upon the outer door. As Reoh left the room to open it, the Very Young Man picked up the bit of stone that the Chemist had just taken from the microscope.

"I wish—may I keep it?" he asked impulsively.

The Chemist smiled and nodded, and the Very Young Man was about to slip it into the pocket of his robe when Reoh hastily reëntered the room, followed by Oteo. The youth was breathing heavily, as though he had been running, and on his face was a frightened look.

"Bad; very bad," said the old man, in a tone of deep concern, as they came through the doorway.

"What is it, Oteo?" asked the Chemist quickly. The boy answered him with a flood of words in his native tongue.

The Chemist listened quietly. Then he turned to his companions.

"Targo has escaped," he said briefly. "They sent word to me at home, and Oteo ran here to tell me. A crowd broke into the court-house and released him. Oteo says they went away by water, and that no one is following them."

The youth, who evidently understood English, added something else in his own language.

"He says Targo vowed death to all who have the magic power. He spoke in the city just now, and promised them deliverance from the giants."

"Good Lord," murmured the Very Young Man.

"He has gone to Orlog probably," the Chemist continued. "We have nothing to fear for the moment. But that he could speak, in the centre of Arite, after this morning, and that the people would listen——"

"It seems to me things are getting worse every minute," said the Big Business Man.

Oteo spoke again. The Chemist translated. "The police did nothing. They simply stood and listened, but took no part."

"Bad; very bad," repeated the old man, shaking his head.

"What we should do I confess I cannot tell," said the Chemist soberly. "But that we should do something drastic is obvious."

"We can't do anything until Lylda gets back," declared

the Very Young Man. "We'll see what she has done. We might have had to let Targo go anyway."

The Chemist started towards the door. "To-night, by the time of sleep, Reoh," he said to the old man, "I expect Lylda will have returned. You had better come to us then with Aura. I do not think you should stay here alone to sleep to-night."

"In a moment—Aura comes," Reoh answered. "We shall be with you—very soon."

The Chemist motioned to his companions, and with obvious reluctance on the part of the Very Young Man they left, followed by Oteo.

On the way back the city seemed quiet—abnormally so. The streets were nearly deserted; what few pedestrians they met avoided them, or passed them sullenly. They were perhaps half-way back to the Chemist's house when the Very Young Man stopped short.

"I forgot that piece of stone," he explained, looking at them queerly. "Go on. I'll be there by the time you are," and disregarding the Chemist's admonition that he might get lost he left them abruptly and walked swiftly back over the way they had come.

Without difficulty, for they had made few turns, the Very Young Man located Reoh's house. As he approached he noticed the figure of a man lounging against a further corner of the building; the figure disappeared almost as soon as he saw it.

It was a trivial incident, but, somehow, to the Very Young Man, it held something in it of impending danger. He did not knock on the outer door, but finding it partly open, he slowly pushed it wider and stepped quietly into the hallway beyond. He was hardly inside when there came from within the house a girl's scream—a cry of horror, abruptly stifled.

For an instant, the Very Young Man stood hesitating.

Then he dashed forward through an open doorway in the direction from which the cry had seemed to come.

The room into which he burst was Reoh's study; the room he had left only a few moments before. On the floor, almost across his path, lay the old man, with the short blade of a sword buried to the hilt in his breast. In a corner of the room a young Oroid girl stood with her back against the wall. Her hands were pressed against her mouth; her eyes were wide with terror. Bending over the body on the floor with a hand at its armpit, knelt the huge, gray figure of a man. At the sound of the intruder's entrance he looked up quickly and sprang to his feet.

The Very Young Man saw it was Targo!

CHAPTER XXVI

THE ABDUCTION

WHEN the Very Young Man left them so unceremoniously the Chemist and his companions continued on their way home, talking earnestly over the serious turn affairs had taken. Of the three, the Big Business Man appeared the most perturbed.

"Lylda isn't going to accomplish anything," he said. "It won't work. The thing has gone too far. It isn't politics any longer; it's a struggle against us—a hatred and fear of our supernatural powers."

"If we had never come——" began the Doctor.

"It probably would have worked out all right," finished the Big Business Man. "But since we're here——"

"We could leave," the Doctor suggested.

"It has gone too far; I agree with you," the Chemist said. "Your going would not help. They would never believe I did not still possess the magic. And now, without the drugs I might not be able to cope with affairs. It is a very serious situation."

"And getting worse all the time," added the Big Business Man.

When they arrived at the Chemist's home Loto did not run out to meet them as the Chemist expected. They called his name, but there was no answer. Inside the house they perceived at once that something was wrong. The living-room was in disorder; some of the pieces of furniture had been overturned, and many of the smaller articles were scattered about the floor. Even the wall-hangings had been torn down.

In sudden fear the Chemist ran through the building, calling to Loto. Everywhere he saw evidence of intruders, who had ransacked the rooms, as though making a hasty search. In one of the rooms, crouched on the floor, he came upon Eena, Lylda's little serving-maid. The girl was stricken dumb with terror. At the sight of her master she sobbed with relief, and after a few moments told him what had happened.

When the Chemist rejoined his friends in the lower room his face was set and white. The girl followed him closely, evidently afraid to be left alone. The Chemist spoke quietly, controlling his emotion with obvious difficulty.

"Loto has been stolen!" he said. "Targo and four of his men were here soon after we left. Eena saw them and hid. They searched the house——"

"For the drugs," muttered the Doctor under his breath.

"——and then left, taking Loto with them."

"Which way did they go?" asked the Big Business Man. "Good God, what a thing!"

"They went by water, in a large boat that was waiting for them here," answered the Chemist.

"How long ago?" asked the Doctor quickly. "We have not been gone very long."

"An hour probably, not much more." Eena said something to her master and began to cry softly.

"She says they left a little while ago. Three of the men took Loto away in the boat. She watched them from the window upstairs."

"*Targo aliá*," said the girl.

"One of the men was Targo," said the Chemist. He went to one of the windows overlooking the lake; the Doctor stood beside him. There was no boat in sight.

"They cannot have got very far," said the Doctor. "Those islands there——"

"They would take him to Orlog," said the Chemist. "About fifty miles."

The Doctor turned back to the room. "We can get them. You forget—these drugs—the power they give us. Oh, Will." He called the Big Business Man over to them; he spoke hurriedly, with growing excitement. "What do you think, Will? That boat—they've got Loto—it can't be very far. We can make ourselves so large in half an hour we can wade all over the lake. We can get it. What do you think?"

The Chemist dropped into a chair with his head in his hands. "Let me think—just a moment, Frank. I know the power we have; I know we can do almost anything. That little boy of mine—they've got him. Let me think —just a moment."

He sat motionless. The Doctor continued talking in a lower tone to the Big Business Man by the window. In the doorway Oteo stood like a statue, motionless, except for his big, soft eyes that roved unceasingly over the scene before him. After a moment Eena ceased her sobbing and knelt beside the Chemist, looking up at him sorrowfully.

"I cannot believe," said the Chemist finally, raising his head, "that the safest way to rescue Loto is by the plan you have suggested." He spoke with his usual calm, judicial manner, having regained control of himself completely. "I understand now, thoroughly, and for the first time, the situation we are facing. It is, as you say, a political issue no longer. Targo and his closest followers have convinced a very large proportion of our entire nation, I am certain, that myself, and my family, and you, the strangers, are possessed of a diabolical power that must be annihilated. Targo will never rest until he has the drugs. That is why he searched this house.

"He has abducted Loto for the same purpose. He will

—not hurt Loto—I am convinced of that. Probably he will send someone to-morrow to demand the drugs as the price of Loto's life. But don't you understand? Targo and his advisers, and even the most ignorant of the people, realize what power we have. Lylda showed them that when she flung Targo's brother out into the lake to-day. But we cannot use this power openly. For, while it makes us invincible, it makes them correspondingly desperate. They are a peculiar people. Throughout the whole history of the race they have been kindly, thoughtless children. Now they are aroused. The pendulum has swung to the other extreme. They care little for their lives. They are still children—children who will go to their death unreasoning, fighting against invincibility.

"That is something we must never overlook, for it is a fact. We cannot run amuck as giants over this world and hope to conquer it. We could conquer it, yes; but only when the last of its inhabitants had been killed; stamped out like ants defending their hill from the attacks of an elephant. Don't you see I am right?"

"Then Lylda——" began the Doctor, as the Chemist paused.

"Lylda will fail. Her venture to-day will make matters immeasureably worse."

"You're right," agreed the Big Business Man. "We should have realized."

"So you see we cannot make ourselves large and recapture Loto by force. They would anticipate us and kill him."

"Then what shall we do?" demanded the Doctor. "We must do something."

"That we must decide carefully, for we must make no more mistakes. But we can do nothing at this moment. The lives of all of us are threatened. We must not allow ourselves to become separated. We must wait here for Lylda. Reoh and Aura must stay with us. Then we can decide how to rescue Loto and what to do after that. But we must keep together."

"Jack ought to be here by now," said the Big Business Man. "I hope Reoh and Aura come with him."

For over an hour they waited, and still the Very Young Man did not come. They had just decided to send Oteo to see what had become of him and to bring down Reoh and his daughter, when Lylda unexpectedly returned. It was Eena, standing at one of the side windows, who first saw her mistress. A cry from the girl brought them all to the window. Far away beyond the city they could see the gigantic figure of Lylda, towering several hundred feet in the air.

As she came closer she seemed to stop, near the outskirts of the city, and then they saw her dwindling in size until she disappeared, hidden from their view by the houses near at hand.

In perhaps half an hour more she reappeared, picking her way carefully down the deserted street towards them. She was at this time about forty feet tall. At the corner, a hundred yards away from them a little group of people ran out, and, with shouts of anger, threw something at her as she passed.

She stooped down towards them, and immediately they scurried for safety out of her reach.

Once inside of her own garden, where the Chemist and his companions were waiting, Lylda lost no time in becoming her normal size again. As she grew smaller, she sat down with her back against a little tree. Her face was white and drawn; her eyes were full of tears as she looked at her husband and his friends.

When the drug had ceased to act, the Chemist sat beside her. She had started out only a few hours before a crusader, dominant, forceful; she came back now, a tired, discouraged little woman. The Chemist put his arm around her protectingly, drawing her drooping body towards him. "Very bad news, Lylda, we know," he said gently.

"Oh, my husband," she cried brokenly. "So sorry I am—so very sorry. The best I knew I did. And it was all so very bad—so very bad——" she broke off abruptly, looking at him with her great, sorrowful eyes.

"Tell us Lylda," he said softly.

"To many cities I went," she answered. "And I told the people all I meant to say. Some of them believed. But they were not many, and of the others who did not believe, they were afraid, and so kept they silent. Then into Orlog I went, and in the public square I spoke—for very long, because, for some reason I know not, at first they listened.

"But no one there believed. And then, my husband, at last I knew why I could not hope to gain my way. It is not because they want Targo's rule that they oppose us. It was, but it is so no longer. It is because they have been made to fear these drugs we have. For now, in Orlog, they are shouting death to all the giants. Forgotten are all their cries for land—the things that Targo promised, and we in Arite would not give. It is death to all the giants they are shouting now: death to you, to me, to us all, because we have these drugs."

"Did they attack you?" asked the Big Business Man.

"Many things they threw," Lylda answered. "But I was so big," she smiled a little sad, twisted smile. "What they could do was as nothing. And because of that they fear and hate us so; yet never have I seen such fearless things as those they did. Death to the giants was their only cry. And I could have killed them—hundreds, thousands—yet never could I have made them stop while yet they were alive.

"I told them Targo I would free.   And in Orlog they laughed.   For they said that he would free himself before I had returned."

"He did," muttered the Big Business Man.

"Targo escaped this afternoon," the Chemist explained. "He went to Orlog by boat and took——" He stopped abruptly.   "Come into the house, Lylda," he added gently; "there are other things, my wife, of which we must speak."   He rose to his feet, pulling her up with him.

"Where is Jack," she asked, looking at the Big Business Man, who stood watching her gravely.   "And where is Loto?   Does he not want to see his mother who tried so——" She put her arms around the Chemist's neck. "So very hard I tried," she finished softly.   "So very hard, because—I thought——"

The Chemist led her gently into the house.   The Doctor started to follow, but the Big Business Man held him back.   "It is better not," he said in an undertone, "don't you think?"   Oteo was standing near them, and the Big Business Man motioned to him.   "Besides," he added, "I'm worried about Jack.   I think we ought to go up after him.   I don't think it ought to take us very long."

"With Oteo—he knows the way," agreed the Doctor. "It's devilish strange what's keeping that boy."

They found that although Oteo spoke only a few words of English, he understood nearly everything they said, and waiting only a moment more, they started up into the city towards Reoh's home.

In the living-room of the house, the Chemist sat Lylda gently down on a cushion in front of the hearth.   Sitting beside her, he laid his hand on hers that rested on her knee.

"For twelve years, Lylda, we have lived together," he began slowly.   "And no sorrow has come to us; no danger has threatened us or those we loved." He met his wife's questioning gaze unflinchingly and went on:

"You have proved yourself a wonderful woman, my wife. You never knew—nor those before you—the conflict of human passions. No danger before has ever threatened you or those you loved." He saw her eyes grow wider.

"Very strange you talk, my husband. There is something——"

"There is something, Lylda. To-day you have seen strife, anger, hate and—and death. You have met them all calmly; you have fought them all justly, like a woman —a brave, honest Oroid woman, who can wrong no one. There is something now that I must tell you." He saw the growing fear in her eyes and hurried on.

"Loto, to-day—this afternoon——"

The woman gave a little, low cry of anguish, instantly repressed. Her hand gripped his tightly.

"No, no, Lylda, not that," he said quickly, "but this afternoon while we were all away—Loto was here alone with Eena—Targo with his men came. They did not hurt Loto; they took him away in a boat to Orlog." He stopped abruptly. Lylda's eyes never left his face. Her breath came fast; she put a hand to her mouth and stifled the cry that rose to her lips.

"They will not hurt him, Lylda; that I know. And soon we will have him back."

For a moment more her searching eyes stared steadily into his. He heard the whispered words, "My little son —with Targo," come slowly from her lips; then with a low, sobbing cry she dropped senseless into his arms.

CHAPTER XXVII

AURA

THE Very Young Man involuntarily took a step backward as he met Targo's eyes, glaring at him across the old man's body. The girl in the corner gave another cry—a cry of fright and horror, yet with a note of relief. The Very Young Man found himself wondering who she was; then he knew.

His first impulse was to leap across the room towards her. He thought of the chemicals and instinctively his hand went to his arm-pit. But he knew there was no time for that. He hesitated one brief instant. As he stood rigid Targo stooped swiftly and grasped the dagger in his victim's breast.

The girl screamed again, louder this time, and like a mask the Very Young Man's indecision fell from him. He stood alert, clear-headed. Here was an enemy threatening him—an enemy he must fight and overcome.

In the second that Targo bent down the Very Young Man bounded forward, and with a leap that his football days had taught him so well how to make, he landed squarely upon the bare, broad back of his antagonist. The impact of his weight forced Targo down upon the floor, and losing his balance he fell, with the Very Young Man on top of him. They hit the leg of the table as they rolled over, and something dropped from it to the floor, striking the stone surface with a thud.

The knife still stuck in the dead man's body. The Very Young Man thought he could reach it, but his opponent's great arms were around him now and held him too tightly. He tried to pull himself loose, but could not. Then he rolled partly over again, and met Targo's eyes above, leering triumphantly down at him. He looked away and wrenched his right arm free. Across the room he could see the girl still crouching in the corner. His right hand sweeping along the floor struck something heavy lying there. His fingers closed over it; he raised it up, and hardly knowing what he did, crashed it against his enemy's head.

He felt the tense muscles of the man relax, and then the weight of his inert body as it pressed down upon him. He wriggled free, and sprang to his feet. As he stood weak and trembling, looking down at the unconscious form of Targo lying upon the floor, the girl suddenly ran over and stood beside him. Her slim little body came only a little above his shoulder; instinctively he put his arm about her.

A voice, calling from outside the room, made the girl look up into his face with new terror.

"Others are coming." she whispered tensely and huddled up against him.

The Very Young Man saw that the room had two doors—the one through which he had entered, and another in one of its other walls. There were no windows. He pulled the girl now towards the further door, but she held him back.

"They come that way," she whispered.

Another voice sounded behind him and the Very Young Man knew that a man was coming up along the passage-way from the front entrance. Targo's men! He remembered now the skulking figure he had seen outside the house. There were more than two, for now he heard other voices, and some one calling Targo's name.

He held the girl closer and stood motionless. Like rats

in a trap, he thought. He felt the fingers of his right hand holding something heavy. It was a piece of stone—the stone he had looked at through the microscope—the stone with which he had struck Targo. He smiled to himself, and slipped it into his pocket.

The girl had slowly pulled him over to the inner wall of the room. The footsteps came closer. They would be here in a moment. The Very Young Man wondered how he should fight them all; then he thought of the knife that was still in the murdered man's body. He thought he ought to get it now while there was still time. He heard a click and the wall against which he and the girl were leaning yielded with their weight. A door swung open—a door the Very Young Man had not seen before. The girl pulled him through the doorway, and swung the door softly closed behind them.

The Very Young Man found himself now in a long, narrow room with a very high ceiling. It had, apparently, no other door, and no windows. It was evidently a store-room—piled high with what looked like boxes, and with bales of silks and other fabrics.

The Very Young Man looked around him hastily. Then he let go of the girl, and, since locks were unknown in this world, began piling as many heavy objects as possible against the door. The girl tried to help him, but he pushed her away. Once he put his ear to the door and listened. He heard voices outside in the strange Oroid tongue.

The girl stood beside him. "They are lifting Targo up. He speaks; he is not dead," she whispered.

For several minutes they stood there listening. The voices continued in a low murmur. "They'll know we are in here," said the Very Young Man finally, in an undertone. "Is there any other way out of this room?"

The girl shook her head. The Very Young Man for-

got the import of her answer, and suddenly found himself
thinking she was the prettiest girl he had ever seen. She
was hardly more than sixteen, with a slender, not yet
matured, yet perfectly rounded little body. She wore,
like Lylda, a short blue silk tunic, with a golden cord
crossing her breast and encircling her waist. Her raven
black hair hung in two twisted locks nearly to her knees.
Her skin was very white and, even more than Lylda's,
gleamed with iridescent color.

"Only this one door," said the girl. The words
brought the Very Young Man to himself with a start.

No other way out of the room! He knew that Targo
and his men would force their way in very soon. He
could not prevent them. But it would take time. The
Very Young Man remembered that now he had time to
take the chemicals. He put his hand to his armpit and
felt the pouch that held the drug. He wondered which to
take. The ceiling was very high; but to fight in the
narrow confines of such a room——

He led the girl over to a pile of cushions and sat down
beside her.

"Listen," he said briefly. "We are going to take a
medicine; it will make us very small. Then we will hide
from Targo and his men till they are gone. This is not
magic; it is science. Do you understand?"

"I understand," the girl answered readily. "One of
the strangers you are—my brother's friend."

"You will not be afraid to take the drug "

"No." But though she spoke confidently, she drew
closer to him and shivered a little.

The Very Young Man handed her one of the tiny pellets. "Just touch it to the tip of your tongue as I do,"
he said warningly.

They took the drug. When it had ceased to act, they
found themselves standing on the rough uneven stone sur-

face that was the floor of the room.   Far overhead in the dim luminous blackness they could just make out the great arching ceiling, stretching away out of sight down the length of the room. Beside them stood a tremendous shaggy pile of coarsely woven objects that were the silk pillows on which they had been sitting a moment before—pillows that seemed forty or fifty feet square now and loomed high above their heads.

The Very Young Man took the frightened girl by the hand and led her along the tremendous length of a pile of boxes, blocks long it seemed.   These boxes, from their size, might have been rectangular, windowless houses, jammed closely together, and piled one upon the other up into the air almost out of sight.

Finally they came to a broad passageway between the boxes—a mere crack it would have been before.   They turned into it, and, a few feet beyond, came to a larger square space with a box making a roof over it some twenty feet above their heads.

From this retreat they could see the lower part of the door leading into the other room and could hear from beyond it a muffled roar—the voices of Targo and his men. Hardly were they hidden when the door opened a little. It struck against the bales the Very Young Man had piled against it.   For a moment it held, but with the united efforts of the men pushing from the other side, it slowly yielded and swung open.

Targo stepped into the room.   To the Very Young Man he seemed nearly a hundred feet high.   Only his feet and ankles were visible at first, from where the Very Young Man was watching.   Three other men came with him.   They stamped back and forth for a time, moving some of the bales and boxes.   Luckily they left undisturbed those nearest the fugitives; after a moment they left, leaving the door open.

The Very Young Man breathed a long sigh of relief. "Gosh, I'm glad that's over." He spoke in a low tone, although the men in the other room seemed so far away they would hardly have heard him if he had shouted at the top of his voice.

Alone with the girl now in this great silent room, the Very Young Man felt suddenly embarrassed. "I am one of your brother's friends," he said. "My name's Jack; is yours Aura?"

"Lylda's sister I am," she answered quietly. "My father told me about you——" Then with a rush came the memory of her father's death, which the startling experiences of the past half-hour had made her forget. Her big, soft eyes filled with tears and her lips quivered. Involuntarily the Very Young Man put his arm about her again and held her close to him. She was so little and frail—so pathetic and so wholly adorable. For a long time they sat in silence; then the girl gently drew away.

At the doorway they stood and listened; Targo and his followers were still in the adjoining room, talking earnestly. "Loto they have captured," Aura whispered suddenly. "Others of Targo's men have taken him—in a boat—to Orlog. To-morrow they send a messenger to my brother to demand he give up these drugs—or Loto they will kill."

The Very Young Man waited, breathless. Suddenly he heard Targo laugh—a cruel, cynical laugh. Aura shuddered.

"And when he has the drug, all of us will he kill. And all in the land too who will not do as he bids."

The men were rising, evidently in preparation to leave. Aura continued: "They go—now—to Orlog—all but Targo. A little way from here, up the lake shore, a boat is waiting. It will take them there fast."

With a last look around, Targo and his followers disappeared through the back door of the room. An outer door clanged noisily, and the Very Young Man and Aura were left alone in the house.

Reoh murdered, Loto stolen! The Very Young Man thought of Lylda and wondered if anything could have happened to her. "Did they speak of your sister?" he asked.

"Targo said—he—he would put her to death," Aura answered with a shudder. "He said—she killed his brother to-day." She turned to the Very Young Man impulsively, putting her little hands up on his shoulders. "Oh, my friend," she exclaimed. "You can do something to save my family? Targo is so strong, so cruel. My father——" She stopped, and choked back a sob.

"Did they say where Lylda was now?"

"They did not know. She grew very big and went away."

"Where is your brother and my two friends?"

"Targo said they were here when he—he took Loto. Now they have gone home. He was afraid of them—now—because they have the drugs."

"To-morrow they are going to send a messenger from Orlog to demand the drugs?"

"He said to-morrow. Oh, you will do something for us? You can save Loto?"

The Very Young Man was beginning to formulate a plan. "And to-night," he asked, "from what they said—are you sure they will not hurt Loto?"

"They said no. But he is so little—so——" The girl burst into tears, and at every sob the Very Young Man's heart leaped in his breast. He wanted to comfort her, but he could think of no word to say; he wanted to help her —to do the best thing in what he saw was a grave crisis. What he should have done was to have taken her back to the Chemist and his friends, and then with them planned the rescue of Loto. But with the girl's hands upon his shoulders, and her sorrowful little tear-stained face looking up to his, he did not think of that. He thought only of her and her pathetic appeal. "You will do something, my friend? You can save Loto?" He could save Loto! With the power of the drugs he could do anything!

The Very Young Man made a sudden decision. "I don't know the way to Orlog; you do?" he asked abruptly.

"Oh yes, I know it well."

"We will go to Orlog, you and I—now, and rescue Loto. You will not be afraid?"

The girl's eyes looked into his with a clear, steady gaze. The Very Young Man stared down into their depths with his heart pounding. "I shall not be afraid—with you," said the girl softly.

The Very Young Man drew a long breath. He knew he must think it all out carefully. The drug would make them very large, and in a short time they could walk to Orlog. No harm could come to them. Once in Orlog they would find Loto—probably in Targo's palace—and bring him back with them. The Very Young Man pictured the surprise and gratification of the Chemist and his friends. Lylda would be back by then; no sooner would she have heard of Loto's loss than he would bring him back to her. Or perhaps they would meet Lylda and she would join them.

The Very Young Man produced the drug and was about to give Aura one of the pellets when another thought occurred to him. Targo would not harm Loto now because he was valuable as a hostage. But suppose he saw these two giants coming to the rescue? The Very Young Man knew that probably the boy would be killed before he could save him. That way would not do. He would have to get to Orlog unseen—rescue Loto by a sudden rush, before they could harm him.

But first it would be necessary for him and Aura to get out of Arite quietly without causing any excitement. Once in the open country they could grow larger and travel rapidly to Orlog. The Very Young Man thought it would be best to be normal size while leaving Arite. He explained his plan to Aura briefly.

It took several successive tastes of the different drugs before this result was accomplished, but in perhaps half an hour they were ready to leave the house. To the Very Young Man this change of size was no longer even startling. Aura, this time, with him beside her, seemed quite unafraid.

"Now we're ready," said the Very Young Man, in a matter-of-fact tone that was far from indicating his true feeling. "Take the way where we are least likely to be noticed—towards Orlog. When we get in the open country we can get bigger."

He led the girl across Reoh's study. She kept her face averted as they passed the body lying on the floor, and in a moment they were outside the house. They walked rapidly, keeping close to the walls of the houses. The streets were nearly deserted and no one seemed to notice them.

The Very Young Man was calculating the time. "Probably they are just getting to Orlog with Loto," he said. "Once we get out of Arite we'll travel fast; we'll have him back in two or three hours."

Aura said nothing, but walked beside him. Once or twice she looked back over her shoulder.

They were in the outskirts of the city, when suddenly the girl gripped her companion by the arm.

"Some one—behind us," she whispered. The Very Young Man resisted an impulse to look around. They had come to a cross street; the Very Young Man abruptly turned the corner, and clutching Aura by the hand ran swiftly forward a short distance. When they had slowed down to a walk again the Very Young Man looked cautiously back over his shoulder. As he did so he caught a glimpse of three men who had just reached the corner, and who darted hastily back out of sight as he turned his head.

CHAPTER XXVIII

THE ATTACK ON THE PALACE

OTEO led the two men swiftly through the city towards Reoh's house. There were few pedestrians about and no one seemed particularly to notice them. Yet somehow, the Big Business Man thought, there hung about the city an ominous air of unrest. Perhaps it was the abnormal quiet—that solemn sinister look of deserted streets; or perhaps it was an occasional face peering at them from a window, or a figure lurking in a doorway disappearing at their approach. The Big Business Man found his heart beating fast. He suddenly felt very much alone. The realization came to him that he was in a strange world, surrounded by beings of another race, most of whom, he knew now, hated and feared him and those who had come with him.

Then his thoughts took another turn. He looked up at the brilliant galaxy of stars overhead. New, unexplored worlds! Thousands, millions of them! In one tiny, little atom of a woman's wedding-ring! Then he thought of his friend the Banker. Perhaps the ring had not been moved from its place in the clubroom. Then—he looked at the sky again—then Broadway—only thirty feet away from him this moment! He smiled a little at this conception, and drew a long breath—awed by his thoughts.

Oteo was plucking at his sleeve and pointing. Across the street stood Reoh's house. The Doctor knocked upon its partially open front door, and, receiving no answer, they entered silently, with the dread sense of impending

234

evil hanging over them. The Doctor led the way into the old man's study. At the threshold he stopped, shocked into immobility. Upon the floor, with the knife still in it, lay Reoh's body. The Doctor made a hasty examination, although the presence of the knife obviously made it unnecessary.

A hurried search of the house convinced them that Aura and the Very Young Man were not there. The two men, confused by this double disaster, were at a loss to know what to do.

"They've got him," said the Big Business Man with conviction. "And the girl too, probably. He must have come back just as they were killing Reoh."

"There wasn't much time," the Doctor said. "He was back here in ten minutes. But they've got him—you're right—or he would have been back with us before this."

"They'll take him and the girl to Orlog. They won't hurt them because they——" The Big Business Man stopped abruptly; his face went white. "Good God, Frank, do you realize? They've got the drugs now!"

Targo had the drugs! The Big Business Man shuddered with fear at the thought. Their situation would be desperate, indeed, if that were so.

The Doctor reasoned it out more calmly. "I hadn't thought of that," he said slowly. "And it makes me think perhaps they have not captured Jack. If they had the drugs they would lose no time in using them. They haven't used them yet—that's evident."

The Big Business Man was about to reply when there came a shouting from the street outside, and the sound of many feet rushing past the house. They hurried to the door. A mob swept by—a mob of nearly a thousand persons. Most of them were men. Some were armed with swords; others brandished huge stones or lengths of beaten gold implements, perhaps with which they had been working, and which now they held as weapons.

The mob ran swiftly, with vainglorious shouts from its leaders. It turned a corner near-by and disappeared.

From every house now people appeared, and soon the streets were full of scurrying pedestrians. Most of them followed the direction taken by the mob. The listeners in the doorway could hear now, from far away, the sound of shouts and cheering. And from all around them came the buzz and hum of busy streets. The city was thoroughly awake—alert and expectant.

The Big Business Man flung the door wide. "I'm going to follow that crowd. See what's going on. We can't stay here in the midst of this."

The Doctor and Oteo followed him out into the street, and they mingled with the hastening crowd. In their excitement they walked freely among the people. No one appeared to notice them, for the crowd was as excited as they, hurrying along, heedless of its immediate surroundings. As they advanced, the street became more congested.

Down another street they saw fighting going on—a weaponless crowd swaying and struggling aimlessly. A number of armed men charged this crowd—men who by their breast-plates and swords the Big Business Man recognized as the police. The crowd ceased struggling and dispersed, only to gather again in another place.

The city was in a turmoil of excitement without apparent reason, or definite object. Yet there was a steady tide in the direction the first armed mob had gone, and with that tide went the Big Business Man and his two companions.

After a time they came to an open park, beyond which, on a prominence, with the lake behind, stood a large building that the Chemist had already pointed out to them as the king's palace.

Oteo led them swiftly into a side street to avoid the dense crowd around the park. Making a slight detour they came back to it again—much nearer the palace now—and approached from behind a house that fronted the open space near the palace.

"Friend of the Master—his house!" Oteo explained as he knocked peremptorily at a side door.

They waited a moment, but no one came. Oteo pushed the door and led them within. The house was deserted, and following Oteo, they went to the roof. Here they could see perfectly what was going on around the palace, and in the park below them.

This park was nearly triangular in shape—a thousand feet possibly on each side. At the base of the triangle, on a bluff with the lake behind it, stood the palace. Its main entrance, two huge golden doors, stood at the top of a broad flight of stone steps. On these steps a fight was in progress. A mob surged up them, repulsed at the top by a score or more of men armed with swords, who were defending the doorway.

The square was thronged with people watching the palace steps and shouting almost continuously. The fight before the palace evidently had been in progress for some time. Many dead were lying in the doorway and on the steps below it. The few defenders had so far resisted successfully against tremendous odds, for the invaders, pressed upward by those behind, could not retreat, and were being killed at the top from lack of space in which to fight.

"Look there," cried the Big Business Man suddenly. Coming down a cross street, marching in orderly array with its commander in front, was a company of soldier police. It came to a halt almost directly beneath the watchers on the roof-tops, and its leader brandishing his sword after a moment of hesitation, ordered his men to charge the crowd. They did not move at the order, but stood sullenly in their places. Again he ordered them forward, and, as they refused to obey, made a threatening move towards them.

In sudden frenzy, those nearest leaped upon him, and in an instant he lay dead upon the ground, with half a dozen swords run through his body. Then the men stood, in formation still, apathetically watching the events that were going on around them.

Meanwhile the fight on the palace steps raged more furiously than ever. The defenders were reduced now to a mere handful.

"A moment more—they'll be in," said the Doctor breathlessly. Hardly had he spoken when, with a sudden, irresistible rush, the last of the guards were swept away, and the invaders surged through the doorway into the palace.

A great cry went up from the crowd in the park as the palace was taken—a cry of applause mingled with awe, for they were a little frightened at what they were seeing.

Perhaps a hundred people crowded through the doorway into the palace; the others stood outside—on the steps and on the terrace below—waiting. Hardly more than five minutes went by when a man appeared on the palace roof. He advanced to the parapet with several others standing respectfully behind him.

"Targo!" murmered Oteo.

It was Targo—Targo triumphantly standing with uplifted arms before the people he was to rule. When the din that was raised at his appearance had subsided a little he spoke; one short sentence, and then he paused. There was a moment of indecision in the crowd before it broke into tumultuous cheers.

"The king—he killed," Oteo said softly, looking at his master's friends with big, frightened eyes.

The Big Business Man stared out over the waving, cheering throng, with the huge, dominant, triumphant figure of Targo above and muttered to himself, "The king is dead; long live the king."

When he could make himself heard, Targo spoke again. The Doctor and the Big Business Man were leaning over the parapet watching the scene, when suddenly a stone flew up from the crowd beneath, and struck the railing within a few feet of where they were standing. They glanced down in surprise, and realized, from the faces that were upturned, that they were recognized. A murmur ran over the crowd directly below, and then someone raised a shout. Four words it seemed to be, repeated over and over. Gradually the shout spread—"Death to the Giants," the Big Business Man knew it was—"Death to the Giants," until the whole mass of people were calling it rhythmically—drowning out Targo's voice completely. A thousand faces now stared up at the men on the roof-top and a rain of stones began falling around them.

The Doctor clutched his friend by the arm and pulled him back from the parapet. "They know us—good God, don't you see?" he said tensely. "Come on. We must get out of this. There'll be trouble." He started across the roof towards the opening that led down into the house.

The Big Business Man jerked himself free from the grasp that held him.

"I do see," he cried a little wildly. "I do see we've been damn fools. There'll be trouble. You're right—there will be trouble; but it won't be ours. I'm through—through with this miserable little atom and its swarm of insects." He gripped the Doctor by both shoulders. "My God, Frank, can't you understand? We're men, you and I—men! These creatures"—he waved his arm back towards the city—"nothing but insects—infinitesimal—

smaller than the smallest thing we ever dreamed of. And we take them seriously. Don't you understand? Seriously! God, man, that's funny, not tragic."

He fumbled at the neck of his robe, and tearing it away, brought out a vial of the drugs.

"Here," he exclaimed, and offered one of the pellets.

"Not too much," warned the Doctor vehemently, "only touch it to your tongue."

Oteo, with pleading eyes, watched them taking the drug, and the Doctor handed him a pellet, showing him how to take it.

As they stood together upon the roof-top, clinging to one another, the city dwindled away rapidly beneath them. By the time the drug had ceased to act there was hardly room for them to stand on the roof, and the house, had it not been built solidly of stone, would have been crushed under their weight. At first they felt a little dizzy, as though they were hanging in mid-air, or were in a balloon, looking down at the city. Then gradually, they seemed to be of normal size again, balancing themselves awkwardly upon a little toy-house whose top was hardly bigger than their feet.

The park, only a step now beneath the house-top, swarmed with tiny figures less than two inches in height. Targo still stood upon the palace roof; they could have reached down and picked him up between thumb and forefinger. The whole city lay within a radius of a few hundred feet around them.

When they had stopped increasing in size, they leaped in turn over the palace, landing upon the broad beach of the lake. Then they began walking along it. There was only room for one on the sand, and the other two, for they walked abreast, waded ankle-deep in the water. From the little city below them they could hear the hum of a myriad of tiny voices—thin, shrill and faint. Suddenly the Big Business Man laughed. There was no hysteria in his voice now—just amusement and relief.

"And we took that seriously," he said. "Funny, isn't it?"

CHAPTER XXIX

ON THE LAKE

"YOU'RE right—we are being followed," the Very Young Man said soberly. He had pulled the girl over close against the wall of a house. "Did you see that?"

"Three, they are," Aura answered. "I saw them before—in the street below—Targo's men."

Evidently the three men had been watching the house from which they had come and had followed them from there. If they were Targo's men, as seemed very probable, the Very Young Man could not understand why they had not already attacked him. Perhaps they intended to as soon as he and Aura had reached a more secluded part of the city. They must know he had the drugs, and to gain possession of those certainly was what they were striving for. The Very Young Man realized he must take no chances; to lose the drugs would be fatal to them all.

"Are we near the edge of the city?" he asked.

"Yes, very near."

"Then we shall get large here. If we make a run for it we will be in the country before we are big enough to attrack too much attention. Understand, Aura?"

"I understand."

"We mustn't stir up the city if we can help it; with giants running around, the people would get worked up to a frenzy. You could see that with Lylda this afternoon. Not that you can blame them altogether, but we want to

get Loto back before we start anything here in Arite."
He took the pellets out as he spoke, and they each touched
one of them to the tip of their tongues.

"Now, then, come on—not too fast, we want to keep
going," said the Very Young Man, taking the girl by the
hand again.

As they started off, running slowly down the street, the
Very Young Man looked back. The three men were
running after them—not fast, seeming content merely to
keep their distance. The Very Young Man laughed.
"Wait till they see us get big. Fine chance they've got."

Aura, her lithe, young body in perfect condition, ran
lightly and easily as a fawn. She made a pretty picture
as she ran, with her long, black hair streaming out behind
her, and the short silk tunic flapping about her lean,
round thighs. She still held the Very Young Man by the
hand, running just in advance of him, guiding him
through the streets, which in this part of the city were
more broken up and irregular.

They had not gone more than a hundred yards when
the pavement began to move unsteadily under them, as the
deck of a plunging ship feels to one who runs its length,
and the houses they were swiftly passing began visibly to
decrease in size. The Very Young Man felt the girl
falter in her stride. He dropped her hand and slipped his
arm about her waist, holding her other hand against it.
She smiled up into his eyes, and thus they ran on, side by
side.

A few moments more and they were in the open
country, running on a road that wound through the hills,
between cultivated fields dotted here and there with
houses. The landscape dwindled beneath them steadily,
until they seemed to be running along a narrow, curving
path, bordered by little patches of different-colored
ground, like a checkerboard. The houses they passed

now hardly reached as high as their knees. Sometimes peasants stood in the doorways of these houses watching them in terror. Occasionally they passed a farmer ploughing his field, who stopped his work, stricken dumb, and stared at them as they went swiftly by.

When they were well out into the country, perhaps a quarter of the way to Orlog—for to beings so huge as they the distance was not great—the Very Young Man slowed down to a walk.

"How far have we gone?" he asked.

Aura stopped abruptly and looked around her. They seemed now to be at the bottom of a huge, circular, shallow bowl. In every direction from where they stood the land curved upward towards the rim of the bowl that was the horizon—a line, not sharp and well defined, but dim and hazy, melting away into the blackness of the star-studded sky. Behind them, hardly more than a mile away, according to their present stature—they had stopped growing entirely now—lay the city of Arite. They could see completely across it and out into the country beyond.

The lake, with whose shore they had been running parallel, was much closer to them. Ahead, up near the rim of the horizon, lay a black smudge. Aura pointed. "Orlog is there," she said. "You see it?"

To the Very Young Man suddenly came the realization that already he was facing the problem of how to get into Orlog unheralded. If they remained in their present size they could easily walk there in an hour or less. But long before that they would be seen and recognized.

The Very Young Man feared for Loto's safety if he allowed that to happen. He seemed to be able to make out the city of Orlog now. It was smaller than Arite, and lay partially behind a hill, with most of its houses strung along the lake shore. If only they were not so tall they could not be seen so readily. But if they became smaller it would take them much longer to get there. And eventually they would have to become normal Oroid size, or even smaller, in order to get into the city unnoticed.. The Very Young Man thought of the lake. Perhaps that would be the best way.

"Can you swim?" he asked. And Aura, with her ready smile, answered that she could. "If we are in the water," she added, seeming to have followed his thoughts, "they would not see us. I can swim very far—can you?"

The Very Young Man nodded.

"If we could get near to Orlog in the water," he said, "we might get a boat. And then when we were small, we could sail up. They wouldn't see us then."

"There are many boats," answered the girl in agreement. "Look!"

There were, indeed, on the lake, within sight of them now, several boats. "We must get the one nearest Orlog," the Very Young Man said. "Or else it will beat us in and carry the news."

In a few minutes more they were at the lake shore. The Very Young Man wore, underneath his robe, a close-fitting knitted garment very much like a bathing-suit. He took off his robe now, and rolling it up, tied it across his back with the cord he had worn around his waist. Aura's tunic was too short to impede her swimming and when the Very Young Man was ready, they waded out into the water together. They found the lake no deeper than to Aura's shoulders, but as it was easier to swim than to wade, they began swimming—away from shore towards the farthest boat that evidently was headed for Orlog.

The Very Young Man thought with satisfaction that, with only their heads visible, huge as they would appear, they could probably reach this boat without being seen by

any one in Orlog.   The boat was perhaps a quarter of a
mile from them—a tiny little toy vessel, it seemed, that
they never would have seen except for its sail.

They came up to it rapidly, for they were swimming
very much faster than it could sail, passing close to one
of the others and nearly swamping it by the waves they
made.   As they neared the boat they were pursuing—it
was different from any the Very Young Man had seen so
far, a single, canoe-shaped hull, with out-riders on both
sides—they could see it held but a single occupant, a man
who sat in its stern—a figure about as long as one of the
Very Young Man's fingers.

The Very Young Man and Aura were swimming side
by side, now.   The water was perfect in temperature—
neither too hot nor too cold; they had not been swimming fast, and were not winded.

"We've got him, what'll we do with him," the Very
Young Man wanted to know in dismay, as the thought
occurred to him,   He might have been more puzzled at
how to take the drug to make them smaller while they
were swimming, but Aura's answer solved both problems.

"There is an island," she said flinging an arm up out of
the water.   "We can push the boat to it, and him we can
leave there.   Is that not the thing to do?"

"You bet your life," the Very Young Man agreed, enthusiastically.   "That's just the thing to do."

As they came within reach of the boat the Very Young
Man stopped swimming and found that the water was
not much deeper than his waist.   The man in the boat appeared now about to throw himself into the lake from
fright.

"Tell him, Aura," the Very Young Man said.   "We
won't hurt him."

Wading through the water, they pushed the boat with
its terrified occupant carefully in front of them towards

the island, which was not more than two or three hundred yards away. The Very Young Man found this rather slow work; becoming impatient, he seized the boat in his hand, pinning the man against its seat with his fore-finger so he would not fall out. Then raising the boat out of the water over his head he waded forward much more rapidly.

The island, which they reached in a few moments more, was circular in shape, and about fifty feet in diameter. It had a beach entirely around it; a hill perhaps ten feet high rose near its center, and at one end it was heavily wooded. There were no houses to be seen.

The Very Young Man set the boat back on the water, and they pushed it up on the beach. When it grounded the tiny man leaped out and ran swiftly along the sand. The Very Young Man and Aura laughed heartily as they stood ankle-deep in the water beside the boat, watching him. For nearly five minutes he ran; then suddenly he ducked inland and disappeared in the woods.

When they were left alone they lost no time in becoming normal Oroid size. The boat now appeared about twenty-five feet long—a narrow, canoe-shaped hull hollowed out of a tree-trunk. They climbed into it, and with a long pole they found lying in its bottom, the Very Young Man shoved it off the beach.

CHAPTER XXX

THE boat had a mast stepped near the bow, and a triangular cloth sail. The Very Young Man sat in the stern, steering with a short, broad-bladed paddle; Aura lay on a pile of rushes in the bottom of the boat, looking up at him.

For about half a mile the Very Young Man sailed along parallel with the beach, looking for the man they had marooned. He was nowhere in sight, and they finally headed out into the lake towards Orlog, which they could just see dimly on the further shore.

The breeze was fresh, and they made good time. The boat steered easily, and the Very Young Man, reclining on one elbow, with Aura at his feet, felt at peace with himself and with the world. Again he thought this girl the prettiest he had ever seen. There was something, too, of a spiritual quality in the delicate smallness of her features —a sweetness of expression in her quick, understanding smile, and an honest clearness in her steady gaze that somehow he seemed never to have seen in a girl's face before.

He felt again, now that he had time to think more of her, that same old diffidence that had come to him before when they were alone in the store-room of her home. That she did not share this feeling was obvious from the frankness and ease of her manner.

For some time after leaving the island neither spoke. The Very Young Man felt the girl's eyes fixed almost constantly upon him—a calm gaze that held in it a great curiosity and wonderment. He steered steadily onward towards Orlog. There was, for the moment, nothing to discuss concerning their adventure, and he wondered what he should say to this girl who stared at him so frankly. Then he met her eyes, and again she smiled with that perfect sense of comradeship he had so seldom felt with women of his own race.

"You're very beautiful," said the Very Young Man abruptly.

The girl's eyes widened a little, but she did not drop her lashes. "I want to be beautiful; if you think it is so, I am very glad."

"I do. I think you're the prettiest girl I ever saw." He blurted out the words impetuously. He was very earnest, very sincere, and very young.

A trace of coquetry came into the girl's manner. "Prettier than the girls of your world? Are they not pretty?"

"Oh, yes—of course; but——"

"What?" she asked when he paused.

The Very Young Man considered a moment. "You're —you're different," he said finally. She waited. "You —you don't know how to flirt, for one thing."

The girl turned her head away and looked at him a little sidewise through lowered lashes.

"How do you know that?" she asked demurely; and the Very Young Man admitted to himself with a shock of surprise that he certainly was totally wrong in that deduction at least.

"Tell me of the girls in your world," she went on after a moment's silence. "My sister's husband many times he has told me of the wonderful things up there in that great land. But more I would like to hear."

He told her, with an eloquence and enthusiasm born of

youth, about his own life and those of his people. She questioned eagerly and with an intelligence that surprised him, for she knew far more of the subject than he realized.

"These girls of your country," she interrupted him once. "They, too, are very beautiful; they wear fine clothes—I know—my brother he has told me."

"Yes," said the Very Young Man.

"And are they very learned—very clever—do they work and govern, like the men?"

"Some are very learned. And they are beginning to govern, like the men; but not so much as you do here."

The girl's forehead wrinkled. "My brother he once told me," she said slowly, "that in your world many women are bad. Is that so?"

"Some are, of course. And some men think that most are. But I don't; I think women are splendid."

"If that is so, then better I can understand what I have heard," the girl answered thoughtfully. "If Oroid women were as I have heard my brother talk of some of yours, this world of ours would soon be full of evil."

"You are different," the Very Young Man said quickly. "You—and Lylda."

"The women here, they have kept the evil out of life," the girl went on. "It is their duty—their responsibility to their race. Your good women—they have not always governed as we have. Why is that?"

"I do not know," the Very Young Man admitted. "Except because the men would not let them."

"Why not, if they are just as learned as the men?" The girl was smiling—a little roguish, twisted smile.

"There are very clever girls," the Very Young Man went on hastily; he found himself a little on the defensive, and he did not know just why. "They are able to do things in the world. But—many men do not like them."

Aura was smiling openly now, and her eyes twinkled with mischief. "Perhaps it is the men are jealous. Could that not be so?"

The Very Young Man did not answer, and the girl went on more seriously. "The women of my race, they are very just. Perhaps you know that, Jack. Often has my brother told us of his own great world and of its problems. And the many things he has told us—Lylda and I—we have often wondered. For every question has its other side, and we cannot judge—from him alone."

The Very Young Man, surprised at the turn their conversation had taken, and confused a little by this calm logic from a girl—particularly from so young and pretty a girl—was at a loss how to go on.

"You cannot understand, Aura," he finally said seriously. "Women may be all kinds; some are bad—some are good. Down here I know it is not that way. Sometimes when a girl is smart she thinks she is smarter than any living man. You would not like that sort of girl would you?"

"My brother never said it just that way," she answered with equal seriousness. "No, that would be bad—very bad. In our land women are only different from men. They know they are not better or worse—only different."

The Very Young Man was thinking of a girl he once knew. "I hate clever girls," he blurted out.

Aura's eyes were teasing him again. "I am so sorry," she said sadly.

The Very Young Man looked his surprise. "Why are you sorry?"

"My sister, she once told me I was clever. My brother said it, too, and I believed them."

The Very Young Man flushed.

"You're different," he repeated.

"How—different?" She was looking at him sidewise again.

"I don't know; I've been trying to think—but you are. And I don't hate you—I like you—very, very much."

"I like you, too," she answered frankly, and the Very Young Man thought of Loto as she said it. He was leaning down towards her, and their hands met for an instant.

The Very Young Man had spread his robe out to dry when he first got into the boat, and now he put it on while Aura steered. Then he sat beside her on the seat, taking the paddle again.

"Do you go often to the theater?" she asked after a time.

"Oh, yes, often."

"Nothing like that do we have here," she added, a little wistfully. "Only once, when we played a game in the field beyond my brother's home. Lylda was the queen and I her lady. And do you go to the opera, too? My brother he has told me of the opera. How wonderful must that be! So beautiful—more beautiful even it must be than Lylda's music. But never shall it be for me." She smiled sadly: "Never shall I be able to hear it."

An eager contradiction sprang to the Very Young Man's lips, but the girl shook her head quietly.

For several minutes they did not speak. The wind behind them blew the girl's long hair forward over her shoulders. A lock of it fell upon the Very Young Man's hand as it lay on the seat between them, and unseen he twisted it about his fingers. The wind against his neck felt warm and pleasant; the murmur of the water flowing past sounded low and sweet and soothing. Overhead the stars hung very big and bright. It was like sailing on a perfect night in his own world. He was very conscious of the girl's nearness now—conscious of the clinging softness of her hair about his fingers. And all at once he found himself softly quoting some half-forgotten lines:

> "If I were king, ah, love! If I were king
> What tributary nations I would bring
> To bow before your scepter and to swear
> Allegiance to your lips and eyes and hair."

Aura's questioning glance of surprise brought him to himself. "That is so pretty—what is that?" she asked eagerly. "Never have I heard one speak like that before."

"Why, that's poetry; haven't you ever heard any poetry?"

The girl shook her head. "It's just like music—it sings. Do it again."

The Very Young Man suddenly felt very self-conscious.

"Do it again—please." She looked pleadingly up into his face and the Very Young Man went on:

> "Beneath your feet what treasures I would fling!
> The stars would be your pearls upon a string;
> The world a ruby for your finger-ring;
> And you could have the sun and moon to wear
> If I were king."

The girl clapped her hands artlessly. "Oh, that is so pretty. Never did I know that words could sound like that. Say it some more, please."

And the Very Young Man, sitting under the stars beside this beautiful little creature of another world, searched into his memory and for her who never before had known that words could rhyme, opened up the realm of poetry.

CHAPTER XXXI

THE PALACE OF ORLOG

ENGROSSED with each other the Very Young Man and Aura sailed close up to the water-front of Orlog before they remembered their situation. It was the Very Young Man who first became aware of the danger. Without explanation he suddenly pulled Aura into the bottom of the boat, leaving it to flutter up into the wind unguided.

"They might see us from here," he said hurriedly. "We must decide what is best for us to do now."

They were then less than a quarter of a mile from the stone quay that marked the city's principal landing-place. Nearer to them was a broad, sandy beach behind which, in a long string along the lake shore, lay the city. Its houses were not unlike those of Arite, although most of them were rather smaller and less pretentious. On a rise of ground just beyond the beach, and nearly in front of them, stood an elaborate building that was Targo's palace.

"We daren't go much closer," the Very Young Man said. "They'd recognize us."

"You they would know for one of the strangers," said Aura. "But if I should steer and you were hidden no one would notice."

The Very Young Man realized a difficulty. "We've got to be very small when we go into the city."

"How small would you think?" asked Aura.

The Very Young Man held his hands about a foot apart. "You see, the trouble is, we must be small enough to get around without too much danger of being seen; but if we get too small it would be a terrible walk up there to Targo's palace."

"We cannot sail this boat if we are such a size," Aura declared. "Too large it would be for us to steer."

"That's just it, but we can't go any closer this way."

Aura thought a moment. "If you lie there," she indicated the bottom of the boat under a forward seat, "no one can see. And I will steer—there to the beach ahead; me they will not notice. Then at the beach we will take the drug."

"We've got to take a chance," said the Very Young Man. "Some one may come along and see us getting small."

They talked it over very carefully for some time. Finally they decided to follow Aura's plan and run the boat to the beach under her guidance; then to take the drug. There were few people around the lake front at this hour; the beach itself, as far as they could see, was entirely deserted, and the danger of discovery seemed slight. Aura pointed out, however, that once on shore, if their stature were so great as a foot they would be even more conspicuous than when of normal size even allowing for the strangeness of the Very Young Man's appearance. The Very Young Man made a calculation and reached the conclusion that with a height of six or seven inches they would have to walk about a mile from the landing-place to reach Targo's palace. They decided to become as near that size as they conveniently could.

When both fully understood what they intended to do, the Very Young Man gave Aura one of the pellets of the drug and lay down in the bow of the boat. Without a word the girl took her seat in the stern and steered for the beach. When they were close inshore Aura signalled her companion and at the same moment both took the drug. Then she left her seat and lay down beside the Very Young Man. The boat, from the momentum it had gained, floated inshore and grounded gently on the beach.

As they lay there, the Very Young Man could see the sides of the boat growing up steadily above their heads. The gunwale was nearly six feet above them before he realized a new danger. Scrambling to his feet he pulled the girl up with him; even when standing upright their heads came below the sides of the vessel.

"We've got to get out right now," the Very Young Man said in an excited whisper. "We'd be too small." He led the girl hastily into the bow and with a running leap clambered up and sat astride the gunwale. Then, reaching down he pulled Aura up beside him.

In a moment they had dropped overboard up to their shoulders in the water. High overhead loomed the hull of the boat—a large sailing vessel it seemed to them now. They started wading towards shore immediately, but, because they were so rapidly diminishing in size, it was nearly five minutes before they could get there.

Once on shore they lay prone upon the sand, waiting for the drug to cease its action. When, by proper administering of both chemicals, they had reached approximately their predetermined stature, which, in itself, required considerable calculation on the Very Young Man's part, they stood up near the water's edge and looked about them.

The beach to them now, with its coarse-grained sand, seemed nearly a quarter of a mile wide; in length it extended as far as they could see in both directions. Beyond the beach, directly in front of them on a hill perhaps a thousand feet above the lake level, and about a mile or more away, stood Targo's palace. To the Very Young Man it looked far larger than any building he had ever seen.

The boat in which they had landed lay on the water with its bow on the beach beside them. It was now a vessel some two hundred and fifty feet in length, with sides twenty feet high and a mast towering over a hundred feet in the air.

There was no one in sight from where they stood. "Come on, Aura," said the Very Young Man, and started off across the beach towards the hill.

It was a long walk through the heavy sand to the foot of the hill. When they arrived they found themselves at the beginning of a broad stone roadway—only a path to those of normal Oroid size—that wound back and forth up the hill to the palace. They walked up this road, and as they progressed, saw that it was laid through a grassy lawn that covered the entire hillside—a lawn with gray-blue blades of grass half as high as their bodies.

After walking about ten minutes they came to a short flight of steps. Each step was twice as high as their heads—impossible of ascent—so they made a detour through the grass.

Suddenly Aura clutched the Very Young Man by the arm with a whispered exclamation, and they both dropped to the ground. A man was coming down the roadway; he was just above the steps when they first saw him—a man so tall that, standing beside him, they would have reached hardy above his ankles. The long grass in which they were lying hid them effectually from his sight and he passed them by unnoticed. When he was gone the Very Young Man drew a long breath. "We must watch that," he said apprehensively. "If any one sees us now it's all off. We must be extremely careful."

It took the two adventurers over an hour to get safely up the hill and into the palace. Its main entrance, approached by a long flight of steps, was an impossible means of ingress, but Aura fortunately knew of a smaller door at the side which led into the basement of the building. This door they found slightly ajar. It was open so little, however, that they could not get past, and as they were not strong enough even with their combined efforts, to swing the door open, they were again brought to a halt.

"We'd better get still smaller," the Very Young Man whispered somewhat nervously. "There's less danger that way."

They reduced their size, perhaps one half, and when that was accomplished the crack in the door had widened sufficiently to let them in. Within the building they found themselves in a hallway several hundred feet wide and half a mile or more in length—its ceiling high as the roof of some great auditorium. The Very Young Man looked about in dismay. "Great Scott," he ejaculated, "this won't do at all."

"Many times I have been here," said Aura. "It looks so very different now, but I think I know the way."

"That may be," agreed the Very Young Man dubiously, "but we'd have to walk miles if we stay as small as this."

A heavy tread sounded far away in the distance. The Very Young Man and Aura shrank back against the wall, close by the door. In a moment a man's feet and the lower part of his legs came into view. He stopped by the door, pulling it inward. The Very Young Man looked up into the air; a hundred and fifty feet, perhaps, above their heads he saw the man's face looking out through the doorway.

In a moment another man joined him, coming from outside, and they spoke together for a time. Their roaring voices, coming down from this great height, were nevertheless distinctly audible.

"In the audience room," Aura whispered, after listening an instant, "Targo's younger brother talks with his counsellors. Big things they are planning." The Very Young Man did not answer; the two men continued their brief conversation and parted.

When the Very Young Man and Aura were left alone, he turned to the girl eagerly. "Did they mention Loto? Is he here?"

"Of him they did not speak," Aura answered. "It is best that we go to the audience room, where they are talking. Then, perhaps, we will know." The Very Young Man agreed, and they started off.

For nearly half an hour they trudged onward along this seemingless endless hallway. Then again they were confronted with a flight of steps—this time steps that were each more than three times their own height.

"We've got to chance it," said the Very Young Man, and after listening carefully and hearing no one about, they again took the drug, making themselves sufficiently large to ascend these steps to the upper story of the building.

It was nearly an hour before the two intruders, after several narrow escapes from discovery, and by alternating doses of both drugs, succeeded in getting into the room where Targo's brother and his advisers were in conference.

They entered through the open door—a doorway so wide that a hundred like them could have marched through it abreast. A thousand feet away across the vastness of the room they could see Targo's brother and ten of his men—sitting on mats upon the floor, talking earnestly. Before them stood a stone bench on which were a number of golden goblets and plates of food.

The adventurers ran swiftly down the length of the room, following its wall. It echoed with their footfalls, but they knew that this sound, so loud to their ears, would be inaudible to the huge figures they were approaching.

"They won't see us," whispered the Very Young Man, "let's get up close." And in a few moments more they were standing beside one of the figures, sheltered from sight by a corner of the mat upon which the man was sitting. His foot, bent sidewise under him upon the floor, was almost within reach of the Very Young Man's hand. The fibre thong that fastened its sandal looked like a huge rope thick as the Very Young Man's ankle, and each of its toes were half as long as his entire body.

Targo's brother, a younger man than those with him, appeared to be doing most of the talking. He it was beside whom Aura and the Very Young Man were standing.

"You tell me if they mention Loto," whispered the Very Young Man. Aura nodded and they stood silent, listening. The men all appeared deeply engrossed with what their leader was saying. The Very Young Man, watching his companion's face, saw an expression of concern and fear upon it. She leaned towards him.

"In Arite, to-night," she whispered, "Targo is organizing men to attack the palace of the king. Him will they kill—then Targo will be proclaimed leader of all the Oroid nation."

"We must get back," the Very Young Man answered in an anxious whisper. "I wish we knew where Loto was; haven't they mentioned him—or any of us?"

Aura did not reply, and the Very Young Man waited silent. Once one of the men laughed—a laugh that drifted out into the immense distances of the room in great waves of sound. Aura gripped her companion by the arm.

"Then when Targo rules the land, they will send a messenger to my brother. Him they will tell that the drugs must be given to Targo, or Loto will be killed—wait—when they have the drugs," Aura translated in a swift, tense whisper, "then all of us they will kill." She shuddered. "And with the drugs they will rule as they desire—for evil."

"They'll never get them," the Very Young Man muttered.

Targo's brother leaned forward and raised a goblet from the table. The movement of his foot upon the floor made the two eavesdroppers jump aside to avoid being struck.

Again Aura grasped her companion by the arm. "He is saying Loto is upstairs," she whispered after a moment. "I know where."

"I knew it," said the Very Young Man exultingly. "You take us there. Come on—let's get out of here—we mustn't waste a minute."

They started back towards the wall nearest them—some fifty feet away—and following along its edge, ran down towards the doorway through which they had entered the room. They were still perhaps a hundred yards away from it, running swiftly, when there appeared in the doorway the feet and legs of two men who were coming in. The Very Young Man and Aura stopped abruptly, shrinking up against the side of the wall. Then there came a a heavy metallic clanging sound; the two men entered the room, closing the door.

CHAPTER XXXII

"WE'LL have to get smaller," said the Doctor. "There's Rogers' house."

They had been walking along the beach from the king's palace hardly more than a hundred yards. The Doctor and the Big Business Man were in front, and Oteo, wide-eyed and solemn, was close behind them.

The Doctor was pointing down at the ground a few feet ahead. There, at a height just above their ankles, stood the Chemist's house—a little building whose roof did not reach more than half-way to their knees, even though it stood on higher ground than the beach upon which they were walking. On the roof they could see two tiny figures—the Chemist and Lylda—waving their arms.

The Big Business Man stopped short. "Now see here, Frank, let's understand this. We've been fooling with this thing too damned long. We've made a hell of a mess of it, you know that." He spoke determinedly, with a profanity unusual with him. The Doctor did not answer.

"We got here—yesterday. We found a peaceful world. Dissatisfaction in it—yes. But certainly a more peaceful world than the one we left. We've been here one day—one day, Frank, and now look at things. This child, Loto—stolen. Jack disappeared—God knows what's happened to him. A revolution—the whole place in an uproar. All in one day, since we took our place in this world and tried to mix up in its affairs."

"It's time to call a halt, Frank. If only we can get Jack back. That's the bad part—we've got to find Jack. And then get out; we don't belong here anyway. It's nothing to us—why, man, look at it." He waved his arm out over the city. In the street beside them they could see a number of little figures no bigger than their fingers, staring up into the air. "What is all that to us now, as we stand here. Nothing. Nothing but a kid's toy; with little animated mannikins for a child to play with."

"We've got to find Jack," said the Doctor.

"Certainly we have—and then get out. We're oniy hurting these little creatures, anyway, by being here."

"But there's Rogers and Lylda," added the Doctor. "And Loto and Lylda's sister."

"Take them with us. They'll have to go—they can't stay here now. But we must find Jack—that's the main thing."

"Look," the Doctor said, moving forward. "They're shouting to us."

They walked up and bent over the Chemist's house. Their friend was making a funnel of his hands and trying to attract their attention. The Big Business Man knelt upon the beach and put his head down beside the house. "Make yourselves smaller," he heard the Chemist shouting in a shrill little voice.

"We think it best not to. You must come up to us. Serious things have happened. Take the drug now— then we'll tell you." The Big Business Man, with his knees upon the beach, had one hand on the sand and the other at the gate of Lylda's garden. His face was just above the roof-top.

The two little figures consulted a moment; then the Chemist shouted up, "All right; wait," and he and Lylda disappeared into the house. A moment afterwards they reappeared in the garden; Eena was with them. They crossed the garden and turned into the street towards the flight of steps that led down to the lake.

The Big Business Man had regained his feet and was standing ankle-deep in the water talking to the Doctor when Oteo suddenly plucked at his sleeve.

"The Master—" he cried. The youth was staring down into the street, with a look of terror on his face. The Big Business Man followed the direction of his glance; at the head of the steps a number of men had rushed upon the Chemist and the two women, and were dragging them back up the hill. The Big Business Man hesitated only a moment; then he reached down and plucking a little figure from one of the struggling groups, flung it back over his shoulder into the lake.

The other assailants did not run, as he had expected, so he gently pried them apart with his fingers from their captives, and, one by one, flung them into the air behind him. One who struck Lylda, he squashed upon the flag-stones of the street with his thumb.

Only one escaped. He had been holding Eena; when he saw he was the last, he suddenly dropped his captive and ran shrieking up the hill into the city.

The Big Business Man laughed grimly, and got upon his feet a little unsteadily. His face was white.

"You see, Frank," he said, and his voice trembled a little. "Good God, suppose we had been that size, too."

In a few moments more the Chemist, Lylda and Eena had taken the drug and were as large as the others. All six stood in the water beside the Chemist's house. The Chemist had not spoken while he was growing; now he greeted his friends quietly. "A close call, gentlemen. I thank you." He smiled approvingly at the Big Business Man.

Eena and Oteo stood apart from the others. The girl was obviously terror-stricken by the experiences she had undergone. Oteo put his arm across her shoulders, and spoke to her reassuringly.

"Where is Jack?" Lylda asked anxiously. "And my father—and Aura?" The Big Business Man thought her face looked years older than when he had last seen it. Her expression was set and stern, but her eyes stared into his with a gentle, sorrowful gaze that belied the sternness of her lips.

They told her, as gently as they could, of the death of her father and the disappearance of the Very Young Man, presumably with Aura. She bore up bravely under the news of her father's death, standing with her hand on her husband's arm, and her sorrowful eyes fixed upon the face of the Big Business Man who haltingly told what had befallen them. When he came to a description of the attack on the palace, the death of the king, and the triumph of Targo, the Chemist raised his hands with a hopeless gesture.

The Doctor put in: "It's a serious situation—most serious."

"There's only one thing we can do," the Big Business Man added quickly. "We must find Jack and your sister," he addressed Lylda, whose eyes had never left his face, "and then get out of this world as quickly as we can—before we do it any more harm."

The Chemist began pacing up and down the strip of the beach. He had evidently reached the same conclusion —that it was hopeless to continue longer to cope with so desperate a situation. But he could not bring himself so easily to a realization that his life in this world, of which he had been so long virtually the leader, was at an end. He strode back and forth thinking deeply; the water that he kicked idly splashed up sometimes over the houses of the tiny city at his side.

The Big Business Man went on, "It's the only way—

the best way for all of us and for this little world, too."

"The best way for you—and you." Lylda spoke softly and with a sweet, gentle sadness. "It is best for you, my friends. But for me——" She shook her head.

The Big Business Man laid his hands gently on her shoulders. "Best for you, too, little woman. And for these people you love so well. Believe me—it is."

The Chemist paused in his walk. "Probably Aura and Jack are together. No harm has come to them so far—that's certain. If his situation were desperate he would have made himself as large as we are and we would see him."

"If he got the chance," the Doctor murmured.

"Certainly he has not been killed or captured," the Chemist reasoned, "for we would have other giants to face immediately that happened."

"Perhaps he took the girl with him and started off to Orlog to find Loto," suggested the Doctor. "That crazy boy might do anything."

"He should be back by now, even if he had," said the Big Business Man. "I don't see how anything could happen to him—having those——" He stopped abruptly.

While they had been talking a crowd of little people had gathered in the city beside them—a crowd that thronged the street before the Chemist's house, filled the open space across from it and overflowed down the steps leading to the beach. It was uncanny, standing there, to see these swarming little creatures, like ants whose hill had been desecrated by the foot of some stray passer-by. They were enraged, and with an ant's unreasoning, desperate courage they were ready to fight and to die, against an enemy irresistibly strong.

"Good God, look at them," murmured the Big Business Man in awe.

The steps leading to the beach were black with them now—a swaying, struggling mass of little human forms, men and women, hardly a finger's length in height, coming down in a steady stream and swarming out upon the beach. In a few moments the sand was black with them, and always more appeared in the city above to take their places.

The Big Business Man felt a sharp sting in his foot above the sandal. One of the tiny figures was clinging to its string and sticking a sword into his flesh. Involuntarily he kicked; a hundred of the little creatures were swept aside, and when he put his foot back upon the sand he could feel them smash under his tread. Their faint, shrill, squeaking shrieks had a ghostly semblance to human voices, and he turned suddenly sick and faint.

Then he glanced at Lylda's face; it bore an expression of sorrow and of horror that made him shudder. To him at first these had been savage, vicious little insects, annoying, but harmless enough if one kept upon one's feet; but to her, he knew, they were men and women— misguided, frenzied—but human, thinking beings like herself. And he found himself wondering, vaguely, what he should do to repel them.

The attack was so unexpected, and came so quickly that the giants had stood motionless, watching it with awe. Before they realized their situation the sand was so crowded with the struggling little figures that none of them could stir without trampling upon scores.

Oteo and Eena, standing ankle-deep in the water, were unattacked, and at a word from the Chemist the others joined them, leaving little heaps of mangled human forms upon the beach where they had trod.

All except Lylda. She stood her ground—her face bloodless, her eyes filled with tears. Her feet were covered now; her ankles bleeding from a dozen tiny knives hacking at her flesh. The Chemist called her to him, but she only raised her arms with a gesture of appeal.

"Oh, my husband," she cried. "Please, I must. Let me take the drug now and grow small—like them. Then will they see we mean them no harm. And I shall tell them we are their friends—and you, the Master, mean only good——"

The Big Business Man started forward. "They'll kill her. God, that's——" But the Chemist held them back.

"Not now, Lylda," he said gently. "Not now. Don't you see? There's nothing you can do; it's too late now." He met her gaze unyielding. For a moment she stared; then her figure swayed and with a low sob she dropped in a heap upon the sand.

As Lylda fell, the Chemist leaped forward, the other three men at his side. A strident cry came up from the swarming multitude, and in an instant hundreds of them were upon her, climbing over her and thrusting their swords into her body.

The Chemist and the Big Business Man picked her up and carried her into the water, brushing off the fighting little figures that still clung to her. There they laid her down, her head supported by Eena, who knelt in the water beside her mistress.

The multitude on the sand crowded up to the water's edge; hundreds, forced forward by the pressure of those behind, plunged in, swam about, or sank and were rolled back by the surf, lifeless upon the shore. The beach crawled with their struggling forms, only the spot where Lylda had fallen was black and still.

"She's all right," said the Doctor after a moment, bending over Lylda. A cry from Oteo made him straighten up quickly. Out over the horizon, towards Orlog, there appeared the dim shape of a gigantic human form, and behind it others, faint and blurred against the stars!

CHAPTER XXXIII

THE RESCUE OF LOTO

THE Very Young Man heard the clang of the closing door with sinking heart. The two newcomers, passing close to him and Aura as they stood shrinking up against the wall, joined their friends at the table. The Very Young Man turned to Aura with a solemn face.

"Are there any other doors?" he asked.

The girl pointed. "One other, there—but see, it, too, is closed."

Far across the room the Very Young Man could make out a heavy metal door similar to that through which they had entered. It was closed—he could see that plainly. And to open it—so huge a door that its great golden handle hung nearly a hundred feet above them—was an utter impossibility.

The Very Young Man looked at the windows. There were four of them, all on one side of the room—enormous curtained apertures, two hundred feet in length and half as broad—but none came even within fifty feet of the floor. The Very Young Man realized with dismay that there was apparently no way of escape out of the room.

"We can't get out, Aura," he said, and in spite of him his voice trembled. "There's no way."

The girl had no answer but a quiet nod of agreement. Her face was serious, but there was on it no sign of panic. The Very Young Man hesitated a moment; then he started off down the room towards one of the doors, with Aura close at his side.

They could not get out in their present size, he knew. Nor would they dare make themselves sufficiently large to open the door, or climb through one of the windows, even if the room had been nearer the ground than it actually was. Long before they could escape they would be discovered and seized.

The Very Young Man tried to think it out clearly. He knew, except for a possible accident, or a miscalculation on his part, that they were in no real danger. But he did not want to make a false move, and now for the first time he realized his responsibility to Aura, and began to regret the rashness of his undertaking.

They could wait, of course, until the conference was over, and then slip out unnoticed. But the Very Young Man felt that the chances of their rescuing Loto were greater now than they would be probably at any time in the future. They must get out now, he was convinced of that. But how?

They were at the door in a moment more. Standing so close it seemed, now, a tremendous shaggy walling of shining metal. They walked its length, and then suddenly the Very Young Man had an idea. He threw himself face down upon the floor. Underneath the door's lower edge there was a tiny crack. To one of normal Oroid size it would have been unnoticeable—a space hardly so great as the thickness of a thin sheet of paper. But the Very Young Man could see it plainly; he gauged its size by slipping the edge of his robe into it.

This crack was formed by the bottom of the door and the level surface of the floor; there was no sill. The door was perfectly hung, for the crack seemed to be of uniform size. The Very Young Man showed it to Aura.

"There's the way out," he whispered. "Through there and then large again on the other side."

He made his calculation of size carefully, and then,

crushing one of the pills into powder, divided a portion of it between himself and the girl. Aura seemed tired and the drug made her very dizzy. They both sat upon the stone floor, close up to the door, and closed their eyes. When, by the feeling of the floor beneath them, they knew the action of the drug was over, they stood up unsteadily and looked around them.

They now found themselves standing upon a great stone plain. The ground beneath their feet was rough, but as far away as they could see, out up to the horizon, it was mathematically level. This great expanse was empty except in one place; over to the right there appeared a huge, irregular, blurred mass that might have been, by its look, a range of mountains. But the mass moved as they stared at it, and the Very Young Man knew it was the nearest one of Targo's men, sitting beside the table.

In the opposite direction, perhaps a hundred yards away from where they were standing, they could see the bottom of the door. It hung in the air some fifty feet above the surface of the ground. They walked over and stood underneath; like a great roof it spread over them—a flat, level surface parallel with the floor beneath.

At this extraordinary change in their surroundings Aura seemed frightened, but seeing the matter-of-fact way in which her companion acted, she maintained her composure and soon was much interested in this new aspect of things. The Very Young Man took a last careful look around and then, holding Aura by the hand, started to cross under the door in a direction he judged to be at right angles to its length.

They walked swiftly, trying to keep their sense of direction, but having no means of knowing whether they were doing so or not. For perhaps ten minutes they walked; then they emerged on the other side of the door and again faced a great level, empty expanse.

"We're under," the Very Young Man remarked with relief. "Do you know where Loto is from here?"

Aura had recovered her self-possession sufficiently to smile.

"I might, perhaps," she answered, with a pretty little shrug. "But it's a long way, don't you think? A hundred miles, it may be?"

"We get large here," said the Very Young Man, with an answering smile. He was greatly relieved to be outside the audience room; the way seemed easy before them now.

They took the opposite drug, and after several successive changes of size, succeeded in locating the upper room in the palace in which Loto was held. At this time they were about the same relative size to their enemies as when they entered the audience chamber on the floor below.

"That must be it," the Very Young Man whispered, as they cautiously turned a hallway corner. A short distance beyond, in front of a closed door, sat two guards.

"That is the room of which they spoke," Aura answered. "Only one door there is, I think."

"That's all right," said the Very Young Man confidently. "We'll do the same thing—go under the door."

They went close up to the guards, who were sitting upon the floor playing some sort of a game with little golden balls. This door, like the other, had a space beneath it, rather wider than the other, and in ten minutes more the Very Young Man and Aura were beneath it, and inside the room.

As they grew larger again the Very Young Man at first thought the room was empty. "There he is," cried Aura happily. The Very Young Man looked and could see across the still huge room, the figure of Loto, standing at a window opening.

"Don't let him see us till we're his size," cautioned the

Very Young Man. "It might frighten him. And if he made any noise——" He looked at the door behind them significantly.

Aura nodded eagerly; her face was radiant. Steadily larger they grew. Loto did not turn round, but stood quiet, looking out of the window.

They crept up close behind him, and when they were normal size Aura whispered his name softly. The boy turned in surprise and she faced him with a warning finger on her lips. He gave a low, happy little cry, and in another instant was in her arms, sobbing as she held him close to her breast.

The Very Young Man's eyes grew moist as he watched them, and heard the soft Oroid words of endearment they whispered to each other. He put his arms around them, too, and all at once he felt very big and very strong beside these two delicate, graceful little creatures of whom he was protector.

A noise in the hallway outside brought the Very Young Man to himself.

"We must get out," he said swiftly. "There's no time to lose." He went to the window; it faced the city, fifty feet or more above the ground.

The Very Young Man make a quick decision. "If we go out the way we came, it will take a very long time," he explained. "And we might be seen. I think we'd better take the quick way; get big here—get right out," he waved his hands towards the roof, "and make a run for it back to Arite."

He made another calculation. The room in which they were was on the top floor of the palace; Aura had told him that. It was a room about fifty feet in length, triangular in shape, and some thirty feet from floor to ceiling. The Very Young Man estimated that when they had grown large enough to fill the room, they could burst through the palace roof and leap to the ground. Then in a short time they could run over the country, back to Arite. He measured out the drug carefully, and without hesitation his companions took what he gave them.

As they all three started growing—it was Loto's first experience, and he gave an exclamation of fright at the sensation and threw his arms around Aura again—the Very Young Man made them sit upon the floor near the center of the room. He sat himself beside them, staring up at the ceiling that was steadily folding up and coming down towards them. For some time he stared, fascinated by its ceaseless movement.

Then suddenly he realized with a start that it was almost down upon them. He put up his hand and touched it, and a thrill of fear ran over him. He looked around. Beside him sat Aura and Loto, huddled close together. The walls of the room had nearly closed in upon them now; its few pieces of furniture had been pushed aside, unnoticed, by the growth of their enormous bodies. It was as though they were crouching in a triangular box, almost entirely filling it.

The Very Young Man laid his hand on Aura's arm, and she met his anxious glance with her fearless, trusting smile.

"We'll have to break through the roof now," whispered the Very Young Man, and the girl answered calmly: "What you say to do, we will do."

Their heads were bent down now by the ever-lowering ceiling; the Very Young Man pressed his shoulder against it and heaved upwards. He could feel the floor under him quiver and the roof give beneath his thrust, but he did not break through. In sudden horror he wondered if he could. If he did not, soon, they would be crushed to death by their own growth within the room.

The Very Young Man knew there was still time to take

the other drug. He shoved again, but with the same result. Their bodies were bent double now. The ceiling was pressing close upon them; the walls of the room were at their elbow. The Very Young Man crooked his arm through the little square orifice window that he found at his side, and, with a signal to his companions, all three in unison heaved upwards with all their strength. There came one agonizing instant of resistance; then with a wrenching of wood, the clatter of falling stones and a sudden crash, they burst through and straightened upright into the open air above.

The Very Young Man sat still for a moment, breathing hard. Overhead stretched the canopy of stars; around lay the city, shrunken now and still steadily diminishing. Then he got unsteadily upon his feet, pulling his companions up with him and shaking the bits of stone and broken wood from him as he did so.

In a moment more the palace roof was down to their knees, and they stepped out of the room. They heard a cry from below and saw the two guards, standing amidst the débris, looking up at them through the torn roof in fright and astonishment.

There came other shouts from within the palace now, and the sound of the hurrying of many little feet. For some minutes more they grew larger, as they stood upon the palace roof, clinging to one another and listening to the spreading cries of excitement within the building and in the city streets below them.

"Come on," said the Very Young Man finally, and he jumped off the roof into the street. A group of little figures scattered as he landed, and he narrowly escaped treading upon them.

So large had they grown that it was hardly more than a step down from the roof; Aura and Loto were by the Very Young Man's side in a moment, and immediately they started off, picking their way single file out of the city. For a short time longer they continued growing; when they had stopped the city houses stood hardly above their ankles.

It was difficult walking, for the street was narrow and the frightened people in it were often unable to avoid their tread, but fortunately the palace stood near the edge of the city, and soon they were past its last houses and out into the open country.

"Well, we did it," said the Very Young Man, exulting. Then he patted Loto affectionately upon the shoulder, adding. "Well, little brother, we got you back, didn't we?"

Aura stopped suddenly. "Look there—at Arite," she said, pointing up at the horizon ahead of them.

Far in the distance, at the edge of the lake, and beside a dim smudge he knew to be the houses of Arite, the Very Young Man saw the giant figure of a man, huge as himself, towering up against the background of sky.

CHAPTER XXXIV

THE DECISION

"GIANTS!" exclaimed the Doctor, staring across the country towards Orlog. There was dismay in his voice.

The Big Business Man, standing beside him, clutched at his robe. "How many do you make out; they look like three to me."

The Doctor strained his eyes into the dim, luminous distance. "Three, I think—one taller than the others; it must be Jack." His voice was a little husky, and held none of the confidence his words were intended to convey.

Lylda was upon her feet now, standing beside the Chemist. She stared towards Orlog searchingly, then turned to him and said quietly, "It must be Jack and Aura, with Loto." She stopped with quivering lips; then with an obvious effort went on confidently. "It cannot be that the God you believe in would let anything happen to them."

"They're coming this way—fast," said the Big Business Man. "We'll know in a few moments."

The figures, plainly visible now against the starry background, were out in the open country, half a mile perhaps from the lake, and were evidently rapidly approaching Arite.

"If it should be Targo's men," the Big Business Man added, "we must take more of the drug. It is death then for them or for us."

In silence the six of them stood ankle deep in the water

waiting. The multitude of little people on the beach and in the near-by city streets were dispersing now. A steady stream was flowing up the steps from the beach, and back into the city. Five minutes more and only a fringe of those in whom frenzy still raged remained at the water's edge; a few of these, more daring, or more unreasoning than the others, plunged into the lake and swam about the giants' ankles unnoticed.

Suddenly Lylda gave a sigh of relief. "Aura it is," she cried. "Can you not see, there at the left? Her short robe—you see—and her hair, flowing down so long; no man is that."

"You're right," said the Big Business Man. "The smallest one on this side is Loto; I can see him. And Jack is leading. It's all right; they're safe. Thank God for that; they're safe, thank God!" The fervent relief in his voice showed what a strain he had been under.

It was Jack; a moment more left no doubt of that. The Big Business Man turned to the Chemist and Lylda, where they stood close together, and laying a hand upon the shoulder of each said with deep feeling: "We have all come through it safely, my friends. And now the way lies clear before us. We must go back, out of this world, to which we have brought only trouble. It is the only way; you must see that."

Lylda avoided his eyes.

"All through it safely," she murmured after him. "All safe except—except my father." Her arm around the Chemist tightened. "All safe—except those." She turned her big, sorrowful eyes towards the beach, where a thousand little mangled figures lay dead and dying. "All safe—except those."

It was only a short time before the adventurers from Orlog arrived, and Loto was in his mother's arms. The Very Young Man, with mixed feelings of pride at his exploit and relief at being freed from so grave a responsibility, happily displayed Aura to his friends.

"Gosh, I'm glad we're all together again; it had me scared, that's a fact." His eye fell upon the beach. "Great Scott, you've been having a fight, too? Look at that." The Big Business Man and the Doctor outlined briefly what had happened, and the Very Young Man answered in turn with an account of his adventures.

Aura joined her sister and Loto. The Chemist after a moment stood apart from the others thinking deeply. He had said little during all the events of the afternoon and evening. Now he reached the inevitable decision that events had forced upon him. His face was very serious as he called his companions around him.

"We must decide at once," he began, looking from one to the other, "what we are to do. Our situation here has become intolerable—desperate. I agree with you," his glance rested on the Big Business Man an instant; "by staying here we can only do harm to these misguided people."

"Of course," the Big Business Man interjected under his breath.

"If the drugs should ever get out of our possession down here, immeasurable harm would result to this world, as well as causing our own deaths. If we leave now, we save ourselves; although we leave the Oroids ruled by Targo. But without the power of the drugs, he can do only temporary harm. Eventually he will be overthrown. It is the best way, I think. And I am ready to leave."

"It's the only way," the Big Business Man agreed. "Don't you think so?" The Doctor and the Very Young Man both assented.

"The sooner the better," the Very Young Man added. He glanced at Aura, and the thought that flashed into his mind made his heart jump violently.

The Chemist turned to Lylda. "To leave your people," he said gently, "I know how hard it is. But your way now lies with me—with us." He pulled Loto up against him as he spoke.

Lylda bowed her head. "You speak true, my husband, my way does lie with you. I cannot help the feeling that we should stay. But with you my way does lie; whither you direct, we shall go—for ever."

The Chemist kissed her tenderly. "My sister also?" he smiled gently at Aura.

"My way lies with you, too," the girl answered simply. "For no man here has held my heart."

The Very Young Man stepped forward. "Do we take them with us?" He indicated Oteo and Eena, who stood silently watching.

"Ask them, Lylda," said the Chemist.

Calling them to her, Lylda spoke to the youth and the girl in her native tongue. They listened quietly; Oteo with an almost expressionless stolidity of face, but with his soft, dog-like eyes fixed upon his mistress; Eena with heaving breast and trembling limbs. When Lylda paused they both fell upon their knees before her. She put her hands upon their heads and smiling wistfully, said in English:

"So it shall be; with me you shall go, because that is what you wish."

The Very Young Man looked around at them all with satisfaction. "Then it's all settled," he said, and again his glance fell on Aura. He wondered why his heart was pounding so, and why he was so thrilled with happiness; and he was glad he was able to speak in so matter-of-fact a tone.

"I don't know how about you," he added, "but, Great Scott, I'm hungry."

"Since we have decided to go," the Chemist said, "we

had better start as soon as possible. Are there things in the house, Lylda, that you care to take?"

Lylda shook her head. "Nothing can I take but memories of this world, and those would I rather leave." She smiled sadly. "There are some things I would wish to do—my father——"

"It might be dangerous to wait," the Big Business Man put in hurriedly. "The sooner we start, the better. Another encounter would only mean more death." He looked significantly at the beach.

"We've got to eat," said the Very Young Man.

"If we handle the drugs right," the Chemist said, "we can make the trip out in a very short time. When we get above the forest and well on our way we can rest safely. Let us start at once."

"We've got to eat," the Very Young Man insisted. "And we've got to have food with us."

The Chemist smiled. "What you say is quite true, Jack, we have got to have food and water; those are the only things necessary to our trip."

"We can make ourselves small now and have supper," suggested the Very Young Man. "Then we can fill up the bottles for our belts and take enough food for the trip."

"No, we won't," interposed the Big Business Man positively. "We won't get small again. Something might happen. Once we get through the tunnels——" He stopped abruptly.

"Great Scott! We never thought of that," ejaculated the Very Young Man, as the same thought occurred to him. "We'll have to get small to get through the tunnels. Suppose there's a mob there that won't let us in?"

"Is there any other way up to the forest?" the Doctor asked.

The Chemist shook his head. "There are a dozen different tunnels, all near here, and several at Orlog, that all lead to the upper surface. But I think that is the only way."

"They might try to stop us," the Big Business Man suggested. "We certainly had better get through them as quickly as we possibly can."

It was Aura who diffidently suggested the plan they finally adopted. They all reduced their size first to about the height of the Chemist's house. Then the Very Young Man prepared to make himself sufficiently small to get the food and water-bottles, and bring them up to the larger size.

"Keep your eye on me," he warned. "Somebody might jump on me."

They stood around the house, while the Very Young Man, in the garden, took the drug and dwindled in stature to Oroid size. There were none of the Oroids in sight, except some on the beach and others up the street silently watching. As he grew smaller the Very Young Man sat down wearily in the wreck of what once had been Lylda's beautiful garden. He felt very tired and hungry, and his head was ringing.

When he was no longer changing size he stood up in the garden path. The house, nearly its proper dimensions once more, was close at hand, silent and deserted. Aura stood in the garden beside it, her shoulders pushing aside the great branches of an overhanging tree, her arm resting upon the roof-top. The Very Young Man waved up at her and shouted: "Be out in a minute," and then plunged into the house.

CHAPTER XXXV

O NCE inside he went swiftly to the room where they had left their water-bottles and other paraphernalia. He found them without difficulty, and retraced his steps to the door he had entered. Depositing his load near it, he went back towards the room which Lylda had described to him, and in which the food was stored.

Walking along this silent hallway, listening to the echoes of his own footsteps on its stone floor, the Very Young Man found himself oppressed by a feeling of impending danger. He looked back over his shoulder—once he stood quite still and listened. But he heard nothing; the house was quite silent, and smiling at his own fear he went on again.

Selecting the food they needed for the trip took him but a moment. He left the storeroom, his arms loaded, and started back toward the garden door. Several doorways opened into the hall below, and all at once the Very Young Man found himself afraid as he passed them. He was within sight of the garden door, not more than twenty feet away, when he hesitated. Just ahead, at his right, an archway opened into a room beside the hall. The Very Young Man paused only an instant; then, ashamed of his fear, started slowly forward. He felt an impulse to run, but he did not. And then, from out of the silence, there came a low, growling cry that made his heart stand still, and the huge gray figure of a man leaped upon him and bore him to the ground.

283

As he went down, with the packages of food flying in all directions, the Very Young Man gripped the naked body of his antagonist tightly. He twisted round as he fell and lay with his foe partly on top of him. He knew instinctively that his situation was desperate. The man's huge torso, with its powerful muscles that his arms encircled, told him that in a contest of strength such as this, inevitably he would find himself overcome.

The man raised his fist to strike, and the Very Young Man caught him by the wrist. Over his foe's shoulder now he could see the open doorway leading into the garden, not more than six or eight feet away. Beyond it lay safety; that he knew. He gave a mighty lunge and succeeded in rolling over toward the doorway. But he could not stay above his opponent, for the man's greater strength lifted him up and over, and again pinned him to the floor.

He was nearer the door now, and just beyond it he caught a glimpse of the white flesh of Aura's ankle as she stood beside the house. The man put a hand on the Very Young Man's throat. The Very Young Man caught it by the wrist, but he could feel the growing pressure of its fingers cutting off his breath. He tried to pull the hand back, but could not; he tried to twist his body free, but the weight of his foe held him tightly against the floor. A great roaring filled his ears; the hallway began fading from his sight. With a last despairing breath, he gave a choking cry: "Aura! Aura!"

The man's fingers at his throat loosened a little; he drew another breath, and his head cleared. His eyes were fixed on the strip of garden he could see beyond the doorway. Suddenly Aura's enormous body came into view, as she stooped and then lay prone upon the ground. Her face was close to the door; she was looking in. The Very Young Man gave another cry, half stifled. And then into the hallway he saw come swiftly a huge hand, whose fingers gripped him and his antagonist and jerked them hurriedly down the hall and out into the garden.

As they lay struggling on the ground outside, the Very Young Man felt himself held less closely. He wrenched himself free and sprang to his feet, standing close beside Aura's face. The man was up almost as quickly, preparing again to spring upon his victim. Something moved behind the Very Young Man, and he looked up into the air hurriedly. The Big Business Man stood behind him; the Very Young Man met his anxious glance.

"I'm all right," he shouted. His antagonist leaped forward and at the same instant a huge, flat object, that was the Big Business Man's foot, swept through the air and mashed the man down into the dirt of the garden. The Very Young Man turned suddenly sick as he heard the agonized shriek and the crunching of the breaking bones. The Big Business Man lifted his foot, and the mangled figure lay still. The Very Young Man sat down suddenly in the garden path and covered his face with his hands.

When he raised his head his friends were all standing round him, crowding the garden. The body of the man who had attacked him had disappeared. The Very Young Man looked up into Aura's face—she was on her feet now with the others—and tried to smile.

"I'm all right," he repeated. "I'll go get the food and things."

In a few minutes more he had made himself as large as his companions, and had brought with him most of the food. There still remained in the smaller size the waterbottles, some of the food, the belts with which to carry it, and a few other articles they needed for the trip.

"I'll get them," said the Big Business Man; "you sit down and rest."

The Very Young Man was glad to do as he was told, and sat beside Aura in the garden, while the Big Business Man brought up to their size the remainder of the supplies.

When they had divided the food, and all were equipped for the journey, they started at once for the tunnels. Lylda's eyes again filled with tears as she left so summarily, and probably for the last time, this home in which she had been so happy.

As they passed the last houses of the city, heading towards the tunnel entrances that the Chemist had selected, the Big Business Man and the Chemist walked in front, the others following close behind them. A crowd of Oroids watched them leave, and many others were to be seen ahead; but these scattered as the giants approached. Occasionally a few stood their ground, and these the Big Business Man mercilessly trampled under foot.

"It's the only way; I'm sorry," he said, half apologetically. "We cannot take any chances now; we must get out."

"It's shorter through these tunnels I'm taking," the Chemist said after a moment.

"My idea," said the Big Business man, "is that we should go through the tunnels that are the largest. They're not all the same size, are they?"

"No," the Chemist answered; "some are a little larger."

"You see," the Big Business Man continued, "I figure we are going to have a fight. They're following us. Look at that crowd over there. They'll never let us out if they can help it. When we get into the tunnels, naturally we'll have to be small enough to walk through them. The larger we are the better; so let's take the very biggest."

"These are," the Chemist answered. "We can make it at about so high." He held his hand about the level of his waist.

"That won't be so bad," the Big Business Man commented.

Meanwhile the Very Young Man, walking with Aura behind the leaders, was talking to her earnestly. He was conscious of a curious sense of companionship with this quiet girl—a companionship unlike anything he had ever felt for a girl before. And now that he was taking her with him, back to his own world——

"Climb out on to the surface of the ring," he was saying, "and then, in a few minutes more, we'll be there. Aura, you cannot realize how wonderful it will be."

The girl smiled her quiet smile; her face was sad with the memory of what she was leaving, but full of youthful, eager anticipation of that which lay ahead.

"So much has happened, and so quickly, I cannot realize it yet, I know," she answered. "But that it will be very wonderful, up there above, I do believe. And I am glad that we are going, only——"

The Very Young Man took her hand, holding it a moment. "Don't, Aura. You mustn't think of that." He spoke gently, with a tender note in his voice.

"Don't think of the past, Aura," he went on earnestly. "Think only of the future—the great cities, the opera, the poetry I am going to teach you."

The girl laid her hand on his arm. "You are so kind, my friend Jack. You will have much to teach me, will you not? Is it sure you will want to? I shall be like a little child up there in your great world."

An answer sprang to the Very Young Man's lips—words the thinking of which made his heart leap into his throat. But before he could voice them Loto ran up to him from behind, crying. "I want to walk by you, Jack; *mamita* talks of things I know not."

The Very Young Man put his arm across the child's

shoulders. "Well, little boy," he said laughing, "how do you like this adventure?"

"Never have I been in the Great Forests," Loto answered, turning his big, serious eyes up to his friend's face. "I shall not be afraid—with my father, and *mamita*, and with you."

"The Great Forests won't seem very big, Loto, after a little while," the Very Young Man said. "And of course you won't be afraid of anything. You're going to see many things, Loto—very many strange and wonderful things for such a little boy."

They reached the entrance to the tunnel in a few moments more, and stopped before it. As they approached, a number of little figures darted into its luminous blackness and disappeared. There were none others in sight now, except far away towards Arite, where perhaps a thousand stood watching intently.

The tunnel entrance, against the side of a hill, stood nearly breast high.

"I'm wrong," said the Chemist, as the others came up. "It's not so high all the way through. We shall have to make ourselves much smaller than this."

"This is a good time to eat," suggested the Very Young Man. The others agreed, and without making themselves any smaller—the Big Business Man objected to that procedure—they sat down before the mouth of the tunnel and ate a somewhat frugal meal.

"Have you any plans for the trip up?" asked the Doctor of the Chemist while they were eating.

"I have," interjected the Big Business Man, and the Chemist answered:

"Yes, I am sure I can make it far easier than it was for me before. I'll tell you as we go up; the first thing is to get through the tunnels."

"I don't anticipate much difficulty in that," the Doctor said. "Do you?"

The Chemist shook his head. "No, I don't."

"But we mustn't take any chances," put in the Big Business Man quickly. "How small do you suppose we should make ourselves?"

The Chemist looked at the tunnel opening. "About half that," he replied.

"Not at the start," said the Big Business Man. "Let's go in as large as possible; we can get smaller when we have to."

It took them but a few minutes to finish the meal. They were all tired from the exciting events of the day, but the Big Business Man would not hear of their resting a moment more than was absolutely necessary.

"It won't be much of a trip up to the forests," he argued. "Once we get well on our way and into one of the larger sizes, we can sleep safely. But not now; it's too dangerous."

They were soon ready to start, and in a moment more all had made themselves small enough to walk into the tunnel opening. They were, at this time, perhaps six times the normal height of an adult Oroid. The city of Arite, apparently much farther away now, was still visible up against the distant horizon. As they were about to start, Lylda, with Aura close behind her, turned to face it.

"Good-by to our own world now we must say, my sister," she said sadly. "The land that bore us—so beautiful a world, and once so kindly. We have been very happy here. And I cannot think it is right for me to leave."

"Your way lies with your husband," Aura said gently. "You yourself have said it, and it is true."

Lylda raised her arms up towards the far-away city with a gesture almost of benediction.

"Good future to you, land that I love." Her voice trembled. "Good future to you, for ever and ever."

The Very Young Man, standing behind them with Loto, was calling: "They're started; come on."

With one last sorrowful glance Lylda turned slowly, and, walking with her arm about her sister, followed the others into the depths of the tunnel.

CHAPTER XXXVI

THE FIGHT IN THE TUNNELS

FOR some time this strange party of refugees from an outraged world walked in silence. Because of their size, the tunnel appeared to them now not more than eight or nine feet in height,, and in most places of nearly similar width. For perhaps ten minutes no one spoke except an occasional monosyllable. The Chemist and Big Business Man, walking abreast, were leading; Aura and Lylda with the Very Young man, and Loto close in front of them, brought up the rear.

The tunnel they were traversing appeared quite deserted; only once, at the intersection of another smaller passageway, a few little figures—not more than a foot high—scurried past and hastily disappeared. Once the party stopped for half an hour to rest.

"I don't think we'll have any trouble getting through," said the Chemist. "The tunnels are usually deserted at the time of sleep."

The Big Business Man appeared not so sanguine, but said nothing. Finally they came to one of the large amphitheaters into which several of the tunnels opened. In size, it appeared to them now a hundred feet in length and with a roof some twelve feet high. The Chemist stopped to let the others come up.

"I think our best route is there," he pointed.

"It is not so high a tunnel; we shall have to get smaller. Beyond it they are larger again. It is not far—half an hour, perhaps, walking as we——"

A cry from Aura interrupted him.

"My brother, see, they come," she exclaimed.

Before them, out of several of the smaller passageways, a crowd of little figures was pouring. There were no shouts; there was seemingly no confusion; just a steady, flowing stream of human forms, emptying from the tunnels into the amphitheater and spreading out over its open surface.

The fugitives stared a moment in horror. "Good God! they've got us," the Doctor muttered, breaking the tenseness of the silence.

The little people kept their distance at first, and then as the open space filled up, slowly they began coming closer, in little waves of movement, irresistible as an incoming tide.

Aura turned towards the passageway through which they had entered. "We can go back," she said. And then. "No—see, they come there, too." A crowd of the little gray figures blocked that entrance also—a crowd that hesitated an instant and then came forward, spreading out fan-shape as it came.

The Big Business Man doubled up his fists.

"It's fight," he said grimly. "By God! we'll——" but Lylda, with a low cry, flung herself before him.

"No, no," she said passionately. "Not that; it cannot be that now, just at the last——"

Aura laid a hand upon her sister's shoulder.

"Wait, my sister," she said gently. "There is no matter of justice here—for you, a woman—to decide. This is for men to deal with—a matter for men—our men. And what they say to do—that must be done."

She turned to the Chemist and the Very Young Man, who were standing side by side.

"A woman—cannot kill," she said slowly. "Unless—her man—says it so. Or if to save him——"

Her eyes flashed fire; she held her slim little body erect and rigid—an Amazon ready to fight to the death for those she loved.

The Chemist hesitated a moment. Before he could answer, a single shrill cry sounded from somewhere out in the silent, menacing throng. As though at a signal, a thousand little voices took it up, and with a great rush the crowd swept forward.

In the first moment of surprise and indecision the group of fugitives stood motionless. As the wave of little, struggling human forms closed in around them, the Very Young Man came to himself with a start. He looked down. They were black around him now, swaying back and forth about his legs. Most of them were men, armed with the short, broad-bladed swords, or with smaller knives. Some brandished other improvised weapons; still others held rocks in their hands.

A little pair of arms clutched the Very Young Man about his leg; he gave a violent kick, scattering a number of the struggling figures and clearing a space into which he leaped.

"Back—Aura, Lylda," he shouted. "Take Loto and Eena. Get back behind us."

The Big Business Man, kicking violently, and sometimes stooping down to sweep the ground with great swings of his arm, had cleared a space before them. Taking Loto, who looked on with frightened eyes, the three women stepped back against the side wall of the amphitheater.

The Very Young Man swiftly discarded his robe, standing in the knitted under-suit in which he had swam the lake; the other men followed his example. For ten minutes or more in ceaseless waves, the little creatures threw themselves forward, and were beaten back. The confined space echoed with their shouts, and with the cries of the wounded. The five men fought silently. Once the Doctor stumbled and fell. Before his friends could get to him, his body was covered with his foes. When he got back upon his feet, knocking them off, he was bleeding profusely from an ugly-looking wound in his shoulder.

"Good God!" he panted as the Chemist and the Big Business Man leaped over to him. "They'll get us—if we go down."

"We can get larger," said the Big Business Man, pointing upwards to the roof overhead. "Larger—and then——" He swayed a trifle, breathing hard. His legs were covered with blood from a dozen wounds.

Oteo, fighting back and forth before them, was holding the crowd in check; a heap of dead lay in a semicircle in front of him.

"I'm going across," shouted the Very Young Man suddenly, and began striding forward into the struggling mass.

The crowd, thus diverted, eased its attack for a moment. Slowly the Very Young Man waded into it. He was perhaps fifty feet out from the side wall when a stone struck him upon the temple. He went down, out of sight in the seething mass.

"Come on," shouted the Big Business Man. But before he could move, Aura dashed past him, fighting her way out to where the Very Young Man lay. In a moment she was beside him. Her fragile body seemed hopelessly inadequate for such a struggle, but the spirit within her made her fight like a wildcat.

Catching one of the little figures by the legs she flung him about like a club, knocking a score of the others back and clearing a space about the Very Young Man. Then abruptly she dropped her victim and knelt down, plucking away the last of the attacking figures who was hacking at the Very Young Man's arm with his sword.

The Chemist and Big Business Man were beside her now, and together they carried the Very Young Man back. He had recovered consciousness, and smiled up at them feebly. They laid him on the ground against the wall, and Aura sat beside him.

"Gosh, I'm all right," he said, waving them away. "Be with you in a minute; give 'em hell!"

The Doctor knelt beside the Very Young Man for a moment, and, finding he was not seriously hurt, left him and rejoined the Chemist and Big Business Man, who, with Oteo, had forced the struggling mass of little figures some distance away.

"I'm going to get larger," shouted the Big Business Man a moment later. "Wipe them all out, damn it; I can do it. We can't keep on this way."

The Doctor was by his side.

"You can't do it—isn't room," he shouted in answer, pausing as he waved one of his assailants in the air above his head. "You might take too much."

The Big Business Man was reaching with one hand under his robe. With his feet he kicked violently to keep the space about him clear. A tiny stone flew by his head; another struck him on the chest, and all at once he realized that he was bruised all over from where other stones had been hitting him. He looked across to the opposite wall of the amphitheater. Through the tunnel entrance there he saw that the stream of little people was flowing the other way now. They were trying to get out, instead of pouring in.

The Big Business Man waved his arms. "They're running away—look," he shouted. "They're running—over there—come on." He dashed forward, and, followed by his companions, redoubled his efforts.

The crowd wavered; the shouting grew less; those further away began running back.

Then suddenly a shrill cry arose—just a single little voice it was at first. After a moment others took it up, and still others, until it sounded from every side—three Oroid words repeated over and over.

The Chemist abruptly stopped fighting. "It's done," he shouted. "Thank God it's over."

The cry continued. The little figures had ceased attacking now and were struggling in a frenzy to get through the tunnels.

"No more," shouted the Chemist. "They're going. See them going? Stop."

His companions stood by his side, panting and weak from loss of blood. The Chemist tried to smile. His face was livid; he swayed unsteadily on his feet. "No more," he repeated. "It's over. Thank God, it's over!"

Meanwhile the Very Young Man, lying on the floor with Aura sitting beside him, revived a little. He tried to sit up after a few moments, but the girl pulled him down.

"But I got to go—give 'em hell," he protested weakly. His head was still confused; he only knew he should be back, fighting beside his friends.

"Not yet," Aura said gently. "There is no need— yet. When there is, you may trust me, Jack; I shall say it."

The Very Young Man closed his eyes. The blurred, iridescent outlines of the rocks confused him; his head was ringing. The girl put an arm under his neck. He found one of her hands, and held it tightly. For a moment he lay silent. Then his head seemed to clear a little; he opened his eyes.

"What are they doing now, Aura?" he asked.

"It is no different," the girl answered softly. "So terrible a thing—so terrible——" she finished almost to her-self.

"I'll wait—just a minute more," he murmured and closed his eyes again.

He held the girl's hand tighter. He seemed to be float-ing away, and her hand steadied him. The sounds of the fighting sounded very distant now—all blurred and con-fused and dreamlike. Only the girl's nearness seemed real—the touch of her little body against his as she sat beside him.

"Aura," he whispered. "Aura."

She put her face down to his. "Yes, Jack," she answered gently.

"It's very bad—there—don't you think?"

She did not answer.

"I was just thinking," he went on; he spoke slowly, al-most in a whisper. "Maybe—you know—we won't come through this." He paused; his thoughts somehow seemed too big to put into words. But he knew he was very happy.

"I was just thinking, Aura, that if we shouldn't come through I just wanted you to know——" Again he stopped. From far away he heard the shrill, rhythmic cry of many voices shouting in unison. He listened, and then it all came back. The battle—his friends there fight-ing—they needed him. He let go of the girl's hand and sat up, brushing back his moist hair.

"Listen, Aura. Hear them shouting; I mustn't stay here." He tried, weakly, to get upon his feet, but the girl's arm about his waist held him down.

"Wait," she said. Surprised by the tenseness of her tone, he relaxed.

The cry grew louder, rolling up from a thousand voices and echoing back and forth across the amphitheater. The Very Young Man wondered vaguely what it could mean. He looked into Aura's face. Her lips were smiling now.

"What is it, Aura?" he whispered.

The girl impulsively put her arms about him and held him close.

"But we are coming through, my friend Jack. We are coming through." The Very Young Man looked wonderingly into her eyes. "Don't you hear? That cry—the cry of fear and despair. It means—life to us; and no more death—to them."

The Chemist's voice came out of the distance shouting: "They're running away. It's over; thank God it's over!"

Then the Very Young Man knew, and life opened up before him again. "Life," he whispered to himself. "Life and love and happiness."

CHAPTER XXXVII

A COMBAT OF TITANS

IN a few minutes the amphitheater was entirely clear, save for the dead and maimed little figures lying scattered about; but it was nearly an hour more before the fugitives were ready to resume their journey.

The attack had come so suddenly, and had demanded such immediate and continuous action that none of the men, with the exception of the Very Young Man, had had time to realize how desperate was the situation in which they had fallen. With the almost equally abrupt cessation of the struggle there came the inevitable reaction; the men bleeding from a score of wounds, weak from loss of blood, and sick from the memory of the things they had been compelled to do, threw themselves upon the ground utterly exhausted.

"We must get out of here," said the Doctor, after they had been lying quiet for a time, with the strident shrieks of hundreds of the dying little creatures sounding in their ears. "That was pretty near the end."

"It isn't far," the Chemist answered, "when we get started."

"We must get water," the Doctor went on. "These cuts——" They had used nearly all their drinking-water washing out their wounds, which Aura and Lylda had bound up with strips of cloth torn from their garments.

The Chemist got upon his feet. "There's no water nearer than the Forest River," he said. "That tunnel over there comes out very near it."

"What makes you think we won't have another scrap getting out?" the Very Young Man wanted to know. He had entirely recovered from the effects of the stone that had struck him on the temple, and was in better condition than any of the other men.

"I'm sure," the Chemist said confidently, "they were through; they will not attack us again; for some time at least. The tunnels will be deserted."

The Big Business Man stood up also.

"We'd better get going while we have the chance," he said. "This getting smaller—I don't like it."

They started soon after, and, true to the Chemist's prediction, met no further obstacle to their safe passage through the tunnels. When they had reached the forest above, none of the little people were in sight.

The Big Business Man heaved a long sigh of relief. "Thank goodness we're here at last," he said. "I didn't realize how good these woods would look."

In a few minutes more they were at the edge of the river, bathing their wounds in its cooling water, and replenishing their drinking-bottles.

"How do we get across?" the Very Young Man asked.

"We won't have to cross it," the Chemist answered with a smile. "The tunnel took us under."

"Let's eat here," the Very Young Man suggested, "and take a sleep; we're about all in."

"We ought to get larger first," protested the Big Business Man. They were at this time about four times Oroid size; the forest trees, so huge when last they had seen them, now seemed only rather large saplings.

"Some one of us must stay awake," the Doctor said. "But there do not seem to be any Oroids up here."

"What do they come up here for, anyway?" asked the Very Young Man.

"There's some hunting," the Chemist answered. "But principally it's the mines beyond, in the deserts."

They agreed finally to stop beside the river and eat another meal, and then, with one of them on guard, to sleep for a time before continuing their journey.

The meal, at the Doctor's insistence, was frugal to the extreme, and was soon over. They selected Oteo to stand guard first. The youth, when he understood what was intended, pleaded so with his master that the Chemist agreed. Utterly worn out, the travelers lay down on a mossy bank at the river's edge, and in a few moments were all fast asleep.

Oteo sat nearby with his back against a tree-trunk. Occasionally he got up and walked to and fro to fight off the drowsiness that came over him.

How long the Very Young Man slept he never knew. He slept dreamlessly for a considerable time. When he struggled back to consciousness it was with a curious feeling of detachment, as though his mind no longer was connected with his body. He thought first of Aura, with a calm peaceful sense of happiness. For a long time he lay, drifting along with his thoughts and wondering whether he were asleep or awake. Then all at once he knew he was not asleep. His eyes were open; before him stood the forest trees at the river's edge. And at the foot of one of the trees he could see the figure of Oteo, sitting hunched up with his head upon his hands, 'fast asleep.

Remembrance came to the Very Young Man, and he sat up with a start. Beside him his friends lay motionless. He looked around, still a little confused. And then his heart leaped into his throat, for at the edge of the woods he saw a small, lean, gray figure—the little figure of a man who stood against a tree-trunk. The man's face was turned towards him; he met the glistening eyes looking down and saw the lips parted in a leering smile.

A thrill of fear ran over the Very Young Man as he recognized the face of Targo. And then his heart seemed to stop beating. For as he stared, fascinated, into the man's mocking eyes, he saw that slowly, steadily he was growing larger. Mechanically the Very Young Man's hand went to his armpit, his fingers fumbling at the pouch strapped underneath. The vial of chemicals was not there!

For an instant more the Very Young Man continued staring. Then, with an effort, he turned his eyes away from the gaze that seemed to hypnotize him. Beside him the Chemist lay sleeping. He looked back at Targo, and saw him larger—almost as large now as he was himself.

Like a cloak discarded, the Very Young Man's bewilderment dropped from him. He recognized the danger, realized that in another moment this enemy would be irresistibly powerful—invincible. His mind was clear now, his nerves steady, his muscles tense. He knew the only thing he could do; he calculated the chances in a flash of thought.

Still staring at the triumphant face of Targo, the Very Young Man jumped to his feet and swiftly bent over the sleeping form of the Chemist. Reaching through the neck of his robe he took out the vial of chemicals, and before his friend was fairly awake had swallowed one of the pills.

As the Very Young Man sprang into action Targo turned and ran swiftly away, perhaps a hundred feet; then again he stopped and stood watching his intended victim with his sardonic smile.

The Very Young Man met the Chemist's startled eyes.

"Targo!" said the Very Young Man swiftly. "He's here; he stole the drug just now, while I was sleeping."

The Chemist opened his mouth to reply, but the Very Young Man bounded away. He could feel the drug beginning to work; the ground under his feet swayed unsteadily.

Swiftly he ran straight towards the figure of Targo, where he stood leaning against a tree. His enemy did not move to run away, but stood quietly awaiting him. The Very Young Man saw he was now nearly the same size that Targo was; if anything, the larger.

A fallen tree separated them; the Very Young Man cleared it with a bound. Still Targo stood motionless, awaiting his onslaught. Then abruptly he stooped to the ground, and a rock whistled through the air, narrowly missing the Very Young Man's head. Before Targo could recover from the throw the Very Young Man was upon him, and they went down together.

Back and forth over the soft ground they rolled, first one on top, then the other. The Very Young Man's hand found a stone on the ground beside them. His fingers clutched it; he raised it above him. But a blow upon his forearm knocked it away before he could strike; and a sudden twist of his antagonist's body rolled him over and pinned him upon his back.

The Very Young Man thought of his encounter with Targo before, and again with sinking heart he realized he was the weaker of the two. He jerked one of his wrists free and, striking upwards with all his force, landed full on his enemy's jaw. The man's head snapped back, but he laughed—a grim, sardonic laugh that ended in a half growl, like a wild beast enraged. The Very Young Man's blood ran cold. A sudden frenzy seized him; he put all his strength into one desperate lunge and, wrenching himself free, sprang to his feet.

Targo was up almost as quickly as he, and for an instant the two stood eyeing each other, breathing hard. At the Very Young Man's feet a little stream was flowing past. Vaguely he found himself thinking how peaceful it looked; how cool and soothing the water would be to his bruised and aching body. Beside the stream his eye caught a number of tiny human figures, standing close together, looking up at him—little forms that a single sweep of his foot would have scattered and killed. A shiver of fear ran across him as in a flash he realized this other danger. With a cry, he leaped sidewise, away from the water. Beside him stood a little tree whose bushy top hardly reached his waist. He clutched its trunk with both hands and jerking it from the ground swung it at his enemy's head, meeting him just as he sprang forward. The tree struck Targo a glancing blow upon the shoulder. With another laugh he grasped its roots and twisted it from the Very Young Man's hand. A second more and they came together again, and the Very Young Man felt his antagonist's powerful arms around his body, bending him backwards.

The Big Business Man stood beside the others at the river's edge, watching the gigantic struggle, the outcome of which meant life or death to them all. The grappling figures were ten times his own height before he fairly realized the situation. At first he thought he should take some of the drug also, and grow larger with them. Then he knew that he could not overtake their growth in time to aid his friend. The Chemist and the Doctor must evidently have reached the same conclusion, for they, too, did nothing, only stood motionless, speechless, staring up at the battling giants.

Loto, with his head buried upon his mother's shoulder, and her arms holding him close, whimpered a little in terror. Only Aura, of all the party, did not get upon her feet. She lay full length upon the ground, a hand under her chin, staring steadily upwards. Her face was expressionless, her eyes unblinking. But her lips moved a little, as though she were breathing a silent prayer, and the fingers of her hand against her face dug their nails into the flesh of her cheek.

Taller far than the tree-tops, the two giants stood facing each other. Then the Very Young Man seized one of the trees, and with a mighty pull tore it up by the roots and swung it through the air. Aura drew a quick breath as in another instant they grappled and came crashing to the ground, falling head and shoulders in the river with a splash that drenched her with its spray. The Very Young Man was underneath, and she seemed to meet the glance of his great eyes when he fell. The trees growing on the river-bank snapped like rushes beneath the huge bodies of the giants, as, still growing larger, they struggled back and forth. The river, stirred into turmoil by the sweep of their great arms, rolled its waves up over the mossy banks, driving the watchers back into the edge of the woods, and even there covering them with its spray.

A moment more and the giants were on their feet again, standing ankle deep, far out in the river. Up against the unbroken blackness of the starless sky their huge forms towered. For a second they stood motionless; then they came together again and Aura could see the Very Young Man sink on his knees, his hand trailing in the water. Then in an instant more he struggled up to his feet; and as his hand left the water Aura saw that it clutched an enormous dripping rock. She held her breath, watching the tremendous figures as they swayed, locked in each other's arms. A single step sidewise and they were back nearly at the river's bank; the water seethed white under their tread.

The Very Young Man's right arm hung limp behind him; the boulder in his hand dangled a hundred feet or more in the air above the water. Slowly the greater strength of his antagonist bent him backwards. Aura's heart stood still as she saw Targo's fingers at the Very Young Man's throat. Then, in a great arc, the Very Young Man swept the hand holding the rock over his head, and brought it down full upon his enemy's skull. The boulder fell into the river with a thundering splash. For a brief instant the giant figures hung swaying; then the titanic hulk of Targo's body came crashing down. It fell full across the river, quivered convulsively and lay still.

And the river, backing up before it a moment, turned aside in its course, and flung the muddy torrent of its water roaring down through the forest.

CHAPTER XXXVIII

THE Very Young Man stood ankle deep in the turgid little rivulet, a tightness clutching at his chest, and with his head whirling. At his feet his antagonist lay motionless. He stepped out of the water, putting his foot into a tiny grove of trees that bent and crackled like twigs under his tread. He wondered if he would faint; he knew he must not. Away to the left he saw a line of tiny hills; beyond that a luminous obscurity into which his sight could not penetrate; behind him there was only darkness. He seemed to be standing in the midst of a great barren waste, with just a little toy river and forest at his feet—a child's plaything, set down in a man's great desert.

The Very Young Man suddenly thought of his friends. He stepped into the middle of the river and out again on the other side. Then he bent down with his face close to the ground, just above the tops of the tiny little trees. He made the human figures out finally. Hardly larger than ants they seemed, and he shuddered as he saw them. The end of his thumb could have smashed them all, they were so small.

One of the figures seemed to be waving something, and the Very Young Man thought he heard the squeak of its voice. He straightened upright, standing rigid, afraid to move his feet. He wondered what he should do, and in sudden fear felt for the vial of the diminishing drug. It was still in place, in the pouch under his armpit. The Very Young Man breathed a sigh of relief.

He decided to take the drug and rejoin his friends. Then as a sudden thought struck him he bent down to the ground again, slowly, with infinite caution. The little figures were still there; and now he thought they were not quite as tiny as before. He watched them; slowly but unmistakably they were growing larger.

The Very Young Man carefully took a step backwards, and then sat down heavily. The forest trees crackled under him. He pulled up his knees, and rested his head upon them. The little rivulet diverted from its course by the body of Targo, swept past through the woods almost at his side. The noise it made mingled with the ringing in his head. His body ached all over; he closed his eyes.

"He's all right now," the Doctor's voice said. "He'll be all right in a moment."

The Very Young Man opened his eyes. He was lying upon the ground, with Aura sitting beside him, and his friends—all his own size again—standing over him.

He met Aura's tender, serious eyes, and smiled. "I'm all right," he said. "What a foolish thing to faint."

Lylda stooped beside him. "You saved us all," she said. "There is nothing we can say—to mean what it should. But you will always know how we feel; how splendid you were."

To the praise they gave him the Very Young Man had no answer save a smile of embarrassment. Aura said nothing, only met his smile with one of her own, and with a tender glance that made his heart beat faster.

"I'm all right," he repeated after a moment of silence. "Let's get started."

They sat down now beside the Very Young Man, and earnestly discussed the best plan for getting out of the ring.

"You said you had calculated the best **way**," suggested the Doctor to the Chemist."

"First of all," interrupted the Big Business Man. "Are we sure none of these Oriods is going to follow us? For Heaven's sake let's have done with these terrible struggles."

The Very Young Man remembered. "He stole one of the vials," he said, pointing to Targo's body.

"He was probably alone," the Chemist reasoned. "If any others had been with him they would have taken some of the drug also. Probably Targo took one of the pills and then dropped the vial to the ground."

"My idea," pursued the Big Business Man, "is for us to get large just as quickly and continuously as possible. Probably you're right about Targo, but don't let's take any chances.

"I've been thinking," he continued, seeing that they agreed with him. "You know this is a curious problem we have facing us. I've been thinking about it a lot. It seemed a frightful long trip down here, but in spite of that, I can't get it out of my mind that we're only a very little distance under the surface of the ring."

"It's absolutely all in the viewpoint," the Chemist said with a smile. "That's what I meant about having an easier method of getting out. The distance depends absolutely on how you view it."

"How far would it be out if we didn't get any larger?" the Very Young Man wanted to know.

"Based on the size of a normal Oroid adult, and using the terrestrial standard of feet and inches as they would seem to us when Oroid size, I should say the distance from Arite to the surface of the ring would be about one hundred and fifty to a hundred and sixty thousand miles."

"Holy mackerel!" exclaimed the Very Young Man.

"Don't let's do much walking while we're small."

"You have the idea exactly," smiled the Chemist.

"Taking the other viewpoint," said the Doctor. "Just where do you figure this Oroid universe is located in the ring?"

"It is contained within one of the atoms of gold," the Chemist answered. "And that golden atom, I estimate, is located probably within one one-hundredth of an inch, possibly even one one-thousandth of an inch away from the circular indentation I made in the bottom of the scratch. In actual distance I suppose Arite is possibly one-sixteenth of an inch below the surface of the ring."

"Certainly makes a difference how you look at it," murmured the Very Young Man in awe.

The Chemist went on. "It is obvious then, that although when coming down the distance must be covered to some extent by physical movement—by traveling geographically, so to speak—going back, that is not altogether the case. Most of the distance may be covered by bodily growth, rather than by a movement of the body from place to place."

"We might get lost," objected the Very Young Man. "Suppose we got started in the wrong direction?"

"Coming in, that is a grave danger," answered the Chemist, "because then distances are opening up and a single false step means many miles of error later on. But going out, just the reverse is true; distances are shortening. A mile in the wrong direction is corrected in an instant later on. Not coming to a realization of that when I made the trip before, led me to undertake many unnecessary hours of most arduous climbing. There is only one condition imperative; the body growing must have free space for its growth, or it will be crushed to death."

"Have you planned exactly how we are to get out?" asked the Big Business Man.

"Yes, I have," the Chemist answered. "In the size we are now, which you must remember is several thousand times Oroid height, it will be only a short distance to a point where as we grow we can move gradually to the centre of the circular pit. That huge inclined plane slides down out of it, you remember. Once in the pit, with its walls closing in upon us, we can at the proper moment get out of it about as I did before."

"Then we'll be in the valley of the scratch," exclaimed the Very Young Man eagerly. "I'll certainly be glad to get back there again."

"Getting out of the valley we'll use the same methods," the Chemist continued. "There we shall have to do some climbing, but not nearly so much as I did."

The Very Young Man was thrilled at the prospect of so speedy a return to his own world. "Let's get going," he suggested quickly. "It sounds a cinch."

They started away in a few minutes more, leaving the body of Targo lying where it had fallen across the river. In half an hour of walking they located without difficulty the huge incline down which the Chemist had fallen when first he came into the ring. Following along the bottom of the incline they reached his landing place—a mass of small rocks and pebbles of a different metallic-looking stone than the ground around marking it plainly. These were the rocks and boulders that had been brought down with him in his fall.

"From here," said the Chemist, as they came to a halt, "we can go up into the valley by growth alone. It is several hours, but we need move very little from this position."

"How about eating?" suggested the Very Young Man.

They sat down at the base of the incline and ate another meal—rather a more lavish one this time, for the rest they had taken, and the prospect of a shorter journey ahead of them than they had anticipated made the Doctor less strict.   Then, the meal over, they took the amount of the drug the Chemist specified.   He measured it carefully—more than ten of the pills.

"We have a long wait," the Chemist said, when the first sickness from this tremendous dose had left them.

The time passed quickly.   They spoke seldom, for the extraordinary rapidity with which the aspect of the landscape was changing, and the remarkable sensations they experienced, absorbed all their attention.

In about two hours after taking the drug the curving, luminous line that was the upper edge of the incline came into view, faint and blurred, but still distinct against the blackness of the sky.   The incline now was noticeably steeper; each moment they saw its top coming down towards them out of the heights above, and its surface smoothing out and becoming more nearly perpendicular.

They were all standing up now.   The ground beneath them seemed in rapid motion, coming towards them from all directions, and dwindling away beneath their feet. The incline too—now in form a vertical concave wall—kept shoving itself forward, and they had to step backwards continually to avoid its thrust.

Within another hour a similar concave wall appeared behind them which they could follow with their eyes entirely around the circumference of the great pit in which they now found themselves.   The sides of this pit soon became completely perpendicular—smooth and shining.

Another hour and the action of the drug was beginning to slacken—the walls encircling them, although steadily closing in, no longer seemed to move with such rapidity. The pit as they saw it now was perhaps a thousand feet in diameter and twice as deep.   Far overhead the blackness of the sky was beginning to be tinged with a faint gray-blue.

At the Chemist's suggestion they walked over near the center of the circular enclosure. Slowly its walls closed in about them. An hour more and its diameter was scarcely fifty feet.

The Chemist called his companions around him.

"There is an obstacle here," he began, "that we can easily overcome; but we must all understand just what we are to do. In perhaps half an hour at the rate we are growing this enclosure will resemble a well twice as deep, approximately, as it is broad. We cannot climb up its sides, therefore we must wait until it is not more than six feet in depth in order to be able to get out. At that time its diameter will be scarcely three feet. There are nine of us here; you can realize there would not be room for us all.

"What we must do is very simple. Since there is not room for us all at once, we must get large from now on only one at a time."

"Quite so," said the Big Business Man in a perfectly matter-of-fact tone.

"All of us but one will stop growing now; one will go on and get out of the pit. He will immediately stop his growth so that he can wait for the others and help them out. Each of us will follow the same method of procedure."

The Chemist then went on to arrange the exact quantities of the drugs they were each to take at specified times, so that at the end they would all be nearly the same size again. When he had explained all this to Oteo and Eena in their native language, they were ready to proceed with the plan.

"Who's first?" asked the Very Young Man. "Let me go with Loto."

They selected the Chemist to go first, and all but him took a little of the other drug and checked their growth. The pit at this time was hardly more than fifteen feet across and about thirty feet deep.

The Chemist stood in the centre of the enclosure, while his friends crowded over against its walls to make room for his growing body. It was nearly half an hour before his head was above its top. He waited only a moment more, then he sprang upwards, clambered out of the pit and disappeared beyond the rim. In a few moments they saw his huge head and shoulders hanging out over the side wall; his hand and arm reached down towards them and they heard his great voice roaring.

"Come on—somebody else."

The Very Young Man went next, with Loto. Nothing unusual marked their growth, and without difficulty, helped by the Chemist's hands reaching down to them, they climbed out of the pit.

In an hour more the entire party was in the valley, standing beside the little circular opening out of which they had come.

The Very Young Man found himself beside Aura, a little apart from the others, who gathered to discuss their plan for growing out of the valley.

"It isn't much of a trip, is it, Aura?" the Very Young Man said. "Do you realize, we're nearly there?"

The girl looked around her curiously. The valley of the scratch appeared to them now hardly more than a quarter of a mile in width. Aura stared upwards between its narrow walls to where, several thousand feet above, a narrow strip of gray-blue sky was visible.

"That sky—is that the sky of your world?" she exclaimed. "How pretty it is!"

The Very Young Man laughed.

"No, Aura, that's not our sky. It's only the space in

the room above the ring.   When we get the size we are
going to be finally, our heads will be right up in there.
The real sky with its stars will be even then as far above
us as your sky at Arite was above you."

Aura breathed a long sigh.   "It's too wonderful—
really to understand, isn't it?" she said.

The Very Young Man pulled her down on the ground
beside him.

"The most wonderful part, Aura, is going to be having
you up there."   He spoke gently; somehow whenever he
thought of this fragile little girl-woman up in his strange
bustling world, he felt himself very big and strong.   He
wanted to be her protector, and her teacher of all the new
and curious things she must learn.

The girl did not reply at once; she simply met his
earnest gaze with her frank answering smile of understanding.

The Chemist was calling to them.

"Oh, you Jack.   We're about ready to start."

The Very Young Man got to his feet, holding down his
hands to help Aura up.

"You're going to make a fine woman, Aura, in this
new world.   You just wait and see if you don't," he said
as they rejoined the others.

The Chemist explained his plans to them.   "This valley
is several times deeper than its breadth; you can see that.
We cannot grow large enough to jump out as we did out
of the pit; we would be crushed by the walls before we
were sufficiently tall to leap out.

"But we're not going to do as I did, and climb all the
way up.   Instead we will stay here at the bottom until
we are as large as we can conveniently get between the
valley walls.   Then we will stop growing and climb up
the side; it will only be a short distance then."

The Very Young Man nodded his comprehension.

"Unless by that time the walls are too smooth to climb up," he remarked.

"If we see them getting too smooth, we'll stop and begin climbing," the Chemist agreed. "We're all ready, aren't we?" He began measuring out the estimated quantities of the drug, handing it to each of them.

"Say, I'm terrible sorry," began the Very Young Man, apologetically interrupting this procedure. "But you know if it wasn't for me, we'd all starve to death."

It was several hours since they had eaten last, and all of them were hungry, although the excitement of their strange journey had kept them from realizing it. They ate—"the last meal in the ring" as the Big Business Man put it—and in half an hour more they were ready to start.

When they had reached a size where it seemed desirable again to stop growing the valley resembled a narrow cañon—hardly more than a deep rift in the ground. They were still standing on its floor; above them, the parallel edges of the rift marked the surface of the ring. The side walls of the cañon were smooth, but there were still many places where they could climb out without much difficulty.

They started up a narrow declivity along the cañon face. The Chemist led the way; the Very Young Man, with Aura just in front of him, was last. They had been walking only a moment when the Chemist called back over his shoulder.

"It's getting very narrow. We'd better stop here and take the drug."

The Chemist had reached a rocky shelf—a ledge some twenty feet square that jutted out from the cañon wall. They gathered upon it, and took enough of the diminishing drug to stop their growth. Then the Chemist again started forward; but, very soon after, a cry of alarm from Aura stopped him.

The party turned in confusion and crowded back. Aura, pale and trembling, was standing on the very brink of the ledge looking down. The Very Young Man had disappeared.

The Big Business Man ran to the brink. "Did he fall? Where is he? I don't see him."

They gathered in confusion about the girl. "No," she said. "He—just a moment ago he was here."

"He couldn't have fallen," the Doctor exclaimed. "It isn't far down there—we'd see him."

The truth suddenly dawned on the Doctor. "Don't move!" he commanded sharply. "Don't any of you move! Don't take a step!"

Uncomprehending, they stood motionless. The Doctor's gaze was at the rocky floor under his feet.

"It's size," he added vehemently. "Don't you understand? He's taken too much of the diminishing drug."

An exclamation from Oteo made them all move towards him, in spite of the Doctor's command. There, close by Oteo's feet, they saw the tiny figure of the Very Young Man, already no more than an inch in height, and rapidly growing smaller.

The Doctor bent down, and the little figure waved its arms in terror.

"Don't get smaller," called the Doctor. But even as he said it, he realized it was a futile command.

The Very Young Man answered, in a voice so minute it seemed coming from an infinite distance.

"I can't stop! I haven't any of the other drug!"

They all remembered then. Targo had stolen the Very Young Man's vial of the enlarging drug. It had never been replaced. Instead the Very Young Man had been borrowing from the others as he went along.

The Big Business Man was seized with sudden panic. "He'll get lost. We must get smaller with him." He turned sidewise, and stumbling over a rock almost crushed the Very Young Man with the step he took to recover his balance.

Aura, with a cry, pushed several of the others back; Oteo and Eena, frightened, started down the declivity.

"We must get smaller!" the Big Business Man reiterated.

The panic was growing among them all. Above their excited cries the Doctor's voice rose.

"Stand still—all of you. If we move—even a few steps—we can never get small and hope to find him."

The Doctor—himself too confused to know whether he should take the diminishing drug at once or not—was bending over the ground. And as he watched, fascinated, the Very Young Man's figure dwindled beyond the vanishing point and was gone!

CHAPTER XXXIX

A MODERN DINOSAUR

THE Very Young Man never knew quite how it happened. The Doctor had told them to check their growth: and he took the drug abstractedly, for his mind was on Aura and how she would feel, coming for the first time into this great outer world.

What quantity he took, the Very Young Man afterward could never decide. But the next thing he knew, the figures of his companions had grown to gigantic size. The rocks about him were expanding enormously. Already he had lost the contour of the ledge. The cañon wall had drawn back almost out of sight in the haze of the distance. He turned around, bewildered. There was no precipice behind him. Instead, a great, rocky plain, tumbling with a mass of boulders, and broken by seams and rifts, spread out to his gaze. And even in that instant, as he regarded it in confusion, it opened up to greater distances.

Near at hand—a hundred yards away, perhaps—a gigantic human figure towered five hundred feet into the air. Around it, further away, others equally large, were blurred into the haze of distance.

The nearer figure stooped, and the Very Young Man, fearful that he might be crushed by its movement, waved his arms in terror. He started to run, leaping over the jagged ground beneath his feet. A great roaring voice from above came down to him—the Doctor's voice.

"Don't get smaller!"

The Very Young Man stopped running, more frightened than ever before with the realization that came to him. He shouted upward:

"I can't stop! I haven't any of the other drug!"

An enormous blurred object came swooping towards him, and went past with a rush of wind—the foot of the Big Business Man, though the Very Young Man did not know it. Above him now the air was filled with roaring —the excited voices of his friends.

A few moments passed while the Very Young Man stood stock still, too frightened to move. The roaring above gradually ceased. The towering figures expanded —faded back into the distance—disappeared.

The Very Young Man was alone in the silence and desolation of a jagged, broken landscape that was still expanding beneath him. For some time he stood there, bewildered. He came to himself suddenly with the thought that although he was too small to be seen by his friends, yet they must be there still within a few steps of him. They might take a step—might crush him to death without seeing him, or knowing that they had done it! There were rocky buttes and hills all about him now. Without stopping to reason what he was doing he began to run. He did not know or care where—anywhere away from those colossal figures who with a single step would crush the very hills and rocks about him and bury him beneath an avalanche of golden quartz.

He ran, in panic, for an hour perhaps, scrambling over little ravines, falling into a crevice—climbing out and running again. At last, with his feet torn and bleeding, he threw himself to the ground, utterly exhausted.

After a time, with returning strength, the Very Young Man began to think more calmly. He was lost—lost in size—the one thing that the Doctor, when they started down into the ring, had warned them against so earnestly.

What a fool he had been to run! He was miles away
from them now. He could not make himself large; and
were they to get smaller—small enough to see him, they
might wander in this barren wilderness for days and never
chance to come upon him.

The Very Young Man cursed himself for a fool.
Why hadn't he kept some of the enlarging drug with
him? And then abruptly, he realized something addition-
ally terrifying. The dose of the diminishing drug which
he had just taken so thoughtlessly, was the last that remained in that vial. He was utterly helpless. Thousands of miles of rocky country surrounded him—a
wilderness devoid of vegetation, of water, and of life.

Lying prone upon the ground, which at last had
stopped expanding, the Very Young Man gave himself
up to terrified reflection. So this was the end—all the
dangers they had passed through—their conquests—and
the journey out of the ring so near to a safe ending. . . . And then this!

For a time the Very Young Man abandoned hope.
There was nothing to do, of course. They could never
find him—probably, with women and a child among them
they would not dare even to try. They would go
safely back to their own world—but he—Jack Bruce—
would remain in the ring. He laughed with bitter cyni-
cism at the thought. Even the habitable world of the
ring itself, was denied him. Like a lost soul, poised between two worlds, he was abandoned, waiting helpless,
until hunger and thirst would put an end to his suffer-
ings.

Then the Very Young Man thought of Aura; and with
the thought came a new determination not to give up
hope. He stood up and looked about him, steeling himself against the flood of despair that again was almost
overwhelming. He must return as nearly as possible to

the point where he had parted from his friends. It was the only chance he had remaining—to be close enough so if one, or all of them, had become small, they would be able to see him.

There was little to choose of direction in the desolate waste around, but dimly the Very Young Man recalled having a low line of hills behind him when he was running. He faced that way now. He had come perhaps six or seven miles; he would return now as nearly as possible over the same route. He selected a gully that seemed to wind in that general direction, and climbing down into it, started off along its floor.

The gully was some forty feet deep and seemed to average considerably wider. Its sides were smooth and precipitous in some places; in others they were broken. The Very Young Man had been walking some thirty minutes when, as he came abruptly around a sharp bend, he saw before him the most terrifying object he had ever beheld. He stood stock still, fascinated with horror. On the floor of the gully, directly in front of him, lay a gigantic lizard—a reptile hideous, grotesque in its enormity. It was lying motionless, with its jaw, longer than his own body, flat on the ground as though it were sunning itself. Its tail, motionless also, wound out behind it. It was a reptile that by its size—it seemed to the Very Young Man at least thirty feet long—might have been a dinosaur reincarnated out of the dark, mysterious ages of the earth's formation. And yet, even in that moment of horror, the Very Young Man recognized it for what it was—the tiny lizard the Chemist had sent into the valley of the scratch to test his drug!

At sight of the Very Young Man the reptile raised its great head. Its tongue licked out hideously; its huge eyes stared unblinking. And then, slowly, hastelessly, it began coming forward, its great feet scratching on the rocks, its tail sliding around a boulder behind it.

The Very Young Man waited no longer, but turning, ran back headlong the way he had come. Curiously enough, this new danger, though it terrified, did not confuse him. It was a situation demanding physical action, and with it he found his mind working clearly. He leaped over a rock, half stumbled, recovered himself and dashed onward.

A glance over his shoulder showed him the reptile coming around the bend in the gully. It slid forward, crawling over the rocks without effort, still hastelessly, as though leisurely to pick up this prey which it knew could not escape it.

The gully here chanced to have smooth, almost perpendicular sides. The Very Young Man saw that he could not climb out; and even if he could, he knew that the reptile would go up the sides as easily as along the floor. It had been over a hundred feet from him when he first saw it. Now it was less than half that distance and gaining rapidly.

For an instant the Very Young Man slackened his flight. To run on would be futile. The reptile would overtake him any moment; even now he knew that with a sudden spring it could land upon him.

A cross rift at right angles in the wall came into sight— a break in the rock as though it had been riven apart by some gigantic wedge. It was as deep as the gully itself and just wide enough to admit the passage of the Very Young Man's body. He darted into it; and heard behind him the spring of the reptile as it landed at the entrance to the rift into which its huge size barred it from advancing.

The Very Young Man stopped—panting for breath.

He could just turn about between the enclosing walls. Behind him, outside in the gully, the lizard lay baffled. And then, seemingly without further interest, it moved away.

The Very Young Man rested. The danger was past. He could get out of the rift, doubtless, further ahead, without reëntering the gully. And, if he kept well away from the reptile, probably it would not bother him.

Exultation filled the Very Young Man. And then again he remembered his situation—lost in size, helpless, without the power to rejoin his friends. He had escaped death in one form only to confront it again in another— worse perhaps, since it was the more lingering.

Ahead of him, the rift seemed ascending and opening up. He followed it, and in a few hundred yards was again on the broken plateau above, level now with the top of the gully.

The winding gully itself, the Very Young Man could see plainly. Its nearest point to him was some six hundred feet away; and in its bottom he knew that hideous reptile lurked. He shuddered and turned away, instinctively walking quietly, fearing to make some noise that might again attract its attention to him.

And then came a sound that drove the blood from his face and turned him cold all over. From the depths of the gully, in another of its bends nearby, the sound of an anxious girl's voice floated upward.

"Jack! Oh Jack!" And again:

"Jack—my friend Jack!"

It was Aura, his own size perhaps, in the gully searching for him!

With frantic, horrified haste, the Very Young Man ran towards the top of the gully. He shouted warningly, as he ran.

Aura must have heard him, for her voice changed from

anxiety to a glad cry of relief. He reached the top of
the gully; at its bottom—forty feet below down its precipitous side—stood Aura, looking up, radiant, to greet
him.

"I took the drug," she cried. "I took it before they
could forbid me. They are waiting—up there for us.
There is no danger now, Jack."

The Very Young Man tried to silence her. A noise
down the gully made him turn. The gigantic reptile appeared around the nearby bend. It saw the girl and
scuttled forward, rattling the loose bowlders beneath its
feet as it came.

Aura saw it the same instant. She looked up helplessly
to the Very Young Man above her; then she turned and
ran down the gully.

The Very Young Man stood transfixed. It was a
sheer drop of forty feet or more to the gully floor beneath him. There was seemingly nothing that he could
do in those few terrible seconds, and yet with subconscious, instinctive reasoning, he did the one and only
thing possible. A loose mass of the jagged, gold quartz
hung over the gully wall. Frantically he tore at it—
pried loose with feet and hands a bowlder that hung
poised. As the lizard approached, the loosened rock slid
forward, and dropped squarely upon the reptile's broad
back.

It was a bowlder nearly as large as the Very Young
Man himself, but the gigantic reptile shook it off, writh-
ing and twisting for an instant, and hurling the smaller
loose rocks about the floor of the gully with its struggles.

The Very Young Man cast about for another missile,
but there were none at hand. Aura, at the confusion,
had stopped about two hundred feet away.

"Run!" shouted the Very Young Man. "Hide somewhere! Run!"

The lizard, momentarily stunned, recovered swiftly. Again it started forward, seemingly now as alert as before. And then, without warning, in the air above his head the Very Young Man heard the rush of gigantic wings. A tremendous grey body swooped past him and into the gully—a bird larger in proportion than the lizard itself. . . . It was the little sparrow the Chemist had sent in from the outside world—maddened now by thirst and hunger, which to the reptile had been much more endurable.

The Very Young Man, shouting again to Aura to run, stood awe-struck, watching the titanic struggle that was raging below him. The great lizard rose high on its forelegs to meet this enemy. Its tremendous jaws opened—and snapped closed; but the bird avoided them. Its huge claws gripped the reptile's back; its flapping wings spread the sixty foot width of the gully as it strove to raise its prey into the air. The roaring of these enormous wings was deafening; the wind from them as they came up tore past the Very Young Man in violent gusts; and as they went down, the suction of air almost swept him over the brink of the precipice. He flung himself prone, clinging desperately to hold his position.

The lizard threshed and squirmed. A swish of its enormous tail struck the gully wall and brought down an avalanche of loose, golden rock. But the giant bird held its grip; its bill—so large that the Very Young Man's body could easily have lain within it—pecked ferociously at the lizard's head.

It was a struggle to the death—an unequal struggle, though it raged for many minutes with an uncanny fury. At last, dragging its adversary to where the gully was wider, the bird flapped its wings with freedom of movement and laboriously rose into the air.

And a moment later the Very Young Man, looking upward, saw through the magic diminishing glass of distance, a little sparrow of his own world, with a tiny, helpless lizard struggling in its grasp.

"Aura! Don't cry, Aura! Gosh, I don't want you to cry—everything's all right now."

The Very Young Man sat awkwardly beside the frightened girl, who, overcome by the strain of what she had been through, was crying silently. It was strange to see Aura crying; she had always been such a Spartan, so different from any other girl he had ever known. It confused him.

"Don't cry, Aura," he repeated. He tried clumsily to soothe her. He wanted to thank her for what she had done in risking her life to find him. He wanted to tell her a thousand tender things that sprang into his heart as he sat there beside her. But when she raised her tear-stained face and smiled at him bravely, all he said was:

"Gosh, that was some fight, wasn't it? It was great of you to come down after me, Aura. Are they waiting for us up there?" And then when she nodded:

"We'd better hurry, Aura. How can we ever find them? We must have come miles from where they are."

She smiled at him quizzically through her tears.

"You forget, Jack, how small we are. They are waiting on the little ledge for us—and all this country—" She spread her arms toward the vast wilderness that surrounded them—"this is all only a very small part of that same ledge on which they are standing."

It was true; and the Very Young Man realized it at once.

Aura had both drugs with her. They took the one to increase their size, and without mishap or moving from where they were, rejoined those on the little ledge who were so anxiously awaiting them.

For half an hour the Very Young Man recounted his adventure, with praises of Aura that made the girl run to her sister to hide her confusion. Then once more the party started its short climb out of the valley of the scratch. In ten minutes they were all safely on the top— on the surface of the ring at last.

CHAPTER XL

THE Banker, lying huddled in his chair in the club-room, awoke with a start. The ring lay at his feet—a shining, golden band gleaming brightly in the light as it lay upon the black silk handkerchief. The Banker shivered a little for the room was cold. Then he realized he had been asleep and looked at his watch. Three o'clock! They had been gone seven hours, and he had not taken the ring back to the Museum as they had told him to. He rose hastily to his feet; then as another thought struck him, he sat down again, staring at the ring.

The honk of an automobile horn in the street outside aroused him from his reverie. He got to his feet and mechanically began straightening up the room, packing up the several suit-cases. Then with obvious awe, and a caution that was almost ludicrous, he fixed the ring in its frame within the valise prepared for it. He lighted the little light in the valise, and, every moment or two, went back to look searchingly down at the ring inside.

When everything was packed the Banker left the room, returning in a moment with two of the club attendants. They carried the suit-cases outside, the Banker himself gingerly holding the bag containing the ring.

"A taxi," he ordered when they were at the door. Then he went to the desk, explaining that his friends had left earlier in the evening and that they had finished with the room.

To the taxi-driver he gave a number that was not the Museum address, but that of his own bachelor apartment on Park Avenue. It was still raining as he got into the taxi; he held the valise tightly on his lap, looking into it occasionally and gruffly ordering the chauffeur to drive slowly.

In the sumptuous living-room of his apartment he spread the handkerchief on the floor under the center electrolier and laid the ring upon it. Dismissing the astonished and only half-awake butler with a growl, he sat down in an easy-chair facing the ring, and in a few minutes more was again fast asleep.

In the morning when the maid entered he was still sleeping. Two hours later he rang for her, and gave tersely a variety of orders. These she and the butler obeyed with an air that plainly showed they thought their master had taken leave of his senses.

They brought him his breakfast and a bath-robe and slippers. And the butler carried in a mattress and a pair of blankets, laying them with a sigh on the hardwood floor in a corner of the room.

Then the Banker waved them away. He undressed, put on his bath-robe and slippers and sat down calmly to eat his breakfast. When he had finished he lighted a cigar and sat again in his easy-chair, staring at the ring, engrossed with his thoughts. Three days he would give them. Three days, to be sure they had made the trip successfully. Then he would take the ring to the Museum. And every Sunday he would visit it; until they came back —if they ever did.

The Banker's living-room with its usually perfect appointments was in thorough disorder. His meals were still being served him there by his dismayed servants. The mattress still lay in the corner; on it the rumpled blankets showed where he had been sleeping. For the hundredth time during his long vigil the Banker, still wearing his dressing-gown and slippers and needing a shave badly, put his face down close to the ring. His heart leaped into his throat; his breath came fast; for along the edge of the ring a tiny little line of figures was slowly moving.

He looked closer, careful lest his laboured breathing blow them away. He saw they were human forms— little upright figures, an eighth of an inch or less in height —moving slowly along one behind the other. He counted nine of them. Nine! he thought, with a shock of surprise. Why, only three had gone in! Then they had found Rogers, and were bringing him and others back with him!

Relief from the strain of many hours surged over the Banker. His eyes filled with tears; he dashed them away —and thought how ridiculous a feeling it was that possessed him. Then suddenly his head felt queer; he was afraid he was going to faint. He rose unsteadily to his feet, and threw himself full-length upon the mattress in the corner of the room. Then his senses faded. He seemed hardly to faint, but rather to drift off into an involuntary but pleasant slumber.

With returning consciousness the Banker heard in the room a confusion of many voices. He opened his eyes; the Doctor was sitting on the mattress beside him. The Banker smiled and parted his lips to speak, but the Doctor interrupted him.

"Well, old friend!" he cried heartily. "What happened to you? Here we are back all safely."

The Banker shook his friend's hand with emotion; then after a moment he sat up and looked about him. The room seemed full of people—strange looking figures, in extraordinary costumes, dirty and torn. The Very Young Man crowded forward.

"We got back, sir, didn't we?" he said.

The Banker saw he was holding a young girl by the hand—the most remarkable-looking girl, the Banker thought, that he had ever beheld. Her single garment, hanging short of her bare knees, was ragged and dirty; her jet black hair fell in tangled masses over her shoulders.

"This is Aura," said the Very Young Man. His voice was full of pride; his manner ingenuous as a child's.

Without a trace of embarrassment the girl smiled and with a pretty little bending of her head, held down her hand to the astonished Banker, who sat speechless upon his mattress.

Loto pushed forward. "That's *mamita* over there," he said, pointing. "Her name is Lylda; she's Aura's sister."

The Banker recovered his wits. "Well, and who are you, little man?" he asked with a smile.

"My name is Loto," the little boy answered earnestly. "That's my father." And he pointed across the room to where the Chemist was coming forward to join them.

CHAPTER XLI

CHRISTMAS EVE in a little village of Northern
New York—a white Christmas, clear and cold. In
the dark, blue-black of the sky the glittering stars were
spread thick; the brilliant moon poured down its silver
light over the whiteness of the sloping roof-tops, and upon
the ghostly white, silently drooping trees. A heaviness
hung in the frosty air—a stillness broken only by the
tinkling of sleigh-bells or sometimes by the merry laughter of the passers-by.

At the outskirts of the village, a little back from the
road, a farmhouse lay snuggled up between two huge
apple-trees—an old-fashioned, rambling farmhouse with
a steeply pitched roof, piled high now, with snow. It
was brilliantly lighted this Christmas Eve, its lower windows sending forth broad yellow beams of light over the
whiteness of the ground outside.

In one of the lower rooms of the house, before a huge,
blazing log-fire, a woman and four men sat talking.
Across the room, at a table, a little boy was looking at a
picture-book by the light of an oil-lamp.

The woman made a striking picture as she sat back at
ease before the fire. She was dressed in a simple black
evening-dress such as a lady of the city would wear. It
covered her shoulders, but left her throat bare. Her
features, particularly her eyes, had a slight Oriental cast,
which the mass of very black hair coiled on her head ac-
centuated. Yet she did not look like an Oriental, nor in-

deed like a woman of any race of this earth. Her cheeks were red—the delicate diffused red of perfect health. But underneath the red there lay a curious mixture of other colours, not only on her cheeks but particularly noticeable on her neck and arms. Her skin was smooth as a pearl; in the mellow firelight it glowed, with the iridescence of a shell.

The four men were dressed in the careless negligee of city men in the country. They were talking gaily now among themselves. The woman spoke seldom, staring dreamily into the fire.

A clock in another room struck eight; the woman glanced over to where the child sat, absorbed with the pictures in his book. The page at which he was looking showed a sleigh loaded with toys, with a team of reindeers and a jolly, fat, white-bearded, red-jacketed old man driving the sleigh over the chimney tops.

"Come Loto, little son," the woman said. "You hear —it is the time of sleep for you."

The boy put down his book reluctantly and went over to the fireplace, standing beside his mother with an arm about her neck.

"Oh, *mamita* dear, will he surely come, this Santa Claus? He never knew about me before; will he surely come?"

Lylda kissed him tenderly. "He will come, Loto, every Christmas Eve; to you and to all the other children of this great world, will he always come."

"But you must be asleep when he comes, Loto," one of the men admonished.

"Yes, my father, that I know," the boy answered gravely. "I will go now."

"Come back Loto, when you have undressed," the Chemist called after him, as he left the room. "Remember you must hang your stocking."

When they were left alone Lylda looked at her companions and smiled.

"His first Christmas," she said. "How wonderful we are going to make it for him."

"I can remember so well," the Big Business Man remarked thoughtfully, "when they first told me there was no Santa Claus. I cried, for I knew Christmas would never be the same to me."

"Loto is nearly twelve years old," the Doctor said. "Just imagine—having his first Christmas."

"We're going to make it a corker," said the Banker. "Where's the tree? We got one."

"In the wood-shed," Lylda answered. "He has not seen it; I was so very careful."

They were silent a moment. Then: "My room is chock full of toys," the Banker said reflectively. "But this is a rotten town for candy canes—they only had little ones." And they all laughed.

"I have a present for you, Lylda," the Chemist said after a moment.

"Oh, but you must not give it until to-morrow; you yourself have told me that."

The Chemist rose. "I want to give it now," he said, and left the room. In a moment he returned, carrying a mahogany pedestal under one arm and a square parcel in the other. He set the pedestal upright on the floor in a corner of the room and began opening the package. It was a mahogany case, cubical in shape. He lifted its cover, disclosing a glass-bell set upon a flat, mahogany slab. Fastened to the center of this was a handsome black plush case, in which lay a gold wedding-ring.

Lylda drew in her breath sharply and held it; the three other men stared at the ring in amazement. The Chemist was saying: "And I decided not to destroy it, Lylda, for your sake. There is no air under this glass cover;

the ring is lying in a vacuum, so that nothing can come out of it and live. It is quite safe for us to keep it—this way. I thought of this plan, afterwards, and decided to keep the ring—for you." He set the glass bell on the pedestal.

Lylda stood before it, bending down close over the glass.

"You give me back—my world," she breathed; then she straightened up, holding out her arms toward the ring. "My birthplace—my people—they are safe." And then abruptly she sank to her knees and began softly sobbing.

Loto called from upstairs and they heard him coming down. Lylda went back hastily to the fire; the Chemist pushed a large chair in front of the pedestal, hiding it from sight.

The boy, in his night clothes, stood on the hearth beside his mother.

"There is the stocking, *mamita*. Where shall I hang it?"

"First the prayer, Loto. Can you remember?"

The child knelt on the hearth, with his head in his mother's lap.

"Now I lay me——" he began softly, halting over the unfamiliar words. Lylda's fingers stroked his brown curly head as it nestled against her knees; the firelight shone golden in his tousled curls.

The Chemist was watching them with moist eyes. "His first Christmas," he murmured, and smiled a little tender smile. "His first Christmas."

The child was finishing.

"And God bless Aura, and Jack, and——"

"And Grandmother Reoh," his mother prompted softly. "And Grandfather Reoh—and *mamita*, and——" The boy ended with a rush—"and me too. Amen. Now where do I hang the stocking, mother?"

In a moment the little stocking dangled from a mantel over the fireplace.

"You are sure he will come?" the child asked anxiously again.

"It is certain, Loto—if you are asleep."

Loto kissed his mother and shook hands solemnly with the men—a grave, dignified little figure.

"Good night, Loto," said the Big Business Man.

"Good night, sir. Good night, my father—good night, *mamita;* I shall be asleep very soon." And with a last look at the stocking he ran out of the room.

"What a Christmas he will have," said the Banker, a little huskily.

A girl stood in the doorway that led into the dining-room adjoining—a curious-looking girl in a gingham apron and cap. Lylda looked up.

"Oh, Eena, please will you say to Oteo we want the tree from the wood-shed—in the dining-room."

The little maid hesitated. Her mistress smiled and added a few words in foreign tongue. The girl disappeared.

"Every window gets a holly wreath," the Doctor said. "They're in a box outside in the wood-shed."

"Look what I've got," said the Big Business Man, and produced from his pocket a little folded object which he opened triumphantly into a long serpent of filigree red paper on a string with little red and green paper bells hanging from it. "Across the doorway," he added, waving his hand.

A moment after there came a stamping of feet on the porch outside, and then the banging of an outer door. A young man and girl burst into the room, kicking the snow from their feet and laughing. The youth carried two pairs of ice-skates slung over his shoulder; as he entered the room he flung them clattering to the floor.

The girl, even at first glance, was extraordinarily pretty. She was small and very slender of build. She wore stout high-laced tan shoes, a heavy woollen skirt that fell to her shoe-tops and a short, belted coat, with a high collar buttoned tight about her throat. She was covered now with snow. Her face and the locks of hair that strayed from under her knitted cap were soaking wet.

"He threw me down," she appealed to the others.

"I didn't—she fell."

"You did; into the snow you threw me—off the road." She laughed. "But I am learning to skate."

"She fell three times," said her companion accusingly.

"Twice only, it was," the girl corrected. She pulled off her cap, and a great mass of black hair came tumbling down about her shoulders.

Lylda, from her chair before the fire, smiled mischievously.

"Aura, my sister," she said in a tone of gentle reproof. "So immodest it is to show all that hair."

The girl in confusion began gathering it up.

"Don't you let her tease you, Aura," said the Big Business Man. "It's very beautiful hair."

"Where's Loto?" asked the Very Young Man, pulling off his hat and coat.

"In bed—see his stocking there."

A childish treble voice was calling from upstairs. "Good night, Aura—good night, my friend Jack."

"Good night, old man—see you to-morrow," the Very Young Man called back in answer.

"You mustn't make so much noise," the Doctor said reprovingly. "He'll never get to sleep."

"No, you mustn't," the Big Business Man agreed. "To-morrow's a very very big day for him."

"Some Christmas," commented the Very Young Man looking around. "Where's the holly and stuff?"

"Oh, we've got it all right, don't you worry," said the Banker.

"And mistletoe," said Lylda, twinkling. "For you, Jack."

Eena again stood in the doorway and said something to her mistress. "The tree is ready," said Lylda.

The Chemist rose to his feet. "Come on, everybody; let's go trim it."

They crowded gaily into the dining-room, leaving the Very Young Man and Aura sitting alone by the fire. For some time they sat silent, listening to the laughter of the others trimming the tree.

The Very Young Man looked at the girl beside him as she sat staring into the fire. She had taken off her heavy coat, and her figure seemed long and very slim in the clothes she was wearing now. She sat bending forward, with her hands clasped over her knees. The long line of her slender arm and shoulder, and the delicacy of her profile turned towards him, made the Very Young Man realize anew how fragile she was, and how beautiful.

Her mass of hair was coiled in a great black pile on her head, with a big, loose knot low at the neck. The iridescence of her skin gleamed under the flaming red of her cheeks. Her lips, too, were red, with the smooth, rich red of coral. The Very Young Man thought with a shock of surprise that he had never noticed before that they were red; in the ring there had been no such color.

In the room adjoining, his friends were proposing a toast over the Christmas punch bowl. The Chemist's voice floated in through the doorway.

"To the Oroids—happiness to them." Then for an instant there was silence as they drank the toast.

Aura met the Very Young Man's eyes and smiled a little wanly. "Happiness—to them! I wonder. We who are so happy to-night—I wonder, are they?"

The Very Young Man leaned towards her. "You are happy, Aura?"

The girl nodded, still staring wistfully into the fire.

"I want you to be," the Very Young Man added simply, and fell silent.

A blazing log in the fire twisted and rolled to one side; the crackling flames leaped higher, bathing the girl's drooping little figure in their golden light.

The Very Young Man after a time found himself murmuring familiar lines of poetry. His memory leaped back. A boat sailing over a silent summer lake—underneath the stars—the warmth of a girl's soft little body touching his—her hair, twisted about his fingers—the thrill in his heart; he felt it now as his lips formed the words:

> "The stars would be your pearls upon a string,
> The world a ruby for your finger-ring,
> And you could have the sun and moon to wear,
> If I were king."

"You remember, Aura, that night in the boat?"

Again the girl nodded. "I shall learn to read it—some day," she said eagerly. "And all the others that you told me. I want to. They sing—so beautifully."

A sleigh passed along the road outside; the jingle of its bells drifted in to them. The Very Young Man reached over and gently touched the girl's hand; her fingers closed over his with an answering pressure. His heart was beating fast.

"Aura," he said earnestly. "I want to be King—for

you—this first Christmas and always. I want to give you—all there is in this life, of happiness, that I can give —just for you."

The girl met his gaze with eyes that were melting with tenderness.

"I love you, Aura," he said softly.

"I love you, too, Jack," she whispered, and held her lips up to his.

THE END

In the Bison Frontiers of Imagination series